A WOMAN TO BLAME

VINCENT PANETTIERE

Copyright © 2019 All rights reserved. This book or any portion thereof may not be reproduced or used in any manner whatsoever without the express written permission of the publisher except for the use of brief quotations in a book review.

Second Edition

Print ISBN: 978-1-54397-978-7

eBook ISBN: 978-1-54397-979-4

Man supposes that he directs his life and governs his actions, when his existence is irretrievably under the control of destiny.
Goethe

ACKNOWLEDGMENTS

I am grateful to Dunya Bean, Joan Howlett, Walter Queren, and Lynn Smith for their encouragement and support as the story progressed.

I was indeed very fortunate to have Susan Hughes edit *A Woman to Blame* with patience and precision. Her pursuit of excellence improved the text and helped the book grow.

Most especially I am grateful to my wife Penny for her love and support through the ages.

CHAPTER ONE

"What's the mystery?" Mike Hegan asked as his boots shuffled a path through the newly fallen snow. They were not the words he would use when called to the scene of the most recent homicide in Chicago. As the icy winds of January sliced into the city from Lake Michigan, Hegan cared less about his destination. He wanted the slog to end so his cheeks, all four of them, could thaw.

"You'll see. We're almost there," a warm, female voice answered with barely a trace of shiver.

Hegan knew the voice belonged to Lucy. As they made their way up Michigan Avenue, she was barely visible. Her head was bent against the wind and snow sprinkles. Her body was swaddled in a floor-length, cranberry-colored down coat.

"I heard a voice, but all I can see is cranberry Bubble Wrap."

"Hush. This coat is the best present you ever gave me. It's warmer than you are some nights."

"What?"

Lucy stopped and pointed at a sign hanging above a stairway between Joe's Shoe Repair and a Subway sandwich shop: MADAME STELLA'S DANCE STUDIO - 2ND FLOOR.

The sign didn't answer Hegan's initial question but prompted a flurry of others he was about to unleash until the fingers of Lucy's woolen mitten gently rested against his lips.

"We're going to be married in six months, and you dance like the creature in *Young Frankenstein*."

"I do not." Hegan stopped protesting and launched into a heavy-footed-shuffle impersonation of Peter Boyle while trying to sing "Puttin' on the Ritz" through pressed lips. Humor had saved Hegan from uncomfortable moments and situations since he was an adolescent. Now, he felt his comedic chops emerging to rescue him again.

"Start climbing," was all Lucy said as she headed up a long flight of steps to the second floor.

During the six months Hegan and Lucy had lived together, he learned not to object or resist when the wind was at her back, otherwise he'd play Wile E. Coyote to her Road Runner. But, if he was creative, and he knew he was, there were alternatives to slavish submission.

Hegan displayed a grumpy reluctance as he tromped up the steps while watching moisture slide off the thick rubber tops of his boots. He joined Lucy at the front door of Madame Stella's studio and made his move. He looked at her with a smile of compliance on his face and not a bone of resistance in his body.

"I see your point—about dancing—and would love to take lessons with you."

Lucy's face flooded with expectation like a child discovering presents under the Christmas tree. *Oh, what a good boy am I*, he thought.

"But, look." Hegan pointed to his thick-soled boots. "Can't. See?" He began a few jerky movements, his feet never once leaving the floor.

Lucy's nod spoke of understanding but not disappointment. She produced a pair of Hegan's tasseled loafers from the gym bag slung on her shoulder. Her smile was more "up yours" than beatific.

"*Apres-vous, monsieur*," she said, not knowing how to say "gotcha" in French.

Caught and trapped, Hegan slowly pushed the door open a crack, clinging to his freedom for another moment.

A shout pierced the opening and echoed in the hall. He stopped trying to enter when he heard "D. E. A. D!"

Hegan listened at the door. No music. Scattering footsteps. Persons fleeing. He popped the snaps on his jacket and reached for his holster. Lucy pushed by him and threw open the door.

Madame Stella, fortyish, a sheaf of red hair tied atop her head by a black velvet ribbon, stood in the middle of the studio with her arms gesturing wildly.

"That's it! D.E.A.D!"

Hegan reached for Lucy's shoulder to pull her to safety until he could determine what bizarre ritual was sucking them into its vortex. She slipped past him to get a better view.

"Drop everything and dance!" Madame Stella encouraged about ten teenagers who immediately turned into a twirling, gyrating explosion of humanity, consumed and directed by their own inner music.

* * *

"D.E.A.D.," Hegan murmured to no one as he awoke and adjusted his eyes to the refracted glare of the Caribbean sun. He felt movement and slowly turned to find Charles approaching. Charles was his pathfinder, his brother-in-arms. Charles was his taxi driver on the island of St. Vincent.

"They are here," Charles said with a solemnity in his voice Hegan regretted hearing. He followed the turn of Charles's head to find an electric baggage tug being driven slowly across the tarmac of the island's Amos Vale airport. Two baggage carts were connected to the tug.

The airport had a runway only long enough to accommodate commuter planes from Barbados and outlying islands in the Grenadines chain. It would never be mistaken for O'Hare.

The lone plane on the runway was the de Havilland turboprop that would initiate the first leg of Hegan's trip back to Chicago. Two coffins were lashed to the top shelves of the carts as the tug stopped before the plane's open cargo door.

Hegan wondered yet again what brought him to this island in the Caribbean, a speck eighteen miles long and eleven wide which he imagined must look like a poppy seed from outer space.

Of course, he remembered.

Burnt fish.

Seven dead.

Two bodies traveling with him to Chicago.

All died because someone cooked and burned fish.

There was an eighth fatality.

For that dead woman, he would always feel completely to blame.

* * *

Johnny Faraci had new neighbors. He heard them moving in one night after ten. Several days later, he smelled what he thought was their dinner. Before the latest inhabitants of condo 32C—which had a partial view of Lake Michigan from high above Chicago's Lake Shore Drive—actually appeared before him in material form, he judged them to be "loud and stinky."

One morning, weeks later, Faraci noticed an imbalance in the molecular particulate of his air. Though he tried, the offensive odor was difficult to ignore as it began to slip into his condo—32A, with a 180-degree view of the lake. Faraci, now remembering his earlier experience, was convinced the odor wafted from Mr. and Mrs. Ivanov's condo. He knew their names from the directory in the lobby, because they were never courteous enough to formally introduce themselves. This lack of civility Faraci added to his carefully maintained list of personal slights.

What was worse, he wondered, *the unsettling beginning of his morning or last month's disruption of his nocturnal solitude?*

Faraci shuddered, remembering how the splintering of his front door by the movers became an "introduction" to his neighbors who never apologized, causing another black mark against their names. Instead, they sent the building manager to arrange for a replacement. The anger that rose in him as a result of such irresponsibility brought Faraci back to the odor.

He tried guessing what kind of meat they were cooking. Could food that malodorous enhance appetite? His mind visited the possibilities. *Liver?* He'd had calves' liver a few times and didn't remember its smell being so foul. *Kidneys? Pigs feet, maybe?* He'd had neither.

Fish! Had to be. He remembered the dish of dry cod and potatoes his paternal grand- mother made for his father because Faraci's mother refused to cook any dish that made her nauseous when not pregnant. The cod looked like a wooden plank and smelled like a burning rubber tire.

On the rare occasion when his father returned home, after visiting Grandma Maria, with a jar of... what to call it? "Stuff" was the only apt description, made especially for her "sonny boy." Mrs. Faraci, Jr.—his mother—refused to heat it or stay in the same room while his father ate. Such was her revulsion that even in the winter all the windows were open. The wind could blow the curtains up to the ceiling, and their breath could freeze into icy droplets, but no window was shut until his father had finished eating that repulsive dish, its remains immediately wrapped in newspaper and buried at the bottom of the trash barrel in the backyard.

During the winter before Grandma Maria died, Faraci remembered, his father ate the dreaded cod dish at the dining room table with his overcoat, hat, and gloves on.

From those early years sprang Faraci's aversion to offensive odor. No matter the source, including his own person. His cigar smoke excluded. He paid a bundle to have Cohibas—the real thing—smuggled across the border from Windsor, Ontario, and anyone who didn't like his cigar smoke could blow smoke up their own ass. Nevertheless, Faraci took a solemn vow never to be offensive—at least in the odor department.

Faraci started the day at peace with himself. After showering, he slipped into the black trousers of his silk suit, put on a starched white shirt, and added an Italian silk tie. For extra comfort he wore his new silk smoking robe. Hefner wore a robe over pajamas, and stupid Gigante wore a moth-eaten one before his conviction. Faraci's was made of a maroon silk delicately festooned with a pattern of gold griffins that were embroidered with actual fourteen-carat-gold thread.

Faraci eased his lean frame into a comfortably matured leather armchair in the corner of his forty-foot living room. He took great pride in maintaining his weight proportionate to his height. Measuring four inches below six feet, he weighed 155 pounds. That frame enabled him to wear contoured Italian silk suits and shirts.

His living room was decorated in the manner of an exclusive British club, the kind he remembered from the movies of his youth. Chippendale this and Chesterfield that. Precisely what didn't matter. He cared about totality more than specifics. The only exception to the decor was the lead-lined drapes. Faraci believed this precaution would prevent him from being harmed by the ultraviolet rays of satellite spy cameras while keeping his exposure to electronic surveillance to a minimum. Certain that many leaders of multinational corporations were safeguarded in like manner, Faraci never thought such precautions to be extreme.

Faraci considered himself part of the managerial class. He directed people and events, took issue when subordinates made mistakes, and meted out appropriate censure. His methods most likely would not be the subject of a *Harvard Business Review* story—not yet.

If at any time in his life Faraci had ever recited "God's in His heaven /All's right with the world," that's what he would have repeated this morning as he opened the *Chicago Tribune*. As was his custom, he turned first to *Doonesbury* because the strip aggravated him. With luck, that would be the only *agita* he got - as offensive as a burp.

He prided himself on an excellent sense of smell and, paradoxically, considering his cigar smoking, an educated palate as well. He enjoyed fine food and wine. His olfactory glands and taste buds could distinguish the ingredients of any dish, including its herbal content. But his patience disappeared when the noxious odor from the adjoining apartment reached his lungs. This was his *agita*.

In the twenty years he'd owned the condo, never had he been so offended, which was his second rule of life. Don't offend and don't be offended. Almost, but not quite, do unto others as they do unto you, though not as benign.

Before acting in haste or prejudging the Ivanovs, he was determined to eliminate all possibilities, sniffing the drain in the sink, the refrigerator and vegetable crispers. The trash can still had a deodorant wafer affixed to the inside. He could check off the kitchen.

The drain in the bathroom sink didn't smell and neither did the drain in the shower. He sniffed above the toilet, confirming no odor came from the bathroom.

When he returned to the living room, the smell intensified. Faraci lit a four-inch Cohiba earlier than usual. He saw no other option. He was in the midst of a malodorous fog that threatened to permeate every porous surface—from drapes to sofa fabric to his prized smoking robe. *Better the smoke on my robe should come from my Cohiba*, he reasoned.

As he drew in and expelled the rich, comforting smoke, Faraci thought he saw the odor actually filter through his walls like in some cheap horror movie and started to panic. But after a few more puffs, he remembered the windows were sealed shut and dismissed any hysterical notions. The only area he had not checked was outside his front door.

With the cigar in his mouth smoking like propitiating incense, Faraci, resolved to know the source of the outrage, headed for the front door. He took big puffs and blew clouds of cigar smoke to deodorize the air and provide a protective wreath around his head. As he put his hand on the door, the possibility that the CIA was trying to smoke him out of his condo using noxious fish odor gas made him stop.

Faraci was a private man, though his business made him a public figure. As he approached his seventieth year, he wanted more privacy than ever before. More than anything, he was determined to prove his mother wrong. She foretold his death when he was fifty. There was the possibility, and he eagerly embraced it, that since she was a native-born American, learning Sicilian dialect from her immigrant Aunt Evelyn, his mother may have mispronounced the word and he'd actually lived years longer than expected.

No matter. He wasn't taking chances. He was too young, too healthy, and too ambitious to die just now. And certainly not at the hands of the CIA or any of the other alphabet soup subsidiaries of Uncle Sam.

Even worse was the thought that the Feds would trick him and haul his ass to some max security dungeon. Just in case, he took a snub nose .38 from the drawer of the lamp table in the foyer and dropped it into the pocket of his robe. Then he felt like a *stunatz*, a first-class jerk. *They're outside—night scopes on M-16s with infrared sights and grenade launchers—and I've got a .38 as big as my limp dick*, he thought.

Nothing mattered. If they killed him, he'd die with a fusillade of bullets turning his body into chopped chuck. If he stayed inside, he'd puke himself to death on their putrid gas. Faraci pushed his right hand into his pocket and gripped the pistol as he flung open the door.

Blam! He was engulfed in smoke. No Feds. The hall was empty, but his new neighbors' door was wide open, propped open by a three-foot-tall silver samovar.

"Holy fuckin'shit! They're killin' themselves and want me to die, too."

The open door was four feet away, and as he reached it, the ghostly shape of what he assumed was the Mrs. half of M&M Ivanov, partially shrouded in smoke, appeared in the foyer waving the latest copy of *Cosmo* and driving the smoke straight into Faraci's face.

"What the fuck are you doing?" he growled as the edge of the magazine almost hit him in the nose. "That shit stinks. You're killing me!" Faraci puffed furiously to mingle his smoke with hers. When she emerged from the haze he was grateful they weren't mingling bodily fluids.

Mrs. I. wore a daffodil-yellow housecoat that matched her slippers. During her progress to the front door, her robe loosened. Thankfully—and here Faraci expressed rare gratitude to the Almighty—the robe didn't open, altogether exposing the round mound of her being.

When Mrs. I. saw Faraci puff, she yelled, "No! No! Out! Bad! Cancer!" But he continued to puff without speaking and pointed to the interior of her condo, pinching his nose with two fingers in a universal language that even she, he hoped, could understand.

"*Schmelt.*" She nodded and flashed an embarrassed smile, exposing symmetrically placed gold teeth above and below each other. "*Schmelt*," she repeated in case Faraci didn't understand.

He did. "Yeah, I schmelt it, and it schtinks 'cause it's shit."

She looked at him quizzically—to smile or not smile?

At this moment, Faraci made a mistake that would set the wheels of fate in motion. They would move as inexorably as the troop trains positioned toward Sarajevo before the start and leading to the outbreak of World War I.

Faraci held his nose with his left hand, leaving his right to communicate his displeasure and agitation. When events of such an urgent nature dictated, he was known to point at the offender in short, punchy strokes. So, Faraci pointed with his right hand.

His right hand held the .38. It was unintentional, of course. How could he explain that to a fat woman who barely spoke English and cooked smelly fish? Nevertheless, his gestures pointed the barrel of the .38 into Mrs. I.'s face.

She was shocked and screamed. The robe fell open, revealing an undulating form with more hollers and valleys than Kentucky coal country. She retreated and slammed the door. He quickly closed his and immediately noticed a twenty percent decrease in the odor's intensity. Now he could join Lenny for breakfast.

Faraci sat in the last booth in the back of Benno's, a small café off LaSalle in the financial district, one of few such establishments that had escaped the urban renewal bulldozer. Benno's was a joint, a hangout where lawyers, politicians, and others like Faraci could meet in solitude. He looked around and saw maybe five booths altogether, with another three or four tables down the center and one lonely table for two squeezed by the front window. The heat from inside met the window chilled by the January air, steaming the glass opaque and making the joint more secluded. Faraci liked joints and didn't feel the least bit uncomfortable eating in a suit that represented six weeks' wages for fifty percent of the patrons and a mile beyond the aspirations of the workers.

He sat alone at the last booth in a corner next to the kitchen. This was his preferred spot for a number of reasons. His back was to the wall, and he observed all who came in and out. If there was need to vacate the premises, he was into the kitchen and away in a second. Last, and most important for Faraci, his proximity to the kitchen insured his food was hot. All the waiters knew who he was and how he was capable of ruining their day, if not their gainful employment or, God forbid, their health if his food was not hot off the stove.

Lenny Santoro was five minutes late, which was unusual considering he taught accounting at the university and believed in being precise in all aspects of his life. Faraci and Lenny knew each other from another lifetime ago—high school.

Lenny graduated from college with a degree in economics, found the field too aggressive, and ultimately settled for a profession more suited to his personality. Faraci found a profession that was aggressive but wasn't, strictly speaking, economics.

Lenny slid into the booth as Faraci looked away from his watch, one eyebrow raised. "So? This is abnormal, Lenny. Five minutes." Faraci spoke across the rim of his coffee cup.

Lenny was contrite and didn't realize Faraci was reliving their high school days when they would take turns "ranking out" the other. Faraci saw the mortification on Lenny's face and relented. "Come on. I know you...what, forty, years? Maybe more? So, you're late." His *pronunciamento* ended, Faraci waved for the waiter to take Lenny's order.

He ordered a cappuccino and explained to Faraci, "I hate being late. You know I'd be here exactly as usual. I got delayed by a colleague. Nice guy. Family man. Tenured. Written a few papers. Speaks at symposia."

"No" from Faraci startled Lenny as he tentatively sipped from the steaming cup of cappuccino.

"No? What?"

"I said no," Faraci insisted. "I won't marry him." What resembled laughter tinkled from Faraci's mouth. "Sounds like you're giving me his pedigree. What do you guys call it? CeeVee?"

Considering the way his day began, Faraci attributed his good mood to the swift and efficient solution to his odor problem. He liked solving mysteries as much as he liked creating them.

"Curriculum vitae," Lenny said before finally getting to the reason for the biographical details. "Johnny, you know, all the years since high school, I never intruded on your business. Never. Whatever I learned from the outside. Didn't matter. You were always Johnny of Johnny and the Harptones, the doo-wop group we sang with down in the high school basement in that space near the boiler."

"The alcove," Faraci corrected.

"Yeah. So, I know this guy, the C.V. guy, who teaches math and got some trouble."

Faraci shrugged. "He teaches math; he should be able to *figure* things out."

Lenny didn't laugh and Faraci said, seriously, "What kind of trouble?" When he saw the you-know-what-I-mean look on Lenny's face, he added "because if he knocked up some coed, that's not my line" and smiled.

"Geez. You took comedian pills this morning. It's the usual." With that, Lenny rubbed the thumb and forefinger of his right hand together, the universal nonverbal gesture for money.

"Sure," Faraci said. "For you, Lenny. Send him to my office. I'll work something out, but not with a slide rule." Again, the tinkle of Faraci's laugh, to which he added a drum rim shot, *ba-da-bum*, on the table with the tips of both index fingers.

Tension eased from Lenny's body, and he managed a weak smile. "Thank you."

They ordered breakfast and then got into an argument over putting a dome on Wrigley Field. Lenny was pro, based on economics. Faraci couldn't care less but argued violently against, based on aesthetics. Faraci made Lenny pay for breakfast, and they left convinced the other was an imbecile. Next week they'd find something else to argue about.

* * *

Vadim Ivanov got a call from his wife, Ivana, in the office of his commodities trading company before he'd had time to finish his second cup of coffee. She was in tears, and he could barely understand her rapid speech. The one word he did understand was *gun*. He rushed home, grateful she was alive and unharmed but worried nevertheless. Could it be a home invasion robbery, like in California? He hoped no one had discovered the concealed safe. He'd spent a million eight on the condo. They were supposed to provide the best security. First, he'd call his lawyer and sue the bastards. Then he'd call Gregori, who was more experienced in such matters.

He called out Ivana's name from the foyer. *What the hell was she cooking?* More importantly, why didn't she answer? Vadim searched the rooms to find Ivana cowering in the kitchen corner where the sink met the stove, a clump of shivering flesh, her eyes red from crying. He held his wife as he would a child who had been awakened by a nightmare. After she stopped crying, he gave her a shot of vodka from the bottle in the freezer. She refused, but he insisted she bolt it down. It would straighten her spine.

Ivana needed two more shots before all her vertebrae were aligned. It was then she told him every detail. She'd gotten a deep yen for fried smelts, the ones he'd caught ice fishing in Wisconsin the previous weekend. The phone rang. Her shrug filled in the gap. The fish started to burn. Smoke billowed throughout the condo. As she cleared out the smoke, the man next door threatened her with his gun.

"The man next door?" he asked without indicating the one he hoped was not involved. "Ruski or Amerikanski?"

Ivana looked at her husband of fifteen years with doubts about his sanity. Of course it was the American; who else would have a gun in his condo?

"We do," Vadim reminded her.

They had to have a gun, she was quick to point out, because all the Americans were armed. Weren't those stories in *Pravda* enough of a warning? Now, all she'd worried about before they left Kiev had come true. Her life had been threatened and she almost died because of a little burnt fish.

Vadim called Gregori and left a message. Only his brother could help them now.

* * *

Dr. Santoro's words during a phone call the day before echoed in professor Steve Gorman's head as he drove downtown toward Navy Pier. "I've got this friend. Says he can help you. Whatever you decide is okay with me. Your business. I know nothing and want to know less.

You're a big boy. It's your call."

When Gorman heard the friend identified as Johnny Faraci, his emotions were jumbled. At first he felt too morally superior to sink so low. The newspapers called Faraci "a reputed mobster." Having to deal with that sort of individual was way beneath a tenured professor. Yet, the reality was he needed help, and he needed it fast. Soon he was convinced that his greater intelligence would rule. Just as he'd gotten a good deal on a used car for his wife, that same combo of daring and intellectual brilliance would see him through to a successful—and favorable for him—negotiation with Faraci.

Gorman smiled as he parked the car and, head down, forced his way against and through the icy wind blowing off Lake Michigan toward the entrance to the Chicago Clipper, an old Lake Michigan steamer-ferry. Decommissioned, the Clipper was now a floating restaurant and catering hall. The veteran of Prohibition was permanently moored to provide barely edible food to tourists and conventioneers. Two satellite dishes and other antennae were prominent aft of its smokestack.

Gorman, intent on visualizing a positive outcome to his negotiation with Faraci, never raised his head to notice.

Gorman's smile faded when he entered the foyer and encountered Jeff. With hooded eyes and a lean, angular face, Jeff presented an aura of controlled mayhem, like a falcon ready to strike. Jeff asked Gorman if he wanted smoking or nonsmoking. When Gorman asked to see Faraci, Jeff ordered, "Stay right here!" Without hesitation, Gorman stood still. Jeff disappeared.

After a few minutes of nervous waiting during which Gorman's eyes stayed riveted on the pattern of red velvet wall covering, Jeff instantly reappeared and beckoned for the professor to ascend a dark staircase. What light there was shone off a highly polished wood banister. Jeff flicked his head toward the top of the stairs and waited for Gorman to go first. After three steps, Gorman looked over his shoulder and saw Jeff follow. Eyes poking out from under heavy lids met Gorman's, and he broke contact only to note Jeff's hand inside his jacket, at the level of his waist. Gorman took the next ten steps as if prodded by the devil's pitchfork, his heart pounding as he reached the top.

The stairs led directly into Faraci's office. The large space, with a semicircle of windows, had been the bridge of the former vessel. Faraci smiled across the room as Gorman tried to compose himself. Gorman inhaled deeply and noticed a bank of television monitors along a far wall. Even at this distance he observed horse races on two of the screens. Gorman didn't expect Old World manners, but he didn't get the barely intelligible speech of Tony Soprano either. What the professor couldn't know was that Faraci liked to play "menace the pigeon," which kept all supplicants off balance and gave him an edge from the first sit-down.

Faraci, business-like, explained that he was in the catering business, and from time to time friends would recommend their friends for a helping hand. That was the occasion of their meeting. Considering the circumstances and nature of their mutual affairs, all involved must maintain decorum and discretion at all times.

Made perfect sense to Gorman, who had a reputation for being a take-no-prisoners professor. In his classes you performed or paid with a diminished grade point average. Across from him sat a man who shared a similar respect for responsibility.

Faraci let Gorman explain his difficulty, holding a long-standing belief that words initiated and spoken in candor were the best traps. When he learned that some non-green-card-holding spic at the university was getting gobs of vigorish from students and faculty alike, he put his hand over his mouth to conceal his shock and surprise. Then, his anger rose.

"That prick is a janitor?" As if social hierarchy should determine who was permitted to charge outrageous interest. Never bothered the banks.

Gorman nodded.

Gorman related he was two months in arrears with payment and asked for more time. Trujillo—that was the prick's name—threatened to visit his wife at home when Gorman was teaching.

"You got a preeeety wife." Trujillo leered at the family photo on Gorman's desk late one afternoon as he went from office to office ostensibly emptying the trash, while also collecting bets and intimidating those he determined were deadbeats.

"Maybe she need a man like me. A real hombre," Trujillo offered as he grabbed his crotch.

Gorman stood up and gave the janitor an impotent shove. The prick blurted a derisive laugh in return and wagged a finger as reminder.

"Maybe it better for her you no pay." His hand shot to the inseam of his grey work pants.

Gorman grabbed a calculus book and prepared to slam it on Trujillo's head when a student arrived for his four o'clock appointment.

Faraci listened to Gorman's tale of woe with inner glee. He was willing to help Gorman as a favor to his good friend Lenny. Gorman's look of relief sealed his fate. Unsaid was Faraci's ire that an interloper—and worse, an illegal noncitizen—was usurping his income and decreasing his profits. American business could not sustain itself if healthy competition replaced cartels and monopolies.

Faraci had to do his part for the economy, but his attention to Gorman was replaced by action on one of the TV screens.

"See that?" Faraci pointed excitedly to a race in progress. "It's some horse running in Bumfuck, Missouri, and I'm gonna win a bundle."

Gorman paused at the interruption, thinking the last subject he wanted to discuss was horse racing. Faraci persisted. "Know why? I bet the trainer." Faraci was pleased with himself and didn't allow Gorman to respond. "I got ten winners this month just betting on this trainer. The beauty part... she's a girl! Ariel something. A sure winner. Look it!"

They watched as Faraci's horse crossed the finish line in an easy gait, ahead by four lengths. "You was sayin'?"

Gorman explained how he owed ten thousand dollars, and each week the total increased by five percent.

"That much?" Faraci was being sarcastic, but Gorman was too consumed with his plight to notice. The ignorant spic and the dumb college guy didn't know what a cheap deal they had in five percent a week. And it never, he reminded himself, ever pays to be an amateur. Faraci told Gorman not to lose sleep; the ten grand was his. No interest. No reimbursement. A gift.

Gorman was speechless, and finally blurted his everlasting gratitude. He thought a little humble prostrating was required, even though he knew deep within it was the brilliance of Professor Steven Gorman that caused such a successful outcome.

But, it also wasn't a gift, per se. It was payment for information that would remove a predator from the scene.

"How?" Gorman gulped and expected Faraci to tell him the less he knew the better. But Faraci surprised him.

"You see the Discovery Channel program on wolves? No? Too bad. See, they catch the wolves, put a radioactive collar on them, and relocate them to another neighborhood. Consider the spic relocated."

Relocation was suitable to Gorman. He hoped Trujillo's new environment would be thousands of miles away from his wife and that the temperature never rose above minus-forty-five degrees. They agreed to think about a proper time and place to pay off Trujillo, and Gorman left. A smile returned to his face as he reached the bottom of the stairs but vanished as soon as Jeff appeared. Gorman waved at falcon eyes and quickly left the Chicago Clipper.

* * *

When Gregori finally returned his brother's call, he apologized for the delay. His new Uzbekistan restaurant was opening in two weeks, and every day was another problem. He could sense the agitation in his older brother's voice, but when asked for specifics, Ivan declined to speak on the phone. They decided to meet at the zoo.

An hour later, in front of the polar bear exhibit at the Lincoln Park Zoo, Vadim gave his baby brother, Gregori, a bear hug. The brothers were surprised to find the polar bears hibernating inside. Only the brothers Ivanov were dumb enough to stand outside in the January cold. For what they had to discuss, speaking outside in hushed tones was preferable. They were used to cold.

Vadim pushed Gregori an arm's length away and eyed him head to shoe. "Little brother, little brother. You a good lookin' guy. Like Putin." In fact, Gregori had the same slim build and angular face as Vladimir Putin. He exuded power, too, but on a lesser, nonnuclear, scale.

Though two months had passed since their last meeting, the brothers consumed by their respective businesses, the relationship had not diminished.

"I hate you," Vadim blurted. Gregori wasn't surprised. He knew the reason and smiled. Vadim tried to grab Gregori's midriff but couldn't. "You got nothing. No fet, no fleb." Vadim played his bulging stomach like a drum. "You eat like a musk ox and drink and smoke. Me, I'm wearing a pickle barrel under my shirt."

And so they ambled down the zoo's paths, acting like a couple of forty something kids until Vadim got to the heart of the problem. All kidding stopped and Gregori paid more attention to his older brother than he did his professors at the polytechnic institute. Vadim recounted the entire story, from the phone call to how Ivana slugged down three shots of vodka, and then identified the gun wielder.

Gregori didn't offer a twitch or tick of expression, and Vadim took this lack of response as either fear or impotency. Then he wondered if Gregori actually grasped the true nature and reputation of the neighbor in Condo 32A.

"If this is too much to ask, Gregori, I'll understand. I just thought, considering you have friends..."

"Shh. Dear older brother. Consider it done. A way will be found. A serpentine way so that the victim will be totally at ease." Gregori had already formed a plan, his eyes told Vadim.

"Do not take on this burden alone," Vadim advised. "You must keep me informed. Likewise, whatever I learn about my neighbor, you will know, too."

"Good. For now, my first call will be to Zendofsky. He changed his name to Zenda, but no matter."

The brothers Ivanov fiercely embraced in a display of affection and strength, each challenging the other to break contact first. Vadim lost and hoped it was not a bad omen.

* * *

Teresa Perino rang the front door to her brother's row house in Chicago's old Polish section where gentrification of the neighborhood was underway. Her children, little Michael and Michelle, stood on either side ready to greet their uncle. When the door opened, the children rushed inside, each grabbing one of Mike Hegan's legs. Their momentum, even for little kids, caused him to take a step back before embracing them.

When Hegan looked up, he saw a wan smile on Teresa's face.

"Eddie working?" he asked, figuring with his brother-in-law—also a member of Chicago's finest—a no-show, he must be in the middle of a case. She shook her head and put a finger to her lips.

"Kids, go see Lucy," she said, and the children left.

Hegan embraced his sister. "We're going to counseling. Trying to work things out. I don't want the kids to know. He decided not to come."

This was not the first time his sister's nearly eight-year marriage had faltered. As tough as it was being a cop, being a cop's wife was tougher. Hegan loved his sister but never thought she'd last this long married to Eddie Perino, one of his former partners, who never appeared marriageable. *Is any cop marriageable, me included?* Hegan thought. He worried about his own future.

Sometimes impulsiveness is more constructive than tortured thought, he reasoned. All life's a risk. A gamble. He was going to take the leap. What was the expression? Leaping into marriage? He knew the word wasn't defined as a track and field term—leaping in the broad jump, truly a double entendre. Clearly, whoever came up with "leaping into marriage" defined leap as jumping off a cliff or a building. That was the kind of leap they meant. Nevertheless, Hegan was determined to take the leap and get married. No matter what.

He kissed the top of Teresa's head and gently led her to the dining room. "Let's eat."

Lucy had coal-black eyes and a sharp, self-deprecating laugh that drew him into the kitchen. He found her playing with Mikey and Michelle. She looked up at Hegan. Her eyes met his, bathing him in a love he could never deserve.

"Eddie not coming?" she asked Teresa intuitively.

"A case..." Mike blurted after an uncomfortable pause.

Teresa swallowed hard and concurred. "Work." She shrugged, covering. "Not easy being a cop's wife."

"Oh" was all Lucy could answer, being polite and returning to the stove.

Mike came up behind Lucy as she stirred a pot. She sensed his presence without hearing his voice and turned to read his face. Mike saw in her eyes that she was wary. Reading his emotions, Lucy threw her arms around his neck as if they hadn't seen each other in a decade. Their lips stayed pressed together for longer than Teresa thought appropriate in front of the children, who giggled and pointed. Just when Teresa was ready to distract the girl and boy, the kiss ended.

Lucy licked her lips. "Needs more salt."

"Salt isn't good for you," Hegan replied. "Raises your blood pressure."

Lucy stirred the sauce on the stove. Suggestively, she pointed the wooden spoon at Hegan for emphasis. "I have enough salt. You need some to raise, ahem, your blood pressure."

"Maybe we should come back at another time," Teresa offered.

Before either could respond, Mikey started chanting, "Uncle Mike's getting married. Uncle Mike's getting married."

"How do you know that?" Hegan said, scooping up Mikey in his arms. "How come?"

Mikey gave him the wisdom of his six years. "When two people kiss, they... they have to get married." There. Cause and effect.

"Thank you very much, Mikey. That will be all. Now, take your place at the table. You too, Michelle." Teresa wrested control from the lovebirds, and order was restored through maternal fiat.

Lucy brought salad to the table and Hegan a bowl of spaghetti and meatballs. Hegan loved Lucy's cooking almost as much as he loved her. Sometimes he wondered which held first place in his heart.

Tonight was special in two ways. Lucy made her special spaghetti sauce. Eddie liked it and she wanted to please Hegan's brother-in-law who would soon become hers as well. That Eddie was a no show did not dampen the occasion. .

Second was the surprise. Hegan poured the adults red wine and raised his glass. They all clinked, the children with their milk.

"Enjoy," he said and waited while everyone sipped and Teresa started eating. Hegan looked over at Lucy and was pierced by her eyes clear back to his vertebrae. "And while you're enjoying, I want you all to know..." Hegan paused, waiting to get maximum attention.

"What, Uncle Mike?" his namesake nephew asked.

"You want to know? Huh? You really want to know?" he asked his five-year-old straight man.

"I don't want to know," Michelle said as Mikey nodded and kept on eating.

"Enough! Tell us!" Teresa was no fun. Hegan decided his attempt at being a stand-up comedian needed to end.

"Lucy and I are getting married," he said soft and quick.

"Yes! I told you!" Mikey said, pumping his fist into the air.

"What?" Teresa's eyes and head shot up at them. "Why didn't you say so? You're such a jerk," she said, standing and slapping Hegan on the shoulder before hugging Lucy and kissing her cheek. "When? Have you decided?"

"In six months. July twenty-sixth. Hope you all can come," Lucy said. Hegan took her hand and kissed it.

"I can't come," Michelle piped up all of a sudden.

"What?" Teresa said.

"I'm not going." Reality intruded on fantasy and it hurt, even to a seven-year-old.

"Young lady." Teresa would brook no petulance or misbehavior from her children. She knew she was as old-fashioned as her mother, but she didn't care. "We'll have none of that" was her conclusion and dictate.

Hegan gently patted his sister's arm, a sign to cool it. "Why aren't you coming, Michelle? We'd love for you to be there."

Michelle bowed her head and scrunched her mouth before deciding to answer. "You're supposed to marry me, Uncle Mike."

Hegan heard the beginnings of a guffaw from Teresa and slapped her leg under the table. She was silent.

"I'm so much older than you, sweetheart. By the time you're old enough, I'll have a long white beard down to my toes." The image made Michelle laugh, and Lucy saw her opportunity.

"We want you both in the wedding party," Lucy said and, as if waiting to present a big surprise, pulled a roll of paper from under the sideboard. She showed Michelle a sketch of the flower girl's dress. "You'll wear this, pink with white lace. And a garland of flowers on your head. You'll carry a big basket of rose petals. As I come down the aisle, you'll strew them on the carpet."

Michelle's eyes brightened. She bounced in her chair. "Yippee!"

"And you, young man," Hegan turned to Mikey, "will carry the rings."

"What's a strew?'" Mikey asked.

Hegan showed him a sketch of the blue suit the boy would wear. "You'll be the most important person in the whole church." Mikey was too young to understand his uncle's words, but the gravity of their sound made him giggle. "Without the rings, we can't get married. Isn't that right?" He looked over at Lucy for confirmation.

"Well, not exactly." She grabbed a hank of his hair and ran her fingers through it possessively.

Lucy saw Teresa look away, only the hint of an ambivalent smile on her face.

"Kids, go play with Uncle Mikey." Hegan was surprised and protested. Dinner wasn't over. He didn't want to play. He was comfortable. Lucy ended the discussion. "Go play or you won't get dessert. And I don't mean chocolate cake."

"Oh. You mean...?"

"Maybe I do and maybe I don't. If you're not out of here in five, four, three—"

"Let's go play with Uncle Mikey," Hegan said.

After they left, Lucy embraced Teresa, who accepted the comfort. The two women had grown to know and appreciate each other over the last few months as Mike made clear in his careful, painfully slow way that Lucy was the woman he wanted above all others.

Lucy looked in Teresa's eyes, noted Eddie's absence, and knew. Teresa put her head on Lucy's shoulder and let a few tears flow. Then she sniffled, wiped the tears from her cheeks, and offered Lucy a grateful smile.

"Call me. Night or day," Lucy said, her intensity sparking a look of surprise in Teresa's eyes. Support was needed and given. "We're practically sisters, or will be officially in six months. I'll always be here for you."

They hugged and Lucy returned to the dessert phase. "Get the kids," she said to Teresa, "and I do mean all three of them."

* * *

Gorman drew back the drapes of the room he used as a study and lit his pipe. Here he maintained order and protected himself from the chaos of his fourteen year marriage and the three children it produced. When all else was unbearable, this one room in his house was his refuge. After a few puffs, he focused on the low, grey sky indicating snow was imminent. He wondered if enough snow would fall on campus to cancel his classes on Monday. For now, only the threat loomed.

As Gorman's organized mind wrestled to a no-decision regarding the weather, his phone rang. That phone rarely, if ever, rang. It was a private line installed in his sanctuary so that the social calls of his wife and children would not intrude. Only a select few had the number: his department chair and the dean of the faculty.

As the ring persisted, Gorman experienced the eerie feeling that the caller actually knew he was in the room. Gorman grabbed the phone and answered.

"Who?" Gorman asked at the voice, which he found deep in tone but uneducated in speech. There was a swagger in the voice that seemed unaware of a world beyond its own existence.

"Metcha at the Clipper. Mr. F. wants to see ya." Jeff's voice was the aural equivalent of walking down the street to the cadence of hip-hop.

Gorman went through a Rolodex in his mind. *Clipper? Mr. F.* Finally, *Faraci*!

"Sure." He recovered. "When does Mr. F. wanna meet?"

"Now," Jeff said.

"Now? I can't. My wife and I have dinner plans."

"Now!" Jeff barked.

"We're meeting friends," sounding lame even to himself.

"What part of *now* don'tcha unnerstan'?" Jeff asked.

Gorman was convinced this Jeff had rehearsed the line as an all-purpose response to any resistance. He tried to construct a logical retort, but the image of Jeff's menacing, hooded eyes intruded.

"I'm waiting," Jeff said playfully, with no interest in fun and games. "Maybe you don't remember, huh?"

Gorman remembered all too well. "Of course. Jeff. From the Clipper. Let me see if I can rearrange my plans." Gorman put Jeff on hold and puffed rapidly. Through the window he saw the grey sky getting darker. He didn't want to venture out in bad weather. He and his wife had no plans except staying inside. If he didn't go, Trujillo would only get worse, and he'd also have Faraci as an enemy.

Gorman reconnected, but Jeff was gone. The phone rang again.

"Hey! What the fuck you think you're doin'? Don't you hang up on me."

Gorman patiently tried to explain the hold process, but it got Jeff more upset. He tried to reclaim the upper hand. "It's possible I can adjust my plans," Gorman began, only to get "I'll adjust your life" from Jeff. When Jeff paused for a second, Gorman agreed to meet that night. He used a sharp tone and felt he'd gained equilibrium, if not a slight edge. He was told they would take care of Trujillo and given a time and meeting place to arrange details.

Gorman was pleased Faraci at last decided to pay off Trujillo. He'd do as asked, and life would return to normalcy—whatever that was. For the last few weeks, Gorman, following Faraci's instructions, had been stringing Trujillo along. He'd pay fifty bucks and, a few days later, two hundred more.

"Pay up. I ain't no Bisa card," Trujillo would say with annoyance. Gorman promised he'd pay all of it if only Trujillo had patience. He was cashing in his IRA. Or was it his 401(k)? Gorman couldn't keep his lies straight, and Trujillo didn't care.

* * *

That night, Lucy hurried out of the bathroom and scrambled, naked, into their Ethan Allen sleigh bed. She snuggled up to Hegan's body, also naked, for warmth from the cool January night air. *This will be the start of sweet dreams*, he thought as her erect nipples brushed his body until she found a comfortable position.

Lucy wasn't interested in more than warmth. Ever since the spaghetti dinner she had been pained by Teresa's unstable marriage. "We'll never break up, will we, Mike? We'll always be together and always be best friends, won't we?"

"You're stuck with me," he replied, caressing the inside of her thigh. She pushed him away.

"Maybe we should run away and get married now. Justice of the peace and all that. Do the ceremony thing for my folks later. At least we'll know we belong to each other."

Hegan wrapped an arm around Lucy and bear hugged her closer. "And what do you call this?" he said, squeezing her again for emphasis.

"Why buy the cow when you can get the milk for free?" She said it in a singsong fashion which was both light and serious.

"I know, I know. The cheerleader who screws the football team never marries the quarterback," he answered.

"I hope you're not teasing me," she said seriously.

Hegan went back to Lucy's thigh, but she expressed more concerns about Teresa's fragile mental health. Next, Lucy worried about Mikey and Michelle. What would happen to their growth and development if their parents divorced or continued to fight?

"Geez," he said with an exaggerated flourish. Lucy chuckled, knowing Hegan's reaction was intended to lighten her concerns. "I've heard of nervous brides, but that's right before the wedding. Will this go on for the next six months? Night after night. On and on and on."

"Shut up," she said playfully.

To prove it, Lucy covered his body with hers, pinned his hands above his head, and gave him a kiss full on his mouth. Her pelvis circled his, and she got the desired response, until finally she sat up, straddled his legs, and rode him with an intensity Hegan had never experienced from her before. There had been plenty of hot and sweaty days and nights with Lucy, going back to the first time the previous summer, but tonight Lucy had a hunger that would never be sated. Like a sailor on the last day in port before embarking on six months at sea, Lucy seemed to be storing up all the exquisite sensations she could receive from Hegan's body for a long, long time.

Hegan didn't know what possessed Lucy but hoped he could replicate it and bottle it for future use, like solar panels collect sunlight. He was going along for the ride, in this case being ridden, and it didn't bother his manhood a bit. *Shake me, bake me, any way you want me*, he thought as Lucy rhythmically impaled herself.

Her intensity was such that he wanted to laugh but knew it would spoil Lucy's enjoyment. Worse, she'd get angry, and that would shrivel his ardor until he could cover her face with kisses and restore the mood. The thought of kissing Lucy made him smile. Lucy would never know.

"I knew I'd bring a smile to your face, big boy," she teased seconds before releasing a spasm of pleasure and dropping the weight of her body down on him in a heap. Hegan rolled her over on her back without uncoupling, threw her limp legs over his shoulders, and a few seconds later they were unconscious in each other's arms.

CHAPTER TWO

What could possibly be worse than driving on a cold January night with heavy snow forecast? Gorman wondered as he backed out of the driveway. Being dead, was the swift answer. Weather inconvenience became a secondary concern.

Fear emerged as the front-runner, even if it had been the unknown variable in a life he managed with mathematical precision. Gorman wondered what the odds were that he'd be dead before morning. Who would give the odds? What was the inside info? Who'd handicap his death like they did the fillies at Arlington Park? Then he remembered it was losing bets on the horses that ultimately got him where he was this night.

He had to endure his darkest fears in the hope of saving his life. *Never again.* What? Another false promise? He tried to stop gambling before, pitting the strength of his will against an unrelenting obsession to beat the odds. Gamblers Anonymous was not for him. All those losers and retards. Not him. His will was stronger. This time, with some luck from the gods—whoever they were—he'd change. He knew he was right, because the calculations were always correct. They were his fortress, and he was always safe from attack. Now, quite suddenly, Gorman had lost his way in a more rigorous discipline: the street.

Gorman was heading for the part of Chicago that never gets extolled in Chamber of Commerce brochures. Kept hidden. More precisely, never acknowledged until some lurid crime called out for attention. This was where the "other" people lived, where pools of light provided the pretense of safety on dark streets. Gorman wanted to speed through these streets. He'd prefer not to be there at all. *Too late now*, he thought, and slowed the car down as he approached the intersection Jeff had designated.

Jeff's instructions were to turn into a parking lot on the corner. As he prepared to do so, a hand banged on his window. Gorman jumped and watched the figure pass through his headlights. Jeff motioned for Gorman to open the door then slid into the front seat.

"'Bout time you showed. I'm freezin' my nuts out here."

Gorman didn't respond. By now he knew there was only one set of rules; they weren't his. Jeff took command.

"Here's the plan. We go over to the bodega. I'm hidin' in the back seat, just in case. My guys will follow and wait a block behind—"

"Guys? Who said...?"

Jeff continued without acknowledging Gorman's question. "You go in and give the spic the money, get back in the car, and drive away. Then we relocate the bastard."

Gorman nodded, but wanted to be sure he understood. All theorems had to be proven. He grasped for some control, even if tentative. "You brought the money?"

Jeff pulled an envelope from inside his coat and showed Gorman, flipping through a wad of bills. To Gorman's surprise, Jeff gave him the envelope. As he tucked the money inside his coat pocket, some of his tension started to subside. Here was tangible proof. Faraci was a man of his word, and, more importantly, Gorman's problem was solved.

Two blocks from the bodega, Jeff had Gorman pull over and stop. He folded his body over the seatback like a pole-vaulter and hid in the dark. "Go ahead. Slow and easy." Gorman proceeded after glancing in his rearview mirror to find they were still being followed by Jeff's "friends." He wouldn't quibble over the description and didn't care to think of his potential saviors as henchmen.

Gorman blocked doubts and distractive thoughts from his mind. On internal cruise control, he parked in front of a nameless bodega on a poorly lit street he would try not to remember. Even in the cold, clumps of men and women huddled on the sidewalk. All eyes turned to him, the stranger who none feared.

Gorman and Trujillo locked onto each other as soon as the bell above the bodega's door rang. Gorman kept his gaze focused directly toward the rear wall, about a foot above Trujillo's head. The less he saw of his tormentor's face, the easier this would be, he decided. Focusing on the wall, Gorman did not see with clarity the eclectic array of items on the periphery of his vision: canned goods containing Latino foodstuffs on the shelves, or the tall votive candles and other implements of sanatoria, or the posters advertising cheap phone cards to Latin American countries.

Trujillo drank from a bottle hidden in a brown paper bag. Gorman noticed a trace of moustache being cultivated on the younger man's upper lip. *Thinks a hairy lip will make him look older*, Gorman thought. He'd gladly take a straight razor to Trujillo's face. Envisioning turning his nemesis into a bloody stump caused Gorman to smile.

Trujillo smiled back. As Gorman reached the midpoint of the store Trujillo stood and reached two arms out in greeting.

"Come, amigo. Come," he said behind a false welcome. Trujillo waved Gorman forward impatiently, pointing to a seat on the opposite side of the booth he occupied. He shoved away a young teenage girl who occupied the same seat, like sweeping crumbs off a table.

Gorman pulled out the envelope as he slid into the booth. "All there. Ten thousand. Like I said on the phone."

Trujillo pulled out a wad of hundred-dollar bills and started counting in English and Spanish, "uno, dos, tres, four, five," alternating languages in a musical tempo underscored by a taunting, disrespectful tone. "One hundred," Trujillo declared and then flipped through the other bundles, comparing their thickness until satisfied.

"I trust you, amigo," he said, putting the envelope next to his thigh on the worn, red vinyl seat. "But if you are short, I just put it on your bill." He brayed a laugh in triumph, exposing yellowed teeth. Trujillo offered Gorman a slug from the bottle, but Gorman declined.

"Thank you," Gorman said as if dealing with the loan officer of his bank.

"No, *gracias a te, señor.*"

Before leaving, Gorman pulled a folded sheet of paper out of another pocket. "This is a receipt for the money." Gorman unfolded the paper and placed it in front of Trujillo.

The receipt was a product of Gorman's obsessive nature. In this context it made no sense. A head-scratcher from the start. To Gorman it was about being tidy. Terms of sale. Buy something and get a receipt—from toothpaste to a car.

Trujillo lifted the paper from the table and waved it in the air. "Hey, he wants me to sign a recipe." He purposely mispronounced the word and laughed. Then, he shook the paper in Gorman's face with a ferocity that forced the smug professor to pull back in his seat.

"It's for my records. A mere formality. I won't show this to anyone." Gorman's tone was flat. He worked hard not to show fear but knew Trujillo could sense it.

Trujillo laughed again. "A mere formality?" he said, mocking Gorman for the benefit of whoever was in his audience. He paused for dramatic effect as if considering a megadeal. "Okay, I sign it."

Gorman was relieved inside and provided the pen. Trujillo signed with a flourish and, after an insincere smile revealed his true feelings, pushed pen and paper back to Gorman with a dismissive backhand.

"Thank you," Gorman said again and slid out of the booth.

"*De nada,*" Trujillo replied, which was exactly what he meant and felt about the paper he'd just signed. It was nothing. His signature was nothing. His word to Gorman was nothing. All Trujillo did was fulfill his cultural imperative, which called for the primacy of self-involvement in all things, no different than an out of control child wanting what he wants when he wants it.

As Gorman pushed open the front door and disappeared into the dark street, Trujillo spit in his direction. He crammed the envelope inside his belt and swaggered outside in time to watch his victim disappear into the night.

"*Cabron!*" he yelled after the car so everyone could hear and waved the envelope in victory. "*Soy grande hombre,*" he added and started planning the next time he'd meet Gorman so he could wring more money out of the stupid gringo.

Intent on savoring the many ways Gorman would squirm next time, Trujillo didn't notice a car glide down the street with its headlights out. Nor did he see Jeff's hand reach out from the shadows before it covered his mouth and pulled him into the open door of the idling car.

Within seconds, Jeff delivered a professional chop to Trujillo's neck. He shut the door, pleased he'd retained the basic skill learned while a member of the army's Special Ops. The blow stunned Trujillo long enough for the small-time loan shark to be snatched without a trace or a sound. Due to the speed and stealth of Jeff and his "friends," the residents on the sidewalk, clumped together against the cold, never heard a thing. Half an hour later, the last thing Trujillo heard was a chainsaw being cranked to life.

* * *

Hegan's pager sounded while the morning was still dark. He rolled out of bed, jolted by adrenalin. Lucy experienced a tectonic shift in the bed but was too exhausted to complain. Hegan grabbed the pager and his cell phone from the top of the retro Ethan Allen dresser and dialed the blinking number while heading to the front bedroom where he could talk without waking Lucy.

From the supervisor at the overnight desk, Hegan learned that a body had been found in the university's swimming pool. Seems some coeds came in for a few early laps and saw the water had a faintly pink hue. Hegan could respond in twenty minutes. "Better make it thirty," the disembodied voice told him. "We got eight inches of snow last night. Now it's freezing rain."

Lucy woke with a start as Hegan turned on the ceiling light to search the closet for his boots.

"What is it?" she asked, sitting up in bed and drawing the covers up to her neck.

"A body in the university pool. Homicide, the uniforms think. Also, there's eight inches of snow and now freezing rain. We'll visit your folks next weekend."

Lucy was willing to wait until he returned, but Hegan didn't know how long his investigation would take. Just as she knew she wanted Hegan for her lifelong mate, Lucy was determined to visit her parents in their suburban home. If Hegan couldn't be with her, she'd give them the happy news about the wedding herself. There was plenty of mother-daughter stuff to discuss. Hegan would only be an afterthought; get in the way; spend time on inconsequential matters with her father. Besides, she had snow tires on the Volvo.

"You saw the commercials with the crash dummies" was Lucy's parting shot.

Hegan finished lacing his boots, the same ones he thought would keep him from taking dancing lessons, and strapped on his holster. "No! I don't want you to go! It's idiotic to drive fifty miles one way in this weather."

"Don't you call me an idiot!" she yelled after him as he raced down the stairs and opened the hall closet for his jacket.

"I will if you act like one."

"Just because you wear a gun doesn't mean you have the power of God Almighty over me," she said, bouncing down the stairs. She was naked, but the cold didn't bother her because her blood was boiling.

"Cut the crap. I want you to stay home!" Hegan turned to give her a kiss, but she turned her cheek away and pushed him toward the door.

"Get out. Just get out, you paternalistic pig!"

Hegan smiled as his face met the cold morning air. That was his hot-blooded Lucy. She was a challenge in and out of bed, and he loved all of her fiery nature. Within seconds, the icy rain wiped the smile off his face.

Hegan tried to determine how the body, lacking head or hands, was deposited in the university pool. The answer to that question would lead him to the reason why. The tile walls and water in the pool created an echo chamber, and Hegan heard one of the uniforms twenty yards behind him whisper, "So this is how you learn the dead man's float here, huh?" "Dead men can't float," his pal whispered back. "Stow that," Hegan said, aiming his words at them in a voice that needed no acoustical help.

Hegan watched as two scuba divers in complete gear—fins, masks, wet suits—entered the pool and secured the body. Pink fluid dripped onto the tile as they maneuvered the body to the shallow end and "walked" it up the steps to the pool deck. Hegan studied the pool, looking for more traces of blood. Its absence was gradually the answer to his first question. For whatever unknown reason, it was becoming evident the corpse was dismembered elsewhere and moved to the pool. Why the pool and how? Like the horse's head in *The Godfather*, this corpse magically appeared and also sent a message. From whom, to whom, wasn't on the card. He knew Latinos' control of the drug trade was being eclipsed by Eastern Europeans. But that was the obvious answer.

Hegan completed his tour of the pool deck and reached the body. According to the driver's license in the victim's pocket, what was left of the body belonged to a twenty-eight-year-old Latino named Trujillo. Without the benefit of fingerprints or dental records, it could be anyone. Hegan was sure of only one thing: being in the heated pool house was preferable when icy rain fell outside.

Hegan's exterior warmth belied the spreading chill of dread emerging in his gut as he recalled Lucy's rant. They'd never separated for work without a kiss in the six months they'd lived together. This was a break in what many would consider routine, but which had become almost a sacred act to him. He shivered remembering.

One of the uniforms noticed Hegan zip his jacket. "You okay, detective?" he asked in jest. "Maybe you need—"

"I need quiet," Hegan shot back. "Have some respect for the dead."

Never again would they part the least bit grumpy with each other, he vowed, determined to whisk away all the ill will of the morning as soon as he got home.

* * *

While Hegan was discerning the meaning of his corpse, Lucy visited her parents. A string of accidents in the near-whiteout conditions caused the fifty-mile trip to take more than two hours. Her parents' joy at her news was worth the delay. Before they could discuss details, the Weather Channel indicated more icy rain for that evening, and her parents advised Lucy to leave while there was enough daylight. They'd talk by phone and she could visit again, this time with Mike, when the weather got better.

The roads iced faster than Lucy expected. At a fork in a road through a heavily wooded area two miles from her parents' house, the Volvo skidded on a hidden patch of ice and hit a thirty-five-year-old oak with a cross-body block, like a pulling guard takes out a charging linebacker to open the hole for the fullback.

Except the oak was the genetic ancestor of those who gave their lives to build Old Ironsides, the USS *Constitution*, famed for its exploits in the American Revolution. The oak had an ancestral reputation to uphold. Its ancestors resisted British cannonballs. Now, it had to stand tall against the metal frame of an out-of-control Swedish car. It did. Steel-belted snow tires were useless as the car spun out of control sideways and lifted for a moment off the ground.

The centrifugal momentum of the Volvo finally ended, its steel bent and glass shattered. The oak stood tall but suffered a large gash in its middle-aged trunk. It was bloody, but unbowed. Its ultimate demise would take some time.

The frame of the Volvo had creased but remained intact. Perhaps it could be restored. What did not survive as well as the oak or car was Lucy. She wore a seat belt and was not thrown forward into the windshield like a crash test dummy, because the car did not have a head-on impact. When the Volvo broadsided the tree, Lucy's head bobbled from side to side, unrestrained by any safety harness. The whipsaw motion caused her brain to slam against the bone of her skull until it shimmied like jelly on a plate.

By the time the wreck was discovered by a passing motorist, the local fire department ambulance called, and Lucy rushed—as fast as the rescuers dared on icy roads—to the local hospital, she was in a vegetative state.

Hegan called Lucy at home. He hoped to calm her down, make plans for dinner. He'd bring flowers. Lucy didn't answer. He got called back to the crime scene and hung up before the answering machine message played.

An hour later he called. Still no Lucy. He listened to their recorded message: "This is Mike... and Lucy," she announced with a chuckle in her voice as if to say "I've got him, and any of you man-stealing ladies out there better give up."

The message continued with each alternating the usual words, "Please leave a message at the beep and we'll call you back." Lucy thought it was cute. Hegan had endured, wanting a message more practical than cloying.

"Hey, Lucy. If you're there, pick up. If not I hope you're shopping. Buy yourself something very expensive, 'cause you're worth it. Love ya." He hung up.

Hegan became more concerned about Lucy than the torso. She was stubborn enough to visit her parents just to show him and the weather gods she could do as she pleased. He expected she'd accuse him of being paternalistic again when he got home. All he wanted was to keep her safe. There was that old double standard again. Show concern and get accused of being a controlling father surrogate; don't, and be called cold and unloving.

Time crawled by, and he resented the assignment but had to continue. The three female student swimmers were kept apart so their stories would not be infected by each other. They shivered on separate sides of the pinkish water, legs quaking involuntarily though wrapped in large towels in the balmy temperature of the pool room. Hegan slowly questioned each one in turn, though a voice in his head kept pulling him elsewhere. At times that voice created tragic scenarios causing him to stop his interrogation, leave the pool area, and take deep breaths in the corridor before his equilibrium was restored.

"This must be tough for you too," one of the coeds said with empathy when Hegan returned, not knowing his reaction was personal, not professional. Hegan nodded at the tone of her voice though not its implication.

Two hours passed while Hegan was getting essentially the same story from each of the young women. They arrived together. Changed in the women's locker room. Entered the pool. The lights were on. That in itself wasn't unusual, as the light switch was outside the pool area and could've been turned on by the janitor without his venturing inside. From a distance, one of them thought somebody's duffel bag was at the bottom of the pool. Another thought it was a trash barrel. Just a prank by stupid, arrogant frat boys.

Hegan took a break and called again. The message played and he hung up. He redialed and this time entered his code to listen to his messages. The first message he heard was the latest. It was his to Lucy. The second message was startling.

Lucy's mother called an hour earlier. "Hi, honey. Hope you're home. Been three hours since you left. Maybe you're in a hot bath. What great news. We love you. You, too, Mike. Bye." There were no more messages. *Four hours*! he thought. *She left at two. Icy rain is still falling. Where is she?*

During his remaining time at the crime scene, Hegan just went through the motions. He was professional enough but tried to move things along to such a degree that he snapped at the uniformed officers, who were surprised at the usually cordial and mellow detective sergeant.

It was dark when Hegan pulled in front of his house. The Volvo was not in its usual place at the end of the driveway. Inside, he checked the messages before turning on the light. There were only the two he'd heard. The phone rang and his stomach rose and fell. He snatched at the receiver, missed it, and knocked it to the floor. He groped in the dark, following the cord until he finally placed the phone to his ear.

"Lucy?" he asked and heard Lucy's mother reply.

"Mike!" She was crying.

"Oh Jesus!" were the only words he could say before hearing the reason she called.

"Goddamned fucking Jesus H. Christ!" he screamed in the dark after hanging up. He ripped the phone out of the wall and threw it across the room.

On instinct, Hegan called Clay on his cell phone. He was the only person he thought to call.

"It's Lucy. She's..."

Clay didn't have to hear more. "I'll be there."

What could Clay do? Hegan would never hear Lucy's voice or her laugh. He'd never feel her body in bed or see her glorious smile. What could anybody do for him now? Fuck it! He crawled toward the liquor cabinet and grabbed the first bottle he found.

Clay's car was blocked in a drift created by snowplows. He ran the remaining ten blocks. Covered in icy rain and snow, Clay resembled a gigantic black Santa. Frosty breath covered his chin as Clay entered the unlocked front door. He turned on the lights and found Hegan huddled in a corner of the living room, clutching a half empty bottle of J&B.

Clay pried the bottle from Hegan's hand and wrapped his behemoth arms around his friend. The rain on Clay's coat mingled with the tears on Hegan's cheeks. They were a tableau, like the male version of the Pietà, the poster boys for humanity, a black man and white man united in grief. Two men able to touch and be touched without hesitation or fear.

Ten years ago, Leon Clay was a defensive end for the Chicago Bears. A decade later, he'd lost none of his quickness, compared to civilians. Now, on the gridiron, he'd be a tortoise, but Clay could still bench press his own weight. He easily lifted Hegan and tossed him, clothed, in the shower. The sooner Hegan was functioning, the better. Then he put the kettle on for tea and warmed a can of soup from the pantry.

Clay checked on Hegan, who was more dazed than awake. He shut off the water and threw a towel at his friend Hegan. "Dry off and change. Heating soup." Clay returned to check on the soup and tried to remember when he first met Hegan. The soup was mushroom barley, and that took Clay back to the deli, which took him back to the day they met five years earlier.

Clay remembered chasing some whippet of a Vikings wide receiver down the sidelines, his lungs screaming for relief and every bone and sinew yelling at him to stop. He made a last desperate effort to keep the receiver from scoring, threw himself at the player, missed and ended up staggering out of control into the sideline crowd. His chest smacked Hegan—at the time, a uniformed cop detailed for crowd control—in the head and knocked him out. Later, when smelling salts revived Hegan and the Bears' defense returned to the bench, Clay formally introduced himself. He also apologized, but Hegan understood completely. Clay really wanted Hegan to know it was unintentional.

Hegan didn't need any more apologies. "The least you could've done was trip the guy and keep him from scoring the go-ahead touchdown."

"What?" Clay went to boil in an instant. "Do you know... do you know...?" Clay looked down at Hegan and saw a big grin on his face. *Gotcha* time. Clay wrapped his gigantic arm around Hegan's shoulder. "Little man,"—at six feet, Hegan was about eight inches shorter—"you are a turkey, and I'm gonna buy you dinner."

"You want a turkey sandwich that'll make your eyes water, I know the only place," Hegan said, playing straight man.

That night they ate turkey sandwiches with Thousand Island dressing and mushroom barley soup at Kaz's deli. So began an enduring friendship between Hegan, Kaz, and the others who played poker every Wednesday night at Henry's, another of Hegan's pals.

Hegan's hair was wet when he entered the kitchen and sat before the bowl of soup Clay presented. "I'm not hungry."

Clay commanded, "Eat. Something. This is the Lord's test."

"Yeah, if it's His test, let Him take it."

"You gotta be strong, whether you want to or not."

"Who says? Nobody told me there'd be a test." The combination of emotional and physical exhaustion fueled by too much Scotch drained Hegan. He slowly passed out.

Clay carried him upstairs. Half asleep, Hegan reacted violently as they got to the master bedroom and refused to enter. He chose to sleep in the double bed of his unattached, bachelor years. It had occupied the small front room since Lucy entered his life and they'd bought the Ethan Allen bedroom suite. He planned to sell all that furniture. He needed to sell it. Give it away. Burn it. No reminders. Nothing but pain. As tears ran down his cheeks, Hegan cried himself to sleep.

In the middle of the night, Hegan felt Lucy's body on his and was relieved that the horrendous nightmare was over. He heard her voice once again. "Knew I'd bring a smile to your face, big boy." Hegan rolled over to get on top of her and hit his hand on the bedroom wall. He flailed in the dark, trying to chase the dread that occupied his bed.

* * *

Steve Gorman saw Lenny Santoro in the faculty lounge for the first time since revealing his particular financial difficulties. He didn't think Lenny was avoiding him, only that their schedules conflicted. Any doubts were dispelled when Lenny greeted him warmly and they shared coffee together.

"I wanted to thank you," Gorman began and was immediately stopped by a metronomic wave of Lenny's finger.

"We won't discuss this. Now, or at any time. All I'll say, and I would appreciate no response from you, is you asked for help, I made a suggestion. Whatever subsequently developed is your business."

Gorman stifled his response and offered a weak smile. Lenny didn't want any awkwardness between them and opened another line of conversation. "How do you feel about putting a dome on Wrigley Field?" he asked.

Gorman shook his head for clarity, the question out of left field, he thought. "You're serious?" He looked at Lenny and saw the question was not idly posed.

"You can't play baseball in Chicago in April. One year it snowed. And in the event the Cubs ever make the World Series, which is played in mid-October, that weather's just as cold."

Gorman seized the question for debate and was about to render his opinion when Isabelle St. Pierre, a young French instructor, intruded breathlessly. "You hear about the body?" She was so intent on dispensing her news she didn't realize the two men were engaged in a serious conversation. "Oh! I'm sorry. Forgive me for interrupting."

Four raised eyebrows fixed her to the spot, and she immediately regretted acting like such a naive airhead with two seasoned and highly respected, not to mention tenured, professors.

"Isabelle," Lenny began and she relaxed, "you told us the headline..."

"Now tell us the rest of the story," Gorman chimed in thinking he sounded like Paul Harvey. Isabelle pulled up a chair and leaned forward so she could speak softly. "By now the whole school knows, but early Sunday morning a body was found in the pool house."

"Any body we know? As long as it wasn't you." Gorman was flirtatious with her, as usual. His eyes frisked her body. "Your figures would make my calculus book blush."

"Oy!" Santoro groaned. "Enough, Gorman. So, who was it?" he asked Isabelle his voice calm. Isabelle did not encourage Gorman, who she knew was a notorious randy goat, and deflected him with a serious and objective "No one knows," followed by a sweet "fuck you" smile.

"Male or female?" Santoro asked without much investment in the details.

Isabelle tried to get her facts straight. One of her students went for an early morning swim with two friends, and they made the discovery. Isabelle related all she knew. "Male. Fully clothed.

Not the kind a student would wear." She paused and drew in a breath. "But somebody cut his head off and his hands. *C'est* très *terrible*," which in French made it seem more gruesome.

"That's too bad," Lenny responded then got lost in thought.

"Guess we'll be the subject of exploitation in the media until they dig their fangs into a more juicy story," Gorman offered.

A quick look at the clock above the faculty lounge door gave Isabelle six minutes to make her next class. She'd unburdened herself, and wasn't ridiculed. Hopefully they didn't regard her as some flighty chick dishing gossip. Talk of the body erased considering a dome for Wrigley Field. They finished their coffee in silence.

By the time Gorman reached his first class that morning, he'd heard the words "body" and "pool" as he passed students in the halls. The words struck him in such a random fashion that their impact was diffuse. After class, he visited his mailbox in the professor's lounge. The room was a collection of sofas and arm chairs, more reminiscent of a hospital waiting room than a sanctuary for intellectuals. One faculty member was hidden behind *The Wall Street Journal*, and another dozed in the far corner.

Gorman found his mail cubicle and sifted through various directives from the chairman's office and a notice from the credit union. One letter, unsealed and without a stamp, bore his last name in handwriting that was unfamiliar. It contained a single page of white paper with instructions to "watch the news at six." The instruction, which he took as a demand, sent an unexpected chill down his spine. His hands trembled while trying to fill a Styrofoam cup with coffee. Two younger faculty members sat in animated discussion near the coffee table. He hoped his fumbling was not apparent to them. At quick glance, Gorman thought they were in the English department or some arts discipline. He nodded coolly and sipped, holding his cup with both hands to keep it steady.

"That's right," Gorman heard one voice behind him say. The words ricocheted in the room, but neither the reader nor the sleeper stirred. "Just like *The Godfather*."

Now, a different voice added its appraisal. "The body is a message to somebody. Like the horse's head!"

"Maybe a faculty member. Ooo!" And they both laughed like two kids on their first camping trip trying to frighten each other.

Gorman considered what he'd heard as another example of irresponsible artistic imagination. Logically, he thought, seeking to calm his mind, the university was near gang territory, and the body was a message to their rivals that they would exact a terrible price from any opponent. And it also told the authorities the gang could operate anywhere in the city with impunity. What part of the city wasn't near the turf of some gang? Gorman had no more time to waste thinking about low-class thugs and left to grade test papers.

Later that afternoon, as numbers from the exam papers swirled in front of his eyes, Gorman lapsed into a momentary hypnotic doze. A ringing phone jarred him into semiconsciousness, and then he realized it was on his desk. He swiveled his chair toward the desk and snatched the phone. A beat for composure and then, "Professor Gorman speaking."

"It's me." Gorman now knew the unforgettable sound of Jeff's voice. "Your benefactor asks for your presence at 1600 hours."

Gorman decided not to make the calculation to civilian time and simply responded, "I'll be there."

* * *

Bob Zenda preferred to be in Ocala, Florida, in January rather than Chicago, Illinois. To be sure, there were brisk days when strong winds would whip inland from the Atlantic, but they were the exception to bright blue skies dotted by puffy white clouds. Occasionally, Zenda wondered if the clouds were actually an artistic work painted by some latter-day Michelangelo while on his back atop a huge scaffold in Orlando. Most of the time, he did not luxuriate in such ruminations. He had businesses to run, and spending part of the winter in Florida was hard work—maybe not as hard as digging ditches in Siberia, but labor nevertheless.

Today his priority was interviewing a candidate to train his stable of five thoroughbred racehorses residing in the lush horse country of central Florida for the winter. Zenda drove his Mercedes up the gravel road to the ranch-style house with red tile roof that served as his office and living quarters whenever he needed a break from the bustle of Chicago.

Ariel Sutherland waited for him on the front porch. He'd read her resume the night before while staying in Hialeah after examining some two-year-olds at an auction. Her experience was extensive, and he thought she'd look much older.

Zenda got out of his car and purposely chose to remove his sunglasses and squint in the sun as an expression of openness and sincerity. "I'm so sorry. Took the turnpike and I'm still late."

"Only a few minutes. No harm, no foul. Or is it foal?" Ariel joked. He smiled politely but couldn't stop trying to determine how this young woman before him amassed such credentials. He took her hand and found her grip firm, though her skin was surprisingly soft to the touch.

Ariel followed him to his office. She was a few inches over five feet tall, and her weight was light enough to qualify her as a jockey. The oversized glasses with dark frames Ariel wore to make her seem five years older reminded Zenda of Audrey Hepburn in that movie *Holly* something. He couldn't remember.

"You're twenty–five?" Zenda asked for confirmation as he scanned her resume from behind his desk. Ariel pulled her wallet out of her backpack and flipped it open to reveal her driver's license.

"I believe you," he responded and waved away her offer of proof. Another glance at the resume. "You started at fifteen?"

She smiled at him with warmth and confidence. "Altoona, Iowa. My first job as a hot-walker. Long hours. Low pay. But the best training. I loved it."

She was animated and driven, with a passion that overwhelmed Zenda.

"The horses weren't much," Ariel continued. "Henry and Harry Fick had a few they dabbled with. One of them never broke her maiden, but they loved her as much as all the winners. Dame Edith was her name. I think that's what kept her from winning."

"Her name?" Though new to the racing game, Zenda couldn't believe a name alone would produce failure.

"Sure." Ariel spoke with authority. "Much too old-fashioned for such a young horse. Too much responsibility."

Zenda liked Ariel immediately. She was fresh, energetic, and knew her onions or apples or whatever the expression was. Even after six years as a citizen, he still couldn't keep the idiomatic expressions straight.

"But why so young?" Zenda asked, unable to envision this child-woman on her own a decade earlier. "Was your father a trainer?"

"In a way, yes." When Zenda didn't catch the sarcasm in her voice, she relented. "It's a joke." She hesitated, and her face was overcome with a look that aged her by a decade. "Actually, I ran away from home."

"Oh. I'm sorry," was all Zenda could express, uncomfortable with such a private disclosure.

"Best thing that ever happened to me," she said as Zenda watched ten years slip off her face, revealing the woman he'd met minutes earlier. "I had to discover the rest of the world," she offered with a shrug.

Zenda felt better. He knew where the desire for exploration and growth could lead. Hadn't he immigrated for just that reason? Of course, he also left his native land for reasons of health. Leave and live. Stay and die. He'd made the reasonable and healthy choice.

Tender emotions made Zenda uneasy. Hate, anger, rage he could handle. Feeling they were at an awkward moment, he needed a smooth segue. Ariel provided one for him.

"Can I see your horses?"

"A wonderful idea." Zenda was relieved.

They made their way down the lane along a white wooden fence that enclosed acres of grazing area closest to a white barn. First, Zenda pointed out a broodmare and gelding. At the halfway point, a chestnut stallion pranced into the center of the field. He kicked up his hind legs, sprinted and stopped, twirled and sprinted again.

Ariel couldn't take her eyes off the magnificent thoroughbred. "Look at him! He's showing off." As he heard her voice, the stallion reared straight up and then trotted toward them with equine insouciance.

"That's Scallion. Italian Scallion. He's our best, and he loves the ladies."

Drawn toward the high-spirited horse, Ariel didn't indicate she'd heard Zenda. As Scallion reached the fence, she climbed onto the top rail, centered her buttocks, and easily balanced herself. Scallion came straight for Ariel without hesitation, as if he understood the meaning of kismet. He gently placed his head on her slender thigh and looked up at her with pleading brown eyes.

"What a beautiful boy you are," Ariel said, greeting Scallion with soothing words and caresses. "We're gonna be good pals." She turned to

Zenda and gave him a worried look, not wanting to be presumptuous. "That is if..."

Scallion sensed her concern and moved away to look directly at Zenda. His whinny was a demand. "There are no ifs," Zenda said, first to Scallion and then to Ariel. "None at all. He's yours. They all are."

Satisfied, Scallion returned to Ariel, who kissed the white of his forelock, leaped off the fence, and shook Zenda's hand. "Thanks. You won't be sorry."

Preoccupied with their lovefest, neither one noticed the dark figure ambling toward them from the foaling barn. Frankie LoFrisco, a bear of a man dressed in a black suit jacket, black T-shirt and black jeans, lurched down the path. Not the kind of clothing one wears in the warm Florida sun. Only the stallion knew of his approach before he got within hailing distance. Scallion's agitated pawing of the ground increased. They heard the intruder call out before they saw him.

"Hey, y'all." The words were southern but the inflection Brooklyn. A forced smile was on his face as he nodded first to Zenda and then to the unknown woman.

"Frankie. Meet Ariel. She's my new trainer."

LoFrisco took a measure of the young woman and produced a toothy smile as insincere as Humphrey Bogart's in *The Caine Mutiny*. He hoped this expression of friendliness hid the seething anger churning in his gut.

"Frankie's been our assistant trainer for a few years now. I'm sure he'll be a great help getting you settled."

"My pleasure," Frankie said. He attempted a courtly bow, but his girth turned a gallant attempt into an awkward comedic skit.

Zenda left Ariel to tour the grounds with Frankie and returned to his office as the phone rang. Gregori Ivanov had a problem in Chicago. A few hours later, Zenda told Ariel he had to return to Chicago; his dress manufacturing business needed attention.

"That's cool," she said, even though she couldn't care less about fashion and had not worn a dress in more than ten years. She preferred jeans, slacks, jodhpurs—anything that protected the personal integrity she'd reclaimed after running away from home. She assured Zenda he had no worries while in Chicago. Zenda worried he would never thaw out.

* * *

Zenda regretted leaving Ocala, but Gregori, his friend and silent business partner, had given him troubling news. *What kind of society allows women to be threatened with violence?* he thought as the taxi brought him from O'Hare. He was willing to do his part in the noble efforts to reclaim Ivana's honor and make a little cash in the process.

The cold, blustery wind all but carried Zenda into the restaurant when he opened the door. There was a red ribbon tied around a tall ficus tree. Gold lettering on its large bow read CONGRATULATIONS AND GOOD LUCK. Such was Zenda's first impression of Gregori's newly opened restaurant featuring cuisine from Uzbekistan, descriptively named Uzbek.

Zenda's arrival at the restaurant's twilight time—too late for lunch and too early for dinner—was convenient for them to talk without being disturbed. He was not impressed by the ficus. What did hold Zenda in awe was the ceiling. Painted in robin's egg blue, it contained large, puffy clouds, their mesmerizing realism catching Zenda spellbound for a moment and transporting his spirit back to the warmth of Ocala. An icy blast from the opening door made his bones brittle and returned Zenda to the present.

Gregori rushed inside and wrapped his arms around Zenda from behind. Gregori was a hugger from the old school, particularly when there was an interval of some time between him and the huggee.

"Such nice tan you have, Mr. Zendofsky," a compliment and criticism from Gregori. The welcoming portion concluded, Gregori escorted Zenda to a booth at the rear of the restaurant where it was warmer and where none of the staff could accidentally overhear. Then he brought a bottle of vodka and two glasses. The first toast was to each other's health. The second was to the success of their endeavor. Now it was time to discuss serious business.

Zenda got the overview from Gregori's earlier call. Johnny Faraci, who Zenda knew only by reputation—and that was only what was printed in the local papers which he read on occasion—disrespected Gregori's sister-in-law. As Gregori elaborated on the details, Zenda was distracted by the brightly colored murals depicting rural scenes from Uzbekistan. Sheepherders were cooking over an open fire. Exotic young women in flaring skirts were frozen in tableau as they leaped in a traditional folk dance to the accompaniment of an elderly violinist.

"Pay attention," Gregori snapped at Zenda, who turned from the murals to face his friend with the uncanny resemblance to Putin.

"You've made a beautiful place here," Zenda replied.

Gregori dismissed the compliment. "S'nothing. You pay and they do what you want. Now, what do we do about Faraci?"

Zenda could not resist a smile across the table. "Nothing. Tell your brother to buy Ivana a present. He could even try to fuck her more often." He grimaced at the thought.

Gregori was not amused and held out his index finger in midair halfway across the table, pointed straight between Zenda's eyes, his lips locked grimly. But the thought of anyone having carnal knowledge of the corpulent Ivana burst the dam, and a laugh exploded out of his face.

"That I will *not* advise my brother," he said, continuing to laugh. "Be serious. This goes beyond Ivana, who I care about only because Vadim is so generous." Zenda knew this was a reminder from Gregori

Vincent Panettiere | 53

that it was Vadim's financing which kept them in business. Now Gregori became serious.

"One of our most productive employees has disappeared. We visited the bodega. No one knows nothing. You know how they are. First, not smart. Too much drinking and..." Gregori held out his arm and made a pantomime of injecting it with drugs.

Zenda knew. "Even in Florida. I ask only simple things of them—keep the stalls clean—and they are too drunk."

Gregori was not much interested in horses and told Zenda how they'd visited the university where "this Jose or Juan; one of those names" also worked as a janitor. On Zenda's raised eyebrows he explained, "So many smart people have bad credit, and they come to us for help. We help them and they pay. And pay. And pay." His laugh was hollow. He related how Juan or Jose was absent from his job at the university for so many weeks that he was terminated.

Gregori had two concerns. With the pipeline at the university broken, all that income was lost. More worrisome was the possibility that Faraci was behind the man's disappearance, which meant he was out to destroy their operation and drive them out of business.

"Because of some smoke?" Zenda had doubts.

"You know those wops. They never forget."

Whatever the reason, and Ivana was the last, though convenient, priority, Gregori insisted Faraci had to be punished or neutralized.

Zenda thoughtfully scratched his chin as if grooming a lush, but invisible, beard. He did not flee the internecine gang rivalries of Odessa to simply replicate them in the United States. He loved his horses and his boutique dress manufacturing business. For both he was indebted to Vadim. Maybe that was the answer, he concluded, just as Gregori seemed to be losing patience. Somehow Zenda had to figure out a way to help Vadim and get his debt canceled in return.

* * *

A week passed before Lucy could be buried, after the ground thawed enough for the grave diggers, behind the small church in her parents' suburban town. In Chicago on that day, three business establishments—Kaz's deli, Henry's bar, and Clay's florist—had similar signs on their front doors: CLOSED. DEATH IN THE FAMILY. The three men were by Hegan's side, supportive but scant comfort.

During much of the ceremony, the grey skies and relentless prairie wind distracted even those who'd been the most intimate with Lucy. Reverence and homage were superseded by a fervent desire to be some place warmer.

Hegan stood alone to witness Lucy's casket being lowered into the ground, when even her parents and other friends fled to the interior of their cars immediately after the group "amen" sounded.

As Hegan settled into the back of the limo, Henry offered to hold an old-fashioned Irish wake in the back room of his place to help Hegan purge his pain.

"You need to tie one on till you black out," Henry advised.

Hegan appreciated the gesture but knew he'd spent too much time with a J&B pacifier over the last two weeks. Tomorrow he wanted to wake up without a hangover and make plans to sell his house and get a job with a two-bit police department in some hick California town. Henry, Kaz, and Clay exchanged worried glances.

"First you gotta eat," Kaz said. "I told the driver. We're going downtown." Hegan waved the notion away. "I know, you're not hungry now, but then.... And if you're still not, you'll watch us eat."

Clay watched Hegan with the eyes of a predator. He was ready to strike if Hegan exhibited the slightest irrational sign. Only in this context, Clay's "strike" would envelope Hegan in his massive arms and keep him safe. Hegan was weary and had no choice but to go downtown with the others. He folded his arms against his chest and leaned his head against the window. He closed his eyes—not to sleep but to obscure reality for as long as he was able.

CHAPTER THREE

SIX MONTHS LATER

Teresa reached the midpoint of the stairs when she heard the Regulator clock in the front hall begin its count to the next hour. It stopped at seven as she reached the first floor landing.

From the early moments of Teresa's memory, that clock occupied the same space on the long hall between the front door and kitchen in the century-old row house she now owned on the edge of downtown Chicago. The clock and the house, formerly owned by her dearly loved grandmother, was a serene connection to her childhood. During those visits of long ago, Teresa would stand mesmerized, watching the mechanism of the clock uncoil just before the chimes spoke.

As she watched the pendulum swing inside the clock's glass-front cabinet Teresa knew something in her world was constant and regular. The face of a person she barely recognized was reflected back. Haggard and lacking... what was it? Stability? A solidified core? So much, she agreed, was lacking. The face appeared at least ten years older than... thirty two? No. A year had gone by without notice. Thirty-three! With a seven-year-old daughter and six-year-old son and a marriage that would never be any older.

No wonder she'd lost a year when the ordinary events of her day were either volcanic or operatic, sometimes both. At least Eddie was out of the house, though not without a struggle. Remembering that victory, she saw a brief smile reflected back at her.

Satisfied that the children had been bathed and were almost ready for bed, all was in place. She now had time for herself. What to do with precious moments before they were wasted either by crisis or exhaustion?

Teresa left the clock and entered the parlor off the hall. In some houses, a similar space was called the living room or family room. But she thought parlor was most appropriate in this old house. She felt protected by the drapes around the bay window, and the cream color of the walls gave her a warm, cozy feeling no matter the time of day. Best of all, there was no television in the room. Solitude would be maintained.

Observing that the children's toys were neatly arranged in nooks beside the furniture made a smile cross her face. They were learning to pick up after themselves. She knew from personal experience that the pace of progress was always too slow.

The waning light of the summer evening sun hung over the street life outside the parlor's bay window. Voices of children at play and the familiar sound of a car slowly passing, though muted by the window glass, contributed to Teresa's feeling of peace and security.

Picking up the paper, she settled into the end of the sofa and began glancing at headlines.

* * *

Crows feet. Age lines. Laugh lines! That's it—laugh lines. Whatever, they're damned attractive, Mike Hegan thought as he looked across the table at Diana, whose broad, open smile and easy laugh caused him to think of a dark-eyed Ingrid Bergman. Does anybody remember Ingrid Bergman?

Diana was a recent addition to the Wednesday night poker game in the back room of Henry's, a local gin mill. The owner, Henry, preferred to call his place a gin mill instead of a bar, saloon, club, or nite spot—all of which he thought pretentious and nondescript.

Hegan remembered meeting Diana at Kaz's deli. One lunchtime, three months after Lucy died, Diana tried to squeeze through a narrow aisle to take her seat at a table across from his. She shifted her overstuffed gym bag and knocked over a newly filled glass of water. In that moment, he thought ice water was an icebreaker. How could he be annoyed at a woman with an Ingrid Bergman smile, particularly when she was sincerely contrite? Female companionship was not on Hegan's mind that day, but Diana had an easy manner.

Contrition led to conversation, beginning with the usual "you come here often?" and "what do you do?" She was a psychotherapist. "A generalist," she told him. "That means anyone who'll pay or has insurance that will pay. Thanks to the government's healthcare plan, or lack of it, the days of hanging out a shingle and raking in the dough are long gone." She was philosophical and also political.

Hegan was impressed; Diana was no longer in denial about healthcare. But then she was a therapist, and if anyone should reject denial, who better?

Before long Hegan described his relationship with Kaz and their Wednesday night poker game.

"I love poker! You have to let me play." The intensity of her request persisted, causing other patrons to look at him like some kind of pervert.

Hegan's remembrance of their first meeting ended when Diana excused herself from the table. "Have to powder my nose," she explained.

"She's watched too many movies on TCM." Clay spoke into the air to no one in particular as he inspected his newly dealt hand through a pair of half-glasses that on his broad, black face looked like they belonged to Lilliputians.

"Powder? She doing a line?" asked Artie. In his late twenties, he was the youngest of the group. Prematurely thinning hair made him appear older—until he spoke.

"Passé." Hegan corrected Artie.

"Bad move," said Kaz whose ascetic, monk-like looks belied the fact that he owned the best deli in town.

"Come on," Hegan pleaded. "She hadda go."

"She just won twenty bucks. The energy's gone. She's lost momentum," Kaz, a new age philosopher from the pastrami school, reasoned. "She won't win another hand."

"Nickels and dimes." Artie dwelled on trivia.

"Twenty bucks is twenty bucks, even in pennies." Kaz closed.

"She looks just like Ingrid Bergman when she laughs," Hegan opined to the others.

"Who?" Artie asked, always the youngest.

"Ingrid Bergman. *Casablanca*. Humphrey Bogart. Black and white film?"

"Come on." Artie could tell when they were pulling his leg. "Nobody watches black and white anymore." He looked up at the TV screen, the sound off, and saw images of a crime scene, yellow police tape. "Shh. Shh. News bulletin."

At that moment, Henry came into the back room and took the remote out of the pocket in his white apron. They all listened to the broadcast.

"The head and hands of a male Latino were found frozen in the basement of a tenement by a city building inspector. The grisly discovery was contained in an abandoned refrigerator, which for some unknown reason was operational. Sources tell TV Eight they suspect the killing was related to a drug deal gone sour. They add this style of revenge is a sign of warfare between gangs of undocumented immigrants. The police commissioner's office declined to comment. Now for the weather... ."

Henry muted the sound. "Undocumented immigrant my ass. If you're an immigrant you got documents. If you don't got documents, you're illegal. Why the fuck is that so difficult to figure out?"

Before Henry could wind up, Artie chimed in. "Debase the language and you debase the culture."

It took Henry a while to place the voice with the face. "For once, you're right," he said to Artie, not entirely certain what Artie meant.

"Black and Tan," Kaz said to Henry. He was after all *the* Henry of Henry's, the creatively named neighborhood joint located ten steps down from the sidewalk—actually in a cellar—about two blocks from the north end of the Lincoln Park Zoo. The back room was empty of patrons except for the four men and one woman now powdering her nose.

Henry turned his back to the table and spoke over his left shoulder.

"By order of municipal code 1842—" Henry began, sounding like a court bailiff, which he had been prior to taking early retirement.

"And a half," the men chimed in on cue.

"There ain't supposed to be no games of chance or gambling, which is games of chance or the possession of instruments of games of chance, which is gambling, including cards, dice, et cetera and so forth within these walls. When I turn around, I don't want to see... what?"

Again, the quartet on cue. "Cards, dice, et cetera and so forth."

Henry spun around a moment after the table had been hastily cleared of incriminating evidence. He circled the table like a general. All four men had their hands folded on top of the table, looking like angelic schoolboys waiting for their daily allotment of cookies and milk.

Diana returned, saw the ritual, and quickly slid into her seat.

"Damn! I almost missed it," she said, folding her hands on the table before her shapely—Hegan noticed—buttocks found their resting place.

"See no evil, speak no evil—" Henry said.

"My deal," Mike announced.

"Hear no evil." Henry finished.

"Black and Tan."

Vincent Panettiere | 61

"Bushmills."

"Old Style. Twice."

"Skyy. Neat." Diana's choice.

Mike skillfully distributed the cards. "Five-card stud. Jacks or better. Dime to open."

While the others reviewed their cards, Mike got up from the table and headed for a quiet corner of the back room. The others exchanged looks, indicating their awareness of Mike's ritual. This time, his first call was to his squad. He wanted the identity of the frozen head and hands, ASAP. Then he made another call.

* * *

The cell phone on the lamp table next to the sofa only rang once before Teresa picked it up. She knew who the caller would be and was not alarmed by the intrusion. It was the same caller every night at about the same time.

"Hello, Mike," she said with confidence. And, it was her brother.

"We're fine. Really. The kids, too. You'd never know. Funny about kids. Listen, you don't have to keep calling every night. I know, I know."

The front doorbell rang.

"Someone's at the door. Hold on. I'll be right back"

Teresa tossed the phone on the sofa, its cover open, still connected to her brother. Rather than going directly to the front door, Teresa, continuing a pre-divorce practice, edged to the furthest side of the window where she would be partly obscured by the drape but still able to see anyone standing by the door, albeit in profile.

A grey Ford sedan was double-parked in front of her house. An unmarked cop car no doubt. Two ends of the ropes that would knot in her stomach began their sinuous dance toward each other.

When the doorbell rang again, the ropes met.

When a fist pounded on the door in rapid succession, the ropes tied a knot in her stomach.

With a slight turn of her head, her eyes brought into focus the profile of Eddie Perino, a Chicago police detective. Only a month ago, their divorce became final. Now her ex-husband was pounding on her front door.

An electric charge of fear she thought long suppressed cemented Teresa in place for an instant before she was able to move from the window, passing the sofa and open phone.

"Who is it?" Her voice became a frazzle of higher frequency.

Pounding on the door was the answer.

"Let me in." Eddie never asked.

"Eddie, you can't! The children... We decided. There's nothing..." All concepts that reached the same conclusion.

Bang! Bang! Bang! The door vibrated.

Hoping to reason, she unlocked the door, and Eddie sauntered inside like the lord of all he surveyed. Instinctively, her arms shot up to shoulder height, palms out in defense mode, as if to protect her breasts. She thought she must look like a rabbit on hind legs sniffing the evening air.

Seeing Teresa's out-turned palms, Eddie was a picture of calm conciliation.

"Don't worry. I'm not here to hurt you."

"Eddie, why—"

"There's loose ends."

"The divorce was settled last month. Everything is final."

Jumping in again. "Between you and the court. Not between you and me."

Eddie glided through the parlor and adjoining dining room, taking a proprietary interest.

"It's done, over. There's nothing to tie up." Her voice pleaded by drawing out the words.

Now accusing. "You changed things since I... uh... left."

"A little." *Why am I being so tentative?* That awareness caused her strength to slowly seep back, though she followed meekly behind Eddie as he sat at the kitchen table.

"Make some coffee," Eddie commanded as he closely examined the kitchen. "Yeah, you changed things. It's... it's brighter."

The brightest day of my life, Teresa thought. *Free at last, free at last. Great God Almighty, free at last.*

But she said, "That's not such a good idea. Coffee, I mean." At last the self-assertiveness training was kicking in. Set boundaries. And she did. No coffee.

"Okay. But there are things that have to be settled."

"You're not supposed to come here without calling first."

"Don't give me that! Listen to what I tell ya!"

Teresa sat at the long side of the table, while Eddie sat at the head, and listened as he spoke.

"I need a break," Teresa heard Eddie begin. She noticed a tentativeness Eddie had kept hidden, at least from her, through the years of their marriage. His exposed vulnerability caused Teresa to look at Eddie with new eyes. No longer was he the sexy, dashing, young police cadet her brother Mike brought home to dinner. The one she mentally undressed in the dining room as the others ate roast pork.

Even with that, her mind remained fixed, fixated—she made the internal correction—on two red splotches, each about the shape of a small rectangle. They were partially hidden among the red and white checks of the tablecloth on the dining room table. The splotches were her anchor. Surely if she stopped examining them, trying to intuit their internal structure, she would slip away and be gone forever.

She eyed the random design of the splotches, examining their size and shape. Gradually, her ache was masked by the comforting distraction. Eddie took her downcast focus as an indication she was weak and afraid in his presence.

"Break?" as if she'd not been paying attention. She looked up at him to find his eyes boring, digging through her head and out the back into space.

"I can't give you all that money."

"What?" blurted out of her without thought or control.

The palm of Eddie's thick hand crashed down hard on the table, made it shake, and the ache returned. "I got bills!" he explained.

"No, no. Not bills." She was gathering strength and courage.

"Don't tell me my business."

"*I* have the children. And *you* have a new..." Girlfriend was too kind. "... mistress."

The Eddie from long ago. The Eddie she sent away. The Eddie she hoped to God she'd never see again now emerged.

Here comes that look and the cycle of violence, she warned herself. Verbal abuse, criticism, physical violence, and then—Goody! Goody!—loving respite. Now she knew the signs; before she was hopefully, lovingly ignorant.

In Eddie's case, the cycle began with a look. The sneer of contempt. Disdain for her as the lowest form of humanity. That look always began the ache. Today, it added intensity.

To what could she compare this distress? A rapidly descending elevator? No, too quick, but even that had the comfort of elevator walls, floor, and other passengers. There's no comfort in this. Roller coaster? So long ago she couldn't recall the boy's name. While the thrill—some thrill ... she'd barfed all over her date—was brief, it didn't last long and was never repeated.

No, the knot in her stomach did not have recognizable, familiar boundaries, nor was it something that she felt for an instant, soon to be thankfully forgotten. Her stomach throbbed with the weight of it; much more than foreboding, it was a deep, constant awareness that this time, very soon, she would die.

How soon? a perverse corner of her brain challenged.

Why was her mind throwing out mental obstacles as her eyes fixated on red, rectangular spots? She didn't know whether to laugh or cry, but quickly knew she'd better do neither. Yet it was enough to make one laugh or cry at the absurdity of the brain working with no connection to the physical environment. Again, the voice asked, *How soon?*

The man's voice raised two octaves, though she didn't hear his words. He was staring at her now as her mind asked yet again, *How soon?*, obliterating his voice.

"All right," she said aloud. It was a response she hoped would silence the voice inside.

Hearing her voice, she knew speaking was a mistake. She knew silence was her best defense, but she'd blurted out the words and they were heard, even though not directed at Eddie but to the nagging question in her head. Before Eddie could respond, her internal voice answered.

In the time it takes to inhale a shallow breath, or as fast as an ant can cross a strand of hair. That's how soon I can die. Satisfied?

"All right, what?" he demanded.

"All right, I'll take care of... this dirty tablecloth." Knowing how quickly she could die gave her the courage to look him straight in the eye, but then she flinched.

"We had rigatoni with sauce last night, and Mikey tried to help himself. He was so cute, but he dropped the macaroni and... See the stain?" Teresa Perino, seeking safety in her role as a mother, pointed to the red, rectangular anchor splotches her eyes had fixated on during

Eddie Perino's tirade. Now she remembered the sauce was made from the recipe she got from Lucy to save their marriage. Dearly departed Lucy. Gone only six months, but so long ago.

Her fusillade of words momentarily obliterated the pain, allowing Teresa to listen for sounds of the children upstairs, not wanting them to hear, see, remember.

Teresa lifted her eyes from the stain and looked at Eddie. Actually, she didn't see his face. Her eyes looked through Eddie's pupils. She imagined her eyes were acupuncture needles, penetrating deep beyond and into his skull, pinning his brain in place, to hold it and paralyze it for her own safety.

"No, Eddie. It's not all right. You have to pay me what you agreed. To change now is... is... not fair to—"

The back of Eddie's hand meeting the right side of Teresa's face stopped her in midsentence, but she continued. "... to the children."

Teresa refused to cry. Inside, she was happy and feeling stronger. Eddie was naked before her and also defenseless. But he hadn't a clue.

"You don't understand," he began.

The momentum had turned in her favor. Eddie was whining and pleading. There was no apology or plea to be forgiven. He had accused her of not understanding. Laughable! She pointed a finger at him to prevent him from saying another word.

"Stop paying what you owe," she said, her words clear and distinct, "leave ten cents off the check, and your face will be seen all over TV on *Deadbeat Dads*."

Teresa knew it was a stretch, but she hoped the reference to deadbeat dads would resonate with Eddie, who, during his early days as a cop, would come home and rail at the irresponsibility of the deadbeat dads he encountered. The fact that the majority of the DBDs Eddie met were black made his disapproval all the more joyous for him. Teresa knew the comparison would be both odious and wounding to Eddie.

No sooner had her words faded into the ether than Eddie lifted the solid maple dining table and turned the long end against Teresa's chest, tipping her and the chair onto the floor.

At the last possible instant, Teresa scrambled free and stood behind the wreckage which protected her, for the moment, against further attack.

"I won't die for you, Eddie."

"You'll do what I want."

The children! Teresa was charged by the very thought of them. Instinctively, she pushed the upended table against Eddie with all the force she could muster, and gained a sliver of space to flee into the hall. A quick glance up the stairs found the children on a middle step, trying to understand. The girl's arm was wrapped protectively around her younger brother.

"Upstairs," she hissed "Go!" But they could not or would not move.

"I'm not finished."

An arm reached out and pulled Teresa back into the parlor, whereupon Eddie, holding her with one hand, began slapping her face with the unoccupied hand. One side of her face quivered and then the other from the rhythm of his blows. She felt like a goat staked out to lure a tiger. *This is how a tiger paws its victim,* she thought, *before devouring it.* Absorbing a quartet of smacks, Teresa tugged at the arm restraining her and broke free, ran down the hall, and threw open the door.

"I want you out!" she screamed so Eddie and the entire neighborhood could hear. If this was her last act of defiance, it would get the most attention.

"Get out!" Teresa was now on the front porch, almost on the first step. Once again, a deeper maternal instinct replaced that of self-preservation. *The kids!*

She turned toward the door and ran into Eddie's arms. Powered by anger, he began shaking her. For a moment she felt the motion would cause her body to shatter in all directions. She slipped his grasp and ran toward the street; Eddie blindly followed. He tried dragging her back into the house and out of the vision of prying eyes, but Teresa held firm to the iron front gate.

* * *

As soon as Teresa put the phone down and Hegan heard Perino's voice in the background, he knew his sister was in trouble. Luckily, his friends understood when he abruptly left the game.

Also lucky, crosstown traffic was light ---- unusual at midweek during the summer's prime vacation period. In ten, twelve minutes tops, he was at Teresa's street and about to make a left turn if the good citizen in the old Buick in front of him would only go through the yellow light instead of stopping. Not a chance. Hegan couldn't wait. He pulled into the oncoming traffic lane and made a reckless left, leaving horns blaring in his wake.

Halfway there he saw Perino's nondescript sedan double-parked. Then his left hand pummeled his horn. He was coming, and they would know it.

* * *

A car horn—loud, persistent, furious—gave Teresa hope. Eddie would be distracted and back off until he could determine its source.

An old Plymouth Valiant stopped quickly within inches of Eddie's Ford. Hegan emerged from the driver's side at a measured speed. Not so fast as to be uncontrollable, yet not so slow to lack authority.

"Eddie! Teresa! Don't!" Hegan yelled, and that brief distraction enabled Teresa to leave the fence and dart toward the porch while Eddie was occupied with Hegan.

Hegan's open palm counseled patience, while his outstretched arm offered consolation.

"Back off, Hegan! I'm talkin' to my wife."

"Ex. Ex-wife. Not yours to talk to, Eddie."

"None of your concern, Hegan."

Teresa saw a red stain on her white blouse and traced the blood to the corner of her lip. At the same time, she realized her right eye throbbed painfully. But, consumed by the near-fatal drama before her, she decided to heal her wounds later.

"She's my sister, Eddie."

"She don't need no fuckin' big brother guardian angel!" Eddie screamed as his anger rose beyond containment.

Teresa had seen this side of Eddie too many times before not to realize what could erupt. Deep inside she knew that her awareness of Eddie's erratic temper, which ultimately led to their divorce, was the only thing that could save her brother.

Eddie reached inside his suit jacket, where a snub-nosed .38 protruded from the inner pocket. When Teresa saw Eddie's hand disappear, she fled from the porch and ran at Hegan, pushing him back toward the street.

"Go away, Mike. Go!" She pushed at her brother's chest again and again.

Hegan backed up as Teresa turned to face Perino, confident she'd removed her brother from the scene. She deliberately advanced into the line of fire from the pistol Eddie openly displayed.

"Enough, Eddie! Kill me! Go ahead. Kill me. You'll still owe child support, you dumb bastard!" The words were meaningless and illogical, she knew. Were she dead, the children would suffer the most. All she had to attack him with were her angry words that became another red cape to distract the bull so it could somehow be corralled.

Eddie'd had enough, too. As he tightened his grip on the pistol, the metal edge of the gun's butt dug into the palm of his right hand. With his forefinger against the trigger, he advanced toward Teresa.

* * *

While Eddie and Teresa danced mano a mano, Hegan circled around them out of their sight. As Eddie got within four feet of Teresa, Hegan sped toward them and dove through the interstice like a football running back slicing for daylight. The upper half of his torso pushed Teresa away, while his legs and feet jostled Eddie enough for the gun to explode.

Sound and feeling merged instantly in Hegan's mind. The sharp, brief—so brief it seemed harmless to all who heard it—bang of the shot blended with the almost simultaneous searing explosion of flesh. His flesh, Hegan was immediately aware. Before he could examine, review, consider, all those actions he'd been taught in an endless series of police department management training courses, Hegan landed face-first on the cement path to the porch.

"I've been shot. Now I know..." were the last words he heard.

* * *

Hegan heard soft whispers and a constant *whoosh-whoosh-whoosh* in his preconscious mind. He didn't know the sounds were emitted by the monitors attached to him in the intensive care unit. He was also unaware that the elevator of his brain was taking him to a nearly sentient state. Hegan wouldn't identify the sounds as the "tick, tick, tock of a stately clock as it stands against the wall," even if he could remember all the words to Cole Porter's "Night and Day." He translated "whoosh" into the pain in the ass sound of a faucet dripping the minute he wanted to go to sleep. He was certain there was a League of Faucets existing in a parallel universe that took turns conspiring against the human world one moment before it entered slumberland. The aim of this cabal was sleep deprivation; of that, Hegan was convinced. No sooner had the victims for that night squooshed their pillows into the right configuration for restful sleep than an insidious *plink* would sound in the distance.

Has there ever been such a slight sound that could produce an intensity far greater than the waves of an earthquake or atomic explosion, he wondered?

Given its magnitude of reach, the first plink would be ignored and maybe the next few. By the time the would-be-sleeper heard plink number twelve, action must not wait. Sleep was not possible. All the plinking eroded the membrane supporting unconsciousness. Now, in a fully wakeful state, the victim was forced to march into the bathroom to confront the offender, only to find, more times than not, the faucet was dry. But where? Outside! The neighbor's outside faucet for his garden hose! Tonight sleep was impossible!

And with grunts and growls of frustration over a neighbor's leaky garden hose, his brain elevator took Hegan to the edge of consciousness, and he stirred in his intensive care unit bed.

Black. Total black.

I'm blind! Hegan thought as his eyes fluttered open. *Christ, I'm blind! That goddamned Eddie Perino. That wife beating, bribe taking, shiftless, worthless hunk of toxic waste made me blind!*

Aware he was supine, Hegan tried to move, but his head would not budge from the pillow. *Paralyzed and blind!* Hegan was convinced and began plotting revenge against Perino. *I'm gonna...* His plotting was interrupted by a deep James-Earl-Jones-esque laugh. *I've seen too many movies,* he thought. Then he remembered he was blind and forever deprived of his lifelong love of cinema

Again the laugh. It had a smooth, chocolate syrup sound. Being a child of the insidious and totalitarian world of political correctness, he thought he could never equate a chocolate sound with an actual person without being called a racist.

No matter. There it was, and that's how he saw—heard—it. *So it's true,* he thought. *Once you lose the sense of sight, the other senses become sharper. Now I can characterize sound by its flavor. Suppose a voice sounded like pomegranate. What would the person look like?*

His inner chatter was interrupted when the black space shifted and a voice came from the darkness.

"That little bitty scar on my left shoulder was from when I got it separated against the Packers. You can hardly see it, Charlotte. That doc sure did fine work. I'm told he did needlepoint in his spare time. Kind of like keeping in shape before the big game," Clay said earnestly, as he worked out his seduction routine in front of and for the benefit of the nurse.

"No foolin'," said a rapturous female voice.

Hegan tried to move his mouth.

"Er... er..."

"Stop!" Charlotte commanded. The black wall in front of Hegan's eyes disappeared. He saw medical equipment and personnel dashing back and forth.

"Mr. Hegan. Can you hear me?" Charlotte asked.

I'm in heaven, he thought, but called out, "Er... Erasmus!" rather than answer the nurse.

"Erasmus?"

"Huh?" Erasmus Leon Clay said, returning to the foot of the bed and buttoning the shirt he'd opened earlier to reveal the broad expanse of his muscular back, to impress the silky voiced nurse tending to Hegan. Clay hoped to gain the empathy and comfort of Charlotte by displaying his numerous football injuries. All his bare back accomplished was to obstruct Hegan's vision.

"His name's Erasmus." Hegan growled and opened his eyes.

"Erasmus?" She looked Clay up and down, trying to find out how such a name could be pinned to such a body. "You told me it was Leon," she said with a laugh.

"My daddy named me after a scholar. Leon is my social name." Crestfallen, Clay approached Hegan. "You had me convinced I'd be overjoyed to see you awake. Until now!"

"Okay, boys. Go to your corners," Charlotte said.

Clay took two steps back, but his six-foot-eight, 315-pound frame still loomed over the bed. Hegan tried to move.

"Mr. Hegan, lie still. You've been thrashing about since the operation. That's why you were restrained."

"What's wrong with me?"

"Lie still!"

A silk glove wrapped around an iron blackjack, Hegan thought until PC intruded.

"I need to know." She'd met her match. "What's wrong with me?"

"You're a goddamn fool, that's what." Clay's face came at Hegan in Cinemascope.

"Erasmus, honey, I need you to do me a big favor."

"Anything for you, Charlotte," Clay said. The wounded warrior approach had won the day once again.

"Sit your big butt down, and shut your big hippo mouth before I call security, or I will give you a scar that you can't show in mixed company."

Hegan laughed for the first time in three days, during most of which, except for these last few moments, he'd been unconscious. He laughed so hard that Charlotte was concerned he would loosen his restraints.

"Lie still or you'll pop your embolism." Charlotte placed the palm of her hand firmly, but professionally, on the center of Hegan's chest and kept him pinned to the bed.

"Embo what?" Clay asked, working to keep the levity flowing.

"Don't think I could pop a balloon," Hegan countered, stressing the double entendre.

"You are still a very sick man, Mr. Hegan."

"She's right, you know."

"Do me a favor, Mr. Former-football-player-now-gone-to-flab. Take your lard ass into the hall. Out!"

With the grin of a conspiratorial schoolboy on his face, Clay gave a faux-meek wave to Hegan and left the intensive care unit.

"I expect the doctor to be here by noon. He'll give you all the medical whoop-de-do, but I'll give you the blow-by-blow," Charlotte said without humor.

Hegan quieted and observed the nurse.

"The bullet entered your back at the T2 level; that is the second thoracic. Had it been a centimeter closer to your spine, you'd be paralyzed from the neck down. You are a very lucky man."

Maybe it was the loud gulp Hegan took, or maybe it was the fact she could no longer distinguish the color of the sheets from the color of his face that caused Charlotte to pull in her sails.

"I saw the X-rays and they got the bullet. Most of it," she said, divulging too much. "But after the operation you threw an embolism, and we've got to keep you still until it's dissolved. That's what this IV drip in your arm is all about."

The news that he'd escaped from a near-fatal injury was comforting to Hegan until the nurse added, "By the way, you also broke your nose. You have two black eyes and look like a raccoon." She gave him her best uninvolved, professional smile and was gone.

Gradually, Hegan became aware of what being on the lip of oblivion, at the edge of death, felt like. He understood Teresa lived that way all those months—years, even—before the divorce and after, like the other day. How many days ago was that? Yesterday? A week? A month?

Vincent Panettiere | 75

His life had to change. Each day had to have value. No day could be wasted. All of his life had to be appreciated, savored, and even loved. Especially the people: Teresa and the kids, that overgrown kindergarten kid Leon Clay, Kaz and Artie. Any moment he expected to hear Captain and Tennille sing "Love Will Keep Us Together."

And Diana. Six months had passed since Lucy died. Maybe now he could ask Diana out on a date. Maybe not. He wasn't ready to get close to another woman. Besides, what would it do to the group dynamic? Look what it did to *Friend*s. Only kept them on the air for a gazillion more years. "Shit! I sound like I'm in an AA meeting. Group dynamic, my ass!"

On impulse, Hegan slowly wiggled his toes. First on the right foot and then the left. That simple, often inconsequential and automatic action made him smile. The more he wiggled, the more important toe wiggling became. Now that he could move his toes at will, the action was not inconsequential. If he could not? He refused to consider any possibility but full and complete recovery. One thing Hegan knew for certain: he might be restrained, flat on his back, but he was alive and he was free.

* * *

Anyone who witnessed Leon Clay barreling down the Northwest Tollway in the direction of Arlington Park race track in his turquoise 1960 Thunderbird a few weeks later would have no doubt as to his former athletic profession – no shred of interest or knowledge of football required. With the top down so Hegan could absorb the healing rays of the sun, the T-Bird looked to be the size of a circus car, the one containing thousands of clowns. Had Clay suddenly stood up and walked off with the car wrapped around his middle like some plastic, inflatable inner tube at a swimming hole, no one viewing that spectacle would have been surprised.

Hegan looked up at Clay from the passenger seat. Every few minutes, he would twist and turn in his seat, trying to ease the pressure on his back.

"You got pain?" A question and a statement from Clay.

"Nah. It's the way you drive that's got me anxious."

"I told you not to push it. Only been a few weeks since you got out of the hospital. Let's go back." Clay moved the car into the extreme right lane, intent on taking the next exit.

Hegan saw the ARLINGTON PARK, TWO EXITS sign and pointed with emphasis. "We're almost there."

Through his pain, Hegan launched into a paean of Homeric proportions. "Feel the sun. Smell the air." Hegan added dramatic coughs for humor. "Better than all the hospitals to make a sick man well, the lame walk, and the blind see. Watch out for that truck!" he yelled as Clay swerved just in time to avoid an SUV.

"That's no truck. SUV with a soccer mom on the phone yakking her fool head off, without a pussy-hair's-length of an idea where in the hell she is or who the hell is around her. Imagine if she had kids in that car and there'd been an accident."

"It'd be your fault."

"I know!"

"Scared the crap outta ya, didn't it?"

"Better believe that."

They exited the tollway and followed signs that read ARLINGTON PARK - PARKING. In the distance they could see parking attendants, wearing yellow vests, taking four bucks from each car as it entered the sprawling expanse of concrete preceding the side view of the grandstand.

Hegan showed his gold detective badge to the parking attendant, who directed them toward the end of the lot closest to the track's entrance.

* * *

From birth, Frankie LoFrisco clearly possessed his father's fat genes. By the seventh grade, he weighed twice as much as the other boys in his class. During recess, when required to jog around the square, cement playground of PS 104 in Brooklyn, Frankie would begin violently wheezing and coughing. His teachers, fearing he could go into convulsions, advised him to rest—partly for his health, but mostly to prevent a possible lawsuit should he, God forbid, collapse and die.

Frankie liked wheezing and coughing. He developed those responses into a fine art. Each recess he would try to run. "Oh, no, Mr. Siegel," he protested, "let me try." And each time he would be told politely to rest.

His teachers never knew Frankie could turn on the jets once school ended. Tina, his mother, made him. He had deliveries to make.

The packages Frankie carried were light and could easily fit into his pocket. No one would suspect this grammar school student with a pudgy, cherubic face and slightly bucktoothed smile was carrying betting slips to his mother and a wad of cash to the occasional lucky winner.

The family's legitimate business was a candy store on Nineteenth Avenue in the Bensonhurst section of Brooklyn. When not ministering to his mother's clients, Frankie would watch the cash register while Tina worked the phones in the back room.

The counterman was Nonno Joe, Frankie's grandfather on his mother's side, slightly built with a full head of wavy, white hair. NJ, as Frankie referred to his grandfather, served cherry cokes and grilled cheese to the neighborhood kids from Saint Finbar's High School.

Their after-school invasion created havoc and allowed Frankie to fuse an occasional twenty to his fingers while making change. When Frankie wasn't making change or trying to steal a sawbuck, he dreamed of being a jockey. Had he known of Sisyphus, Frankie would have realized pushing a rock uphill was an easier goal.

Once his father, Leo, returned from a six-month stretch on Rikers Island, Frankie begged to be taken to the track. That year, when the summer season in Saratoga ended and the horses returned to the New York area, father and son drove to Aqueduct.

Life was sweet for Frankie, though his dream of guiding an Arabian stallion around the far pole and down the stretch evaporated after two excursions with his father. One day at the paddock observing the jockeys astride, an epiphany.

"My thigh's as big as his two legs," Frankie exulted to soothe his hurt.

He always knew he could beat the odds, but there was no beating genetics. Still, his luck held in high school. No PT classes. While the other boys were grunting through pushups, Frankie was required to spend that hour in study hall. There, prevailing educator wisdom opined, he would actually *study*. That is how Frankie went into competition with his mother. Only small stuff. A dollar. Fifty cents. At first. Gradually adding up to real money. As with all the overreachers of the world, Frankie's luck started running away from him.

The leap from taking bets to giving loans was not that great. His returns increased exponentially. Word of mouth created demand for his services, not only from his fellow students at Saint Finbar's but from their friends as well. There was one priest. Frankie cut his vigorish to a single buck. "I gotta charge you somethin', Father. It's a business. Wouldn't be fair to the others." Father Gleason understood and promised Frankie the reward for his charity would come in the next life. He also guaranteed no less than a D in his physics class.

But Frankie's reward would not be meted out in the next life. He soon learned that a broken nose and chipped teeth were prizes he earned in the present.

"You fuckin' bum!" his mother screamed when she saw Frankie's face and ripped school jacket, the embroidered "SF" on its outer pocket dangling by a thread. Frankie protested the scuffle was nothing, just the cost of doing business. He ego-stroked his mother with the revelation that he so wanted to be a success in business like "my mom." That approach had its effect.

"My angel," she said, patting his smooth, pudgy face. Frankie's face slowly bloomed into a smile before a quick backhand-forehand combo reddened his cheeks, replacing grimace with pain. He cried out in protest, but his mother's hand squeezed his mouth shut.

"You're an idiot, and you'll get yourself killed. Or worse. Paralyzed from the neck down and I'll have to care for you for the rest of my life. And then what? Who'll babysit a fat cripple? There'll be no grandchildren. I'll be alone, except for you." Her body shuddered in disgust.

"But mom..." did not penetrate.

"Quiet. You wanna be in business? The store is your business. But when you start giving loans, you're taking money away from guys who'll put you away. And I don't mean Rikers."

Frankie tried to muster indignation. "Look at you..." It didn't last long.

"Me? Don't look at me. You're out there with your ass hanging out. I'm protected."

"How? I don't see nobody hangin' around here."

That's how Frankie met Faraci, the man saved by Leo's girth during a jailhouse scuffle years ago when both were starting out. Leo drifted to the New York area and married Tina. Faraci worked his way up the ladder, acquiring wealth and power and the ability to offer protection from afar.

Frankie resisted his mother's anger and continued taking bets and making loans. He returned from school one day to find an ambulance in front of the candy store. *NJ*, he thought.

The ambulance screamed away revealing NJ sweeping up glass from the shattered front window. NJ saw Frankie approach and raised the broom as if ready to smack a Spaldeen three sewers. He relented and instead smacked Frankie on his ample ass, sweeping him into the store.

A shambles. Syrup from the broken fountain turned the floor into a sticky mess. Magazines, candy, cigarettes littered the floor.

"They beat your mother." Frankie bit his fist. "She told you to stop. Now see what you've done?"

That night after Leo came home from the hospital, he had two kinds of good news. His wife had bruises and contusions. She would survive. Frankie would be moving to Chicago, serving at the pleasure of Johnny Faraci.

* * *

The wannabe loan shark/bookie had less than zero status in Chicago. He was no more than a high school dropout and gofer. Faraci referred to Frankie as "that punk kid." He loved the sound of the phrase whenever he'd say to an associate "send the punk kid" or "get the punk kid." But his favorite, addressed to Frankie's face was "you're nuthin' but a punk kid, kid." Then he'd laugh as the overweight teenager lowered his head in what Faraci knew was embarrassment.

Frankie had stopped being embarrassed a decade ago. Just after he learned the translation of *gordo*, he bloodied Cruz Millan's nose. No one called him fat from the start of third grade until high school. By then, he had a reputation as a fighter and a businessman. Frankie heard Faraci and remembered Cruz Millan.

At times, when the memory of his Puerto Rican tormenter was not enough, Frankie began biting the inside of his cheek until he tasted blood seeping into his throat. All the while, Faraci smiled with delight. Frankie endured Faraci's taunts but seethed with a determination that vowed payback. How, when, or where, he didn't know. He was fueled by an inner belief that he could beat any odds. This conviction helped him escape his fate in Brooklyn, and it would allow him to escape servitude in Chicago.

Over the next four or five years, Frankie, the hapless fat guy, seeped into Faraci's soft corners. His attitude toward the boy evolved from contempt to a bit less than complete acceptance. Gradually, Faraci's scale of regard went from "that punk kid" to "the kid" to "not a bad kid." That last label remained forever etched in Faraci's mind, as he had no cause to adjust it up or down. Under the guise of being harmless, Frankie learned more than any Brooklyn candy store could teach him.

With his rise in status, Frankie started driving Faraci around the city. One day he drove the older man to Arlington Park, where he could enjoy his one indulgence—after cigars. This was before certain immigrant groups decided to peck away at his territory and made venturing out in public precarious.

By now, Frankie had endured enough taunts and begrudging respect, if not total trust. In truth, Faraci never trusted anyone—another of his rules to live by.

The track valet parked the car, and Faraci held back while Frankie moved ahead. It wasn't an act of security. Faraci tried over the years to instruct Frankie in the finer arts of proper posture and dress. After all that time, he was dismayed by the results.

"Hey! Wait up!" got Frankie to stop in midstep.

Frankie started to apologize, but stopped at "shut it." Faraci spun Frankie around.

"Look at you. Your father never took care of his health. You're gonna go the same way, only younger."

Frankie nodded and hit on an idea. "Mr. Faraci..." The man's silence encouraged Frankie to continue. "I been meaning to come see you. Formal-like."

More silent permission.

"You've been very good to me and all. I need your help... and part of it is getting into better shape and all." No point stopping now. "Could you help me get into the horse business?"

"Buying or selling? I'm sure you don't mean as a jockey."

"Training." He said it directly and with strength. "I been readin' and watchin' these days when we come here and me by myself. I could be good."

Frankie had carefully prepared for this moment. He spilled out the yearnings that fueled his dreams. He was willing to start at the bottom. To learn all he needed from anyone who would give him a chance.

Standing before Faraci was a new Frankie, one who was earnest and determined. Beyond beneficence, Faraci sensed Frankie could be more useful at some unknown date in the future.

"I may know a guy who knows a guy in Florida."

Frankie the supplicant gave a nod, his brow furrowed It was his attempt to indicate he was serious and understood.

Faraci was pleased Frankie's response was not like that of a joyful Cocker Spaniel puppy.

"He'll work your ass off. Like me. Who knows? Could work. You're a good kid, Frankie."

A few days later, Frankie arrived in Miami.

* * *

Frankie's return to Chicago five years later was not as triumphant as he imagined. True, this was the first time he brought a favored horse to Arlington Park. But as an assistant trainer? What kind of progress was that? He'd been so sure the top spot was his, but the Ruskie and the bitch wrecked his dream.

Yet things were starting to break his way. He reconnected with Faraci. Breakfast at Benno's was set for the following morning the instant Faraci heard "I got news on the Commies." The intervening years had been a struggle for Faraci. Not that anyone should pity him. Too much competition from the uncivilized. Smelly fish. Disrespect for territory. He'd get ulcers before his time.

"I'm not a dumb guy," Frankie said, forking up a quarter of his stack as Faraci looked on with a saintly smile. "I hear things. I know... ." Faraci paid more attention when Frankie provided the workout times of Italian Scallion. He would surely win, Frankie opined. "The Commie's lookin' to clean up."

Faraci favored another horse and paid the kid no heed. He hid his surprise at how Frankie had wheedled his way into the Zenda stable. By now he figured Frankie would have crapped out, but the kid didn't fade. Different horses for different tracks. Go with God and be somebody else's *agita*, Faraci concluded.

While Frankie may have changed, he hadn't become a hair-shirt-wearing monk overnight. His need for revenge caused him to fume at "that bitch." Faraci cared not a crumb for Frankie's romantic experiences, but inwardly was delighted to learn that Ariel Sutherland, the bitch in question, was Italian Scallion's trainer. That was a change in fate.

Faraci had nothing against Zenda. It was the Ivanov brothers who gave him acid reflux. Inside information was always valuable, but he never had reason to believe Frankie was reliable.

Faraci needed someone who was mathematically precise. Someone who could get more accurate "inside" information. Maybe they both could clean up.

CHAPTER FOUR

Frankie recalled the breakfast as he loped toward the Personnel Only gate. He gave Faraci and Zenda—"all them guys"—a chance. Not his worry any more.

His two front teeth stuck out as if doing a beaver impersonation. The glint in his eye all but shouted the taste of victory. Frankie moved quickly for a big, fat man. Although *moved* is not the exact word. Frankie rumbled. Invariably, which is to say most of the time, Frankie's clothes were rumpled as well.

Rumpled Frankie rumbled through the employee entrance to the track, consumed by his own self-importance. He flashed his beaver teeth and, one hand stuffed into his jacket pocket as if concealing contraband, wagged the plastic ID card dangling from his neck by a cloth lanyard in a way that both distracted and informed the security guard at the gate.

Along the track's backside, Frankie, fat legs pumping with purpose, maneuvered his way through the grooms and exercise boys and girls. At nearly one hour before post time, he knew the workers had too many other concerns and wouldn't bother to take much notice of him.

Eyes planted only a few feet in front and intent on not making eye contact, Frankie slammed into the left hindquarter of a chestnut mare. The collision jostled the animal and left Frankie with a face full of mare sweat.

The female cold-walker, having experienced what seemed to be a disturbance of seismic proportions, looked first to the health of her charge. Two thousand pounds of bone and muscle could snap fragile ankles under the best of circumstances. Any inordinate strain was to be avoided at all costs.

She saw the mare was unharmed and racked her focus on the offender. "Watch it, asshole!" she yelled over at Frankie who was wiping the mare's sweat off his face without acknowledging his involvement in the incident.

The girl stopped her work to watch Frankie disappear from sight before she resumed leading the mare. Some of the other stable hands silently indicated they'd observed the collision. All exchanged knowing looks, agreeing with her description of Frankie.

One of the young Latino boys nodded in Frankie's direction and called him *maricon* as he flashed a broad, gold-filled smile at the girl, sharing an inside joke and making her laugh.

Turning a corner, Frankie was now invisible to the workers on the main street of stable row. As he approached Barn Seven, Frankie saw Rojas, the barn's stableman, nervously pacing, a long-tined pitchfork in his hand.

"Get inside," Frankie commanded, pushing Rojas into the barn. "You want the world to see?"

"I been waiting and you no come."

"Don't tell me my business. He inside?"

"*Si*. But I no like this."

Frankie's hands were proportionate to his body, which meant they were the size of grizzly bear paws. Frankie's right paw snatched Rojas by the throat and pushed him against the barn wall, while his bulk pinned Rojas' arms, including the handle of the pitchfork, against the young man's body, effectively ending all resistance.

"Do you have a green card?"

"No, you know—"

"Shh." Frankie tightened his grip on Rojas' throat. "And you don't have a permit to work?"

Rojas was about to speak, thought better of it and shook his head.

"Right. So you do what I want and shut up. Where is he?"

Rojas turned his head toward the center of the barn. Frankie then grabbed the pitchfork from Rojas, threw it to the side, and pushed the stableman ahead. "Show me."

Rojas led Frankie to the center stall on the left side of the barn. A shiny brass plaque on the stall door read ZENDA FARMS - ITALIAN SCALLION.

Through the iron grillwork that decorated the front wall of the stall, Frankie could see a chestnut stallion breathing heavily. Bridled and tethered to an iron ring attached to the brick rear wall, Italian Scallion gave Frankie the equine version of the evil eye.

Frankie gave it back. Holding up the pinky and index finger of his right hand, Frankie wagged it back at the stallion. "And back atcha, you neurotic prick." Then Frankie found time to taunt his nemesis. "You never liked me, did ya? Not since the first day in Florida."

Rojas was becoming more agitated as he watched the two-legged/four-legged confrontation. "Do it! Do it! Do it!" he chanted, his voice rising with each repetition.

Frankie turned toward Rojas who instinctively took a giant step back, causing Frankie to move forward. Annoyed at the additional expenditure of energy, Frankie grabbed Rojas with one hand and gave his face a backhanded smash that all but knocked the smaller man to the straw-covered floor.

"This is the second time you told me my business. You better pray there won't be a third time, Rojas."

Then Frankie relented and felt the need to soften his position. *Rather than bullying, I should teach,* he thought. "You know *béisbol* in your country? Three strikes and you're out. Sabe?"

Rojas nodded, not understanding the connection between a horse and baseball.

"When I strike you out, Rojas, you won't get to bat no more. *Finito! Sabe?*"

Frankie drew his pudgy index finger across his neck, figuring Rojas never took English as a second language. Then Frankie pointed that same finger at Rojas, fixing him to the spot at one side of the stall door.

Satisfied, Frankie eased open the stall door. "Easy boy, easy." His words were calming, but the spirit behind them was more "I've gotcha."

Italian Scallion was no fool. He'd been absorbing human emotions since a colt. While his head was tethered, preventing complete escape, his delicate legs skittered in response to Frankie's entreaty.

Nimbly, Frankie dodged the stallion's agitated hindquarter and reached its head. He stroked its forelock in as gentle a way as he could. Just when the horse had calmed its huge body, Frankie smashed an open palm against the side of its head, reminding Scallion that all resistance was futile.

Rojas, observing through the bars of the front wall, could not contain himself at the sight.

"Hey! What you doing?"

Frankie silenced Rojas with the maniacal smile of a kid who likes to burn ants with matches and then immediately returned to his task. Taking a pair of disposable gloves out of one jacket pocket and a large syringe and vial of clear liquid out of the other, Frankie picked up the pace. The gloves went on with a snap, and the cover was removed from the point of the syringe. He filled the syringe from the vial and turned to face his target.

The stallion sensed Frankie was not a benevolent visitor. He became more agitated, his whinny high-pitched and strained. In a last desperate attempt at freedom, the stallion tried to rear up, but its tethered head resisted. It kicked his hind legs out in desperation.

Frankie took a step, raised his right arm, and plunged the point of the syringe into Italian Scallion's neck. Rojas covered his eyes. Frankie picked up the syringe cover to insure no evidence remained and capped the needle. He took off his gloves, and returned them, along with the empty vial to his pocket.

Satisfied, Frankie left the stall, peeled off three hundred-dollar bills, and gave them to Rojas, who quickly stuffed them into his pocket as if they were nuclear waste. Frankie lifted Rojas' downcast chin and gave the flinching stable hand a condescending pat on the cheek.

"Good boy."

Regaining what little self-respect remained, Rojas could not resist a parting shot. "Hope you got a good place to hide, Frankie. This blow up, he finger you."

Frankie's enigmatically evil smile froze Rojas, who wished he'd kept silent. Just when he thought Frankie would strike him out for good, Frankie was gone.

Rumbling, rumpled Frankie stepped out of Barn Seven. His head swiveled left to right as if guided by remote control. His broad back was stooped at the shoulders. A nod here, a two-fingered Papal blessing of a wave there, without losing a step. All the while his head was aimed more at the ground than at the middle distance. *This is my stealth pose*, he thought. A way to be seen, but not seen at the same time.

He imagined a courtroom scenario as the DA questioned a witness, something like:

DA: "Did you see Frankie LoFrisco on the day of (fill in the date)?"
WITNESS: "I think so."
DA: "You think? Can you be sure?"

WITNESS: "Yeah, well. I dunno."

DA: "What was he wearing? Can you recall that?"

WITNESS: "I dunno if I seen him. How can I remember what he's wearin'?"

Frankie imagined the courtroom bursting into laughter before the judge gaveled them to silence.

By now, his eyes had started twinkling and a moronic, semi—some would say more like full-blown—evil grin pushed the corners of his mouth in an uphill direction and forced his chubby cheeks into his eye sockets, giving him the look of a fat Mandarin.

Keeping in the shadows, Frankie made his way to the administrative portion of the track out of public view. He opened a door deep in the shadows and blended into the dark maw beyond. The reflection of stray light off the chrome handles as the door opened and closed gave the only indication of movement.

The hall deep within the basement of Arlington Park was cool when Frankie entered. As his eyes adjusted to the dim light, he smelled the faint residue of industrial-strength cleaner and soon noticed the janitor swabbing away at the far end. *So far, so good*, he thought. Then he entered the office identified by an exterior sign as Horseman's Bookkeeper.

* * *

She was asleep, and he took the time to look out the window from the back seat of a Lincoln Town Car. Without thinking, he picked a pink thread off her skirt. The windows were tinted on all sides—even the partition between the back seat and the driver, who didn't know a thing. Sure, he's on the hook, but he did like he was told: go over there to that place, a place we all know. Be there at a certain time and, at that exact time, get into the driver's seat of a Lincoln Town Car and drive it to that other place. Where? We'll tell you.

No one knows I'm back here. No one knows I'm in town, except those who have to know, and that's all right. 'Cause I'm on the hook, too. Like I need to remind myself.

He felt the hook daily, which was the reason he was in the back seat of the Lincoln Town car to begin with. Anything to get the pain of obligation out of his skin. By the end of the day, that is what he would have to do. Anything.

He noticed the refurbished Soldier's Field as the limo headed north. Too many changes.

He liked the original better. *Luxury boxes, my ass.* A write-off for high-class thieves, a bribe for the pols, and an up-your-ass to the slobs who spent forty hours a week slowly dying so that the high-class thieves could make more money to give bigger bribes to the pols.

She stirred, coming out of the haze he'd created, and softly moaned. The moan was muffled and only he could hear it, because her mouth was taped. Her eyes were blindfolded and her hands tied at the wrists. Only her feet were free.

"Quiet. No one can hear you." He spoke softly as if calming a child.

The words echoed in her partially conscious mind, revealing images from her recessed and repressed, memory. Those big hands, the white hair, the burning sensation. Her eyes were squeezed shut so tight she felt her eyeballs would burst, turn to liquid, and flow out from under her lids and down her cheeks. Later she learned the liquid on her cheeks was tears.

"No one can hear you. This is the price you pay."

What was she paying for? What did she owe? Or see? That was it. Maybe she saw something. That day. They'd never get the tape. She knew resistance was futile. She learned that long ago. At least now payback was possible. Her thoughts were again interrupted by more burning in the other place.

He looked over at the woman tied, gagged, and blindfolded in the back seat of the Lincoln. *I'm speaking softly, for what? Suddenly I'm gentle.* Who was he kidding?

Not her, as she struggled into full consciousness, increasing the volume of her muted cries. If she knew only he could hear them, maybe she'd save her strength. For what? Any strength she saved could be put to no use. Never. His gentleness was a ruse. He had to try once more to get the information. But as he waited for her to regain consciousness, his eyes wandered to her feet, in stylish black pumps and crossed at the ankles, and followed them north toward her bare thighs.

He stared at her white skin and rewound his memory to the night before. *Maybe I didn't rape her. It was so easy; easier than I ever expected. Maybe it wasn't rape. She liked me? She wanted it? A fair exchange? So, I manipulated her. I lied. Men lie, cheat, steal, commit treason, murder just to thrust their light into a dark cave.*

Thinking about last night made him stiffen; his mind became an out-of-control carrousel of sexual feelings that blurred his vision. He snapped his eyes off her thighs and caught a glimpse of Buckingham Fountain spewing a steady stream of water into the air.

Had he been a devotee of Freud, this image might have been meaningful, but he wasn't and it wasn't.

"I'm going to remove the tape," he told her and watched for a sign that she was paying attention. She nodded once.

"At the same time, I will put the barrel of my gun between your eyes. If you scream, I will kill you here, and we'll keep on driving into the woods and dump your body. Do you understand?"

If there was an IQ test for nods, hers displayed a high degree of intelligence.

"Good. I knew you were a smart girl."

He slowly pulled half the tape off, aware it was less painful to pull it off in one fast tug. He wanted to be sure she wouldn't trick him. When it was half removed, he placed the barrel of his snub-nosed .38 at the point where her nose blended with her forehead. Then he removed the tape entirely.

"Okay, now take some breaths. But be quiet."

She took in three deep, measured breaths without speaking.

There is something about the way she takes orders, he thought. *I'm not an authority figure, just the guy who snatched and shtupped her.* He remembered telling her the night before, "This is the price you pay for having an asshole boyfriend." Next, he'd reached under her skirt, ripped off her plain, white, cotton panties, and threw them on the floor. *What young woman wears those?* He expected to find a wispy thong. *Maybe she was trying to feel like a little girl again. A virgin? Ridiculous. Why?* He didn't know or care. A curiosity to trick his brain.

She hadn't yelled or tried to get away, as if she'd learned to submit. She'd never moved or kissed him. And never looked him in the face. Always her face was turned to the wall.

"Look, it doesn't have to be this way," he'd lied. "You tied and gagged."

"What do you want?" Each word measured slowly and carefully to contain no hint of emotion. The words brought him back to the car and present.

She was in her surreal mode, now as in the past, and would reveal no trace of feelings. It was a practiced response.

"Where is the tape?" he asked using the same slow, measured speech as she had.

"I told you, I don't know anything about a tape." There was an edge in her voice, and she wondered if it was noticeable.

It was. He tapped the tip of the .38 gently on her forehead then withdrew it and returned it to his jacket pocket.

She'd wondered since the previous night why anyone would know of or be interested in her tape and concluded it was her only leverage—the only thing that kept her alive, prevented her death. She'd hold on as long as possible.

He hit her hard with the back of his right hand and, at the same time, covered her mouth with his left to muffle any cries.

Her chest heaved with sobs, but no sound escaped.

"Don't hurt me anymore." She recalled saying those words before in her shadow world.

"The tape. That's what we want. It's easy. Tell us and you're free."

"I don't—"

He grabbed her by the front of her black dress and shook her so that her head snapped back against the Corinthian leather of the seat.

"This is the price you pay for having an asshole for a boyfriend."

"I paid last night." She surprised him, reading his mind.

"That was a deposit. The tape is a balloon payment. Then we mark you paid in full."

He heard her thinking and slapped her again before any thoughts coalesced into a counterattack. Not that she was in any position to do him harm.

She's an attractive woman, not gorgeous, he thought. But when she was about to cry and twisted her mouth as if trying to evade a spoonful of castor oil, she looked like an ugly, premenstrual adolescent. Another slap and tears leaked from under her bandaged eyes.

She crossed and uncrossed her legs, pressing them together under her skirt as they pulled back in fear of what might come. The inevitable, she was convinced. Even with that, she'd maintain her leverage. No point in telling the truth now.

"Okay. No more. In my bedroom." The words rushed out, and she all but collapsed.

He was pleased. A price had been paid, but he got value for the expense. He prepared to return the tape to her mouth.

"Don't hurt—"

The tape was in place.

"Be quiet." He was firm. No need to be calm any more. He got what he wanted.

Out the window he saw they were cruising up Lake Shore Drive and past Oak Beach.

On schedule, he thought as he took disposable gloves out of his inside jacket pocket and put them on with a snap. The sound made her jump, but, absorbed in the next step, he didn't pay attention.

He opened the drink cabinet—standard equipment in the luxury car—and removed a syringe and vial of clear liquid. With steady hands he filled the syringe, replaced the vial in the drink cabinet, and removed a tampon.

Deprived of sight, touch, and the ability to make sound, Ariel Sutherland tried to sharpen her hearing. *What was he doing?* Before any possibilities emerged in her mind, the alarm on her watch sounded twice. *Post time.*

"Hey, two o'clock. It's post time," he said, trying to put a razzle-dazzle in his voice, imitating the track announcer. He laughed softly to himself in amusement, not caring if she heard or not, returned the syringe to the console, and shut the doors.

I got something for you, he thought, feeling hostile toward her. Hatred was a part of his power. How it developed he couldn't tell. Must he hate to have power, or did the possession of power develop hatred over those he controlled? But the physical dominated his thoughts, and he knelt down on the floor facing Ariel and the back seat. Her hands were tied together at the wrists and then tied to the strap attached to the side of the car above the rear window.

In one motion, he scooped her legs in one arm and pulled her torso to the edge of the seat as far as it would go. She squirmed and tried to edge back, but stopped after she felt the sting of his gloved backhand on her face. She didn't resist as he roughly pulled her skirt up and legs apart. *Like opening the cavity of a turkey for stuffing*, he thought. Now, that most holy grail in the vast dominion of femininity was exposed for his gaze and penetration.

Geez, this is hard, he admitted to himself, acknowledging he spoke for his head and his dick. Surrendering to the latter, he started fingering her, rationalizing that this would make his other task easier—for both of them.

He wished he could understand the meaning of her muffled sound. Pain? Pleasure? A little more to the left? Soon he decided to stop that line of questioning, knowing the more he fingered her, the harder he got. Get it over and done with.

Even with gloves on he could feel she was ready for the next step. Without another thought, he worked the moist tampon into her, forced her thighs closed, and pushed her back to a normal position on the seat. He stayed kneeling, with his arms pressing her thighs together for another few minutes to make sure. Not much she could do anyway, being trussed like she was. All he had to do now was wait. Another half an hour and it would all be over. No more hooks.

CHAPTER FIVE

Clay towered above Hegan as they ambled along the concourse behind the grandstand. Using a cane to keep his legs steady, Hegan was not agile enough to dodge and weave away from the pulsing mass of horse players coming toward him from every direction like random atomic particles. The mad scramble before the next race had begun. Hegan was determined not to end up like Wile E. Coyote with hundreds of footprints on his back and picked up his pace as he hobbled toward the two dollar window.

"Easy, big fella. Remember what the doc said. 'Slow and steady steps.' Clay couldn't resist adding, in a singsongy, kindergarten way, "S.S.S. Slow. Steady. Steps."

"I was there. Your head was swiveling around looking for what's-her-name."

"Charlotte is a very fine woman. Did you know she sings in her church choir?"

"Most of the time I spent in her company, I was unconscious."

They were fifth in line for the window, and Hegan took the time to call Captain Rosen, the precinct commander. He asked if the identity of frozen-head-and-hands matched the driver's license from the body in the university pool. The news that Rosen had a team working on it did not satisfy Hegan. He pressed Rosen and was told to focus on his complete recovery. But Hegan insisted, reminding Rosen that he'd been the first on the scene. He'd opened the case and needed all available information. Rosen would not be swayed and told Hegan they'd "have a talk." Over and out.

Clay could tell the pain on Hegan's face was more than physical. "This is my fourth win today. Four straight winners. Today is a beautiful day. Just like you said." Clay looked over at Hegan, trying to determine if his jibe had any effect, but found only that his friend looked painfully uncomfortable. "How you feelin'?"

"Me? Oh." Hegan's brain fired rapidly, searching for an answer. "Me? I'm great!"

"And I'm Jamie Foxx," Clay said softly to himself before handing his ticket through the wicket and collecting his winnings. "$37.45. Not bad for a two-buck bet. Come on, I'll buy you a beer."

The crowd thinned out a little by the time Hegan and Clay made their way back through the concourse toward the blue sky outside. "Two," Clay told the attendant stationed at the top row of an aisle leading to the rail. He expertly lifted two eight-ounce cups from a stack and, in one motion, placed them under spigots and turned on the beer tap.

Clay paid for the beer, providing the attendant with a large enough tip to receive an enthusiastic "Thank you, sir" in return, and picked up the two cups.

"Thanks," Hegan said with uncertainty in his voice—not because he'd never had a beer in his life, but because he was now faced with the prospect of leaning on the cane with his left hand and drinking with his right, all while trying to move forward and out of a crowd.

"Gimme that." Clay took the beer and Hegan regained his equilibrium.

They stepped back out of the crowd and found a place close enough to watch the groundskeepers going over the race course, fluffing the dirt to make the surface softer for the next race.

"How you holdin' up? And don't give me any of your John Wayne true grit."

"Me? I'm fine. Yeah. Got nothing to complain about. Once I get back to work—"

"Work?" Clay couldn't wait to interrupt and in the process sputtered some of his beer.

Hegan chuckled. "Nice! Look at you, dribbling all over yourself. Some people should never go out in public."

"Don't change the subject. You're pushin' it, man. Fifteen years of your life you gave to the city. Retire. Go out a stud."

"I'm not old enough." Hegan seemed offended by the idea.

"Work-related disability." Clay reasoned his logic was impeccable.

"Not exactly work related. My ex-brother-in-law accidentally shot me in the back after beating up my sister."

"Yeah, but that's not what you—"

"Told the police review board? Hell, no. I want that little roach to pay alimony for the rest of his unnatural life and beyond. The board believed it was an accident or something. I can't remember, but whatever I said worked out. For me and Teresa. I think Eddie'd rather go to jail."

"Why? In jail he'd either get shanked or turned into a fairy."

"And both are too good for him."

Clay considered those possibilities for a moment and finished with them. "Yeah, at least that problem is solved. Now, about work-related disability. I'm an expert on that subject and got the scars to prove it."

"Please. Don't. Keep your shirt on. Let Charlotte—"

"She's already seen all the itty-bitty stitches on my body," Clay leered at Hegan making certain there was doubt how Charlotte managed to see all the injuries he'd experienced in his football career.

Hegan was intent on making his case, though it was more to convince himself than Clay or anyone else.

"As a rookie cop, I swore to uphold the law and protect the people."

"Rookie?" Now it was Clay's turn to interrupt.

"Would you let me finish? It's my oath."

All of it was too much for Clay, and the dam broke."Wake up! The system chewed on your butt and spit you into a safety net. Use it."

There was wisdom in Clay's advice, but he knew Hegan had doubts. Was it familiarity? Comfort of a set routine? Questions of self-worth? Too many questions for this day. Too soon to decide.

"Let's get some sun." Hegan changed the subject and pointed with his cane toward the paddock area where a small crowd had gathered to watch the lineup of horses pass by before the start of the featured race.

"Saving all your money for the featured race?" Clay asked, change of subject accepted. "Nothing like a few winners to put the peck back in your pecker."

"I don't bet anymore." Hegan's words were flat. Was he not convinced of this decision, or had the words blown out some flicker of life in his soul?

"You stopped gambling? Bullshit."

"No horses, sports cards, lotteries. Nothing."

"No poker?"

"Not even poker." Hegan tried to sound determined like a bozo in an AA meeting.

Clay looked at Hegan as though seeing a stranger for the first time. "Man, whatever nerve that bullet hit in your back must've cut the sensible part of your brain. 'Cause you gone crazy!"

There was something about the sun that seemed to touch Hegan deep in his core. He stopped and closed his eyes for a few moments. Clay waited suspicions still intact.

"I've got a second chance now," Hegan said.

Clay watched Hegan slowly open his eyes.

"Nah, Hegan. This is one of your tricks. You're betting on something."

"I swear. In that hospital bed... there was a time when I tried to move and couldn't. That is the scariest feeling. Then and there, I took an oath. If I could walk again, I'd never gamble."

Clay had no doubt Hegan was sincere. And while he wanted to believe he was witnessing a rebirth of some kind in his long-time friend, the immortal words of Ronald Reagan rang in his head – trust, but verify.

"Oh, no. You won't sucker me. You set me up the same way over the years."

"How?" Hegan said with a tinge of genuine hurt in his voice.

"You got me to bet Gore over Bush."

"At the time—"

"Then Sacramento over the Lakers!"

"I ask your forgiveness, my friend," Hegan said allowing his shoulders to sag; becoming a forlorn creature.

* * *

Hegan fell into a hundred-mile stare. *That was the past*, Hegan vowed as he disappeared inside himself. Where the future led, he didn't know. But despite his talk with Rosen, nothing was written in stone.

"Where'd you go, Hegan?"

Clay's voice got Hegan to focus. Once again he saw the flow of humanity leisurely making its way to inspect the horse flesh parading through the paddock area. Directly across, Hegan spotted a slow procession of the two-legged kind featuring an elegantly tailored gentleman. Even Hegan, whose sartorial splendor began and ended with the L.L. Bean catalog, could appreciate fine threads.

Geez, its Don Barzini from The Godfather *come to life. Just when I want to get serious, the movies pull me back*, he thought, pleased that he sounded in his head like Pacino in *GF3*. While he wanted to turn away from the procession, he was fixed to the obvious display of hierarchy and underlying drama of its movement.

Hegan's persistent gaze was rewarded as the face and figure of Johnny Faraci materialized by the rail opposite. He knew Faraci was at least sixty, but he looked ten or fifteen years younger. Even wisps of grey over the temples didn't add age to his unwrinkled face. *Must be olive oil acts as a preservative*, he decided, realizing that if the politically correct police could read his mind, he'd be in lockup right now.

Faraci's suit was by Cerutti. Hegan had seen an ad in the paper for the same suit, same color and cut; everything about it said it cost a couple thousand dollars.

"Look at that." Hegan elbowed Clay in the side of his stomach, which felt like colliding with a mountain of pillows.

"What? Hey, watch your bony elbow."

"The guy in the suit. See that? He's wearing a coupla thou on his bones, and he risks getting horse shit on it." As if on cue, a dappled gelding lifted its tail right in front of Faraci.

"Hah! See that? Do I have ESP or what?"

Before Clay could respond, Faraci was pulled back from the rail by two members of his entourage. One was older and bald, with a massive upper-body build. *There's a prison pump job, if I ever saw one*, Hegan observed, his eyes sliding over to locate the slimmer, younger, more reptilian member of the rescue team who emulated Faraci's style of dress. *But that one's more dangerous.* Hegan didn't recognize Faraci's associates. *Must be imports*, he thought, *not the usual goombas*.

Escaping in the nick of time from the hind end of a dappled gelding did not deter Faraci from his principle reason for venturing to the paddock rail. Hegan noticed Faraci take a keen interest in the stallion with pink silks and the number *seven* on his saddle blanket.

"What's that seven horse?" Hegan asked Clay.

Clay checked his program. "Italian Scallion. Owned by Zenda Farms, ridden by Jesus da Silva, trained by Ariel Sutherland. Up from Florida. Won three races in a row."

"You said Ariel. That's a girl's name?"

"Girl." Clay pushed the program under Hegan's nose, and he peered at the photo of Ariel Sutherland.

"She looks like she just graduated high school" was Hegan's response. The headshot of Ariel showed a young woman in her midtwenties wearing oversized, dark-rimmed glasses that made her look older.

Yet beneath that artifice, Hegan saw another woman. *Put her in a pleated skirt with knee socks and ribbons in her braids and she could pass for fifteen*, he thought.

Hegan didn't focus long on the photo. He was more interested in Faraci's nod at the lumbering, rumpled figure of Frankie LoFrisco, who clearly was no girl. Why was that lummox holding the bridle of Italian Scallion while it made its way to the edge of the track where the outrider and jockey took over? *With any number of busy trainers*, Hegan recalled, *it was not unusual for an assistant trainer to take a horse out.*

But this was the favorite. The crowd had come to see and wager on Italian Scallion, who had sped up from nowhere—actually from Ocala, Florida, but to the provincial thoroughbred cognoscenti, Florida was not Kentucky where all pretenders to the thoroughbred throne needed to originate.

The buzz around his young female trainer, who'd become an overnight curiosity as her charge thundered up from the Sunshine State, brought celebrity devotees to the track along with members of the twenty-something generation. Even the program indicated Italian Scallion was the most successful horse she'd ever trained. You would think she'd want to be here for its first race in Chicago.

As Frankie turned, his eyes met Faraci's and he nodded in return. *Just like watching tennis*, Hegan thought. *Serve and volley.*

Hegan felt his instincts primed for the first time since he intervened in front of Teresa's house. His acute sense of the reality beneath the reality made him feel more energized than he had in weeks. *This is what the CIA boys call chatter*, he thought.

"Who you got in this race?" Hegan asked

"Number six. Bet A Me Mucho. Why?"

"Put your money on Italian Scallion."

"No way I'll take a tip from Mr. I'mnotbetting! Look at the tote board. He's going off at even money. With three wins in a row and not the favorite?"

"He's my favorite. Bet it all to win." Hegan's voice was devoid of urgency or emotion.

"All? I made five hundred bucks so far today betting against the favorite. You tell me you're not betting. Why should I listen?"

"I smell Johnny Faraci running this race," Hegan whispered as he watched Faraci saunter from the paddock with his fat and skinny bookends.

"Okay," Clay said, doubt resting on every syllable. "I'll meet you at the rail below section fifteen."

As Clay left to place his bet, Hegan's looping gait took him from the paddock toward the front of the grandstand and then through the sparse crowd at the rail near the finish line. The impact of off-track betting and the internet left only those patrons needing the experience—to many it was a fix—of in-person attendance at the track. For them, betting was never the holy end. It was visiting with familiar faces, feeling the rush of the last three seconds as horses careened toward the finish line, a day in the open air, rain or shine, that mattered.

The more technology advances, the less interaction we have with our fellow humans, was his conjecture. And surely there would be those who'd accuse him of overgeneralization, as if he had to name each and every instance when technological advances reduced the opportunity for human intercourse. Radio replaced town meetings. Records replaced concerts. VHS replaced going to the movies—not to mention DVDs. And the Internet created a phony virtual community where certifiable cretins stayed up all night typing gibberish to one another. And the ultimate: porno replaced fucking.

Once, an entire society agreed that in unity there is strength. Now anonymity created security. Except that the Patriot Act destroyed privacy, and not even the anonymity of a chat room was secure with Big Brother—more like Big Tyrant—spying on everyone just like in the bad old days when Communism kept the country from turning fascist.

Must've given me some strong stuff in the hospital, Hegan thought as Clay returned, a fist full of tickets peeking from the side of his paw. When Clay pointed toward the starting gate, Hegan shook tangential thoughts from his head and fully returned to the conscious world.

Number seven was the last horse nudged into position in the last and seventh gate. Within seconds, the track announcer's voice came over the public address system for the sake of those not paying attention.

"The horses are now in the starting gate. Annnnd they're off!"

The double doors on all seven gates swung open in unison, and seven sets of front legs left the ground, grabbing for air, followed by an explosive push from their hindquarters. The three and five horse gained an immediate advantage and forged ahead of the others.

Hegan could focus only on Italian Scallion. "Lookit! Italian Scallion's really moving. You're gonna make a killing!"

"I'd better or the killing I make will be you." Clay was not being serious, though Hegan wasn't altogether convinced.

As the pack passed before their eyes, Italian Scallion was a close fifth behind horses three and five, with more than eighty percent of the course left to cover. In theory, Hegan's pick had ground to cover, but plenty of time to make his move and return home a winner.

"We gotta keep hope alive," Hegan said as they watched seven tails pass from view.

"Amen, brother." Clay was jiving and his canary-eating grin broadcast that fact to Hegan loud and clear.

The track announcer returned with "It's Bet A Me Mucho by half a length, followed by Lucky Dodger, Winsome Sister, Reckless George, Funny Boy, Lunch-N-Et, and Italian Scallion."

"He's dropped back. Italian Scallion's last, Mike."

"I can see and I can hear."

Hegan wondered what happened to all that promise as Italian Scallion left the starting gate bunched up in fifth position. *Ain't the start,* a little voice buried deep inside reminded him. We all come out of the birth canal with a scream and a whoop, pawing at the air with little red fists, ready to grab what's out there for the taking—some, like the Bush boys, at what for them is preordained. But nothing's preordained—not success, not happiness. *It's the finish and maybe the in-between that matters the most, not the start,* the inner voice concluded.

Hegan turned to look for Faraci, but he was gone. Not likely he'd rub elbows with the great unwashed.

As the horses made their way around the far turn, Clay's rhythmic tapping on Hegan's shoulder snapped him out of what could only take him into a slide down the chute into darker places than he was ready to go.

"Quit smacking me on the shoulder!" Hegan sidestepped away. Clay moved toward him but stopped tapping.

"Not smacking. Just keeping time. Giving my boy moral support."

"Your boy is last."

"Keep hope alive," said with a lilting chortle in every word.

As the horses rounded the final turn, Bet A Me Mucho was first by three lengths. The horses closest were running out of gas at the same time and all but conceded.

The track announcer continued his recitation of the obvious. "Coming down the stretch, it's Bet A Me Mucho, followed by Winsome Sister, Reckless George, Lucky Dodger, Lunch-N-Et, Funny Boy, and Italian Scallion."

Hegan and Clay edged their way through the crowd of restless horse players, but Hegan had to stop. "We lost," Hegan said watching Italian Scallion finally cross the finish, ten lengths behind the sixth horse, cantering down the track as if in slow motion, a toy car winding down.

"Damn you, Hegan....Oh well, easy come....."

"Guess my perception of humanity is rusty," Hegan said in disbelief, crushed though the outcome had not been in doubt for the last forty-five seconds of the race. "I was so sure. I'd bet the family jewels."

"Good thing you didn't. They'd be mine now," Clay said with a wicked grin as he reached his huge hand out to grasp Hegan's metaphorical jewels and squeezed tight. Hegan grimaced like a bad amateur actor and Clay looked pleased.

"Come on. I'll buy you a beer," Hegan offered apologetically. "A few beers."

As they reached the concourse leading toward the parking lot, Clay, struggling to keep his emotions in check, began fidgeting like a six-year-old with a secret. Ultimately, he couldn't keep the secret any longer and lost control.

"Aha! Gotcha! Finally gotcha! No way I'd bet more than two dollars on Italian Scallion. Which left me $498 on Bet A Me Mucho!"

Clay was laughing so loud and pointing at him with such intensity, Hegan thought the vein in his neck would burst. He absorbed the jibes with good-natured grace, but couldn't resist countering, if weakly. "Don't think I didn't know."

"Bull pucky."

"Hey, I'm a detective. My eyes are trained through experience to detect human behavior, and I saw a furtiveness transmitted to my antenna." Hegan was scamming Clay and they both knew it.

"Yeah, yeah. Talk that blather all you want. You're still gonna buy me a beer."

"A few beers," Hegan reminded him.

"Even better. First, I gotta collect my winnings."

Hegan waited for Clay to move up to the window. He noted most of the torn tickets littering the floor were for the seven horse, Italian Scallion. Glancing up, he saw the Faraci wannabe collecting a fat envelope. A large payday for some horse other than the Scallion, he was sure.

* * *

Once Frankie delivered Italian Scallion to the outrider at the entrance to the track, his job was finished. He deserved a drink. A nod to Faraci across the paddock and Frankie was on his way. Within the hour. Adios. Sayonara. Good-bye. So long. Farewell. Over and out. The words poured forth at a pace in keeping with his quick steps toward the elevator that would take him up to the Sky Bar on the top floor of the grandstand.

Frankie let his eyes adjust to the bar's dim light and checked for familiar faces. None. Perfect. He ambled over to the end of the long oak bar which ran the length of a thirty-foot window of smoked glass panels.

At first Frankie was pleased that the barman poured out his usual Seven and Seven. *Being well-known is a good thing if I'm gonna get moldy in this place*, he thought. He paid for the drink, left his usual one-buck tip and sat alone at a table by the window. There he had an unimpeded 180-degree view of the track. *The fewer notice me the better*, he told himself.

At the first gulp of his drink, the doors of the portable starting gate silently snapped open, and Frankie was able to observe the results of his efforts. His eyes never left the pink silks with the number seven large enough to be seen five stories in the sky.

When the lead horse rounded the far turn, Frankie finished his drink and waited until the barman was otherwise occupied before he made a stealthy exit. He reached the elevator but wanted to enjoy a few additional stolen moments before his flight. Frankie stopped in front of a door that bore the large, black seven logo of Zenda Farms and pulled a set of keys from his pocket. The first didn't work. Neither did the second and Frankie had to choose between his curiosity and his security. The third opened the door. Frankie entered the Zenda Farms skybox. Actually it was two boxes in one. Here the owner of the stable could entertain fifty of his close personal friends at one time. Frankie sat in a modernistic leather chair at the edge of the window, where he felt like the lord and master of all within his vantage. *Maybe not now*, he thought, *and maybe not here, but soon and in an even better place.*

Then he noticed the half-filled glasses and cigarette butts. Someone had been there recently and left before fully extinguishing one of the cigarettes.

He didn't want to get caught exercising his fantasy, but he remained curious about the suite he would never visit again. At the last moment, he pushed open the sliding door that separated both suites and was surprised to find stacks of pink material on wooden pallets. Some of the material had been scattered on the floor and was badly wrinkled, like somebody trampled or even slept on it.

Frankie picked up a piece of the fabric – *silk or what?* – and tried to figure out why all that material was stored in a suite meant for eating and drinking. He shook his head: it would have to wait.

He locked the door, jiggled the handle to make sure, and headed for the elevator. Once inside, he pushed the button for the basement. On the next floor down, a loud group of winners and drinkers entered. Frankie edged deeper into the back of the car. A glum group of losers and drinkers got on next and cringed at the noise the winners made behind them, surely at their expense. Losers and winners got off on the first floor, and Frankie was alone until the doors opened in the basement.

Frankie, with singular focus, strode down the corridor and entered a door marked Horseman's Bookkeeper. Beyond bulletproof Plexiglas, a floor-to-ceiling safe stood open, its shelves stocked with currency. An assistant trainer with ingenuity in his brain and larceny in his heart, Frankie LoFrisco would make them all pay for under appreciating his talent. For thinking he was just a fat slob. He'd strike at their hearts and their wallets, going straight to their personal piggy bank at the track, the horseman's bookkeeper. He'd used their own money as his stake to bet a fixed race and then stole back the winnings they never knew they had by simply cashing a check he'd written to himself.

Frankie handed the clerk a check.

"A Zenda Farms check. I'll have to get authorization—"

"No need." Frankie's tone was matter-of-fact. "Check the initials and franking symbol on the back."

The clerk flipped the check over, noticed the initials and symbol, and compared them to a ledger next to the phone on the counter. All looked legit and the clerk, a bureaucrat at heart, was satisfied he'd have to expend no more effort.

"Things are looking up, Frankie."

Frankie flashed the clerk an insincere smile as he tapped his thick fingers on the counter and whistled with feigned insouciance. *Mind your own goddamned business or you'll be lookin' up from the inside of a casket.*

The clerk stuffed four large stacks of bills into a manila envelope and slipped it under the opening in the Plexiglas. "850 big ones," he said.

When is this prick gonna shut his mouth? I know how much it is, smart-ass, Frankie thought as he muttered a simple thank you. He waited half an eternity as the envelope moved through the opening.

Almost as slowly as Italian Scallion crossed the finish line. The thought made him chuckle.

With a flash of his bucked teeth and a wave like a Papal blessing, Frankie was out the door. But once in the dimly lit corridor, his eyes darted about in search of familiar faces. All clear. Frankie stuffed the envelope under his shirt, buttoned his rumpled jacket, and headed for the exit.

* * *

Hegan and Clay sat at the bar in Henry's surrounded by half a dozen midafternoon drinkers. The muted television showed film of a truck jackknifed on an interstate overpass and the resulting backup of commuters during early morning rush hour, but no one paid it any notice because Clay was holding court.

"Not only did Hegan guarantee the fix was in—" Clay neared the punch line with glee.

"That horse died!" Henry said.

"You're kidding," a voice of disbelief said from the far corner of the bar.

"Saw it on the TV. A bulletin and all," Henry confirmed.

"Holy shit!" Clay and Hegan at once. Nervous laughter echoed around the bar as the group tried to understand the meaning of Henry's bulletin.

Hegan decided to join in. "When's the last time you saw a horse drop dead at the track?" he asked.

Henry quieted the group and raised the sound on the television which showed film of Italian Scallion collapsing about twenty lengths past the finish line. The sportscaster's voice dropped two octaves to indicate the solemnity of the moment as he provided narrative for the picture.

"Illinois State Racing officials promise a full-scale inquiry into the collapse and death of Italian Scallion after the completion of the seventh race today at Arlington."

Henry placed another mug of beer in front of Hegan. "Gotta hand it to you, Mike. Your picks at the track are drop-dead on the money."

The laughter rose once again, silenced only as the photo of Ariel Sutherland replaced the film of Italian Scallion on the screen above the bar. It was the same picture as the one in Clay's program.

The TV announcer told viewers, "So far, investigators have been unable to locate twenty-five-year-old Ariel Sutherland, Italian Scallion's trainer."

"That's a trainer?" Henry asked. "Those glasses don't fool me. That's a high school kid."

"Right on, Henry," someone said.

Hegan stared at Ariel's photo on the screen as if in a trance. He was not captivated by beauty so much as he was trying to intuitively connect. What was she thinking when that photo was taken? What had she done moments before? How did that day start? What is she thinking now? Where is she? *What am I doing?* Hegan didn't know. And he didn't remember ever taking this approach before on any other case, not that this was his case—or anybody else's. Yet.

Next, the photo of Frankie LoFrisco appeared on the TV screen.

"Hey!" Hegan yelled over to Clay. "That's the guy in the paddock. The one who nodded."

Once the words were out, Hegan thought better of it and quickly put a finger to his lips, hoping to silence Clay.

"Yeah, That's him. He nodded…" Clay got the signal and switched gears. "like he knew us or something. Weird."

Henry saw the sign language. *What the hell is that all about?* Henry wondered.

Hegan was saved by the voice of the TV announcer informing the viewers that "in her absence, the two-year-old stallion was saddled by assistant trainer Frank LoFrisco. Track officials have yet to locate Mr. LoFrisco..."

"Enough of this crap." Henry shut off the TV by remote, came out from behind the bar, and plugged in the jukebox. Jimmy Buffett's "Margaritaville" soon wafted around them.

"We were suckered, Leon."

"We? What you mean we, Kemo Sabe?" Clay pulled two one-dollar bills out of his pocket and used them to fan Hegan. "I only lost two bucks. You got all the credibility of 'I did not have sex with that woman.'"

"Or maybe Iraqi oil will pay for the war," another patron said.

One more in the group had to have his say. "Or we will bring democracy to Iraq."

Hegan shook his head in self-disgust, then caught the refrain of the Buffett song and adapted it slowly. "Some people say it's a woman to blame, but I know it's my own damn fault."

* * *

The Lincoln Town Car slowly crept to the edge of a deserted parking lot at the loneliest and furthest end of Wilmette Beach. Without stopping, the door of the car swung open and Ariel Sutherland, without restraints or blindfold, was pushed out on wobbly legs. The rear wheels of the car sprayed sand at Ariel as it sped off. Instinctively, she tried to defend herself against the tiny buckshot-like particles, but in the effort lost her balance and knocked off her glasses. After being in prolonged darkness, the sudden harsh light hurt her eyes as Ariel knelt to find the glasses, groping about in a widening circle to no avail.

Disoriented and her vision greatly impaired, Ariel stumbled unaware of her direction that ultimately would lead her to the beach.

Her mind raced to embrace her freedom. "*They let me go!*" her mind sang as she staggered forward. Only blurred vision muted her joy in being alive.

Several joggers gave her a quick glance as they ran past Ariel on the hard sand near the water's edge. They were too far away for her to hear their steps, and their shapes were meaningless to her. Silhouetted by the setting sun, Ariel made drunken progress down the beach toward the water.

Someone must see me. Someone could hear me. She started to speak, but no words came out. At the same time, her purse, dangling from a long strap, dropped from her shoulder and onto the sand. She didn't notice, more intent on trying to speak. Soon her voice was less important. She couldn't breathe. Though she tried as hard as she could, pulling air into her lungs took greater and greater effort. She flashed on an old memory but eventually gave up, accepting the burning sensation that followed. Something was terribly wrong. She stopped trying to breathe, surrendering to the inevitable. Instead of a burning sensation, her knees felt like jelly. Then her legs failed and she crashed facedown in the sand. A stray breeze made her skirt billow, but slim pink threads held fast to the back of her dress.

* * *

Johnny Faraci got out of a black Cadillac Escalade in front of a thirty-two-story condominium on Lake Shore Drive. He waved back inside the SUV to the fat and skinny bookends who had accompanied him to the track earlier in the day. Tonight he needed to be alone. Too much happened that he didn't understand. At that moment, an intermittent gust of wind blew at his back, lifting him from behind and causing him to skip a few steps. As important as Johnny thought—knew—he was, the wind was a reminder that the elements could treat him like any flotsam in the water, to be pushed around at will.

Larry, the doorman who had taken the only job he could get after being downsized by an Enron subsidiary which later folded, watched Faraci leave the Escalade and, with head down to make himself a smaller obstacle for the wind, approach the entrance. Larry, a fifty-eight-year-old father of four who had never done any physical labor, used all his strength and will to push the door open for Faraci.

"Thanks. All of a sudden, the wind." Faraci spoke to Larry as if they'd been longtime friends. The crisp twenty Faraci stuffed into Larry's hand proved otherwise.

Larry knew the denomination without looking. He got the same tip each time Faraci entered the lobby. That could be four or five times a day. Larry also knew, thanks to building management personnel, that Faraci had made inquiries about him. He figured the man's act of charity was his way of making amends to society somehow, though he had no clue why Faraci would feel the need to do so. He called out a humble thank you, but Faraci entered an elevator without acknowledging Larry further.

As Faraci exited the elevator on the thirtieth floor, his nose crinkled in disgust.

"Cabbage, every night cabbage." Hopefully the smell hadn't permeated his condo like before. "Fuckin Russians. Every night they eat the same thing. Do I eat pizza every night? No. Do I eat calamari every night? No. They got no taste," Faraci muttered as he opened the door to his condo. He couldn't resist. Turning, he addressed the empty corridor. "Eat a steak, for Christ's sake!" No one answered.

Light from the setting sun glistened off the lake's surface and was reflected into the sky, providing the only light in the living room at the end of the foyer as Faraci entered. No lights were on, but Faraci didn't need any as he made his way down a hall and into his office. When he turned the table lamp on, full-length black drapes kept any residual light from leaking through his window. *Anybody trying to send a missile into my house from some black CIA helicopter won't know where I am*, he thought. He was aware that some acquaintances and rivals who knew about the drapes ridiculed him. Maybe he saw too many movies with that Arnold guy. So what? It was his life.

He turned on the television in time to watch a replay of the seventh race. The phone rang. He muted the TV and answered.

"Yeah, I know. I know." Faraci couldn't understand why nobody realized he knew. Whatever. "Yeah, I saw. He's a fuckin' moron. By tomorrow mornin' he'll be a dead moron. Yeah, I lost... never mind. Money don't matter. It's the principle. He fucked me. I took the bastard when even his own mama didn't want him, and he fucked me. *Basta*. Forget it. You don't have to know what *basta* means. I know and that's good enough." He paused to listen, but not for long. "I never worry," Faraci said then slammed down the phone.

* * *

A customer entered the Uzbekistan restaurant. The slim, male host approached with cautious deference.

"May I help you?"

There was no answer; in fact, he was ignored as if not one word had been uttered. Alarmed, the host looked around for help, but the restaurant was empty except for a two waiters arranging table settings for dinner. The customer looked toward the end of the line of booths, and the host tried to block his view. The man slipped around him.

"Wait!" the host called out as loud as he could without drawing attention to himself. The quaver in his voice was unmistakable.

Gregori poked his head out from the last booth. He held a loaded and cocked Glock on his knee. His guest had arrived. He brushed the host away with the wave of his other hand.

"You find it?" the question firm and fast before his guest could sit opposite.

"Not yet..."

"What are you waiting for?" Gregori's voice resounded in the empty room. "Find it!"

"I know where it is. Don't worry."

The impudence, Gregori thought. Calmly, he reminded the visitor, "I don't worry. You're the one who worries for me." The guest was waved away quicker than his employee.

Zenda entered the restaurant nearly in tears and didn't notice the stranger quickly leaving. They bumped shoulders, but the stranger kept his head turned down and away without acknowledging the contact.

"Who was that?"

"Nobody. A salesman. Selling insurance or something."

"Did you hear? I can't... ." Zenda gasped for air.

Gregori poured a shot of vodka. "Take it." Then he poured Zenda another. But Zenda's anguish could not be blunted by alcohol.

"My horse, the favorite, loses and dies! My trainer is missing. I don't understand. What? Why me?"

"A tragedy not even Chekov would understand."

"And then... I was swindled."

This was new to Gregori. "Swindled how?"

"That fat slob wop. He stole $850,000 from my account at the track."

Gregori didn't understand horses. Another would be born any day. But money lost... that was tragic. He sat back, bearing the weight of Zenda's loss as though in mourning.

* * *

Hegan only wanted a few more minutes to sleep, but the Department of Sanitation truck's roaring, heavy-duty engine, accompanied by the cymbal crash of dashed trash can lids, had other plans for him. He lifted his head from the pillow and twisted his shoulders right to left and left to right. Not too bad. His back was improving. Could be the doctor's suggestion that he sleep on the floor a few nights a week was helping. Then again, could be Mother Nature.

This morning he was on the floor, stretched out on an old quilt that covered the hardwood floor of the front bedroom where he'd slept for the last six months. As he tossed off the sheet, Hegan started humming a disconnected tune.

"Oh, make me a pallet on the floor... dum de dum." He couldn't remember the rest of the words from that old Louis Armstrong tune. He got up, his motions slow and cautious so as not to injure his back or pull any muscles, and shuffled to the window. He opened it and looked out on the street and the Department of Sanitation merrymakers. Though he never wore pajamas, he knew anyone noticing him at the window would only see him bare from the waist up.

"Louder! I can't hear you!" he yelled at the three men, one of whom was his cousin Billy.

"Hey, Mike," Billy replied. "You can't hear?" Billy threw two trash can lids in the air and watched as they fell to earth in front of an oncoming station wagon filled with grade-schoolers on their way to St. Barnabas grammar school up the block. "Can you hear me now?" Billy yelled up at Hegan.

"What are you, a moron?" the carpooling mom yelled out her window. "You almost killed us here, and I got a car fulla kids."

Hegan saw the three workmen turn their backs on the crashing lids and screech of brakes to hide their laughter. At the sound of the mother's voice, Gus, the oldest of the three, took matters into his own hands.

"Easy, ma'am. Ain't nobody killed and nobody tried to hurt ya."

"He threw—"

"Sorry, ma'am. You was speedin' up the block."

"Speeding? I just slowed down for a speed bump. Can't you see?"

"And you were speedin'." Gus was on a roll and facts were immaterial. "That guy over there thought he was gonna get runned over, and the covers just flew in the air."

"You're nuts. You think we pay hard-earned tax dollars to you so you can endanger the lives of our children?"

"Sorry, ma'am, they don't pay us to think. We do dirty, heavy work, and you almost killed a valuable member of the Chicago Department of Sanitation."

The squeals of preadolescent girls distracted the mother.

"All right, all right. Let us go."

"Nobody's stoppin' ya."

Just as the woman applied pressure to the accelerator, Gus put his palm out to stop her. She slammed on the brakes.

"Stop. I don't want none a my men hurt." Gus waved his men out of the street. "Men, I want ya on the sidewalk. Now!"

Sputtering at Gus and shushing the children, the woman started past the D of S truck as Gus waved her Godspeed.

Billy dropped an empty trash barrel in front of Hegan's door and looked up to find him laughing in the window.

"Feelin' better?" Hegan continued to laugh as he gave Billy a thumbs-up and shut the window.

Half an hour later, Hegan was dressed for work: chinos, boots, and short-sleeve, button-down cotton shirt—all from L.L. Bean. He went out the side door of his stucco and frame house, where he'd lived since a child, picked up two trash cans and lids and returned them to their place in the driveway.

Hegan gave his street a quick glance. Five years ago, all the houses were the same dull grey stucco. Then came gentrification, and the once Irish immigrant neighborhood seemed to change overnight. Only his house resembled any of the original houses built in the early 1930s. Most now had three stories. One had an elevator. And another had a pool!

Hegan opened the door to his blue 1968 Plymouth Valiant and stopped. In the time it took him to pick up the trash cans, turn around, and walk up the driveway, someone had placed a parking ticket on his windshield. He looked up the street and spotted the scooter of a meter maid.

"Hey! Hey!" Hegan yelled and waved his gold detective's shield in the air as the meter maid turned around. "I'm a cop. A cop!" The meter maid shrugged back at him. Hegan looked up and down the street. His was the only car that hadn't obeyed the alternate side of the street parking rule. Next he checked the sign, which hung on a pole above his left headlight, and then his watch.

"Five minutes! Five minutes over?"

Hegan loved his nearly forty-year-old Valiant and got razzed plenty of times. "Can't you afford a new car? Where can you get parts? What kind of an old fart drives a Valiant?" Until they rode in it and learned the legendary Slant 6 had been replaced and a 425 hemi engine lurked under its hood. *Bats in hell are slow compared to my baby*, Hegan thought, turning on the engine and the radio.

A country-western tune faded as the DJ came back on. "Now for the news at the top of the hour. Police have identified a body found on a Wilmette beach as that of race horse trainer Ariel Sutherland. A preliminary autopsy is under way. Italian Scallion, the horse Sutherland trained, also died yesterday. In other—"

Hegan heard enough. He switched off the radio, put the clutch in first gear, and drove away. He'd intended to confront Rosen at the precinct, but after hearing the news thought Randy Crimmins would be of more use.

The city morgue was hidden away behind Cook County Hospital in a building that looked like it predated the Chicago fire. As Hegan entered he couldn't decide which was worse—the natural smell of age, decay, and death or the scent of night-blooming Jasmine pumped into the air by atomizers affixed intermittently along the ceiling of the main corridor.

Some slick PR type trying to earn his expense account money thought of this one, Hegan mused as he turned right and headed straight for the chief coroner's office to meet Randy. Once away from the main corridor, the familiar mix of age, decay, and death overpowered Hegan and made him gag. If he ran, he'd feel like a wuss so Hegan did a fast-paced "shuffle" to Crimmins office two doors away, thus saving his breakfast bagel with cream cheese and grape jelly from regurgitation.

Inside he found Randy Crimmins, a scholarly-looking young man in his late thirties who had, an instant sooner, said or done something the chief coroner's secretary found amusing. Her smile and the sparkle in her eyes—the kind reserved for a woman encouraging a future swain –disappeared when she spied Hegan.

"May I help you?"

"Hiya, Mike" Randy greeted him before the question could be answered. "Back on duty?"

"Getting there. Your boss in?"

"Dr. Prokop is at lunch," she replied in a manner that questioned Hegan's business with her boss.

"Good. I didn't really want to see him." Hegan gave her his version of a flirtatious smile, but she was not going to favor a transient. "Is he eating downstairs?" Hegan knew the answer as he pointed in the direction of the autopsy lab below.

"Of course not."

"Really? I thought all the ghouls laid out their salami sandwiches on the bellies of some stiff like a picnic table."

"That's disgusting. He'd never... . It's unethical."

Before she could continue, Randy helped out and gave Hegan a perfunctory snort, mixing disdain with disbelief at all civilian, nonscientific types who couldn't pass high school chemistry and, more importantly, didn't want to.

"Mike's an old friend. He's kind of warped but in a harmless way."

The secretary gave Randy a goofy smile. Only moments ago she'd found him amusing, and whatever excuse he made for that idiot was okay with her.

"Come over to my office, Mike. Don't think I have any salami, but I do have some blood pudding I think you'll like."

Hegan didn't flinch. "Yum. My favorite."

"You're both—"

In the hallway, before the door closed, they could hear her say "disgusting." Hegan gagged again.

"You'll get used to it soon enough," Randy said as he directed Hegan toward his office further down the corridor.

"How long does it take?"

"Coupla years."

Hegan was first through the open door and Randy closed it behind them. As much as Randy was pleased to see Hegan had recovered from the "accident," he knew the visit was not social.

"So who is it?"

"Who is what?" Hegan saw Randy change from affable to impatient, like sun to rain squall. *Probably itching to get back to the secretary.* "Okay. Heard they found that horse trainer."

"We get all the celebrities, from Anton Cermak to Chris Farley and now Ariel Sutherland."

"Cermak? Geez, Randy. Didn't think you were that old."

"I'm not, but they say you've been around since the blizzard of '08."

Hegan saluted Randy with his middle finger and they both laughed. "How'd she die?"

"Don't know. She was assigned to Cevasco. He'll sign off."

"Not Cevasco! All he'll find is her heart stopped. Maybe you can help me...?"

Randy knew the 64-thousand-dollar question was on its way, but it came faster than ever before. "This official?" When Hegan's face looked like it'd been slapped with a frozen flounder, Randy's dread arrived.

Hegan paused thoughtfully and pulled a piece of paper from his pocket. Slowly, for effect, he unfolded it with a quiet reverence and held it under his chin. "This is Ariel Sutherland. Looks like anybody's kid sister. Now she's a stiff downstairs. There's something rotten here, Randy."

Randy covered his eyes and then pressed his hand over his mouth, but not from anguish. He'd seen Hegan in action before. First came the wash. Then the rinse.

"If that was your kid sister, Randy, you'd want me to do something, wouldn't ya?"

Now time to spin dry. Randy pressed his hand to his mouth until he could no longer contain his laughter.

"What?" Hurt was Hegan's forte. "Why the laugh? I mean, this is serious."

Randy surrendered. "Give me two days."

"Thanks," Hegan said with deep sincerity as he leaned on his cane with one hand and gripped Randy's shoulder in appreciation with the other.

CHAPTER SIX

Hegan bolted upright. Inky black. Quiet blaring. Faint light from the red digital numbers on his clock radio. 3 a.m. Hegan had enough. The scenes of his life played endlessly while he slept—or tried to. This morning he shut off the film projector and got up.

He no longer wanted to see this continuous loop of roads not taken, options ignored, people disappointed. His own wounds, from failed high school romances to... to Lucy's face. Images of Eddie, Teresa, Eddie's gun, Hegan diving, pushing Teresa away, and the face of Ariel Sutherland looking up from the page in the program and straight into his eyes.

Now fully awake despite the hour, he fast-forwarded the tape in his mind. It always stopped on Ariel's face, like a crooked roulette wheel. Alone, with nothing to intrude except feelings of guilt and inadequacy, Hegan determined he was the one. The job was his. He accepted.

As the eastern sky turned light grey in anticipation of the sunrise, Hegan drove his Valiant to Arlington Park. At the commercial entrance he found trucks from vendors delivering food, beverages, and other provisions. A flip of his badge later, he was through the gate and parked in a space reserved for owners, trainers, and other racing personnel. He shut the car door, took a step and stumbled. "The goddamned cane," he muttered as he returned to the car to retrieve it.

Hegan felt his heart trying to tear a hole in his shirt. He was on the hunt. Randy had asked if it was official business. His answer now was yes! Yes, it is officially my business. While his mind sifted through all the information he had on Ariel, his nervous system kept his legs moving forward by remote control.

He was alone, slowly making his way through the empty distance to the backstretch rail, when an invisible resistance met him. A brief, unseen impediment, he realized moments later, that he had pushed through and felt flow around his body. Omen or warning? Ariel's spirit urging him forward? He had no time for woo-woo. Yet he realized this was the closest thing to an out-of-body experience he'd had since grade school when, trudging the inside staircase, eight-year-old Hegan had seen himself from the ceiling in real time. He would not share his most recent experience, but neither could he ignore it.

The mild, sweet aroma of tobacco smoke brought Hegan's mind and body back together. His eyes focused on a trim man smoking a pipe. He looked to be about seventy, but with the bearing that said, "I may have white hair and seem mellow, but look in my eyes. They don't know fear, and they don't take crap."

"Gilroy?" The profile was familiar, but the setting was not.

"You blind? Of course it's me."

"I thought when you retired..." Hegan was purposely tentative, aware of Gilroy's combative nature from experience and reputation.

"You think retirement is death? Wait, bucko, till it's your turn. I only retired from the cops, not from life. Now, I got the perfect job. Watchin' after poor unfortunates who can't take care of themselves. Horses! Beautiful horses. Which is a damn sight better than those two-legged animals you go after."

For all the flint in Gilroy's spine, there was warmth in his eyes when he took a full look at Hegan.

"You filled out some, Mike. I remember your first day as a probie—"

"That was fifteen years ago, after I graduated from the academy."

"Don't interrupt." Gilroy smiled at Hegan. "It's good to see ya." His eyes focused on the cane. "How's progress?"

Hegan shrugged and twirled the cane like a baton. "Getting better every day."

"Now I know you didn't drive way the hell over here to help me watch the sun rise."

"Radio said they found Ariel Sutherland."

Her name struck Gilroy like the point of a steel dart. "Cryin' shame. A sweet little thing. And smart. Why'd she do it? Takin' the life of a beautiful, dumb animal. That's a sin."

"You don't believe 'a sweet little thing' could do it?"

"You got the badge. You tell me."

Hegan absorbed Gilroy's presumption of guilt. "When I was a rookie, this old cop—very old, must've been close to a hundred years old—"

"That old, huh?" Gilroy caught on fast, as Hegan knew he would.

Hegan continued undeterred. "He once told me, 'Nothing hard is ever easy.' At the time, I flicked it off as the babbling of an aging man."

"Oh, yeah!" There was only so much Gilroy would take.

"Now what he said makes perfect sense. Easy answers to hard questions are the wrong answers. Isn't that right, Gilroy?"

"You still got the badge." Gilroy softened. "But, I tell ya, Mike, life is so hard these days, at least for some. They want easy answers where none exist." He took a few puffs on his pipe to re-examine that notion. "Maybe we all do."

"Maybe so. How often did you see Ariel?"

"Every morning since Zenda brought his stable north. She'd come through the gate, just about now, bringing the light with her. Never fail. A pro. Always a smile and a wave hello. She kinda skip-walked. Fast. Some days I swear her feet never moved. There must have been one of those conveyer belt things under her feet. She glided by. So much joy. So much life."

Gilroy's eyes misted over, and he turned away from Hegan who found reason to inspect his cane.

"And two days ago?"

Gilroy composed himself and carried on. "Since I heard, I've been trying to remember. But the mind can't always be trusted. If I said yes, you couldn't take it to the bank. Sorry."

"What about family? Parents? Brothers? She ever mention where she was from?"

Gilroy took a few thoughtful puffs on his pipe. "I know she had a sister. Brought her out one morning. An artist. Maybe a gallery or something. You might want to check the phone book."

"Gee, Gilroy. Where've you been all my life?"

"Now, see, that wiseass business will get you no place, lad. But if you ask me, she was a man-hater."

"Ariel?" Hegan was surprised until Gilroy set him straight.

"No, no. The sister. The artist or whatever."

"Man-hater? In all the years I've known you, Sergeant Gilroy, I never heard you call a woman... . You never judged people. Just their actions. What happened?"

"Dunno. Way she stood. Look in her eyes. On guard. Protecting her turf from the past or the future."

Gilroy's composure was slipping, and he ended the conversation by turning his back on Hegan and waving his pipe in the air.

"Thanks, Gilroy."

His only response was removing a handkerchief, quietly blowing his nose, and wiping the corner of one eye. Then he moved into the morning mist.

* * *

Hegan thought the woman who answered the door could have easily been the double for the "concierge" in Mel Brooks' film *The Producers*. But just when he expected to hear "I'm no madam; I'm the concierge," which the celluloid character said to Zero Mostel and Gene Wilder, the woman before Hegan took a long drag on her cigarette, adjusted a mangy cat against her left breast, and blew smoke into his face.

"Yeah? I don't want any." Before Hegan could speak, she shut the door halfway.

"Mrs. LoFrisco?" were the magic words that swung the door open and caused the woman to laugh with such wild gusto that she dropped the cat and the cigarette.

"Me? You think... that I..." She searched for a proper response while stubbing out the cigarette with the sole of a pink velour slipper. "I'd rather kiss a pig's ass."

She wound up enumerating the many alternative routes she'd take before being wed to Frankie LoFrisco, until Hegan flashed his gold badge.

"I was told he lives here, uh..." Hegan wanted her name, but she wasn't forthcoming. He decided to wait her out before explaining the reason for his visit.

"So?" She waited as he stared a hole through her. "Monica," she blurted unwillingly, "that's my name." And, by way of explanation, "He rents. The basement room." Monica liked cops even less than she did door-to-door salesmen, and her attitude was not couched in gentility. She gave a quick nod toward the driveway. "On the side. So?"

Knowing further dialogue was unnecessary, Hegan put his badge back into his jacket pocket and started for the side of the house.

"He ain't there. But, for the record, you got a search warrant?"

Hegan stopped, turned around, and returned to his car without speaking. Monica also saw no need for more conversation. A self-satisfied smirk filled her face as she watched the Valiant reach the next corner.

Stopped at a red light, Hegan's pager sounded. He recognized Rosen's number blinking at him in red. "There's another week of sick leave. No reason to page me. I've got an answering machine. Unless..." Hegan spoke to the air. The looming, unfilled blank troubled him. But he had better things to do and shut off the pager.

The warehouse district near the backwater of the Chicago River had been revitalized over the years. Driving through the area Hegan was surprised to find not only the usual artists' lofts but an active community of shops, galleries, and the obligatory vegetarian restaurants. He located a sign that read SUTHERLAND GALLERY, the object of his visit.

Crossing the street to the gallery, Hegan noticed the adjacent storefront, a restaurant called The Good Grass. *A vegetarian place*, he thought. To be certain, he gave the menu taped inside the front window a perusal. "Wheatgrass, bulgur, seaweed." The menu made him long to finish the half-eaten burger he bought for breakfast. But it was too late, he decided as he stood in front of Sutherland Gallery, transfixed by the instruments of destruction he saw displayed in the window as works of art.

Hegan entered under an archway of scythes as large as elephant tusks, fused together and precariously balanced upright on narrow handles. *One tremor*, he thought, *and instant guillotine.* He was drawn into the force field of a cavernous room where collages of various sizes adorned stark white walls, the space between highlighting and dramatizing each piece.

Up close, Hegan saw that the metal sculptures were composed of old knives, hammers, ice picks, sickles, swords, and jagged pieces of metal that formerly belonged on automobile bodies. He saw bits of rust on some of the pieces, but the smudges, he imagined, could also be blood.

Hegan recalled some of the various crimes of violence he'd investigated over the years.

Gunshots, even up close, did not inflict the massive, deliberate, and mutilating injuries that came from sharp or blunt objects. A bullet or two—or three, even—can end life like that. Hegan automatically snapped his fingers. But the use of one of these weapons could lead to an agonizing death.

The finger snap distracted Portia as she left her office. Wary, she ducked her head around the separating partition and gave Hegan a visual frisking. Before she could confront him, two matronly women tiptoed into the adjoining space. Each was dressed in the tasteful-expensive-casual style acceptable in the upper-class suburbs. This was their cultural day in the big city, which gave them a patina of cosmopolitan sophistication when compared to other women of their acquaintance as well as ammunition against the excess and decay of urban life. Portia observed an almost audible gasp as the women tried to take a sophisticated approach to material they initially found abhorrent.

"May I help you?" Portia asked.

One of the women, wearing a fearful expression and a multihued scarf affixed near her sternum by a gold lion's-head pin, could only recite the obvious. "Knives, hammers, ice picks... ?"

Portia wanted to dispel their aversion through an objective, even clinical approach. "I want to establish a new reality for tools of destruction," she began. "Apart, each is deadly, but forged into a work of art, they become benign."

The two women exchanged looks. This was one cultural experience they might not be able to translate back home. "You're the artist?" the scarf-clad woman asked.

"Yes," Portia said quietly and with more solemn self-importance than needed.

The second woman got the courage to step forward and tried to engage Portia on the basis of common gender. She wore sensible walking shoes—the kind Queen Elizabeth might wear touring the Scottish countryside. "Ah. That explains everything," she said. "I was convinced a man had made these..." She stumbled for the artistically correct word. "... pieces." She finished and smiled.

"How so?" Portia stiffened. The women noticed and took a step back.

"Why, because men are so much more violent than women," scarf woman said with authority.

Portia stepped toward them. "Do you know how many women are on death row in this country?"

"I'm afraid I don't. We've never given it any thought," the second woman said. Then she turned to scarf woman. "Perhaps we should?" It was more a plea for reinforcement and rescue than a question.

Scarf woman couldn't care less. She went to the heart of the matter. "Are you married, dear?" she asked Portia.

"What? It's none of your—"

"Excuse me. I wasn't trying to pry." She tried to placate Portia and turned back to her friend. "After all, life is more difficult for women today than when we were young."

The phone in the office rang, giving Portia an opportunity to excuse herself. Approaching the office, she saw Hegan wander over from the adjoining space. She gave him the one finger give-me-a-minute signal and took the call as Hegan moved closer.

"This is Portia Sutherland," she said.

Hegan studied Portia as she listened to her caller. Though she was a few years older than Ariel, the difference was in her bearing. More self-assured, Portia looked like a young Sigourney Weaver; Ariel a gangling teen. Portia smoldered sensuality surrounded by an electronic force field that could energize or repel. Their style of dress was different. Ariel stuck by the preppy, horsey outfits. And Portia? Hegan, admittedly deprived of fashion consciousness, couldn't figure out what Portia wore. Seemed like a mixture of Goth and retro hippie. Severe and cuddly at the same time.

She listened for a few more seconds. "I'm sorry," she said as if recovering from an amnesiac flash. "Could you repeat that?"

Hegan crept past the open office door and took up a position where he could feign interest in the sculpture while being close enough to eavesdrop. From his vantage point, Hegan also observed Portia's reflection in the curve of a chrome panel that once graced a Rolls Royce. He watched Portia change before his eyes. She went from the serious person in charge to caffeine-induced edginess without touching a drop of coffee.

"Ariel Sutherland is my sister!" After a rushed intake of air, she regained control. "If this is some kind of joke, I'm hanging up." And then she froze. "I see. You must be mistaken. Yes, I'm *sure*. No, I don't watch television news or read the papers. I am an artist. Noooooooo! No!" Hegan heard Portia struggling to breathe as he moved to the open door.

"What do you want? Get out of here!" Portia turned on Hegan, the body of an enemy, just when she needed a friend. "Give me the address." She scribbled it on a piece of scratch paper, slammed down the phone, and rushed into the gallery.

"Leave!" she demanded, grabbing Hegan by the sleeve. "Out! Out! Out!" She corralled the two women and pushed all three of them out the door, shutting and locking it behind her before dashing to the end of the block and flagging a cab at the intersection.

Hegan watched her disappear, the words he'd wanted to say still partially formed on his lips. The two women acted wobbly, as if they'd just exited a roller coaster. Hegan looked at them and shrugged before crossing back to the Valiant.

"It takes all kinds," scarf lady chirped after him.

* * *

Immediately on entering the precinct, Hegan felt he'd been transported to an alien land. Only a month removed from his daily routine and he felt like a stranger. Despite some familiar, distant-but-friendly nods and waves, the feeling persisted to such an extent that Hegan came to regard it as an omen of his future. The institution grinds ahead no matter who inhabits its buildings or wears its uniforms. A merry-go-round in perpetual motion with interchangeable jockeys, he concluded.

Hegan had known Jack Rosen for years. The captain of detectives graduated from the police academy a few years before him. Rosen was known as a decent guy. Not some political, by-the-book paper pusher like some of the other bosses, more concerned about protecting their asses than the public they were sworn to serve and defend.

From the elevator, Hegan turned right, carefully stepping down the corridor without the aid of his cane, trying to affect a normal gait. He paused at Rosen's door and took in a few deep breaths to calm himself before knocking.

"Yeah. Come in," Rosen said. Hegan was now looking at the man who had the power to allow Hegan's career to continue or force him to retire while in prime of his life.

Rosen quickly tried to balance his professional task with genuine admiration and respect for Hegan. Though a bit older and mostly desk bound, Rosen looked as lean and tough as any cop on an LAPD recruitment poster. Rumor in law enforcement circles had it that the men and women on those posters were actually professional models, not frontline personnel.

"Good to see you, Mike. Off the cane?"

Hegan inhaled a stash of bravado and gushed back. "Great to be back, Captain! Cane? What cane?"

Rosen's raised eyebrows told Hegan "you can't kid a kidder," so Hegan changed tactics.

"You look marvelous, Cap." Hegan resisted the urge to provide Billy Crystal's Fernando Lamas accent. But, he did know how to disarm Rosen with. It was a routine that Hegan had used many times in the past. "Here you are chained to your desk, and you look like one of those guys on the LAPD recruiting poster." Rosen began to protest the LAPD image connection, but Hegan was on a roll. "And it's not true they were professional models. One of my pals..."

Rosen was not buying the bravado and came out from behind his desk to shake Hegan's hand and embrace him. "Have a seat, Mike."

Hegan knew the chair was electrified. Many cops who came before him had sat in that chair and never put on their uniform again. That chair brings bad luck. He noticed how Rosen eyeballed him during the handshake and embrace. *He thinks I'll break in a light breeze.* Hegan split the difference and gently rested his right butt cheek on the padded leather arm of the chair, while Rosen hung his left butt cheek off the corner of his desk.

"Mike—" was the only word Rosen was able to speak before Hegan launched into his best-defense-is-a-good-offense tactic. Rosen let him fire a salvo.

"I got the feeling Johnny Faraci's behind that dead horse, and before I'm through, I'll tie him to the trainer as well. That girl... Ariel. I was at the track. I saw—"

"Whoa! Who's talking dead horses? Relax."

Hegan tried. *Maybe it's not what I thought. Maybe my offense is a well-oiled machine.* As Rosen started leafing through papers on his desk, Hegan got the sense that maybe horses could fly.

"*Dies Irae*, Mike. The day of reckoning." Not only was Rosen a straight shooter, but he also knew Latin. "Happens to all of us. You've got to retire."

"No!"

"What?"

"No, Captain?" Hegan was sure Rosen wasn't interested in a little humor. "I'm not a horse with a broken leg. You won't put me down."

"Disability. Come on, Mike. Be reasonable. Don't make it harder on you... or me. It's for your own good."

"No, no." Hegan was up and pacing what little space there was left to pace in the office. For a moment, Rosen figured Hegan should go out on a mental disability rather than a physical one.

"Root canal is good for you. Angioplasty is good for you. Retirement at thirty-six is not good for me or you or the department or Chicago or the memory of that sweet-looking young woman, Ariel. Here, let me show you." Hegan took out the page from the program, dramatically unfolded it, and held it out so Rosen could get a good look.

Part of Rosen admired Hegan. He had fire, determination, courage, passion. There wasn't a whiny, wimpy bone in his body. He deserved the time to make his case. But, and there was always a but with Hegan, he'd dig up his grandmother from her grave to get his way. He'd batter, bludgeon, wheedle, and cajole St. Peter. Not anymore. Another part of Rosen was getting angry—not only because Hegan was being unreasonable, but because he was risking his life and future.

"Goddamnit, Mike. You've still got a piece of that slug in your back."

"Oh, no. In the hospital I was told they got the bullet."

"They lied, Hegan!" Rosen yelled for emphasis. Something had to get through to Hegan. He watched the truth penetrate as the hope in Hegan's face faded. Then Rosen softened his position. "I don't know; I wasn't there. But the x-rays you took a week ago show a fragment. The police surgeon reviewed them and made his decision."

Hegan had no comeback. *Where's the offense? Where's the pointed quip?* He asked his brain, but got back silence.

"Know what that means? That fragment moves and you can be paralyzed from the neck down. Not healthy for your sex life. You've been a great cop. I admire you. I'll miss you."

Rosen spoke the words, but all Hegan heard was a death sentence from some old English movie like *Sea Hawk* with Errol Flynn. "... and ye shall be taken hence and hanged by the neck until dead. And may God have mercy on your soul."

"You've been disabled in the line of duty."

"Disabled my ass!" Hegan leapt up onto Rosen's desk and kicked the medical reports onto the floor. Once up there, Hegan tried to figure out what the hell he was doing. And there was the pain. Hegan squeezed his eyes shut, feigning deep thought and hoping Rosen missed the wince.

"Does this look disabled?" Hegan demanded.

"For Christ's sake, come down from there. You're no Gene Kelly."

"You're right for once; I'm no Gene Kelly. I'm a cop, with fifteen years of training and instinct and experience. And besides, I... I'm..."

Leaning from the waist, head cocked and jaw out at a jaunty, Jimmy Cagney angle, Hegan began pumping his arms and shuffling his feet, bellowing "I'm a Yankee Doodle Dandy, a Yankee Doodle do or die. A real life nephew of my Uncle Sam. Born on the Fourth of July."

Rosen's temples began to throb, and as he massaged them, Hegan stopped singing and jumped down from the desk. More pain. Not his best move. He was unsure if Rosen saw any of the pained expressions shoot through his face, if only for a split second.

"Look, my hands are tied. The police surgeon says you're unfit to return. And the insurance policy won't cover you."

"I knew it. Some fuckin' thieves at the insurance company end my life."

"In two weeks you'll be on disability pay for the rest of your life. Take it while you're young enough and healthy. Get married. Have kids. Enjoy!"

Vincent Panettiere | 137

"Okay, Captain." Hegan reached out and shook Rosen's hand. *The best offense is a good lie,* Hegan thought. Not exactly what Sun Tzu would do, but it was all he had. "When will the papers be ready?"

Rosen was briefly caught off guard at the question but rallied, knowing the wild bronc in front of his desk had stopped snorting and he'd better not waste time. "End of next week," he replied with casual indifference.

"I'll come by then and sign them," Hegan said as Rosen gave him a "good boy" pat on the back and opened the office door. "But what about Italian Scallion?"

"Who?"

"The dead horse."

Rosen gave Hegan a gentle push out the door and closed it.

* * *

The cab stopped in front of the police station. Portia paid the driver and slowly got out. She looked up at the old masonry building. Foreboding, fear, trepidation—a *Roget's Thesaurus* of feelings flooded through her. Emotional pain was a familiar neighbor in Portia's life. But what she faced now was more than she'd experienced or imagined enduring. Knowing she'd survived the hurts of her childhood did not give Portia much comfort as she opened the front door, took a deep breath, and willed herself composed.

The desk sergeant glanced up in time to see a young woman enter. Her body visibly stiffened before she spoke.

"I'm here to see Detective Perino."

He observed Portia's clothes and decided she might seem weird, but she wasn't a nutjob or vagrant. He dialed. "Eddie, there's a woman here to see you."

He asked Portia her name, but she was somewhere else, trying to be anywhere else, becoming one with the dull grey-green paint on the walls. Viscerally she knew some words were being directed to her.

"Huh?"

"Your name?"

"Portia Sutherland."

"A Miss Sutherland," the desk sergeant said into the phone. He listened for a minute and then spoke again. "He said you can go down the corridor, and it's the first door on the left."

Portia could see the end of the corridor which bisected a bullpen area where uniformed and plainclothes officers worked at desks piled with stuffed file folders. She had no idea what they were doing or if they noticed her. She concentrated on taking each step down the corridor, feeling like she was on a rickety rope bridge spanning a gorge cut deep by an icy river in the Andes. One false move and she'd plummet to her death.

A young, attractive woman, dressed more for a bohemian soirée than a corporate board meeting, entered the bullpen. More than style caused her to be noticed. It was her sensuality mixed with a combative attitude that made her stand out.

Portia reached the office door marked HOMICIDE. A foreign word. One that was not part of her vocabulary, until now, except for oblique references that she'd tried to rid from her life experience.

Portia had perfected a life, she thought, free of the toxic drip that sometimes seeped and other times blared out from radio, TV, and the newspapers. She did not want to be influenced by actions or words that were harmful to her spiritual, mental, or physical health. All the media should display the same warning label as on a pack of cigarettes. *This information is hazardous to your health.*

Admittedly, certain information was useful. She wasn't a Luddite entirely. The weather report came to mind as helpful. But she doubted even that. She knew if it was hot or cold, wet or dry, without the radio. Portia was convinced the really important information—the truth behind the World Trade Center's destruction, President Kennedy's assassination, and the bombing of Pearl Harbor—would never be revealed. She found it hard to imagine living in Los Angeles during the OJ trial, information she gleaned by chance during a flight delay at O'Hare. She'd lose her mind. Words like *drive-by shooting*, *gang-related death*, *gang rape*, and *homicide*, were driven from her vocabulary because she refused to give them legitimacy and let them into her reality, her consciousness.

And Portia's reality? There was her work. Perfecting her art was all-consuming. Ariel was the other half of her existence. Now half of her life was gone.

Portia knocked tentatively, and heard a gruff, loud voice command her to "Come! She opened the door to find Eddie Perino sitting behind one of four desks in the office. The other desks, contained stacks of file folders overflowing with details of death. Eddie's desk contained only one file folder placed in its center. Eddie stood up and came out from behind the desk. He extended his hand to her.

"I'm Portia Sutherland," she murmured, almost with defeat, but did not extend her hand.

"Yeah, we spoke on the phone."

The unclasped but still outstretched hand directed her to a chair by his desk. She waited for him to remove a pile of papers from the chair before she could sit. He dumped the load on the floor behind his desk with impatience and disregard. Then, without any words of courtesy or social grace, he returned to his chair and took up a manila folder.

Mechanically and without looking at Portia, Perino opened the folder. "I sympathize with your loss, Miss Sutherland." When she did not respond, he lifted his head and made eye contact, regretting that act as soon as he saw—what was it? Anger? Hatred? It wasn't fear, of that he was certain. "I really do," he added as an afterthought, hoping to blunt her edge.

Portia's eyes went from his to the folder. It contained the harshest reality of her life. Her spirit flagged until rejuvenated unintentionally by Perino.

"She was young," he read from the file. "Only twenty-five. And she trained horses. Now, that's a unique job," he added with insincere, patronizing surprise masking chauvinistic disdain.

"You mean, for a woman, don't you? Unique for a woman. She was my sister, Detective. I know her life better than you do." Portia's edge, shrouded by the solemnity of the occasion and profound sadness, had lost none of its sting.

Perino was not a modern womenslimpified male and issued his own challenge. "But I know her death."

"How many race horse trainers do you find dead on the beach every day, Detective?"

With a certain crude theatricality he had mastered over the years in dealing with many situations and practically all women, Perino scrunched his face, scratched his head and, playing the bumpkin, answered, "Not many." Even peripherally, he tried to avoid her eyes. There had not been many broads in his life who repelled him as much as this one. But even those had a soft underbelly, and he didn't mean the part above their pussy hair. "Not ever. Particularly not a suicide." Read 'em and weep. Full house, aces high. Whatever. Now he looked in her eyes.

Perino was sure the lightning bolt he hurled at Portia frazzled her circuit. For a brief moment, he convinced himself her eyeballs actually spun around.

Portia's force field absorbed the blow and issued a charge of its own. "You've made a mistake. My sister did not commit suicide."

How do I begin? Perino wondered. *She's off balance. I could go in for the kill now or paw with the mouse a bit longer.* That was the answer. Perino issued an audible scoff.

"Only an hour ago you refused to believe she was dead. And now you're questioning the cause. Half an hour ago you were wrong. And you're wrong again."

Something was going on in her head. Univac was sorting the cards for a response. Perino switched from confrontation to conciliation to keep her disoriented.

"If this job has taught me one thing, it's that we never really know anyone very well. Huh? Do we?" *This is easy*, Perino thought. *Rope-a-dope is alive and well.* Savoring each word, rolling it around on his tongue like fine claret, Perino continued. "That's why I let the District Attorney make the decisions, which is what he did... based on the evidence." *Ta-da!*

"What evidence?"

There is a God, and Perino was grateful. She took the bait. Assuming an official pose, he read from the report. "The coroner's report says, and I quote, 'Cause of death was acute overdose of narcotics. Phenobarbital' end quote." He leveled his gaze at the spot where her nose blended into her forehead and pulled the trigger with his eyes. "As soon as we get a search warrant, I'm sure we'll find bottles of pills in her house. DA says it's open and shut."

Open and shut? Portia played the term over in her head. *How fast is something open and shut? Can you see inside? Speed determines what is found. Too fast*, she concluded. *Nothing is open and shut about my sister.*

Portia leaned into the center of Perino's desk. "Ariel never even took an aspirin. Pheno... what?"

"Barbital."

"Quiet! *Never!* My sister was full of life when we spoke last week. She was *very* happy and *very* successful. In a <u>man's</u> game. I won't let you or the DA or any motherfucker on the planet tell me she took her own life. Got it?"

Perino's eyes locked onto the edge of a red index card protruding from the middle of a book atop a bookshelf behind Portia's right shoulder. She'd never know he wasn't paying rapt attention. Outside he was a professional stoic. Inside he seethed. *I'll give her motherfucker. She won't tell me...*

Portia finished and Perino gave her an I've-done-my-job shrug. But, for good measure, there was a final salvo.

"Then there's the note."

Now it was Portia's turn to supply the audible scoff. "Note? Don't joke with me. Ariel was a true child of the MTV generation. E-mail, tape recorders, CDs, video cameras. Even Christmas or birthday cards were electronic."

Tape recorder, Perino reminded himself before taking a slip of paper out of the folder. He held it up so she could see it existed, but not close enough to read it. Another contradicting reality came crashing in on Portia.

"May I?"

Her tone had changed. Now she was a supplicant. Perino was always ready to be magnanimous with a compliant woman. "Hold it by the corners. It's evidence."

Portia took the top corners of the note between the tips of her fingers, as if it was as fragile as the Shroud of Turin. She read its contents out loud, needing to hear and see the actual words before she could believe them. "Be happy for me. I am no longer in pain." The note concluded with a large scrawl that looked like the handwriting of a first grader or an illiterate trying to write for the first time. Or a person with a severe mental disability.

The existence of the note was not good enough for Portia. "That's not her signature. Some idiot wrote that. Not Ariel." She crumpled the note into a ball and tossed it at Perino.

"Hey, hey. This is evidence. You're tampering."

As he bent down to retrieve the paper, Portia gave him the finger, which he did not see. He slowly sat erect again, smoothed out the wrinkles in the note, and returned it to the file folder. *Just who do you think you're dealing with?* he thought as he prepared another set of professional barbs.

"Handwriting changes under duress. It's a scientific fact. I know how hard this must be." Perino actually heard violins. "What a shock... ."

"Really? Don't be so goddamned sure. Like I said, that's not her signature."

Perino decided to wrap up playtime. He had a nooner scheduled with Louise, and she didn't want him to be late. He opened the bottom drawer of his desk and took out a large quilted envelope.

"Her personal effects. Found with her at the time of her death." He could have used a euphemism or phrased it differently, but he wanted her to hear the word *death* again. Her sister was dead. Get used to it.

Portia took the envelope in her hands, embracing her sister. She became aware that something else was being handed to her, interrupting the connection she was making.

"Here's my card." Perino waved his business card between two fingers and reached over the desk. "If you've got any questions or need any help."

"Call you? I don't think so."

"I'm sorry," Perino said with what therapists would call a flat affect, as he let his business card drop on the desk with a smirk.

Portia felt his words connecting to her past, and it brought a chill to her body. Then she recovered. "I'm sorry isn't good enough."

"I'll call the morgue and have them release the body." Perino concluded and stood up so she would get the message. She did. Stood. Opened the door and left, embracing the envelope in both arms, without saying another word.

* * *

A lively birthday celebration was underway at Uzbek. Vadim entered the restaurant and was met with a blast of sound. A three-man band—balalaika, guitar, and accordion—dressed in purple tunics and black trousers worked its way through an up-tempo version of "Moscow Nights." *Such a cliché,* he thought as he ogled the petite blonde singer. For a moment Vadim was caught up in the gaiety.

As usual, Gregori watched the room from his booth at the rear, nearest the kitchen.

"Happy birthday?" Vadim asked, slipping into the opposite side of booth.

In answer he got Gregori's shrug and chin pointed at a fifty-something woman at the head of a long table. The gold paper crown on her head distracted no one from the billowing curves of her cleavage.

"I should look so good at that age" was Vadim's reaction as he ignored the crown.

"You've been there. Don't ask for miracles."

"So? It's done?"

A furtive nod as answer.

"You know what I'm talking about?"

Gregori picked up a half-full vodka bottle and thrust it up to Vadim's lips. "Talk to the bottle so the boys in Langley can hear you better."

A weak nervous laugh. "You drink too much."

Any sense of camaraderie slipped off Gregori's face and was replaced by a look that said, "Shut up, schmuck."

Vadim got the message. "The noise, the party... I thought..."

Gregori turned conciliatory. "You are right, dear brother. The noise is too much. Let us walk."

To any observer outside the restaurant, they were two friends smoking and talking. Vadim had to wait until Gregori finished two cigarettes before receiving any more news.

"I'm told she talked. He knows where it is."

"Yes, yes. But... ?"

"She won't talk anymore."

"Done?"

"Done."

"Our friend?"

"Came to see me. Like losing a child. Two children."

"We had to. Imagine if she..."

"Shh. No need to imagine. There is a way we can help our friend. He lost his children, but he also lost lots cash money."

* * *

While the birthday celebrants danced at Uzbek, Frankie slept, bills of large denominations dancing in his dreams. When he awoke the next morning, his hands still clutched the envelope under his pillow. In one position for so long, he could barely bend either arm at the elbow.

Frankie gave the motel room careful scrutiny. So close to freedom, he didn't want to leave any clues that could trace his disappearance. Pleased with his stealthy escape, he remembered getting a cab at the hack stand in front of the main entrance to Arlington. He made the cab take him into The Loop and bought a flimsy carry-on bag in a cheap luggage store run by Korean immigrants. It was large enough to hold a few shirts, a pair of shoes, some underwear, and the envelope he got at the horseman's bookkeeper's office. The envelope was most important of all.

A third cab took him to the Merchandise Mart where he wandered around, checking out long-legged models as they exited cabs, garment bags in hand, on their way to work in one of the fashion showrooms. Twenty minutes later, Frankie took another cab to the Super 8 motel near O'Hare Airport.

Frankie knew by the time Faraci or the cops or whoever found out he left Arlington in a cab, and then thought to give his description to every cab company in the city, and then through the dumbest of luck followed his trail in the other cabs, he'd be long gone.

Again, he mentally reviewed the precautions he'd taken to avoid detection. Once in the motel room, Frankie closed the drapes and called Dominos for a large pepperoni and sixty-four ounces of Coke. Frankie's dinner made him sleepy, and he decided to turn in without watching television. Before shutting off the lights, Frankie took the envelope out of his carry-on and placed it under his pillow. Frankie laid the side of his head on the pillow, his hands gripping the envelope. Frankie had never slept in the same bed with 850 grand before. He wondered if the money would keep him awake. Maybe it would cause nightmares.

Awake now, Frankie moved into the next phase of his plan. He stuffed the money into his carry-on, brought the bag into the bathroom, closed the door, and showered with the curtain open so he could keep watch over his money even through half–closed, soap-filled eyes.

Convinced the room was clean of anything incriminating, Frankie took a towel and wiped every surface he remembered touching—the phone, doorknobs, counter. For a moment he thought all that extra work was crazy. *Gettin' caught is crazy*, Frankie reminded himself. Then he picked up his bag, as well as the empty pizza box and Coke bottle, and left. After dropping the trash in a dumpster around the corner from the building, Frankie joined the cab waiting for him in front of the motel's office.

"Merchandise Mart," Frankie instructed. When he heaved his bulk into a second cab half an hour later, he told the cabbie, "O'Hare. Delta."

Frankie sat back in the cab, relaxed and self-satisfied. He started dum-de-dumming softly to himself. The cabbie saw Frankie's smiley face and had to smile himself.

"You're in a good mood. Goin' somewhere special?"

"Yeah," Frankie had to admit, "I am. Atlanta."

"Business or pleasure?"

Under other circumstances, Frankie would have bristled at questions, but today was different. "Seein' my sister. She had a baby. I'm an uncle."

"Hey, congratulations."

In response, Frankie patted his jacket with theatrical flourish. "I'd give you a cigar, but I got none."

Frankie gave the cabbie a decent tip. Nothing extravagant so he'd be remembered, but he didn't stiff him either, which would also be remembered. Before entering the Delta terminal, Frankie swept the area with his survival antenna. No boys from Faraci. No cops. A maniacal grin spread over Frankie's fat face as he disappeared inside the terminal.

CHAPTER SEVEN

Leon Clay owned a combination flower shop and nursery housed between a kosher butcher and an Indian sari shop. Across the street were a Hunan-style Chinese restaurant and a Mexican tortilleria. During slow midweek afternoons, Clay liked to stroll along the street, observing the mini United Nations that flowed by his door. He was encouraged by the potential for human integration. There was no easy way to explain the proximity of such diversity. Clay preferred to believe all the establishments were placed in this part of the world when an ethnic Noah's Ark dropped them off two by two—after each got the appropriate SBA loan, of course.

Clay's reverie was broken when a teenage boy and girl entered the shop. He figured both to be about fourteen. They were tentative, seeing no one at first.

"Welcome!" Clay's voice boomed out at them from behind a potted fern. "You have entered the finest flower shop in all of Chicago. How may I help you?"

The blue-eyed, pink-cheeked girl seemed shy and the dark-haired boy determined, yet nervous. Clay felt he was looking at the future of humanity.

"This is a special occasion, isn't it?"

The girl's eyes widened as she looked at the boy, seeking reassurance that it was, in fact, a special occasion and wondering how Clay could have guessed their secret.

"Yes," she answered softly.

"Let me guess," Clay continued. "This your first wedding anniversary?"

"Nooo." The girl giggled. "We're not married."

"You just graduated from college?"

"Nooo. We're too young."

Finally, the boy took charge, directing Clay to the refrigerator case where vases filled with ornate floral arrangements and dozens of fresh red, pink, and yellow roses awaited.

"Is it possible, sir? Um... to buy, uh, one red rose?"

Clay was quiet as he considered the request—not to give the boy any difficulty or cause additional embarrassment. He'd seen the excesses of life, particularly his life. Now he was confronted with innocence and naïveté that he thought had disappeared forever. He wanted to examine and admire the moment a little longer.

"You see, this is our first date and all, and—"

Clay's beefy hand gently patted the boy's shoulder. "Don't you worry. I'll take care of it. Stay with her. She's too pretty to leave alone. Could disappear on you."

"You think so? Oh, okay," the boy said, his tone indicating he was grateful for manly advice. Clay disappeared into the back of the shop.

Hegan entered the flower shop. "You see the owner?" he asked the boy who pointed to the arranging room.

Clay emerged from the back with a beatific smile and a long, rectangular box. Then he spied Hegan.

"Now there's a dude good for a dozen, make that two dozen, long-stemmed red ones," he said for Hegan's benefit. Before Hegan could respond, Clay presented the box containing a single red rose tied with a pink bow to the boy, who gave it to the girl.

"This is for you," the boy said. She blushed and smiled as she admired the rose through the clear cellophane cover.

"Oh, Tommy, it's beautiful. Thank you," she said and kissed him on the cheek.

Tommy reached his hand into his pocket to pay, but Clay stopped him.

"Nope. On the house. It's our first-date special."

Before the couple was out the door, the boy turned and waved back at Clay. "We'll buy all the flowers for our wedding from you."

"Coupla nice kids," he said then turned to Hegan who seemed lost in sad thoughts. "You still want a coupla dozen roses for your lady friend?"

"Soon as I find her, you'll be the second or third to know."

"You mean to say you came here for a social visit? You must have plenty of long green in your pocket since you stopped leaving it at the track." Something was bothering Hegan and Clay thought silly banter would get Hegan talking. "You sure ain't spendin' it with me. What are you spendin' all your money on?"

From a planet far, far away, Hegan began. "Ever hear of a horse and its trainer dying on the same day?"

"Oh, no. You need Prozac. But, it could be a coincidence There's horses I wished died before they left the gate."

"Some bozo on the radio says the cops are calling it a murder-suicide. I haven't found one person who saw her at the track that day. I don't believe it. Smells like a setup," Hegan said, reasoning out loud.

"Just 'cause the radio says it, doesn't mean it's true." Clay tried to introduce his own brand of sanity. "Mike. Why do you always go for long shots?"

"They're forcing me to retire, Leon."

Clay knew Hegan was only telling part of the story.

"There's still this thing." Mike let the words drift into the air.

"Ain't no thing. Just you droppin' the second shoe. You always do this, Mike." Clay was getting wound up. "Nothing is ever settled. What you see in you is not what you get from you."

"Somebody put Ariel where she couldn't fight for herself."

"Geez," he said, realizing what Hegan planned. "You givin' odds?"

"Forty to one she did it. But I don't bet. Remember?"

"And I'm Michael Jackson." Clay lurched into a Michael Jackson spin and moonwalked away as Hegan left the shop.

* * *

Portia got out of a cab in front of a modest, brick house shaded by plane trees and sitting on half an acre of lawn bordered by flower beds. Facing Ariel's house, she was convulsed by a spasm of deep sorrow.

Portia turned to escape, but the cab had reached the corner. She watched the cab make an unusually wide turn to avoid colliding with a car parked halfway into the street. Perhaps it ran out of gas or had been stolen and abandoned. *Curious,* she thought, *how the mind fixates on the insignificant almost as a defense mechanism against... what? Pain? Threat? Sorrow?*

Portia knew sorrow was a wasted emotion. What good would feeling hurt and loss do for her when all she wanted was revenge, to exercise her hate in the most violent way? Only by that means could she reduce the pain. Only then could the suffering have a reason. If not that, all she'd have was the empty emotion of what-might-have-beens and what-I-shouldn't-have-dones.

Her father saying "I'm sorry" all those times—to her and later to Ariel—was an expression of sorrow that no longer had any meaning for her. She wanted to expunge those words from her life. *Expunge,* she thought, *like mopping up a foul liquid with a sponge and squeezing it down the drain to oblivion.* It was with the same passion and commitment that she wanted to find out the truth about Ariel's death.

Portia replaced sorrow with duty and reached into her backpack to find the keys to Ariel's front door. For a moment, her eyes saw the door swing open. Standing there was Ariel, smiling and bubbling with happiness. But when Portia blinked to focus on the image, the memory of the last time she saw Ariel disappeared. Portia kicked something as she stepped toward the door, key in hand, and looked down to find three editions of the morning paper—one for each of the days since Ariel died—strewn about on the welcome mat. The oldest headline blared up at her: HORSE TRAINER KILLS HORSE, THEN SELF. "Bad Love Affair or Revenge?" was the subhead.

For a moment the pain and anguish flooding her face threatened to shatter the protective emotional shell she created to survive. As release, she kicked the papers out of the way until the various sections separated, opened, and were picked up by a stray breeze, scattering them across the well-manicured front lawn.

"Goddamnit!" Portia said as she unlocked the door and pushed it open. She gave a quick glance to the papers now dancing toward the street and decided they were better flying through the neighborhood than by the front door, where any burglar would become instantly aware the house was vacant. *My sister is dead and I'm worrying about burglars?* she asked herself as she stepped inside.

* * *

Hegan exited the expressway and checked a piece of paper he'd slipped under the wrapper of a half-eaten cheeseburger. Through a grease stain he read directions to proceed two blocks and turn left at the light. Hegan took a bite of the burger and a gulp of tepid coffee then turned on the radio.

"Turning to other news," the radio announcer began, "Chicago police today are calling the deaths of thoroughbred race horse Italian Scallion and trainer Ariel Sutherland the most bizarre murder-suicide in the city's history."

Hegan directed his rebuke at the radio. "Murder-suicide? You need drug rehab, pal."

"The Cook County coroner's report indicated both Sutherland and the prize stallion owned by Zenda Farms died of acute Phenobarbital poisoning," the radio report continued.

"Bullshit!" Hegan shouted back and then noticed the intersection where he had to make a left turn. The light was red, and Hegan took another bite of burger and swig of coffee.

As the light turned green and Hegan began his turn, the radio report concluded. "According to investigating detective Edward Perino, Ariel Sutherland had been despondent over a failed romance."

Hearing the name of his ex-brother-in-law on the radio gave Hegan more purpose as he located Ariel's house on the corner of a quiet street.

"Eddie, Eddie. Now you're an expert on failed romance as well as an asshole?" he answered back to the dashboard radio. Hegan switched off the radio and parked in front of a house where stray sheets of newspaper littered the lawn.

* * *

Portia stood in the center of Ariel's living room trying to recall bits of conversations, glimpses of images from the now and forever past. *Only the past is safe from change,* she thought, abandoning the fruitless exercise. A photo in a silver frame on the mantle seemed new, and she picked it up. It contained the last photo she'd taken with Ariel. One month ago, in front of that very fireplace. Taken, Portia remembered, by that man Ariel called her "friend." A full moon later and Ariel was gone. Portia clung to the memory of that evening.

"I want you to meet my friend," Ariel had said as Portia entered the house that night. Ariel had been hosting a dinner party to celebrate the purchase of her first house. Soon after coming north, Zenda had decided to headquarter part of his growing racing stable in the Chicago area. Portia remembered Ariel deciding to put down roots. Her career had started to move, and she wanted permanency, a home base. A place where they could create their own life as sisters, independent and exclusive of parents.

Portia had guessed the man who came across the room to greet her was in his midforties but looked younger.

"This is my friend Steve Gorman," Ariel had said.

Portia had shaken his hand, which was soft and limp. She was convinced those kinds of handshakes always mean the other person couldn't be bothered making physical contact.

She knew he was Ariel's married lover. A fortyish man who needed the "friendship" of a woman twenty years his junior was not looking for a pen pal; he was looking for a steady fuck, she'd concluded. Before she could project her theory on May-November liaisons any further, Gorman had insisted the sisters pose for a photo together in front of the fireplace.

Ariel had been girlishly exuberant that evening, gushing about the horses in her care as if they were complaisant lovers. Portia had sensed Ariel was happy with her life for the first time in years, maybe for the first time ever. For that Portia held no bitterness or regret. Not even a twinge of jealousy.

The only glaring intrusion on their newfound appreciation of each other had been Gorman. Portia considered him an interloper. A spy for the other side. Someone she found Ariel deferring to on more than one occasion—moments that made the hair on her arms tingle with discomfort. Ariel's almost manic gaiety that night had kept Portia from learning any more about Gorman. How did they meet? What was the attraction beyond the physical? The time for discovery had passed.

Portia left the reverie of that evening when the sound of footsteps clomping activated her defenses.

Portia's position enabled her to see a reflection of the front door in the glass of a picture frame over the fireplace. She heard and saw the screen door open. In one motion, she grabbed a leaded crystal vase from the mantle, whirled around, and hurled it toward the door where it shattered at the intruder's feet.

* * *

Hegan noticed a glimmer of recognition flicker across Portia's face as she assumed a combat-ready posture.

"What... ? What do you want?"

Hegan took a step toward her and leaned on his cane. Surprised to find her, he vamped for a moment before spurting out, "You're the woman from the gallery...I'm..."

"The gallery? This is insane! You're stalking me! Get out! I'm calling the police." Portia reached into her backpack for her cell phone, but couldn't seem to find it.

Hegan revealed the badge clipped to his belt. "Lady, I am the police. My name's Hegan."

Portia recovered the phone as she eyed the badge but didn't place the call. "Studies show that every cop has the potential to be a criminal," she offered with authority.

Hegan had to chuckle recalling how many times that shibboleth had been hurled at him—brandished, actually. He must remember to use five-dollar words in their proper context. "Very good," he said. "Sociology 101, right?"

"Do you always break into homes uninvited?"

Hegan thought she sounded like Lauren Bacall in *The Big Sleep*. "The door was open. Only thing broken you broke," he replied, trying not to sound like Bogie. *Let's see how she reacts to a strong offense*, he thought as he scanned her body with his eyes. "Too hip to be from the Junior League. Too wicked to be selling Bibles door-to-door. I got it! Transvestite interior decorator."

"Very amusing. Now I remember. You were at the gallery when I got... got the call. I'm Portia Sutherland. This is my sister's house."

"Yes, I remember that morning. I'm sorry."

"Why should you be sorry?"

"I didn't know her, but I'm sorry she died. First time I saw her face was in the program at the track. Then on TV. She had kind eyes. Guess that's why I'm sorry." As Hegan moved deeper into the house and closer to Portia, he saw her eyes begin to glisten.

"She was kind."

"Why are you listed as her next of kin?" he asked. "No parents... ?"

"I'm her only family," Portia said. Her body language spoke otherwise, as she erased the existence of their parents.

Hegan moved closer and extended his arm to comfort her, but she jerked her body away. Portia deflected the need to answer with a question of her own.

"Why are you here? Detective Perino said the police inquiry is finished."

"I know Perino. I mean, I know what he said." Hegan drifted away from Portia, not wanting to discuss Perino any further. Before Portia could ask another question, he focused the conversation elsewhere. "Looks like she really loved horses," Hegan said as he noticed for the first time that the living room had been decorated in an equine motif, with sculptures of horses on tables and horse lamps and lamp shades. Prints and photos of horses adorned the walls.

Hegan paused at the wall by the staircase. He found photos of Ariel with the horses she'd trained draped with blankets of flowers in the winner's circle at various tracks across the country.

"She has photos of every horse she ever rode or trained," Portia said.

Hegan took special interest in one photo of Ariel standing awkwardly next to Frankie LoFrisco alongside Italian Scallion. "Over the years, I've learned to value my intuition. Even at this early stage in the investigation, I've got a feeling... I came here hoping—"

"You're blowing smoke," Portia said as she crossed the room to look at the same photos by the stairs.

"Could be, but don't bet on it. It's all so easy, how Ariel is being blamed. Sounds like a plot from an old episode of *Murder, She Wrote*."

Both saw that one of the photos was askew and reached to straighten it at the same time. While they avoided making physical contact, Hegan experienced an electric charge, the kind that emerges between passionate antagonists. The look on Portia's face told him she'd felt a spark that she was fighting to ignore. He was glad when Portia headed for safer ground.

"My sister didn't just train horses. She lived for horses. Every minute of her life."

Hegan heard a floorboard creak above, but didn't reveal his awareness in posture or word.

"Someone with so much to live for doesn't take her own life," Hegan said with both conviction and nonchalance as he moved to the base of the stairs, taking a furtive glance up to the second floor.

As soon as she realized they shared a common belief about Ariel, Portia's attitude toward Hegan seemed to soften. She joined Hegan at the base of the stairs. Relieved by the look of gratitude on Portia's face, Hegan took a quick glance up the staircase and noticing how the light changed intensity and direction upstairs, sensed movement. He wanted to act quickly without spooking Portia.

Hegan drew his forty-five and, with his back against the wall, eased up the stairs, his eyes and gun sweeping left to right as he finally reached the top. The second floor contained three rooms, and Hegan had to search each one of them. The room directly across from the stairs was a bedroom --- Ariel's he assumed from the photos of horses on the wall. He could see the end of a queen-size bed and dark dresser beyond. As far as he could tell, there was no one lurking in the shadows.

To the right Hegan spied an open bathroom door. He determined that whatever the intruder wanted to find would not be in the bathroom.

Sun streamed into the upstairs hall from the room immediately to Hegan's left. The shadow Hegan spotted earlier had seemed to move into that room. *All this for a creak and a shadow?* Hegan questioned his instincts. Holding the forty-five in a combat grip, Hegan crouched low and eased his body into the doorway. The room was unoccupied, but someone had ransacked the closet and opened cabinet drawers. That someone had also left the French doors to the balcony wide open.

Hegan swept the room with his gun, checking to see if the intruder had hidden in the closet or behind a leather couch. Then he crept to the open doors and listened for any movement. Hegan determined there were only two ways the intruder could have made his escape—down the stairs and out the front door or over the balcony railing. *If there is an intruder*, Hegan thought. He'd been second-guessing his instincts since being shot at his sister's house; even wondered if he had become gun shy.

But, Hegan's self doubt stopped the moment his heavy stomp onto the balcony achieved the response he had hoped to get. The intruder scrambled down the supports under the balcony. Hegan, preceded by his gun, leaned over the balcony in time to see the back of a man.

"Stop!" he yelled. *Now I sound like a TV cop*, he thought reminding himself that *deeds, not words are required*.

Adrenaline replaced doubt and Hegan rushed to the stairs. He heard Portia's voice as she came toward him. He heard her say "Where did you go?" before colliding with her. They both tumbled to the base of the stairs.

"Out of my way!" Hegan screamed intent on his pursuit while entangled with Portia until he broke away. Hegan crashed through the front door and limped through the remaining sections of the daily paper drifting across the lawn, in the direction he believed the intruder would take around the corner of the house. He was too late.

Hegan followed the sound of a car engine revving and watched as a grey sedan without licensed plates pulled out from its haphazard parking spot near the corner. On instinct, Hegan yelled for the driver to stop. Not a chance, he knew. The driver turned right giving Hegan an indistinct profile.

Hegan holstered his gun and fumbled in his jacket for his car keys as he hobbled toward the Valiant, knowing full well the intruder was gone. He slammed two fists down on the hood of his car, and then thought better of it. Instead, he pummeled his legs with his fists. "Goddamn legs! God-fucking-dammit!"

Portia exited the house after Hegan and could only watch his fury, half in consolation and half in perverse attraction. Propelled by both, she drew closer. Hegan, his eyes flashing more anger at her than she ever expected to see from him, spoke while catching his breath.

"Someone was in her bedroom. I had him trapped on the balcony. If you'd stayed the fuck out of my way I would've had him." Unconsciously, he waved his fist in her face for emphasis.

Whatever feelings of consolation Portia had for Hegan, were flushed away and replaced by her old friend, the iron mask.

"How typical. Take the easy way out. Blame the woman." That was not enough. She wanted to give him more. "I didn't make you fail. You're a cripple! Admit it!"

Hegan's anger knew no boundaries. It enveloped him and, for an instant, he observed himself step out of his body, extend his right hand, and grab Portia by the neck. He squeezed it until he felt the cords of her throat tighten. His left hand joined the right and, together, they throttled Portia until her head snapped off her neck and flew into the street.

Hegan could not remember the last time he'd experienced such overpowering, blind fury. Instead of responding to Portia, he opened the car door and got into the Valiant.

But Portia wasn't finished. "Go ahead. Run away. You're just like every other goddamned man in the goddamned world," she screamed at him as the car pulled away from the curb.

Whatever she screamed, Hegan didn't hear. It didn't matter anymore. He'd wanted to beat a woman within an inch of her life. He hated himself more for losing his temper and self control than for losing the intruder.

"Holy shit!" was the only intelligent response he could make. What cave inside him harbored such anger and violence? His sister had been terrorized and brutalized in her marriage. What stopped him from allowing his anger to erupt into similar abuse? Was it part of his male DNA? The answer was as elusive as the source of the anger, he concluded. "Holy shit."

* * *

Portia was drained of emotion when she reentered Ariel's house. The anger that had shot out of her was a defense. On previous occasions she'd never think twice about expressing such emotions. But today, the person who was becoming her ally, the one who could help her vindicate Ariel's name and life, accused her without cause. It was a betrayal she could not accept. Once again, a man wanted to commit violence against her. This could never happen again. Ally or not. She reminded herself once again not to create and trust false gods, false humans. They always crumble and fall. That Hegan person would, too.

From now on, she was the only hope for Ariel. She didn't need anyone. Portia would avenge her sister. Alone.

* * *

Hegan opened the door to the *Tribune* employees' cafeteria and saw Artie's arm reach into the air above the crowd from a far corner table. Dressed in his best and only blue suit and carrying a leather portfolio with a bronze clasp, Hegan tried to present the bearing of an insurance salesman. Whatever that looked like. A well-dressed thief, he imagined.

Artie watched Hegan weave his way around tables and tray-carrying *Tribune* employees. He was both surprised and impressed. The last time they met, he recalled, Hegan was flat on his back in a hospital bed. With the trained eye of a journalist, he concentrated on Hegan's gait but couldn't tell if Hegan was limping with all the bobbing and weaving he was doing, clutching the portfolio like a fullback bucking toward the goal line. Finally, Hegan reached an aisle between tables and was able to walk normally, without limp, Artie was pleased to observe.

"Where the hell did you get that suit?" Artie asked, rising and extending his hand.

"Mr. Broxton, pleased to meet you," sitting down opposite Artie at the table.

Hegan was into his insurance salesman role. "I think our new policy is just what you and your young family need." Artie almost leveled a mouth full of Coke at Hegan in response, covering his mouth at the last second.

"What new family?" Artie asked.

"Shh." Hegan looked around to see if anyone was listening, though the likelihood was remote. "I forgot to tell you. Mrs. Broxton is expecting twins."

Artie blew his nose and cleared his head. "Are you nuts? There is no Mrs. Broxton, except for my mother, and the only twins she cares about play baseball in Minnesota."

"But if there were a twin-expecting Mrs. Broxton, I have just the policy for her. See?"

Hegan opened the portfolio and showed it to Artie. The portfolio was empty. Almost on cue, Artie took a manila envelope from under his right thigh and placed it toward the edge of the table, near the salt and pepper shakers and sugar dispenser.

Hegan watched the envelope emerge from hiding and set his portfolio down on top of it. "So what's the *spécialité de maison*?" he asked as he got to his feet and fastened the center button of his suit jacket.

"If you hurry, you can try the chipped beef," Artie advised as Hegan left to join a dwindling line.

Artie wondered for the seventeen thousandth time whether or not he was doing the right thing helping Hegan. The information he copied on Portia Sutherland from the paper's morgue files was not incendiary. That wasn't the issue. Here he was, a journalist—really a reporter and rewrite man-person—who respected the ethics of the profession as he believed and practiced. How could he aid a police investigation? That wasn't his job. What happened to the concept of journalism as the fifth estate and watchdog for society? *Co-opted by celebrity and money and turned into the lapdog of the establishment, that's what happened*, he answered.

Ethics was one of those words that had as much validity in reality as virginity. Fifty years ago you could walk into a crowd of singles with certainty that ninety-eight eight percent were virgins waiting for a marriage bed deflowering. Today, only the bed part was left. There wasn't even a marriage.

Hegan returned with a cheeseburger and fries on a tray. "All out of chipped beef," he said as he set the tray down. He reached for the ketchup bottle next to the sugar dispenser and smothered the burger in what he knew was really red-colored sugar. "That good ol' ketchup high," he said. Arnie watched in disbelief as Hegan left no bit of burger unadorned.

Fussing with the sugar dispenser and ketchup bottle, Hegan casually tidied up by placing the manila envelope inside his portfolio.

"Now if any KGB agents are watching," he said to Artie between bites of a slice of onion that slipped out of the bun, "they'll think I'm a neatness freak and you're my lunch buddy."

Artie watched the envelope disappear, relieved it was hidden. "I've never seen you in a suit before."

Hegan noticed Artie was on the edge of agog. "You want my autograph?"

"Only on an IOU, but Clay says you stopped betting."

"Clay's right." Hegan didn't want to provide any more details. "I only wear the suit to funerals," he said without thinking.

To which Artie asked, "Who died?"

Both realized they'd been too glib with repartee for no reason than the sport of dueling witticisms. They looked across the table at each other and silently recalled the most important death in Hegan's life. Hegan took a bite and was the first to move on. "It's also my posing-as-a-phony-insurance-agent suit."

Relieved the awkward moment had passed. Artie stood to go and stuck out his hand.

"Thanks for the info on that insurance policy."

Hegan returned the gesture without wiping a smidgen of ketchup from his hand. "You're quite welcome. Give it some thought. Talk to the missus. Lemme know."

Hegan left and Artie looked for a napkin.

CHAPTER EIGHT

Hegan parked in the employees' lot at Arlington. He looked over at the portfolio on the front seat of the Valiant and loosened his tie. Whatever Artie uncovered Hegan would read when he got home. A few more questions for Gilroy.

Hegan, blue suit blaring like neon, strolled down the center of stable row, carefully avoiding a mini-minefield of digested oats and hay. Pre-race activity was in full swing as Hegan, without a cane, passed exercise boys and grooms taking thoroughbreds through their daily ritual. He stopped a uniformed guard and learned Gilroy had the day off. The guard, also an ex-Chicago cop, directed him toward barn seven. Hegan found the barn door open and stepped into the cool, dark interior redolent of damp hay and urine.

The Zenda barn had eight stalls, four on each side of a wide corridor, with double doors at either end. Italian Scallion's stall, the identifying sign not yet removed, was one third the length of the barn. Hegan opened the door but did not enter. Even in the low light, he could observe signs of struggle. Hay and horse apples at the rear had been kicked up and plastered with force onto the back wall.

"Hey, mister! Whachu doin'?"

The voice, getting louder and closer, came from over Hegan's left shoulder. Hegan turned to find Rojas. The way he held the pitchfork in both hands was more confrontational than agricultural, Hegan noted and immediately waved his badge.

"Chicago Police Department. No la migra," he said as Rojas took a startled step back.

Rojas stood still "Whachu wan'?"

"Where's Mr. Zenda?" Hegan thought he should start at the top.

"He don' live here."

"No shit, Sherlock. But is he at the track today? You see him?"

"I dunno. He maybe in de skybox." Rojas pointed to the grandstand.

"Okay, the skybox. I'll check." Hegan started to leave the barn but had second thoughts. He came back to face Rojas, who responded with a frozen stare.

"I bet you know who killed Italian Scallion." Hegan pointed his finger at Rojas and then at the empty stall. "Was it Frankie LoFrisco?"

Hegan watched Rojas avoid eye contact and vigorously shake his head. "Don't lie to me. Frankie saddled Italian Scallion and led him to the paddock. Either he killed Scallion or you did. Two choices."

Hegan grabbed Rojas's cheeks with one hand and squeezed them together, making the man's mouth pucker out like a grouper.

Finally he blurted out, "Frankie, he did it." As the words left his mouth he saw a shadow pass behind Hegan. A second later he saw a black blur connect with the back of Hegan's head.

He felt Hegan's hand release its grip on his face, and watched as Hegan fell onto the straw-covered floor.

Rojas looked up able to see two eyes staring at him. It was as if they belonged to a predator. He was transfixed and mesmerized; unable to look away.

While locked in the penetrating and powerful stare, Rojas did not realize that Jeff, the owner of those eyes, had slipped closer. A moment later, Rojas felt a steel wire encircle his neck.. Then he stopped feeling anything at all.

* * *

Hegan rose on wobbly legs and struggled to clear his senses. Then he got angry. This recent habit of falling in and out of consciousness had to stop. He wondered how he could let himself be blindsided and began to doubt his competency. Then he remembered the stable hand. Gone. This is a habit he'd have to break.

Picking the last bits of straw from his sleeve, Hegan stumbled out of the barn and into the flank of a well-lathered chestnut mare as she slowly stepped away.

"Nice tail," Hegan said loud enough for the exercise girl aboard the mare to turn around and smile at him.

"Thanks," she said. She was pretty and young. Not much older than Ariel, Hegan noted. He wasn't sure if she thought he was admiring the horse's tail or hers. Though he had to admit, based on the shape of her jeans, she had a good seat - as riders liked to comment.

Hegan returned the smile and, with it still plastered on, came face-to-face with Portia.

"What brings that moronic grin to your face?" she inquired as her initial look of surprise evolved into hurt and hardened into contempt. In an instant she recalled how much she felt Hegan was different. Actually someone she could trust. But he'd betrayed her. Like all men did... and do.

Hegan wanted to say "It takes one to know one," but he resisted.

"What are you... ? I'm, I'm..." He waved his arms, gesturing in a circular fashion like a windmill.

Portia filled in the blanks. "Following another hunch? Or looking for another woman to abuse?"

"Or blowing smoke up your own ass?" Eddie Perino's voice was unmistakable as he stepped out from behind a passing string of horses, a cloud of pent-up anger settling on his face. Swagger was in Perino's gait as he sidled up to Portia, assuming the position of both bodyguard and royal consort.

Portia did the introductions. "You know Sergeant Perino, Mr. Hegan?"

Hegan nodded, ashamed of how he'd reacted at Ariel's house and determined to control his anger in front of Portia.

"He's been a great help to me," Portia added. "I've finally met a policeman who is calm, considerate, and gentle." Portia abruptly turned her back on Hegan and walked away. Perino waited until Portia's back was turned, and then blew Hegan a kiss. It was not a kiss of affection.

"This is where you belong, Hegan. Up to your ass in horse piss."

For emphasis, Perino plucked several strands of damp straw from Hegan's suit, took a sniff, and said "horse piss!" before letting out a loud, triumphant guffaw.

Perino thought it a stroke of genius when he called Portia and suggested he help her reconstruct Ariel's last day at the track. He hoped to control the direction of her inquiry. Better to know what she was thinking and feeling and doing, he reasoned. He never expected her to be so willing after their first meeting in his office. Just goes to prove you can never be certain about any broad.

* * *

Portia looked out the window of the cab, her eyes empty of images but her mind active. Perino seemed helpful. And though it was nice of him to take her to lunch, he found too many occasions to pat her thigh. Each time, his hand moved further toward her crotch until, finally, she "accidentally" speared it with her fork. *What is his game,* she wondered, *apart from the usual "see woman, fuck woman?"*

The cab slowly rolled to a stop. Through the window she saw the word *Mortuary* above a double doorway. When she didn't move, the cab driver turned his head to her.

"This it, lady?" She nodded. "Thought so. That'll be eight forty-five."

Mechanically, Portia reached into her purse and extracted a twenty-dollar bill. She slipped it through the opening in the bulletproof glass and opened the door without waiting for her change.

The cabbie called after her, but she didn't hear—or didn't want to. When a symphony of car horns sounded began behind the cab, the driver gave up, considered himself lucky, and drove away.

Once the mortuary doors closed, Portia was covered in a blanket of silence. Her feet moved, but no sound came up from the thick carpet to her ears. She was all alone in the main hall. The reception desk a few feet inside the entrance was empty. *All the people in here must be dead,* she thought, bypassing the obvious absurdity of the idea.

Soon, a thin, ascetic-looking young man entered the lobby from a side corridor. Portia heard him arrive before she saw him: first, the rustling of fabric; then, the sound she knew too well—his zipper closing. The young man covered his zipping with an officious welcome.

"Good afternoon, madam." His greeting held the hint of a practiced British accent. "What may I do for you?"

"Isn't it more what I can do for you?" Her retort did not shiver his timbers. Why was it that service people, who achieved fiscal solvency by providing their only talent to the consumer, took the position that they were performing a superior act? The Downstairs considered itself better than, even in control of, the Upstairs.

The young man cocked his head as if trying to receive a faraway signal from an extraterrestrial. "How so, madam?"

"The money I spend here pays your salary."

He found a cuticle to be of intense interest and studied it before looking up. "We are quite busy today, madam. What may I do for you?"

She steeled herself and cleared her throat. "Caskets," she said firmly. She needed to be rock-steady, without a trace of emotion in her voice. "I need to see caskets."

"Oh. Why didn't you say so?" His cuticle-challenged right hand shot straight out from his side, and, with index finger pointed down the corridor, he dismissed Portia from his sight.

Portia did not thank the young man. With her back stiff and straight, she headed down the corridor. Through a glass window, Portia saw an astonishing array of caskets—from finely polished woods to plain pine and a selection in between she couldn't identify, as if one mattered more than the other except to the egos of the living.

Two men had their backs to her. The younger man moved nervously, as if his core being was out of sync with his shell. The other was taller and older with a mane of long, snow-white hair that touched the top of his shoulders. This was the one man she truly loathed to the depths of her soul, in every morsel of marrow in her bones. It was a hatred that could grow exponentially, without restraint, without bounds. Just add water and stir—like instant pancakes. Sometimes the ingredients were secret. Sometimes they were obvious. The resulting mixture was always the same.

Her father. Dr. George Sutherland. How she dreaded this moment, but it was inevitable. News of Ariel's death was in the papers and on TV. Even her ivory tower father and reclusive mother could not escape the deluge. Through a sprinkling of tears, Portia's mother negotiated a temporary truce between daughter and father. "For Ariel's sake" was all her mother had to implore. The dreaded meeting was arranged. The principals would limit their exposure to each other.

When Portia entered the room, the men did not immediately notice. She registered with the young mortician first, and once he turned toward her, Dr. Sutherland did as well.

First she noticed the imperious expression on her father's face. She never knew him to express any other emotion, as if it were sewn on. The cheeks were jowlier. The soft, slightly effeminate lips were pursed in disdain.

She wondered if he'd had any collagen injections in the years since they'd been in the same room together. *Wouldn't doubt it.* The hair was still cut so it could be combed into a *V*, with the tip barely touching the top of his forehead, making Dr. Sutherland look like the reincarnation of Caesar Augustus from the front and an aging drag queen from behind.

The moment Dr. Sutherland saw Portia his eyelids fluttered, and he called out to her through mournful sobs. His arms opened to her from the far side of the room, embracing the world. She thought he looked like the statue of Christ in Rio and vowed to give up her life if she could turn him to stone at that instant.

The young mortician tried to be reserved and professional, but nevertheless was affected by Dr. Sutherland's sobs. With some reluctance, he tried to put a comforting arm around the older man who, without acknowledgment, walked out from under the arm toward his daughter.

"My deepest—" was all the young man managed to say before Portia addressed him.

"It's an act. He doesn't have a sorrowful bone in his body."

Portia's words bounced harmlessly off Dr. Sutherland as he reached to take her hand. She recoiled and eluded him without physical contact. Then came the Shakespearean tones.

"We have been estranged lo these many years, my child. Why do you reproach me?"

"Must you?" She started but considered that too mild. "How dare you! Have you no decency? That is never the question. You have no decency. Not a shred. You make a scene and exploit the death of your daughter for your own ego. You vain, contemptible, felonious excuse for... what? How can I describe you and not insult all of humanity?"

"Vengeance! Plague! Death! Confusion! Woe, that too late repents," was his response.

"I don't suppose you've repented, Father?"

How she hated to say that word. He seemed surprised by her sudden step toward him and the intensity with which she looked into his eyes, and he took a step back.

"I didn't think so," she said after getting the confirming answer from his blue eyes, which acknowledged no criticism or sin.

"Was that Shakespeare?" the mortician asked, trying to break the tension.

"Indeed," Dr. Sutherland said to the more appreciative member of the audience.

"You're an actor?" the young man asked.

"You could say that," Portia answered with denigrating amusement. "And a bad one."

"Certainly not!" The Shakespearean tones rang out.

"My father teaches Shakespeare at the university."

"Oh. I graduated from mortician school last week, and you are my first clients," he revealed with an eager grin.

Portia felt revulsion in her stomach, the kind that usually climaxed with spewing vomit. In defense and to preserve her digestive tract, she leveled her eyes at both men. "Right now, your lives are less important than my sister's death."

"Yes, of course. I'm sorry. Well. Uh... I know what you're feeling."

"Only King Lear knows what I'm feeling," Dr. Sutherland said, self-pity reeking from his voice. Then he began to sob. With eyes closed, but directed by a secret compass, he reached out to grab Portia's shoulder for support.

Portia smacked his hand away and backed out of range, causing Dr. Sutherland to totter and almost fall on his face before the mortician grabbed the older man's waist with both hands and pulled him upright. Responses overlapped each other from opposite poles of emotion.

"Are you all right?" the mortician said.

"I told you never to touch me!"

"Ingratitude, thy marble-hearted fiend, more hideous when thou show'st in a child than in a sea monster," Dr. Sutherland responded to his daughter.

I'll get some water. Maybe smelling salts," the young man offered.

"Thankee dear sir. No. I'll manage," Sutherland said affecting deep sadness and hurt.

The mortician tried to figure out what was happening. He looked from one to the other, conflicted by his need to assist a customer while avoiding a familial feud. The old man was harmless enough, but the woman? She might have a weapon in her pocket. He imagined her violent outburst leading to the spurting of blood all over the lining of the expensive caskets. What could he do if that happened? He'd lose his job. For what? Not diagnosing a psycho?

Portia moved to another part of the room, two caskets separating her from her father. He'd never get that close to her again.

"You still have plenty of charm for strangers. But only abuse for your daughters, living and dead." As her verbal smack reverberated, she made eye contact with the mortician and indicated a mahogany casket as her selection.

"Portia, my eldest, you always were a willful, selfish child. But as an adult you've become a hideous mutant."

Portia returned serve. "Whatever I've become I owe to you."

"I absolve you of any debt."

"Ah, the great scholar overflows with generosity." Portia tried to avoid sarcasm because it could be swatted away deftly by her father. She preferred direct and hopefully lethal assault.

"What about the scars? The nightmares? The years of guilt? At least poor Ariel is free. What about me? Do you think I've forgotten what you did after all these years?"

The mortician recorded the mahogany casket's model number in his notebook, feigning disinterest in the conversation around him. But there was more here than he needed to know or could handle. After all, his expertise was with the compliant dead, not with the contentious living. He could do no more and handed his card to Portia.

"Call me. We can discuss bunting at another time."

The mortician left the room, and Portia, searing her father with her eyes, headed out on his heels. She left her father amid the sea of caskets and hoped it would be the next to last time she'd ever see his face or hear his voice.

* * *

As Hegan entered the station house, leather portfolio under his arm, he heard a wolf whistle, tossed in his direction like a lazy lasso. He remembered Jessica, one of his partners when he rode patrol before being promoted to plainclothes, had been a good whistler. She was a petite brunette—newly divorced, he'd learned—who Hegan was convinced had her uniform specially altered to accentuate her curves.

"Nice threads, Hegan. You should dress like that more often."

"Don't feel natural."

"You could give a girl ideas." Jessica slipped her riot baton in and out of its leather holster.

Hegan showed his badge to the desk sergeant as a way of easing away from Jessica, but she was still shining her dark eyes in his direction. "You've got enough ideas, already Jessica. See ya." He turned to the sergeant. "I'm going to see Eddie."

"Not back yet," the sergeant replied without looking up from his computer screen.

"I know." It was a lie. "He said I could wait." Another lie.

The sergeant's shrug was good enough for Hegan. Before he could move toward the back and Eddie Perino's office, he felt the sting of Jessica's riot baton on his butt. When he turned around, he bumped right into her.

"Bye, Mike," she said, returning the baton to its holster.

"Wha... ? That stung."

"It's supposed to. So you have something to remember. I can kiss it and make it better."

"Jessica..." He pointed his finger at her as if readying a profound dissertation, but thought it better not to continue. "Gotta go. Bye."

"Mike?" She whispered provocatively enough to make Hegan stop again. He turned back in time to be on the receiving end of Jessica's good-bye kiss, which she blew to him across the reception area. She kept her lips open as the kiss went airborne, forming a perfect oval to leave Hegan with a lasting image.

Hegan made a pantomime of catching the kiss, being staggered and knocked backward by the force of it. He sent Jessica a farewell wave and turned down the corridor to Perino' office.

Jessica had put the peck back in his pecker. Clay's phrase. After Lucy died, the vitality of his heart and groin did too. Jessica was a wicked flirt. Her intention made him smile until he realized that soon he would no longer be with his fellow officers to endure the daily routine. It was the minuscule, rote activities among colleagues—telling jokes, filing papers, sipping coffee—that Hegan would miss the most.

He received the occasional nod of recognition, but from none who had been close personal friends. *No man is an island*, he thought, *except in a large bureaucracy.* There you can live separate lives while working with strangers who you only get to know for the moments of interaction.

Perino's door was closed. Hegan knocked for effect, just in case he was being spied upon. *In this business, paranoia is a swinging door,* Hegan reminded himself while noticing the clutter on Perino's file-filled desk. He sat opposite and pulled a newspaper from his leather portfolio to cover his search.

He peeked over the top of the paper to check the flow of traffic passing the door he'd left open on purpose. With the open paper as cover, Hegan snooped at the index tabs of various files until he found one marked SUTHER. He eased that file out from the stack and slipped it over to the edge of the desk.

"Looking for something?" Perino asked from the open doorway.

Hegan crashed the paper down under his chin and wriggled his body in mock surprise, enough to distract Perino while the obscured hand pulled the SUTHER file inside the newspaper.

Ending the charade, Hegan looked up at Perino and replied, "A warm bag of shit.

And there you are. My, isn't the universe good to me? Must be my karma. How's your karma today, Eddie?"

Perino held his own newspaper, and he wagged it like a sword at Hegan from the doorway. Hegan saw it was the *Daily Racing Form.* Not a surprise, but he'd hoped Eddie would see the light, considering his alimony and child support responsibilities.

"Someday your wise mouth is gonna open for the last time." Perino gestured with the paper as he spoke.

"I'm bulletproof. Remember?"

"Tell your sister I sent the alimony check. Now, what's this shit about me expecting you? I'd look forward to getting herpes before seeing you again."

"Oh? Is that the one STD you don't have?"

"Funny," Perino said without humor.

Then Hegan noticed the bandage on the back of Perino's hand. "What happened to your hand?"

"I cut it." Perino tossed off the answer, but Hegan couldn't resist.

"I bet you cut it shaving. You always had simian tendencies." Hegan did not show the pleasure he felt when Perino's brow furrowed, in simian fashion, as he tried to figure out the meaning of the word.

Hegan didn't wait for Perino to respond. He stood, tucked his portfolio and the newspaper-wrapped file folder under his arm, and approached Perino, who didn't move until Hegan jammed a finger into his gut. Perino was surprised, and his reaction was to move out of the doorway, giving Hegan clear access to the corridor.

"You're liable to get a hernia if you don't lose that gut and tone up those muscles." Hegan paused for reflection. "A sound mind in a sound body. Makes you a two-time loser."

Perino sought the safety of his desk and made a fumbling effort to check it for missing items, his distrust of Hegan apparent. "If you're going, go. In a few days you'll be an ex-cop. Makes you as valuable as a used rubber."

Hegan realized that in any second, Perino would notice the file was missing. But, he wanted to annoy Eddie by sticking a few well-placed barbs into his skin.

"I like these little chats, Eddie. Think I'll stay awhile." Hegan returned to the chair and propped his legs on the desk to get Perino's attention and stop his inspection. "You heard I'm retiring? Who said that?"

"Good news spreads like horseshit. Come on, what the fuck are you doin' here?"

"A mission of charity."

"A what?"

"I forgive you for shooting me in the back."

"For Christ's sake! How many times—"

"As many as I want." The light, teasing playfulness disappeared from Hegan's voice. His new voice came from the wellspring of his anger—at Perino and himself. "After you beat Teresa the first time, I told her she had to forgive you because cops work under terrible strain. That you didn't mean it. That it would never happen again." His voice was rising in a powerful cadence. "I gambled with her life! Not anymore!"

Hegan's anger propelled him to his feet. As he stood, he kicked the files off Perino's desk, sending them into a jumbled mass of police reports, scraps of notes, and crime scene photos. Ordinarily, Perino would be quick to anger and retaliate, but today he knew not to push Hegan any further.

"If I hadn't covered up for you six months ago, you'd be the Sissy Mary of a dozen bubbas at Joliet by now. And you'd be grateful to them. Because the only other role left for you up there would be that of a corpse." Hegan headed for the door.

"Fuck you" was all Perino could reply, and even that lacked conviction.

"And my sister would be out on the street with no support for the kids. Just leave her alone and keep up the payments."

"You son of a bitch," Perino said, throwing a stapler—the only projectile remaining on the desk. Hegan quickly closed the door and then opened it again after the stapler clattered to the floor.

"You can't fool me, Eddie. She was no suicide, and you know it. In my professional opinion, you suck as a dick."

Perino came out from behind his desk, waded through the jumble of paper on the floor, and halved the distance between them.

"What do you care?" The question was a taunt.

"A simple horse player's hunch." Hegan said, pleased to be noticing his voice had taken on a kind of Errol Flynn insouciance.

"You're a loser, not a player."

"But I'd never gamble and lose money I needed for my kids—if I had any."

An El Nino's worth of storm clouds passed over Perino's face. He was speechless, but the anger in his eyes spoke loud and clear. Hegan was elated. He'd struck gold. He'd spilled blood.

"Good luck, Eddie," he said, closing the door and hoping the blood he'd spilled would not be his own.

As Hegan started back down the corridor through the squad room, Perino quickly got in step behind. "Better be careful walking around without your crutch," Perino whispered loud enough to be heard by only one.

Hegan stopped abruptly and turned, causing Perino to stumble into his chest. Before he could step away, Hegan grabbed the end of Perino's tie and yanked him closer.

"I'm not a cripple anymore, Eddie." Hegan released the tie and pushed Perino away.

* * *

The safelight in the photography darkroom bathed Hegan and Marv in an eerie red glow. The photographer was shorter and older than Hegan, with thinning gray hair and a chest that sloped into his abdomen. But his eyes, even in the dim light, were mischievous. He resembled a middle-aged cherub, with the spirit, mind, and attitude of a fun loving, easy going kid. *My idol*, Hegan thought as he watched Marv take a piece of exposed photographic paper and slip it into the developing solution.

"A few ticks of the second hand and we'll have an image, Mikey." He ended the sentence with a playful pat of Hegan's cheek.

As they waited, Marv examined Hegan with a photographer's eye. "You look good. For a guy who coulda, mighta—God forbid, shoulda—been dead... or worse. Not bad."

"Thanks. How's business? Everybody's gone digital."

"Digital. I'll give them digital." Marv showed Hegan his middle digit. "And business? I'm lucky I got a wife who works." Hegan always laughed when he heard that line, and Marv laughed with him. "Harriet and the girls are fine. Thank God."

Marv turned to the developing tray. "Ah, we got something." He gently lifted the paper with tongs and deposited it in the fixing bath. "This will make the image permanent. As permanent as anything can be in a changing world."

"Geez. A photographer and a philosopher. That's a combo that should be franchised," Hegan said. "Philosophy while you wait. Philosophers R Us."

"If there is permanency, why do we die? If there is no change, why do we die? You're so smart, how come you're risking your health instead of retiring?"

"Who said—?"

"What? It's on the street. All over town. Written on the subway walls and tenement halls. That's who said."

"You talked to Clay, didn't you?"

"I can't buy flowers for my wife? What kind of world... . Here!"

Marv lifted the wet print out of the fixing bath and held it up for Hegan's inspection.

"There. There it is," Hegan said as he examined the wet print. "See? That's Ariel's hand." Above her hand Hegan saw something scrawled in the sand: 8-0-0 S-T-V. "Musta written this as she was dying, Hegan said.

"It's gotta dry." Marv took the print and placed it image-down on the curved steel drum of a print drying machine.

"She was trying to give us a clue. With the last ounce of life. She knew somebody'd killed her. That idiot Perino called it a suicide."

"They put your brother-in-law in charge of the case?" It was only one question, but it had many implications. Marv had taken the photos at the wedding of Teresa and Eddie. His opinion went way back.

"Ex. Ex-brother-in-law," Hegan said.

"At last. Good for Teresa. And you."

Even in the dim red glow, the surprise on Hegan's face was obvious.

"Look," Marv began by way of explanation. "I take pictures, right? But it's not the click, click, look-this-way-and-say-cheese kind. My camera records the moment. The event. But also the soul." Hegan looked up from the dryer, anxious for the process to end. "You think I'm kidding, but once I get the pictures developed…" He searched for the exact description. "Something mystical happens. I dunno. Maybe it's me. You can call me crazy. But once the faces appear, I see different people. Not like Stephen King. It's like I can tell in the picture who they really are."

When Hegan didn't respond, Marv shrugged and took the print out of the dryer.

"Thanks for everything, Marv." Hegan took another look at the photo and put it into his portfolio. "You're a great guy, Marv."

"So, listen," Marv said. "About these parking tickets I've got…"

"I've got two words for you, Marv."

"Yeah?"

"Pay them."

* * *

Hegan paid another visit to Monica, LoFrisco's landlady. She opened the screen door wearing the same housecoat and pink velour slippers. She held the same cat. All cats looked the same to Hegan, but it seemed the same. And she smoked a cigarette, which was different. *Ah! Good deduction, Hegan,* his mind said as his face gave her a pleasant "I've gotcha! Up yours!" smile.

"Good afternoon ma'am... er... Monica."

Hegan held up his badge and a white piece of paper, which from a distance could be construed as the requested search warrant.

"I know you're not Mrs. LoFrisco," he taunted to give himself an edge.

He got it. Monica was not a beautiful woman when there was a neutral-pleasant look on her face. Now, with the steam from Hades rising within, she was not even plain.

"But, I want you to know I have a search warrant which enables me to inspect Mr. LoFrisco's residence. Such as it is."

Hegan noted the annoyed look on Monica's face. Clearly she never expected to see him again and was determined the easiest way to rid herself of this pest was to let him into the apartment. Hegan watched as Monica trudged down the front steps, key in hand, and turned into the driveway. She unlocked the side door and was about to precede Hegan into the basement apartment, when blocked by Hegan's arm. He maneuvered into the favored angle and smiled at her until she got the hint. Now it was Hegan's turn to shut the door in her face.

Hegan flicked on the wall switch at the top of the stairs, illuminating the apartment below.

Before he reached the bottom, Hegan knew someone had been there first. Frankie was a slob, but even a street person wouldn't live in the conditions he found. Bedclothes tossed onto the floor. The dresser lacking drawers, its backing ripped off. The same for the nightstand. The lamp was tossed on the floor. It's shade missing and bulb broken.

No clothes, not even a speck of lint in the clothes closet. Medicine cabinet shelves sparkled. Bathroom sink was dry. At the refrigerator, he found the crisper draws scattered on the floor. Half-melted ice crunching under his foot proved he was not too far behind the visitors. He wondered how they got past Monica the gargoyle.

Desperately seeking some shred of evidence in all the chaos, Hegan looked under the bed. Dust bunnies. Nothing and more nothing. Twenty minutes too late, with hope lost.

Then he got a strange idea, an idea that had never occurred to him before in all the cases he'd worked. From some other planet the words spoke to him. He decided to stop looking and, instead, *wait* to be found. He took a deep breath and stood still at the entrance to the living area. His eyes gave it one more careful scan. All the furniture wrecked, TV smashed. A La-Z-Boy lounger ripped to shreds, stuffing strewn everywhere.

He stopped looking and took another breath. Then his eyes fixed on the phone. It sat on the table, seemingly the only item undisturbed. The phone drew him forward.

A small white pad, insignificant to the searchers, rested by the phone. No different than the kind hotels provide guests for jotting down quick phone messages—like phone numbers. *Duh!* Hegan glided to the phone pad with elation in his heart.

He lifted the pad by its edges. It was blank. He tilted the pad under the light of the lamp and made out a series of impressions. He took his time and, with care, rubbed the side of a pencil over the impressions until the numbers were revealed: 800-555-6545. *This might not be gold*, he thought, *but it's the only shred of evidence in the apartment, and it will have to do.*

When Hegan exited the apartment door, Monica was waiting for him.

"Happy?" she asked, probably hoping he wouldn't be.

"Very," Hegan answered.

"You think I'd have a bum in my house? Even in the cellar?"

"You don't have a bum in your house, madam. And, the guys looking for Frankie know that too."

"See? I told ya. Wait, what?"

"Frankie's gone. Not been there for days. No clothes. No toothbrush. Somebody trashed it when you weren't looking."

"That no-good bastard! Told me he'd take me to New York." Then, as quickly as the outburst escaped her lips, she covered so Hegan wouldn't suspect. "He owes me rent, too." Her voice was a low quiver meant to convey the fragility of her gender.

Hegan wasn't fooled. "Thanks, madam" was his dismissal notice. Without waiting for a reply, he returned to his Valiant and drove away. *Oh, what a good dick am I,* he thought, patting the phone number in his shirt pocket until reality intruded from the radio.

"Zenda farms suffered another tragedy today. Days after their prize stallion and its trainer died, track workers found the partially decapitated body of stable hand Julio Rojas in a dumpster behind barn seven. Police are looking to question one of their own. Detective Eddie Perino reported seeing Mike Hegan leaving barn seven—"

Hegan shut off the radio.

"Fuckin' Eddie... ."

CHAPTER NINE

Hegan stopped to see Kaz at the deli near Clark Street in the middle of singles town.

Someone should research the human genome for the lemming factor, Hegan thought while scanning both sides of the street for a place to park. *Why do humans, who arguably use only ten percent of the capacity of their brains, congregate in packs instead of living independently?* He was specifically thinking of all the singles that lived in little rabbit hutches throughout the North End. For what, the expectation of romance? Better, sex? How? Eyes smoldering in the elevator? At the mailbox? In the laundry room? The odds at the track were better.

Lemmings, was his only answer. There must be a prehistoric tendency, almost visceral, that compels humans to clump together for safety and security. If the appendix is nonfunctioning because humans don't consume large quantities of raw meat—only raw fish in sushi bars or posh restaurants where one can pay twenty-five bucks for uncooked hamburger called steak tartare—how is it that, despite a more powerful brain, the lemming factor has not gone the way of the appendix?

Hegan couldn't come up with the answer, and finding a parking spot was even less successful. He parked in a red zone and stuck his OFFICIAL POLICE BUSINESS sign on the console above the steering wheel. Hegan hoped the sign worked this time, or he'd have another ticket to pay.

Hegan entered the deli to find a lunchtime crowd. Kaz was wrapping a tuna salad sandwich for a customer when Hegan caught his eye.

Kaz rang up the sale. "Manny, take over," he yelled to a young Latino counterman, who Hegan hoped, for Kaz's sake, was legal. Kaz directed Hegan to a table in the corner that was being cleaned off to seat two women in their thirties who waited nearby. By all appearances, they were stay-at-home wives with children currently in preschool, so they could indulge in an hour-long lunch featuring grown-up talk instead of a discourse on Bobby Square Pants or whatever juvenile fad held their kids' interest, much to the glee of marketers.

"Hey, we're next!" The dowdier-looking but most assertive member of the duo raised her voice at the young hostess, now faced with displacing her boss from the back table.

Julie, holding a sheaf of menus, went over to Kaz. "You know, they were waiting a long time, Kaz, and their kids get out of school in half an hour." She pleaded logic, sympathy, and mothers' rights.

"I know, Julie. But we got important business here. Tell them they can have the next table, and lunch is on the house. Hmm? Please."

Julie returned to the women, a forced, pleasant smile on her face, her shoulders slumped, weighed down by the knowledge she'd betrayed her gender. Kaz gave a quick glance over his shoulder and saw the women fume a bit then brighten. Satisfied his tactic had worked, Kaz turned to Hegan who was ordering pastrami on rye with coleslaw and Russian dressing. And a cream soda.

Kaz waited for the waitress to move away with the order before grabbing the sleeve of Hegan's jacket and pulling his arm across the table. This was not a hostile act, and Hegan was familiar with Kaz's manner of intimacy.

"Your face is so long," Kaz began with his deli diplomacy, "it slipped under the door two hours before your behind."

Hegan's eyes shot up from the table, where he was diddling with packets of sugar, and he looked at Kaz, who cocked his head in anticipation of Hegan's response. Hegan struggled with the words, once again surprised by what he'd termed Kaz's deli sensory perception.

"You gonna tell me," Kaz asked, "or do I have to beat it out of you with that three-foot-long salami hanging in the window?"

Hegan smiled. "You and your DSP." The words came, but not easily. "They want me to retire."

"Good. You need a job, come make sandwiches with me." Kaz had a way of deflecting pain and reticence with a skewed take on reality. He provided just enough of the surreal to cause a smile or a laugh, but mostly a momentary disconnect to persistent pain. Some space to perceive blue sky between the clouds.

"Sure, I'll make sandwiches. Hope your customers don't mind a little of my blood with their Russian, 'cause I'll cut myself on that slicing machine."

Hegan's sandwich arrived, and he didn't wait to fill his mouth with a bite of soft rye, creamy Russian dressing, crunchy coleslaw, and salty pastrami. Kaz watched as the troubles immediately vanished from Hegan's face, as if he went from crumpled old man to superhero in one bite.

"Good, eh?" Kaz asked.

Hegan could only nod with his mouth full. "Great," he finally responded. "I'm saved."

"You came in looking like a sad sack of potatoes and now you could save the world. Pastrami has magical powers."

"Not the world, Kaz. What I want is to know why Ariel Sutherland was killed. Who killed her and the horse she trained? If I can find those answers, I'll retire."

"You've got no luck, Hegan. You stink at poker. I wouldn't put a penny on any horse you pick. But now you're asking the impossible."

"What?" Hegan couldn't imagine the convolutions of Kaz's mind.

"Listen to yourself. 'Who killed the girl? Who killed the horse?' Pastrami can help you save the world, but it can't solve the mysteries of life."

Hegan almost lost a gulp of cream soda. "You've been standing on your brains too long."

"Look, Mike. The horse and trainer died on the same day. Coincidence—that's all I hear on TV and in the papers. Nonsense. Things happen for a reason."

"Exactly! Why do you think I'm not buying this suicide bullshit?"

"You miss the point. Think Kennedy assassination. Nine Eleven." Kaz nodded once for emphasis. "You'll never know the truth."

"Ay." Hegan sighed and stood to leave.

"Oy. It's oy, not ay. All these years and you can't speak right." Kaz embraced Hegan. "God bless."

Hegan left the deli and found a parking ticket blocking his side of the windshield. For no conscious reason, he drove toward Portia's gallery. Though another conversation with the next of kin made logical sense, Hegan knew he had an apology to make. But a verbal apology would not be good enough for him or Portia. That day at Ariel's house, his blind anger was his own failure. Instead of taking responsibility, he conveniently directed his anger at Portia. Was this a human trait or only his deficiency? Slick philosophizing would not work, he concluded. Inside, he knew he was wrong and he had to apologize.

Hegan parked across the street from the gallery. Before he could get out of his car, he saw Portia lock the gallery door and hail a cab. Hegan didn't expect to notice the two casually dressed men who responded to Portia's exit by hurrying across the street and driving away in a nondescript Sable. Car of choice of Mr. and Mrs. Frugal American. At this time, he doubted the Frugal Americans. It was obvious she was being tailed. *Who's behind it and who are those guys?* Hegan wondered as he pulled away from the curb to follow the Sable following the cab.

When the informal caravan left city limits, Hegan knew Portia's destination was the Wilmette beach where Ariel's body had been found. He enjoyed playing hopscotch with Portia's tail. From his position a few cars behind, Hegan pulled into the passing lane and drew abreast. The driver, who Hegan still didn't recognize, cast a disdainful glance at the ancient Valiant before Hegan screamed past and pulled in front. Even with a mission, the driver could not resist the challenge. He pulled out to pass Hegan, who would then speed up just enough to stay ahead for a while before allowing the Sable to gain the lead.

Hegan pulled into the passing lane and flew past the Sable and the cab. He took the beach exit and turned into the parking lot, hoping his intuition did not fail. He parked the Valiant behind a camper and hid himself in a picnic area near the stairs leading to the beach. A few minutes later, the cab arrived. He saw Portia gesturing for the driver to get closer to the sign marked BEACH ACCESS, its arrow pointing to the stairs. Hegan noted the Sable enter and move to a position at the far end of the parking lot where there was a clear view of the cab.

Portia got out of the cab and looked down the stairs. Hegan saw her body stiffen with resolve as she stepped off toward the beach. He waited a beat to see what the men in the sedan would do. When there was no movement from the Sable, Hegan left his vantage point and started toward Portia.

Hegan spotted Portia on the beach pacing, around and around, robot-like in a tight circle. From a distance it looked to Hegan like the ritual of Druids. Or zombies. He cautiously descended. While his back was much improved, he didn't want to frighten Portia and then have to chase her on the soft sand.

Hegan reached the beach and stayed behind Portia, opposite from her field of concentration.

"What are you doing?" he asked when he got close enough for her to hear him.

Surprised, Portia whirled, frustration etched on her face. Seeing Hegan, she didn't perceive any danger, but kept silent and quickly moved away. Hegan narrowed the distance before her lead became too great for him. He grabbed her by both arms to control her fury and get her attention.

"Let go of me!"

"This won't bring her back." He was determined to be gentler with her.

"She died here." Portia was standing where her sister died. She didn't simply vanish off the radar screen in a plane over the Atlantic or get vaporized in a battlefield bomb blast. She died on a beach within driving distance of her home. The proximity of her death and its banality left nothing to imagine.

"I know" was all Hegan could say.

"Sometimes I think it would be better not to have her body to bury. Then I could imagine it was all a mistake and she would suddenly return. Or she could have run away to a Brazilian jungle with a handsome native. Happily living in a sarong. Having *café au lait* babies."

Hegan released her arms and put his around her shoulder. "Goddamn it! Let me go." She pushed Hegan away and he stumbled, landing hard on the sand. Portia stood over him, her nostrils flared. *She looks like a mare in heat*, he thought as he stood, arms out like a supplicant.

Portia didn't move. Her hurt and anger held her in place. Yet, there was a force gathering within her, more like a pull coming from and flowing to Hegan. She could only describe it as a uterine pull. She refused to examine the source, because she would not allow such an attraction to happen.

Instead, she nurtured her obsession for revenge. A constant companion for years. Ariel's death was another opportunity to let her violent side out of confinement. Portia grabbed one of Hegan's outstretched arms and executed a classic karate flip, sending him crashing onto the sand on his back.

"If you've come to apologize for the other day, don't bother," she said, directing her words down on Hegan's prone body.

Hegan struggled to conceal his pain, propping himself up on his elbows before rolling to his side and planting one foot to propel himself upright. He brushed sand from his suit and directed his intensity at Portia through his words and body as she stared out toward the lake.

"Your sister needs the apology more than you do. I care more about finding who killed her than healing your wounded feelings."

"I can take care of myself," Portia said, her eyes darting to the impression in the sand where she'd flung Hegan.

"Yeah, I know. You're an artist trained in metal sculpture with a brown belt in karate." Artie's info on Portia was helpful. "Wish I'd remembered the karate part a few seconds ago."

"I never told you... have you been spying?" With theatrical flair, she beseeched the heavens. "Please let me fight!"

"I'm a cop. Remember?"

"I've been trying to forget," she said, her anger subsiding so that it was only a few percentage points greater than the physical pull she felt. *Attract and repel. Attract and repel*, she thought, disturbed at how her body was betraying her.

"You're pretty good at karate." Hegan watched her anger subside as she got more control over her feelings.

"Self defense is one of the social graces for women living in urban America, Detective Hegan." Portia felt confident inside knowing that mere compliments could not cause a chink in her defenses.

"All women in urban America, or just you?" he said, unwilling to let her feel too confident. His response worked as Portia turned and looked directly at him with softened eyes. Hegan took the look as encouragement to press on and did. "I also know your career as an artist never took off."

"Now you're an art critic. Just what are your credentials for judging me?"

"Your sister paid the rent on your gallery."

Portia slapped Hegan across the face. "Bastard! I have talent."

Hegan refused to acknowledge the sting on his cheek. "I never said you lacked talent. Just wonder what kind of people want rusty butcher knives hanging in their living room."

Portia ignored the comment and countered. "What's my bra size, if you're so smart."

"You don't wear one." Hegan's eyes blazed back at her. "Because you don't need one."

This time, Hegan was able to deflect Portia's right cross by grabbing her wrist. He was surprised that Portia let him hold her wrist by her side. He discovered the reason as Portia became lost in a fond memory.

"Ariel always encouraged my work. We'd been through so much together. She was finally tasting success..." Portia pulled away, kicking and stomping on the sand. "Goddamnit!" she screamed at the sky, and her words echoed off the bluff above the empty beach.

They walked to the stairs. Portia shrugged off Hegan as he took her arm.

"In some ways... okay, in a lot of ways, I'm not a perfect man."

"Don't tell me. Call Dr. Phil."

"Once I commit to something—"

"That remains to be seen, Hegan. Deeds, not words."

"Megaforce," he whispered, remembering the motto in an old, awful movie. "Deeds, not words, Megaforce," he repeated, unsure how or why he allowed such triviality to intrude.

Having no idea what he said, Portia quickly outpaced him, and Hegan hurried to catch up.

"You were followed," he said, and she stopped.

"Yeah, by you."

"I was here before you. I followed a Sable. Just the car Mr. and Mrs. Frugal American would buy. Only why should they care about you?"

"Maybe Perino sent them." Portia seemed certain there was a plausible explanation.

"Why didn't he tell you? If the investigation is closed, is he protecting you? From whom? From what? If the investigation is not closed, is he spying on you? Why?"

"I don't know," she whispered.

Hegan preceded Portia up the stairs and could see the sedan had not moved. "When you get to the top, walk toward the picnic table on the right. I'll be casually walking behind you. There'll be a blue Valiant parked next to a camper. Door's open. Get in."

Portia got to the top of the stairs and followed Hegan's instructions. A few beats later, Hegan emerged and heard an engine revving in the distance. He stopped and feigned tying an imaginary shoelace on his cordovan loafers while keeping his eyes on the car. It didn't move.

Hegan strolled toward the camper, keeping peripheral watch. He slipped around the camper and then behind the wheel of the Valiant. Portia was tossing old newspapers and brown paper bags into the back seat.

"This car is a trash heap. How can you—?"

Hegan fired the engine and pulled out.

"Slump down until we get out of the parking lot." Portia looked over, questioning him. "Do it now!"

Portia slid forward, lowering her head below the window as the Valiant passed the sedan and headed toward the exit. Hegan saw one of the men get out of the car and walk toward the camper.

Hegan looked into his rearview mirror. They weren't being followed. The rush of adrenaline made him giddy. After a few seconds of experiencing the pleasure of escaping, outwitting, and indulging in that oh-what-a-good-boy-am-I feeling, he was brought back to the present by Portia.

"How much longer?" she asked. "My neck is ready to snap off."

"We're safe." He again took a quick look behind. "All clear."

"Gee, thanks," she said sliding her butt back into the seat and rotating her neck to encourage her blood into circulation. "When did you plan on telling me? When hell froze over?"

What a pain in the butt, he thought. *Whining. Angry. Wiseass. If this were James Bond's Aston Martin, I'd push the eject button and she'd fly into the air.*

"I'm only trying to protect your boney ass." He knew calling her ass boney was gratuitous, self-indulgent, and capricious. And probably against the law somewhere in the universe, but he didn't care.

"Boney?" she shouted. Portia turned her back to Hegan, stuck her left cheek out, and gave it a solid smack to show its substance.

"Bottom line," he said without thinking.

"Very funny," she said. It was obviously not a compliment.

"Didn't mean it that way," he said, changing the subject before the day disintegrated into a verbal duel. "Open the glove compartment and take out that envelope." He waited until she held it in her hands. "Inside is a computer printout." Again he waited while Portia unfolded the four-page document. Many of the lines were crossed out in red. Those that were not had questions marks in the adjacent margin.

"That's the list of doctors who *supposedly* prescribed drugs for Ariel."

"Where did you get it?"

"I took it from Perino's file. Rather, I took his entire file."

"He seemed like he wanted to help," she said, the lilt of naiveté in her voice. "What does this mean?"

"The police department or the investigation team or Perino or whoever is behind this... they all claim Ariel took drugs—prescription and otherwise. Thus proving she had the means to kill herself and Italian Scallion."

"Yes, yes, yes. Tell me something new." She grew impatient.

"I liked you better when you were showing me your butt."

"That has nothing—"

"Shut up. Just shut up and let me finish." Hegan paused for Portia's irritation to subside. "I'm spelling this out in very short words to make it crystal clear: Ariel was framed."

Portia opened her mouth to respond.

"Quiet! It doesn't matter what you know or feel in your heart. What matters is evidence that can be taken into court. Feelings are not admissible evidence. But a list where sixty percent of the names are bogus—those are the red lines—and the other forty percent are questionable, meaning they are real doctors but don't know and have never treated Ariel, is an indication that someone went to a lot of trouble to create a false and misleading trail. Open-and-shut proof she did it."

"Open and shut. Those were the words Perino used that day in his office."

"The fact that he had the printout in his possession isn't proof of anything. But it is a beginning. You need to know that I'm on your side."

Portia looked up at Hegan, who was speaking while keeping his eyes on traffic. If he had turned toward her he would've seen a softening in her gaze and concluded that he was reaching her again.

"Yeah," she said softly to conceal the question mark in her head.

* * *

Jeff glided up the stairs to Faraci's office and stood like a wraith in the doorway for five or more seconds before being observed.

This fuckin' ghost, Faraci said to himself once he spotted Jeff's form blocking the opening. The hard part came next. Discipline. Self control. In this case, mastery of every muscle and nervous impulse so he did not exhibit surprise—or worse, fright—in the presence of his employee, one whose mercenary profession could not be trusted.

"You're back," he said with a distracted yawn, not glancing up for two beats.

"Yeah." There was a slight trace of a laugh in his voice. A tinkle that insinuated "no biggie."

"And?" Faraci's gaze fixed Jeff to the doorjamb. There was no polite come-in-sit-down-have-a-drink collegiality. A report was due.

"He won't bother you no more."

"Who?"

"The spick. But—"

Faraci's antenna did not convert the reception. "Don't *but* me. Tell me."

"I had to remove another guy."

"One a them the fat pig?" Too much to expect? He was right.

"Nah. Some guy in a blue suit. Gave him a headache he won't forget." In a flash, Jeff brought his right arm straight down to demonstrate how he slugged Hegan with his blackjack.

"He see you?"

"Didn't notice any eyes in back of his head."

"Is that an answer? Yes? Or. No?"

"Noooooooo." Jeff did his Steve Martin impersonation.

Faraci, who went to sleep precisely at ten, had missed the early years of *Saturday Night Live* and failed to make the connection. He thought it impertinent and made a note to deal with Jeff at a date of his choosing. For the moment he simply replied, "Thank you," lowered his eyes to the page on his desk, and dismissed his minion with a few waves of his right hand.

Faraci watched Jeff's back disappear down the stairs. *First we had wise guys*, he thought. *Now all we got is wiseasses.* Too impressed with themselves. No discipline, which compromises security.

* * *

Zenda downed his second shot of vodka before he felt the warmth of the first spread through his stomach. He and Gregori were alone in the restaurant, and he found comfort in his native tongue. Someone was trying to destroy his business. Who? Why? His horse, the girl, and the spick—all dead. Who? Why? He pressed Gregori.

Gregori's outward response was a shrug and upturned palms. "Could be a personal feud. You know how those spicks are. Hot blood. Act first, think later. If ever."

Gregori wondered if in placating Zenda, he was also trying to calm his own concerns and fears.

CHAPTER TEN

Not a day to be buried, Hegan thought as he worked his way around tombstones and headed up a knoll toward the open grave where Ariel Sutherland's remains would permanently rest.

Not a day to be missed. He looked at the sky, a cerulean quilt of puffy clouds dotting the sky. *Burials should only be on rainy days or in the cold...* He stopped, remembering the last funeral, a more personal and tragic experience. He saw his heart and Lucy's coffin sink into the open, frozen earth. Those thoughts caused his chest to pound until he changed his internal narrative by allowing his rambling thoughts to intrude again. *When the sky pours down tears for the dead and mourners are wet and uncomfortable that is when burials should take place. Too bad. Try being closed up in a box.* He hoped... then gave up hoping. Humans don't change, only circumstances.

The glint from the windshield of the approaching hearse caused Hegan to consider the somber ritual he was about to witness. He noticed the gravediggers arranging artificial turf, while other workers opened folding chairs on three sides of the grave. Hegan purposely arrived early so he could find a suitable hiding place from which to watch the mourners as they assembled. He took his position behind a weathered statue of Michael the Archangel and read the inscription. For Our Beloved Matthew. May the Sun Warm Him Through Eternity. b. 1905 - d. 1911. The angel's extended arms pointed to the east and the rising sun.

Hegan watched as the hearse drew up to the curb below the grave site. Following were two limousines. They were joined by eight private cars. The chauffeur of the first limo got out and crossed to the passenger side. He opened the door and helped a woman, frail beyond her years, as she carefully placed her feet on the grass. A tall gentleman with long white hair exited after her and took hold of the woman's arm. By the time Ariel's parents had readied themselves to approach the gravesite, the other mourners were heading in the same direction.

Portia stepped out of the second limo which she shared with a well-dressed, middle-aged man and woman. She didn't speak as she took her mother's free arm and, without looking at Dr. Sutherland, helped her to the single row of chairs at the head of the grave.

Many of the other mourners appeared to be workers from the track, some of whom Hegan recognized. That was all. Family and coworkers. For a woman in her midtwenties, Hegan observed, Ariel didn't have many—or any—friends from her own generation or social sphere.

Hegan saw the minister approach Ariel's family and briskly express his regrets. At least that's what Hegan figured the cleric would say under the circumstances. The introductions concluded as the pallbearers brought the coffin and placed it in the center of the gathering.

Hegan watched as the minister stood at the open end of the quadrangle around the coffin. He also noted how Portia deftly separated the older woman—her mother, no doubt—from the long-haired old man, as if only the two females deserved to participate in the burial rite. He didn't know why the observation mattered, but it was noticeable at the time and so registered.

Hegan couldn't hear much of the ceremony because of distance. His eyes wandered across the group of mourners. Half the men were dark-complected Latinos. One of the others was Gilroy. Another was the Exercise Girl with the cute cheeks. Now, he had a better look at her face.

As his gaze returned to the minister, Hegan spotted a dark shape stealing toward the gravesite from a distance. Someone who wanted to observe the service rather than participate. Most likely not a terrorist or mob assassin. A professional ghoul? Or someone who cared from afar.

Hegan decided discretion could wait and moved closer to the group as the minister wound to a conclusion with "Man is from earth and to the earth he shall return."

It was followed by Portia's angry outburst. "She was a woman! Godammit! Say *woman!*"

The minister absorbed the barrage, hastily blessed the grave, and retreated downhill to the safety of his car without a backward glance to Portia or formal adieu to the Sutherlands. Slowly, the other mourners gathered to pay their respects to Ariel's family.

* * *

Portia didn't know many of those who shook her hand and offered condolences. For her it was a mechanical exercise - shake offered hand and respond with a soft "thank you". Portia disengaged from this activity for a brief moment. The figure she'd spotted during the graveside ceremony became more distinct as he boldly moved closer. It was Gorman, Ariel's suspected lover. Portia darted from the group, determined to chase him away and deprive him of one last good-bye. She had stamped Gorman as undeserving and unsuitable for her sister in life, and now that Ariel was gone, he had even less value.

As Portia sped off, Hegan moved closer to watch her dart around headstones and down another knoll with the instincts of a predator. Her fury increased as she got closer to Gorman. Ten yards from the grave, they saw each other. Gorman turned and fled downhill. Portia stopped in full flight, mission accomplished.

Satisfied she'd repelled the interloper, Portia returned to her parents, caught her breath, and guided her mother back down the knoll toward the waiting limo. She turned for one last look at the coffin as it was being lowered out of sight. Before that parting look could increase Portia's pain at the loss of her sister, she felt a gentle hand on her elbow. She saw the urgency in Hegan's eyes as he drew her away from the others.

"I need to see you tonight."

Portia tried reading his eyes. This urgency was for what? "Why? You want to go dancing on the day my sister was buried?"

"For Christ's sake!" Hegan blurted. "I know how she died."

Portia's knees almost buckled, and she grabbed Hegan's shoulder for support before heading for the car. Halfway there, she stopped and looked back at him.

"Pick me up..."

* * *

The observer, hidden behind an ornate mausoleum, couldn't hear all the words, but he did hear *gallery* and *eight o'clock*, and that was all he needed.

* * *

Hegan slowly turned the Valiant into the alley behind Portia's gallery. Even with headlights on, the alley revealed little until Hegan saw a flash of light. The light got brighter and directed him to the rear of the building. The screech of metal against metal greeted Hegan as he followed it to an open door. Once inside, Hegan was enveloped by sound and light that pulled him to its source.

Portia was dressed in the same clothes she'd worn to the funeral. She'd accessorized them with a pair of protective goggles and heavy, heat-resistant gloves. Hegan watched as she slammed a hammer down on a piece of molten metal. Sparks flew. The noise grew in proportion to the speed of her hammer. Ash billowed in the air. Matted by sweat, Portia's hair became wild clumps. Drops of sweat sprang from her forehead and glistened in the light of the glowing forge. Hegan saw a woman trying to destroy herself through exhaustion or spontaneous combustion. He didn't know which would come first. But he did know this was no way to spend an evening.

Hegan didn't think she was aware of his presence. At least she gave no indication. As the pounding got louder, Hegan crept behind Portia and grabbed her right arm on the upswing. Automatically, she swung her left arm out in defense. Hegan backed away until the arm was fully extended so that he wouldn't be burned by the molten metal gripped in a pair of tongs.

With his face buried in the back of her head, Hegan ordered Portia to drop the tongs.

For good measure, he grasped her left forearm and banged the tongs against the furnace until the hot metal disappeared in the fire and the tongs were flung to the floor. He pulled her away from the heat and twisted the hammer out of her hand until it, too, dropped with a clang.

Trance-like, Portia slumped in his arms, her dead weight pulling him down as he dragged her to an old wooden chair. Hegan cleaned her sweaty face with his handkerchief and gently tapped her cheeks.

"Portia. Come on. Stay with me, Portia. Wake up."

Portia's head bobbled sideways and then her chin dove toward her chest, causing her eyes to pop open. Hegan knelt in front of the chair, holding her arms to keep her from falling.

"It's me, Portia." It took a few seconds for her to recognize Hegan. "I need your help," he said. On hearing the words she snapped awake, made the connection, and struggled to her feet. Silently, she shut down the furnace, picked up her tools, and put them away.

Just as they were about to turn out the lights and leave, Portia darted over to a cabinet and took out the manila envelope she'd received from Perino. "I almost forgot. Ariel's personal effects. Perino gave them to me." Hegan regarded the package and wondered what cards Perino was dealing. No doubt from the bottom up.

Hegan parked on the opposite side of Daley Plaza. Picasso's 50-foot statue of a woman loomed above them. Illumination on the statue's face made it look more eerie and grotesque at night than it did in daylight.

The streets were empty. Only the echo of their footsteps could be heard until replaced by the roar of a high-powered truck engine. The sound, in the quiet of a weeknight, was too unusual for Hegan. When the engine revved again he ordered Portia to hurry, grabbing her elbow and propelling her toward the door of the office building ahead.

"What?" she asked as he quickened the pace. Hegan pulled harder, causing Portia to yelp.

A black Ram pickup, all 350 of its horses galloping at full tilt, bounced over the curb and entered Daley Plaza.

"Run!" Hegan took Portia by the hand and set a quicker pace. They were twenty yards from the building when Portia stopped suddenly and turned to look back at the Picasso. She jerked Hegan to a standstill.

"What are you doing?"

"Picasso." Portia looked at the impressionistic sculpture. "What a pity. Churning out environmental art for any Babbitt with a buck."

Hegan didn't wait for the Ram to get any closer. He grabbed Portia's hand. She resisted and tried to shake him away like an unwanted suitor. "Come on! Now!" A powerful tug set her in motion, but she was unsteady, tripped and dropped the envelope.

"I'll get it," he said pushing her forward. As he reached for the envelope, the soft discharge of a silenced M-16 showered Hegan with puffs of granite. He grabbed the envelope and reached Portia who fiercely tugged on the locked door.

The truck made a quick circle. Again its headlights found Hegan and Portia, trying another door. Locked. Hegan saw the Ram gaining on them and pulled his forty-five. He pushed Portia behind a pillar and fired a defensive shot, webbing the center of the Ram's windshield.

The truck moved out of range and then circled back like a hungry shark as Portia pounded on the door's glass panel and rattled its handle.

"Someone's coming!" she told Hegan, and they watched the elderly night watchman enter the lobby and shuffle toward the front door, a newspaper tucked under his arm. He took one look at them and dismissed them with a perfunctory wave.

They were exposed and without refuge. Hegan heard the truck returning. He pushed Portia behind another pillar seconds before a fusillade from the M-16 blew out the glass door. The Ram bounced off the adjacent curb, exited the plaza and disappeared into the night.

The sound of crashing glass drew the night watchman back to the lobby as Hegan and Portia stepped carefully through the debris.

"What the hell?" the watchman said tiptoeing through the shards of glass that littered the lobby floor. Then he spotted the vandals. "Hey!" he yelled as Hegan and Portia headed for the elevator.

"Call the cops," Hegan told the old man, flashing his badge before the elevator doors closed.

* * *

By the time they'd reached the twenty-second floor, Portia had achieved a degree of equilibrium. Her breathing and heart rate slowed to normal speed so that she once again could feel the ache of dread in her stomach.

They stepped into a dimly lit corridor. As they left the elevator Portia slipped her arm under his. It was an act of solidarity but not surrender. She wanted him to know it indicated partnership, not dependency. He looked first at her arm in his and then into her eyes. Hegan felt Portia draw him closer without speaking. He understood.

Hegan opened a door marked FORENSIC PATHOLOGIST. Randy Crimmins from the coroner's office was waiting and led them back through semidarkness to a cramped laboratory. A quick burst of fluorescent light from overhead brought Portia out of her trance-like existence and into the present. It was a world she knew would produce more pain. She gained control of her urge to flee when Hegan spoke.

"Thanks for staying open late, Randy. This is Portia Sutherland, Ariel's sister." Randy Crimmins, forensic pathologist for the coroner's office, offered his hand as introductions were made. "Portia, I asked him to re-examine Ariel's autopsy results."

"I'm sorry for your trouble, Ms. Sutherland."

Portia's first instinct was to snap back "I've heard that before," but the race for her life had caused an epiphany of sorts during the elevator ride and she whispered "Thank you" instead.

Hegan handed the manila envelope, still officially sealed with police tape, to Randy. "This is what the cops found on Ariel at the beach."

"You haven't opened it?" Randy looked first at Hegan and then at Portia.

"I couldn't just yet. The funeral. You know," she stammered.

Randy nodded and broke the seal. He eased opened the out sized, padded envelope and tilted it so the contents could slowly fall onto the counter. The cascade of items began with what appeared to be the contents of Ariel's purse: It was followed by her checkbook, a pen, her wallet, and a small packet of tissues.

The last item was a travel brochure. Hegan picked it up and read out loud. "The Blue Lagoon. Excellent view of the Grenadines. Where the hell is this place?"

Portia didn't want to be excluded and took the brochure from Hegan. "It's on St. Vincent. An island in the Caribbean."

"Never heard of it." Hegan seemed dismissive. "Anything else?"

Randy spread the items on the table as if a three-card-Monte dealer trying to hide the elusive pea. In the process he discovered a packet of condoms tucked into the tissue packet.

"Condoms. It's not here. As I suspected," Randy concluded.

The condoms were an indication of her sister's sexuality. Portia didn't know how she felt about that. Was it any of her business? If she made it so, was she being judgmental? At least Ariel had the good sense not to get knocked up by that man. Too many questions. She turned her focus on Randy instead.

"Share the joke," she said, her edge returning. "What did you expect to find?"

Surprisingly, Randy deferred to Hegan. "We hoped to find tampons."

This was not the kind of conversation Portia wanted to have with two men. Professional or not. Maybe it was the purposeful disguise and suppression of her own sexual nature. Or maybe it was her exploitation when younger. Whatever the reasons, and there could be more, Portia conceded, she assiduously avoided any conversation or thoughts of sex with anyone at any time.

"Do either of you have a personal need? Or is this some bizarre male ritual?"

Hegan caught the virulence and was clinically direct. "The autopsy found she was using a tampon."

"Big clue. Call the FBI." Clinical didn't work.

"She didn't need a tampon," Randy explained. "The one I found—"

"The one Cevasco missed," Hegan added.

"Uh, yes. It was saturated with curare. A muscle relaxant which caused her death. And there were also traces of semen."

"Wait, wait, wait." Portia tried to get a grip before it all sailed out of sight. "What are you telling me?"

"Your sister had sexual intercourse before using a tampon," Randy began to explain.

"How many women do you know who use tampons after sex?" Portia spoke from the authority of her gender.

Randy passed the torch and to Hegan, who again tried a direct and clinical approach. "She didn't use it voluntarily."

"Come on!" Portia was incredulous. "No woman *lets* someone—"

"Right," Hegan interrupted. "Unless she can't stop him."

"Now... wait!" The pace was almost too much for Portia, but Hegan didn't slow down.

"If she was drunk. Or forced."

"Ariel didn't get drunk."

"There was no evidence of alcohol in her blood," Randy said, "but there were multiple vaginal abrasions. And rope burns on her wrists. She had forced sex—"

"Rape," Hegan said.

Portia inhaled deeply as if the intake of air itself would bring clarity. "Hold it! You're telling me that someone had sex... uh, raped my sister and then killed her with a poisoned tampon?"

"That's what the facts support."

"What?" Hegan watched Portia's emotions shape-shift her face like scenes from the old Michael Jackson music video. Anger, hate, pain, revenge, regret all played out on her face, bringing Portia to the point of hyperventilation.

Randy broke open a vial of smelling salts and offered it. Portia knocked it away.

"Leave me... Wait. How did she... ?" Her question was directed at Randy.

"The poison, absorbed by the vaginal tissue, entered her bloodstream. Like the AIDS virus does."

"How could anyone... . Bastards!" She stopped to inhale deeply again. "But, what about the note... the suicide report?" She grasped for any shred of logic. Any explanation. "And... and Perino said he was waiting for a search warrant."

"Forget Perino. Forget everything you know. This, here and now, is Day One. And, on Day One we know..." Hegan gave a nod to Randy.

". . . more than Cevasco. A poison forcibly induced into Ariel's bloodstream killed her," Randy said. "But we don't know who did it. We also know Perino was holding a list of doctors he claims gave your sister prescriptions. We don't know why or what the prescriptions are for."

"He was so sure about the note. Waving it in my face like a taunt. Like, 'See? I gotcha.'"

Hegan explained to Portia that a sensational case demanded a quick, even superficial solution. Not for the sake of truth, but to stop heartburn in the city and police brass. Once they got the autopsy results, someone wanted a quick resolution supported by doctors and suicide notes. He didn't know if or how Perino was involved beyond being assigned the case.

Portia had to ask. "And you're sure this is true?"

"Somebody killed your sister," Hegan said gently. "And that pickup truck was not bringing us the key to the city." Portia slowly absorbed his words.

"Thanks, Randy," he said, returning Ariel's belongings to the envelope and waving good bye.

Police and a cleaning crew were busy with their respective chores in the lobby as Hegan and Portia left without drawing any attention. Portia didn't glance up at the Picasso as they crossed Daley Plaza and headed for the Valiant.

"Won't Detective Perino be surprised? He was so sure Ariel killed herself." Portia was looking forward to vindication, no matter its size.

"Don't tell anyone about what you learned tonight. Not your parents. Particularly not Eddie Perino."

"I thought he was your friend."

"Friend? Maybe once. Not now. He's my ex-brother-in-law."

"You married his sister?"

Figures, Hegan thought to himself. A woman would pose such a question in only that way.

"*My sister* married the psycho." Hegan felt he heard Portia exhale at his answer. He was more surprised to hear her response.

"Are you... ?"

When Hegan realized Portia could not say the word, he did. "Married? Almost. Once. Her name was Lucy." Hegan fought with himself to reveal more. "But... what about you?" It was a gratuitous question; nevertheless, he asked it.

"My personal life is... personal."

"Hey, I believe you. But I'll take that as a no. Never married."

Portia was drained and let Hegan's remark disappear. As Hegan unlocked the car door, Portia's attention drifted elsewhere, and she stared at something in the distance. Hegan reached for his gun and sped around to find that Portia's interest was in the Joan Miro sculpture. The steel, concrete, and bronze interpretation of a feminine figure held a pitchfork.

"That's by Miro. Come on. Get in."

Portia stood before the opened car door. "What every woman needs," she said before entering the car.

"A statue?"

"A pitchfork." Before Hegan could start the engine, she said, "Yecch! What am I stepping on?"

Hegan reached over, picked up a white bag from under Portia's foot, and held it up for her inspection. "What is that?"

"A double cheeseburger. About a day old. But if you're *that* hungry..." Portia put her palms up to ward off the offensive offering, and Hegan tossed it into the back seat.

They rode in silence for a few minutes. Portia held the envelope close to her chest, trying to absorb Ariel's energy from her personal items.

"There's only one possibility." Portia broke the silence. "Steve Gorman killed Ariel."

"Who the hell is Steve Gorman?"

"He's a mathematics professor at the university. Same place my, you should pardon the expression, father teaches."

"Let me see... . You deduce that, because Gorman teaches with your father, he killed Ariel?"

"No, no. Pay attention. Steve Gorman was that older guy I told you about. The one who took our picture in front of the fireplace. Remember?"

"Yes. But what's that have to do with your father?"

"Nothing! It's an aside. You know, a Shakespearean aside. He just happens to teach at the same university, *and* I believe he killed Ariel."

"Okay. That's clear. Now, tell me why he killed Ariel."

"They were having an affair. That's why he was invited to dinner. So she could introduce him to me."

"You know this for a fact? He couldn't be a friend? An acquaintance?"

"I told you..." She was convinced Hegan would never understand. "Obviously you don't have much life experience with the opposite sex."

"I've had one hell of a life experience with one member in the last few days."

"That's not what I... leave me out of this. Now pay attention. As I told you at Ariel's house, a man twenty years older than a woman wants sex. He doesn't want companionship. That's why God made dogs. And as old as he is, he doesn't want or need a friend."

"Okay. Suppose you're right. Why would he kill Ariel?"

"Because he's married."

Hegan started laughing and it took him a while to stop, much to Portia's displeasure. "And you tell me I lack life experience. That's not enough reason."

"What kind of cop are you?" Portia asked without malice. "Gorman is very manipulative. He's a Svengali, afraid she'd wreck his career. So he killed her."

"And you determined this after meeting him how many times?"

"I told you. I was invited to dinner."

"Once!" Hegan didn't want to pounce on Portia and scare her away. He wanted her input.

He also wanted her to think logically.

"Then why was he skulking about at the funeral? I saw him sneaking up to watch."

"The guy you chased?"

"You saw him?" Portia was surprised.

"Why did you chase away our prime suspect?"

"Don't belittle me. He didn't deserve to say good-bye."

"And the horse. Did he kill Italian Scallion, too?"

"That was a coincidence," Portia said, her tone dismissive.

"The next sound you hear will be me guffawing."

"Why? There's nothing to laugh about. You don't believe in coincidence?"

"Not unless it's on *CSI* and the case can be solved in less than sixty minutes."

"We met by accident."

"Should've worn my seatbelt. But, you'll remember, I came to see you."

Hegan parked the car in front of Kaz's deli.

"Why are we stopping?" Portia asked.

"We need some supplies." Hegan got out of the car and stepped onto the curb.

Portia rolled down the passenger-side window and leaned her head out. "We?"

"*Your* investigation is now closed. But *our* investigation is just beginning."

Whether it was Hegan's words or her awareness of his support, Portia couldn't determine. But a growing sense of serenity in her core was partially replacing the constant ache of dread. She hoped it would grow to be all-consuming so that someday her nightmare would be over.

Portia opened the envelope and took out Ariel's wallet. She had no purpose or goal in mind as she looked at Ariel's driver's license. *Awful picture*, she thought. She noted the license expired in two years and reminded herself to tell Ariel to take a better picture next time. Grief flooded back and overwhelmed the serenity. There would be no next time.

Portia's fingers rested on the wallet's change compartment. Aimlessly she ran her fingers over the leather and felt something other than coins. She unsnapped the flap and rummaged through the coins until she found the alien object—a key to a safe-deposit box.

Inside the billfold she found a photo of Ariel with Gorman. She held it so that Ariel's side of the photo was in light and Gorman was obscured by the dark.

When Hegan left the deli with a bag of food, cheerily humming to himself, Portia put away the photo and the wallet. *He's unreal. The guy must pop happiness pills all day.*

Hegan opened her door and tossed the bag into Portia's lap.

"What?" she said instinctively, taking hold of the bag.

"Be careful, there's soup in there."

"What am I supposed to do with it?"

"Just hold it steady. Or do you expect me to hold it and drive at the same time?"

Portia was silent for a moment. *Cheery and assertive*, she thought for no reason.

"What are you so happy about?" she asked as the car pulled away from the curb.

"I'm happy?" Hegan had no clue why she asked the question.

"You seemed cheerful. Upbeat. Humming as you left the deli. If you were a character in a romance novel, you would be described as having a 'jaunty bounce in your step.'"

"You read romance novels?"

"Of course not! Ariel had some one time and I paged through—"

"Yeah. I read *Playboy* for the essays on existentialism."

"Sure. Don't change the subject. You came out of the deli... happy."

"Now it's proscribed by the political correctness committee to express happiness?"

"Stop with that crap. You've changed, and all I'm asking is, if that is so, why."

"It's not happiness... but I'm not unhappy. I'm... I'm ready to go. My engine is running. I've got a goal. I can be useful. I can help. It's me against the bad guys, and I am gonna win."

Portia envied Hegan's overt enthusiasm. It was rare in her and in her life.

"This is what I do best. I'm not waiting for permission. I don't care who gets annoyed. All I care about is finding out who killed your sister. And why. And making them pay."

Portia had been lost in Hegan's enthusiasm and surprised when the car stopped in front of Ariel's house. "Here? Why?"

"This is where our investigation starts," he said.

Portia got out of the car reluctantly and handed the deli bag to Hegan while she fumbled for the key.

Hegan was on his way to the kitchen before Portia had the first lamp lit. "Be careful. You're wound up enough to trip," he said.

By the time she reached the kitchen, Hegan had plates out and the soup warming in a pot. He rummaged for silverware and headed for the dining room table.

"Let me." Portia took the place settings from him.

"Beef with barley soup and pastrami sandwiches," he announced. "Doesn't get much better."

Portia looked at the food and discovered she'd suppressed her appetite. She was hungry, but still had concerns.

"Are you sure we'll be safe here?" she asked as Hegan inhaled one end of his sandwich.

His words were incomprehensible until he swallowed. "Nobody followed us. Besides, lightning doesn't—"

"Strike twice?" she said, nibbling at her sandwich. "As long as we're exchanging clichés, what about the criminal returning to the scene—"

"Of the crime? No crime was committed here."

"The room with the balcony was trashed."

"We'll be safe here. I promise," he said looking across the table and directly into her eyes.

Portia looked away and finished her soup. The nourishment was both physical and emotional. She took a bite of the sandwich and her nostrils flared with pleasure as she tried to smile and chew at the same time, resulting in a sliver of coleslaw falling back on her plate.

"I'm such a..." but she couldn't finish and had to laugh at the Annie Hall moment she'd been through. "I'm not like this."

Hegan rested his hand on top of hers and gave it a gentle pat. She felt his hand but chose not to react verbally or physically. A reciprocal gesture would indicate more intimacy than she could give. Instead, she ate and let him continue talking. The pastrami was the best she'd eaten and she was still hungry.

"Look," he started awkwardly. "There's something I've wanted to ask you."

Her mouth full, she nodded to him to continue.

"At the beach?" She continued chewing. "You let the cab go," he said.

She swallowed. "Right."

"Did you have a prearranged time for the cab to return?"

"No."

"How did you expect to get back to town?"

"I didn't."

"You were going to stay out there all night?"

"No."

"You weren't going to stay, and you weren't going to go back." Hegan frowned. "What, then?"

"There was the lake," she said.

"Lake? I know the lake. But—"

"The lake was for me," she explained without a trace of emotion.

Hegan let her implication swirl around in his head. He knew he'd have to choose his words carefully. She was distraught. Self-destructive thoughts in such a time of stress and loss are to be expected. What he didn't need was someone willing to jump off the building holding his hand.

"Okay." Hegan tried for his best laid-back surfer approach. "I hear ya."

Portia stopped chewing. "Anybody with an otic nerve and bone can hear, Hegan. It's do you understand that matters. Understanding takes intelligence. That's what I need from you, not some 'I hear you, dude' crap."

"Fine," he said. "What I need to know from you now is, do you still want to kill yourself?"

"I don't know." She saw Hegan getting riled and before she received another barrage from him said, "But I could kill you right now."

"Me?"

"You. And you haven't a clue why." She smirked at Hegan's silence. "I'll tell you why. Out of the deli, you're all bouncy. In here you're all domestic. You make me feel comfortable and protected. Then you're serious. But it's a little boy serious and I'm hooked. I'd tell you anything you asked. And I do tell you my plans to kill myself that afternoon. And what is your response?"

Hegan opened his mouth to speak but didn't get the chance. "Quiet. I'll tell you what you said: 'I hear ya.' And you said that because you were afraid to handle my decision to kill myself. That's why."

Hegan knew she had passion, but this was the first time he thought she had rational, controlled passion. Directed for a purpose.

And never before had she revealed herself to him in such detail. He wanted to tell her about his near-death experience, and Lucy, but thought it was better that he not.

"You're right. I can't handle the thought of anyone wanting to commit suicide. Intellectually, I can accept there may be some people in some situations that are so unbearable et cetera. But I'm not one of them and I would disagree."

"You'd disagree?"

"Yes. Every breath brings new possibility. Change. For the better. No matter what. All death changes is the opportunity to make life better."

"You and Mary Poppins. Come on... ."

"Hey! What do you know? Huh? Your sister died. I am deeply sorry. For you and her. In the last ten years I have seen and investigated more than one thousand deaths. Murders. stabbings, shootings, chokings, bludgeonings. I'm not Mary Poppins. I've just seen all the waste death brings."

He paused and took a breath. "Do you still want to kill yourself?"

She began to speak and he stopped her. "If the answer is yes, I'll continue alone. I won't carry an irrational person on my back, someone who could endanger my life and/or my work. Do you hear..." He said the word with purpose. "Uh, understand me?"

"I understand you," she said softly and stopped talking for a moment. "My answer is no. I no longer want to kill myself."

"Selfishly, I'm glad that's your answer."

"Selfishly?" she asked. "Why selfishly?"

"I need your help." He remained silent. Stopping to choose, choose his words. "And I don't want you to die."

She broke eye contact on hearing his words and closed her eyes, choking back any sound.

She inhaled a few deep breaths and opened her eyes, grateful that Hegan chose not to acknowledge the light she knew must glisten in them.

"I've had enough cops and robbers for one day." Hegan yawned and headed for the living room. "I'm going to sleep. No, that's okay. I'll take the sofa. I insist." Hegan took off his shoes and stretched out on the sofa. "Tomorrow we'll search the house." Portia turned off the kitchen light and passed the sofa. "Good night, Hegan." When he didn't answer she looked again. He was asleep. She headed up the stairs to Ariel's bedroom.

Portia undressed in the dark and slid under Ariel's sheets more easily than she'd expected. Instead of thinking about losing Ariel, she focused on finding another way to connect. She inhaled the pillowcase, trying to make herself believe that Ariel's scent remained. Some hint of perfume or soap. What did Ariel smell like? Such a basic quality of identity. Animals have it. Humans lost interest in such olfactory intimacy, unless it was voluntary—meaning sexually induced—or involuntary in the form of body odor in a crowded, unair-conditioned El car in the middle of summer.

Still, she closed her eyes, thought of Ariel, and tried to inhale a trace of her. Sleep would not come and the uncertain scent kept fading. She opened her eyes, alarmed to see moon shadows flickering on the wall opposite the bed. She tried to identify the shapes, but even with full concentration, the flickering had a hypnotic effect and soon she was asleep.

It was not the sleep of the exhausted whose every cell conspires to pull them into oblivion. Or the innocent whose cares are not weighty enough to bend a pine needle.

Portia's sleep took her back into the home movies of her unconscious mind.

In the first, there was a young teenage girl lying face down on her bed, paging through a magazine, looking at fashions, reading advice on acne and kissing on the first date. She heard the door open and turned to see the silhouette of a man, hefty enough to fill the doorway. His face was in shadow, but she knew his identity and her body tensed. When she tried to get up, he firmly pushed one hand down on her back to keep her in place. The other hand slipped under her skirt. Her buttocks tensed and the man slapped her thigh. His finger moved forward. She could feel the nail was too long; it needed cutting and scraped her skin. The burning began. Her eyes filled with tears.

Portia rolled over and the dream disappeared. For a few moments, she could hear her own breathing and then gradually returned to unconsciousness.

Once again a young teenager was in the bedroom. At a desk. Homework. The door burst open and a younger girl flew into the room. In an instant, she threw shoes out from under the bed like a dog digging a hole for a bone. The bone the young girl hid was herself. She crawled under the bed. The older girl called to her, but there was no answer.

The older girl got on the floor and peeked under the bed. The younger girl would not respond, covered her ears and shut her eyes.

Portia sat up in bed with a gasp. The moon had passed and the room was dark. She closed her eyes and again tried to sleep. Portia saw herself in a dark tunnel. There was light ahead and the figure of a younger woman emerged. It was Ariel, laughing, dancing with joy. She joined Ariel in the light and saw the horses. They were jumping, laughing, cheering as the horses thundered past. Ariel was overjoyed. They hugged and shed tears both bitter and sweet. Ariel's face, her smile permanently fixed, started to fade. Portia tried to hang on to the image. The smile. The laughter. But it would not remain. If the muffled sounds that came from the bed could be translated, the words would be *No! No!* And then they dissolved into sobs of loss.

Portia woke herself from the dream. She was not enough awake to perceive the grey light of dawn. She wanted to run. To escape her mind, to escape her life. She threw off the sheet and in full stride ripped open the door. Then the world was in a jumble.

Hegan sat upright against the bedroom door. The speed of its opening caused him to fall flat toward the inside of the bedroom just as Portia raced out. She tripped over his shoulders and fell facedown into the corridor, splayed out in what some would call a sixty-nine position.

"What the hell?" was all she could say as her head hit his knee and rested on his thigh. She heard "You okay?" and realized she was only wearing panties. She scrambled for the shadows while covering her breasts with her hands. "Hegan? What are you doing—?"

"The sofa was too soft," he explained. "Besides, I could protect you better here."

Hiding her breasts with one arm, she gently touched his face. "You were here all night for me?"

Hegan's nod was more about his responsibility than need for praise. Her face told him how deeply she was affected by his sacrifice. An unusual experience for her to consider. Someone could genuinely care. Once again, her brow furrowed and she inhaled deeply to keep her emotions from escaping.

She got up from the floor, arms around her chest, and slid past him toward the bedroom. He averted his eyes from her breasts. "I'll make breakfast," she said before closing the door.

Though the light was dim, Hegan had seen her bare breasts while she was controlling her feelings. It wasn't a prurient experience. *Sweet!* Is all he thought about her breasts. He realized seeing them symbolized another stage in the gradual unmasking of Portia. He also knew in that amateur psychologist portion of his soul, that the more Portia revealed, the sooner she might become whole.

CHAPTER ELEVEN

The sun woke Hegan as it filtered into the hall where he'd slept through the rest of the night. No breakfast as promised. Stiff and aching, he rolled himself upright. Before coffee could make him a new man, Hegan searched Ariel's medicine cabinet and bathroom shelves. Tylenol PM was the strongest drug he found. Not a surprise.

A mirror at the bottom of the stairs told him he was a rumpled mess. A quick sniff of his armpits confirmed he was not ripe enough to offend.

"Coffee," Hegan said out loud to the empty room and shuffled into the kitchen knowing he was the only one to make it.

Later that morning, after he and Portia finished the coffee in silence, Hegan prepared to re-examine the contents found in Ariel's purse and on her body. Portia at first kept her distance from the process by being overly attentive to cleaning the coffeepot.

Hegan spread the purse and its items—checkbook, wallet, resort brochure, condoms, and other bits and pieces—across the tablecloth on the dining room table. To this mix, Hegan added the photos of Ariel's body as well as others containing enlarge sections from the originals.

Hegan glanced over at Portia and watched her give undue attention to the countertop. He decided she was not ready to see her sister's body. Before returning the wide-angle photos to the envelope, his eyes bore in on the letters in the sand. A mantra of *S-T-V, S-T-V, S-T-V* began playing in his head. When repetition of the letters blurred without meaning, he broke away from the photo and joined Portia in the kitchen. She was folding a dish towel as if it was the most meaningful activity of her life.

Hegan gently patted her back. "You ready?" She nodded and followed him to the dining table. Hegan held back the photos from Portia until he felt she had adjusted to seeing Ariel's belongings. He studied her as she touched and rearranged.

Her face was more serene. With her hair tousled and only partially dry from showering, her unadorned face seemed enveloped in a rosy glow that melted age and stress. She wore one of Ariel's robes, which was too short. The sleeves stopped two inches above Portia's wrists, and the hem ended halfway up her shin. She looked like a girl who went to bed one night an adolescent and woke the next morning as a woman.

* * *

When he didn't speak, Portia glanced up to find him looking directly at her. Where the next words came from, she could not imagine. "I know I must look a fright. First thing in the morning," she said, eyes downcast. "And this robe. It's the best I could find." *What a girlishly flirtatious, shameless tart I've become,* she thought.

"No, no. You look... I mean..." The words came in spurts. He measured and considered each one to reduce her agitation.

"What I mean is... Considering we've been spied on, chased, and shot at. You look... ."

"How *do* I look?" she asked, not trying to give him agony, but not making it any easier.

"You look..." She made him forget Diana *and* Ingrid Bergman. Of course there was Lucy, and thoughts of her made him restrain his enthusiasm "... very nice." His words were soft and shy and Portia wondered what was left unsaid.

More than that. Some latent flattery mechanism inside wanted to know what else. "Nice." She scoffed at such a banal description. "And? What are you not saying?" Portia sipped the last of her coffee to give him some time.

"You... look like you... justhadanorgasm." There! It was out. Inside, Hegan winced. Portia gagged on her coffee but managed to swallow, which sent her into a coughing fit. Hegan went to her aid, gently patting her back.

"I'm okay," she meant the coughing and turned away. "Well.," She almost smiled, but wouldn't let Hegan see it. "Never have I—"

"What I meant was, you look warm. A little tired. Cuddly. There's a glow around you."

She allowed a slight smile to escape briefly, her eyes downcast like a sincere and bashful ingénue.

"You smiled! True, it wasn't a Richter scale smile, but you smiled. And me without my camera to catch this rarity."

She looked up at him and endured his good-natured teasing. As a child, she had never liked being teased, but didn't want past memories to spoil what had happened between them. "I wasn't a happy child."

Hegan thought it best not to go down that road until another time. He showed her the first close-up photo of Ariel.

"This is an enlargement of the photos that were taken right after they found Ariel. See the letters S, T, V? Any idea what they mean?"

"S, T, and V," she began the same way he did. "Stehv... stehv! Of course. Steve. Steve Gorman. I told you."

"Not so fast. You can't get S-T-E-V-E from S, T, V."

"Why not?"

Hegan tried to inject a certain professionalism. "I know you want to nail this guy for boffing... having an affair with your sister. But a few stray letters aren't enough."

Portia tossed the photo onto the table with disregard.

"*If* we're working on this together, you have to be open to my suggestions."

She had him and he knew it. He's the one who gave her the half-time locker-room speech. He told her he needed her help. Now he was patronizing her. "Okay. Fair enough. Let's say he's a *possible* suspect. And I say possible because without incontrovertible proof... ." He looked over at her. Portia was satisfied and she understood about the need for proof.

"Maybe we can get the proof from this." Portia picked up Ariel's wallet, opened the change purse and extracted the safe-deposit box key. "I found it last night."

Hegan examined the key and was about to respond with "good girl" but instead focused on the obvious. "Safe-deposit box key." He considered the possibilities. "You'll have to become Ariel for a day."

Portia waved her hand in the air like she was erasing a chalkboard. "It won't work. I don't look a bit like her, and I'll never be able to forge her signature."

"We'll find a way."

Before they went to the bank, Hegan explained he had to keep his regular visit with Teresa, his sister. Portia insisted they first stop at her apartment so she could change, and Hegan drove to the loft area near the gallery.

"I won't be a minute," she said, which served as a polite way of telling Hegan to stay in the car.

Hegan knew she'd take longer than a minute to get ready. He'd grown up with a sister who, despite his parents' pleading and threatening and her own good intentions, always managed to be late for family functions.

Good intentions, he thought. Hell is paved with good intentions. An overused expression, to be sure. Why should it be so? The idea of hell as a fiery furnace worked against the need for some fixed road surface.

Where was anybody going? They were already at their everlasting destination. *Go to hell* was also an expression. It meant only one thing. It didn't mean go to hell and call the auto club for your Triptik to some exotic distant location, which then required a paved surface.

"Oy," Hegan said. *A mind is a terrible thing to leave untended*, he thought. Tired of sitting, he got out of the car and found the safe-deposit box key in his pocket. He began twisting it between his fingers like a mystical amulet, feeling its edges and curves to better commune with the key and its power.

"I'm back." He heard Portia and looked up to find her approaching him at a brisk pace. The earth mother dominatrix look was gone, replaced by black tailored slacks and a dark grey, short-sleeve blouse. From Red Sonja to Sigourney Weaver in—he looked at his watch—only twenty-five minutes. A new world's record? Probably not even her personal best.

Absorbed in her profound change, he let his fingers move without concentration and the key bounced from his hand onto the sidewalk and then seemed to skip by magnetic pull toward the storm drain in front of the car. Portia blocked the key with her foot like a soccer midfielder. She picked it up and, in silent movie fashion, held it up for Hegan to see before depositing it in her purse for safekeeping.

"You need a keeper," she said and then picked at his wrinkled jacket and pulled at a strand of unruly hair. "A shower and a change of clothes too." Hegan was so grateful he hadn't lost the key in the storm drain, he was ready, if asked, to tie a bungee cord around his ankles and fall off the Hancock building.

He thought it best if he remained silent while driving across town to his house.

* * *

Hegan led Portia down the front hall of his row house, going first to the phone to call Teresa and tell her he'd be late and would be bringing a friend.

"A friend or a, you know, 'friend-friend'?" Teresa could not resist a sibling zotz. She was on a roll and continued. "If it's a 'friend-friend', maybe I won't have the right thing to wear. Could you make it another day so I can shop for clothes that fit the occasion?"

"Will you stop?" he said. "I'm taking a shower and I'll... we'll be there in fifteen minutes." He heard his sister ask insinuating questions, he'd had enough conversation. "Bye Teresa" he said before hanging up the phone.

He turned to Portia and found her wandering around the living room, glancing at books in his bookcase and a collection of old maps framed and hanging above a leather sofa.

"Do you want a drink? Anything?" he asked and got a slight shake of her head in response. "Okay. I'm taking a shower and will be ready in exactly twelve minutes."

"Twelve?"

"Yeah. I've timed it. That's all it takes. Some people say 'give me a minute' and then show up twenty-four minutes later. I know that once I'm in the shower I can be finished in a total of twelve minutes."

Portia looked at her watch. "I'll time you."

Hegan left and Portia wandered into the kitchen where she found enough utensils and special pans to equip a half a dozen restaurants. "This is a guy that let's hamburgers ossify in his car," she muttered.

Back in the living room, she peeked under an old blanket covering a three-foot-tall object to discover a tenor sax on a hard plastic stand. She checked her watch and noted six minutes had elapsed. "What you can learn about someone in six minutes," she said with a chuckle.

Hegan returned six minutes later dressed in pressed chinos, a patterned shirt, and topsiders.

"Twelve minutes flat," he announced.

"Thirteen," she corrected.

Hegan lost no momentum. "Your watch is fast." He stopped Portia as she moved toward the front door. "We have to go photo shopping." When Portia objected, he led her to his computer. Before she could think of a question, he directed her to have a seat. In quick succession, Hegan managed to get Portia still long enough for him to take a digital photo.

Hegan downloaded the photo to his computer and printed a small copy. He took Ariel's driver's license out of his pocket and pasted Portia's picture on top. Portia struggled to get words out.

"Y-you planned this!" A head bob and a grin were his answer. "It can't be legal." Before she could be concerned with Hegan's nonresponse, he showed her what on quick glance could be a new license for Ariel Sutherland.

"Let's go," Hegan said.

* * *

The front door to Teresa's house was wide open, and Hegan expected the worst when no one immediately responded in voice or presence to the sound of the doorbell. He found the screen door locked when he pulled the handle.

At the moment when he'd determined to rip the door open, he heard and saw Teresa approaching.

"I'm coming. I'm coming," she said, the high pitch of her voice piercing the air. She unlocked the screen door and opened it for them.

"The front door was open. I've told you—"

"I know. Everything's fine. We can't live in a prison."

Through the interplay, Hegan let Portia enter ahead while he engaged his sister in the necessity for security. But Teresa had enough and stuck out her hand to Portia.

"Hi. I'm Teresa. My brother has no manners."

"This is Portia. Portia, Teresa."

"I introduced myself," she reminded him. Then a chorus of "Uncle Mike! Uncle Mike!" preceded his niece and nephew.

Teresa ushered Portia into the parlor as Michelle and Mikey ran into Hegan's arms and he embraced them.

Said the spider to the fly, Portia said to herself as she saw how genuinely happy uncle, niece, and nephew were together.

"Look, what I've got," Hegan said as he pulled two wind-up clowns from his pockets. He wound each in turn and set them on the floor in the front hall. Mikey was intent on capturing his clown before it got too far away. Michelle just glared at him.

"Is she your girlfriend?"

Trapped, Hegan didn't answer directly. "Let's go into the parlor," he said, trying to distract Michelle.

She trailed behind, insisting the question be answered. "But I want to know. Is she your girlfriend?"

They entered the parlor, interrupting Teresa's discussion of fabric for the bay window seat. The women turned together and their silence prompted Hegan to answer.

"Of course. Yes. She's a girl and... she's an old... older girl. And she's my friend. So, girl friend." Hegan felt he was through the rapids.

Portia and Teresa raised their eyebrows at the answer but for different reasons. "See, Mom? I told you." She turned to Hegan. "Is she going to die, too?"

"Michelle! That's enough." Teresa interrupted.

"Uncle Mike only brings over special girls." Michelle whispered, but in the small, quiet room it was clearly heard.

"Have there been many others?" Portia whispered back to Michelle, becoming a willing co-conspirator in the parlor game of Let's Make Uncle Mikey Squirm.

Michelle considered the question with all the gravity of a seven-year-old and whispered back, "One. But that was a long, long time ago."

Teresa put the answer in perspective but didn't elaborate. "About six months ago. But, that's a 'long, long time ago' when you're seven."

Portia chose not to press for specifics, and Hegan's agenda did not include parlor games. He introduced Portia to Michelle and was ready to move on.

Michelle stuck out her right hand and Portia took it. "Hi. You're very pretty."

"Thank you. So are you," Portia said.

Michelle had some of her uncle's reticent genes and excused herself. "I have to watch Mikey. To see he doesn't get into trouble," she said shouldering grown-up responsibilities.

Hegan had to right the ship. He was sinking fast in the silence that asked for more of an explanation to his lame definition of girlfriend.

"This is not a social visit. Is he doing what's right?" he asked Teresa.

"He gives me more now than when we were married. What did you say to him?"

"Nothing special. Maybe he learned it was better for his welfare to act more responsibly."

Hegan moved on. "How's the job?"

"Great. I got a raise."

The news that Teresa was gaining stability eased some of the fraternal burden he carried since the divorce, but he wasn't ready to involve Portia. "Okay. We gotta go."

"Kids. Uncle Mike's leaving, I'm pleased to meet you, Portia. Hope you can visit us again."

Oy, Hegan thought. "Teresa..." He made her name sound like it had eight syllables. "This is business."

"Oh. Are you a cop, too?" she asked Portia.

"No, I'm an environmental artist."

"What other kind of business are you into together, Mike?" she said, hoping his non-girlfriend, girl friend would see him blush.

He did, but the children arrived before Teresa could take full advantage.

"Goodbye, Uncle Mike!" they said in unison. "Thanks for the presents." They hugged Hegan.

"We're fine and we're getting better. Really. Take care of yourself." She hugged her brother affectionately.

She followed them outside and called after Portia. "Take care of him for me. He needs a keeper." Portia's slight glance told Teresa they were kindred spirits. Hegan could only shake his head and unlock the car.

As the car pulled away from Teresa's house, Portia couldn't resist. "I suppose now that I've met your family, you'll want to meet mine. Isn't that traditional?" She turned her head away from him and smiled.

Hegan changed the subject. "Before we go to the bank, we need to make some changes with your anatomy."

* * *

It took Hegan thirty minutes to change Portia's hand into a claw of gauze and tape.

"How's your hand?" he said as they drove away.

"Fine," she answered automatically.

"How can it be fine when you cut it in a blender?"

"Oh!" Portia looked at her bandaged right hand. Only her thumb and forefinger were uncovered. The rest was swathed in white gauze and tape. Streaks of dried reddish disinfectant smeared the fingers and bandage. A closer look might reveal traces of what looked like blood. Hegan counted on the size of the bandage to repel anyone wanting a closer inspection of the injury.

* * *

The bank was either Depression-era or retro Depression-era, Hegan couldn't tell. It's not enough banks should safeguard your money. *They have to create ambience too*, he thought, searching for the safe-deposit box vault. Some bank marketing genius probably would pontificate that banks need to "modernize their outreach to consumers," blah, blah, blah. "Competitive market forces..." More blah. What they need to do is provide more than one percent interest on savings and you'll see how many customers they get. Give me ten percent interest and watch me save!

Gingerly holding Portia by her left arm, the right hand being bandaged, Hegan guided her over to the safe-deposit box counter. The young woman smiled at Hegan first before realizing Portia held the key. The woman read the number on the key and opened a file drawer.

"Name?"

"Ariel Sutherland."

"Thank you, Grace," Hegan said, reading the woman's name tag. She acknowledged the personal recognition with another smile. *We all want recognition*, Hegan said to himself. *For some it's ego. All most of us want is to know we're not alone. And yet, calling strangers by their first names is intrusive and presumptuous. Then why do they wear the tags? To create a false sense of intimacy,* Hegan concluded. He regretted calling Grace by her first name and thereby perpetuating a social scam.

A signature card was placed in front of Portia. She looked to Hegan for support and saw he was engaged in a smile contest with

Grace. "Dear," she said, yanking on Hegan's earlobe with her good hand, "please hold this steady for me."

Hegan held the card as Portia tried to duplicate Ariel's signature with the tips of two fingers.

"Oooowww! What did you do?" Grace said, finally noticed Portia's bandage.

Piece of cake, Hegan thought, and coughed into his hand to stifle a bubbling chuckle. But Portia was too intent on the forgery to answer.

"Chopping shrimp for finger sandwiches." Hegan saw the woman wince and grimace. "And," he chuckled ironically for effect, "her fingers got caught in the blender."

"No, no. I can't listen."

"It was a bloody mess. But the shrimp were pretty tasty, weren't they darling?" He patted Portia on her shoulder.

Portia finished and knew the signature wasn't even close. She watched Grace try to decipher the scrawl and mentally make the signatures conform.

"I'll need to see your driver's license, Ms. Sutherland."

Hegan noticed her dilemma as well. "This was the first time that bits of actual fingers were in finger sandwiches." He seemed to quote from the *Guinness Book of Records*.

"You're making me nauseous." Grace shivered as she gave the license a quick glance. "Please come this way." Grace led them to the vault, her hands clapped over her ears in case Hegan wanted to provide more gory details.

Hegan carried the safe-deposit box into a private cubicle and shut the door. He placed the box on the counter and waited for Portia to open it. They sat for a few moments looking at each other and at the box. "It won't explode."

"Easy for you." Portia pulled the hasp and opened the lid. Hegan restrained the impulse to take charge and let Portia make the discoveries.

The first item she found was an insurance policy. "I'm cold," she said and slid the policy over to Hegan.

"We're under a vent," Hegan explained, knowing it wasn't the air conditioning that was making Portia cold.

"Some stocks," she said, taking them out of an envelope.

Hegan decided to provide comic relief. "Hope she didn't have Enron."

"No Enron. No dot-com. All pretty solid. That's the kind of person she is... was."

Hegan thought she'd start to crumble, but Portia remained steady.

"Tickets! Plane tickets. Look Chicago to Miami. Miami to St. Lucia. St. Lucia to St. Vincent! S-T-V!"

Hegan's look back was encouraging but noncommittal. "Anything else?" Hegan knew there had to be more. "Somebody went to a lot of trouble. Tossing Ariel's house.... The attack at Daley Plaza was a warning. Which means they need us and we'll stay alive until they get their Cracker Jack prize."

Portia struggled to feel into the box with her left hand then took the easy way and stood the box on end. A mini audiotape dropped to the counter.

"Bingo!" he said, knowing it was the key. "This is why Ariel's house was searched."

Portia paid more attention to the last item out of the box. It was a plain envelope with the word *WILL* marked on the outside in Ariel's hand. Slowly she removed it from the envelope and read the first page. Her sobs sputtered softly at first but built to an uncontrollable, system-wracking explosion. Hegan thought she'd shatter into pieces and wrapped his arms around her to keep her whole. To his surprise, she didn't recoil from his embrace. Her cries were muffled by his chest and her tears seeped into his shirt.

Slowly she stopped crying and wiped her eyes with his handkerchief. "I'm sorry. The will. Everything came crashing down at once."

Uncomfortable with the raw power of Portia's emotions, Hegan opted for a vain attempt at humor. "Don't worry. I'll never tell."

"What a comfort you are to us poor women in need. A regular confidante. First your sister. Now me. It's a full time job." Portia had no idea why she lashed out, and the look of surprise and hurt on Hegan's face brought immediate regret. "I'm sorry." She grasped his hand. "I can be a bitch."

Hegan opened the lion's mouth and inserted his head. "No! Say it isn't so. I could never believe..."

With eyes watery and her nose running, she laughed. "I deserve that."

"You deserve to laugh more," Hegan said and squeezed her hand.

* * *

Portia left the bank feeling more kindly, she thought, toward Hegan. Better than the vindictive or hateful emotions she preferred to have toward her father. Considering her experiences with that seminal male relationship, where did this kindliness, an unfamiliar part of her being, come from? Supposedly, all humans shared a capacity for love and hate, good and evil acceptance and rejection. Yet, she was not ready to be magnanimous toward mankind, to any kind. The scabs of too many wounds would not let her. Kindliness toward Hegan would have to wait.

In the car, Portia looked over at Hegan as he pulled away from the bank. She understood him better than on that disastrous day at Ariel's. He was being helpful. But... . Could she accept him as more than her instrument for avenging Ariel's death? If he helped achieve her goal, what then? Would she raise him up to stand alone in her Pantheon of honorable, useful men? Would the scabs melt away and the scars fade?

All these questions were premature, she concluded. There's no need to diffuse the journey's goal by tacking on a confectionary ending.

"Hand me that" were the words from Hegan that stopped her mind from roving too far.

"Huh? Oh, sorry."

* * *

For the last few minutes Hegan had observed a Ram truck following them from the bank. In the universe of Ram trucks, it could be an overwhelming majority were located, by coincidence, in the Chicago area, he reasoned. Then he remembered a line from *Marathon Man*. Something about once was coincidence, twice happenstance and the third time—watch your ass.

While Portia was preoccupied in another realm, Hegan made several evasive turns that took them away from Ariel's house, their intended destination. With each turn, the smiling chrome of the Ram reappeared in Hegan's rear mirror. Not a coincidence. He'd have to tell her.

"Reach in the back and hand me that hamburger bag," he repeated.

"You can't be hungry. At least not for that."

"Please. Do it."

His soft tone made Portia realize sating hunger was not Hegan's intent. She reached into the back seat and retrieved the paper bag. Before she could further consider Hegan's qualities, he turned sharply onto lower Wacker Drive and they were cruising along the river. "This isn't the way."

Hegan gestured to the paper bag. "Unwrap the hamburger."

"Please don't tell me..." She saw Hegan pay close attention to his rear and side mirrors, did as he instructed, and waited until he told her to take off the bun while keeping watch over the traffic that followed them. "Ugh. There's green slime all over it. I'm gonna throw it—"

"No! Yum. Not slime. My favorite burger, old guacamole."

"You can't be serious."

Hegan didn't respond. He looked into his side mirror and found the Ram drawing abreast. "That's my burger. Don't you eat any of it." He made exaggerated gestures so that whoever was following would think they were undetected. Then he reached into his shirt pocket, took out the mini audiotape, and placed it on top of the burger.

Portia questioned his sanity.

"Wrap it up." She delayed. "Quickly. And make sure your seat belt is tight." His last instruction set Portia into motion. She wrapped the burger, returned it to the bag, and dropped it onto the back seat.

"Hang on." Hegan cut across two lanes of traffic and exited into an industrial area. He sped through a red light and turned into an alley. Not only did his Valiant have cojones under its hood, it had the agility to swerve through the debris-strewn alley. So did the Ram.

The only obstacle in their escape route was the delivery truck ahead which seemed to be backing up into the loading dock. With some luck he'd have enough room to squeeze past.

"I've been hanging on."

"Look straight ahead. Don't look back."

"Could you tell me why?"

"A Ram truck's been following us since we left the bank. I tried to shake him to be sure it was not the same one as the other night."

"And?"

"It's the same."

With twenty yards to go, the delivery truck pulled out of the loading dock and abruptly stopped, blocking the alley. Hegan slammed on his brakes and skidded to a stop. Portia was thrown forward. Hegan's outstretched arm helped break the sudden forward thrust of her body.

CHAPTER TWELVE

Breaking glass froze words unspoken. Hegan and Portia instinctively covered their eyes at the sound. Glass splinters blasted through the front seat of the Valiant. Doors flung open. Portia and Hegan were pulled from the car, keeping their eyes shut to protect from flying debris.

Hegan's eyes popped open to find a man with one functioning eye. A black patch covered the other. Short and stocky. A human bunker buster. Hard body pushing through rough clothes. *A weight lifter's physique*, Hegan thought. The man's stubby but strong hands grabbed Hegan's shirt, shook him like a dirty rug, and banged him up against the side of the car. The rush of air from Hegan could be heard as the sound of surprise or mask for pain. He rallied his strength and found his voice.

"Look, there must be a mistake." *Maybe a wrestler from Eastern Europe.* "Hey, I know you. The wrestler from Milwaukee… ."

"Sure," he said.

Hegan thought he might now have an edge. "The Moldovan Menace. I saw you. Great."

With one hand he banged Hegan's back against the car again. Hegan struggled through the pain.

"My Visa bill's paid in full. I don't need any self-help courses. And besides…"

One hand firmly gripped Hegan's throat while the other frisked the outside of his pants and jacket pocket containing Hegan's badge. The man looked at the shield with contempt and tossed it over his shoulder into a pile of rubbish.

"You're absolutely right. I'm a cop—" A backhand-forehand smash stopped Hegan in midsentence and caused him to consider what a closed fist might feel like. The salty taste of blood trickled between his gum and lip. One last frisk mashed Hegan's jewels.

While Hegan was trying to keep the one-eyed attacker at bay, Portia was struggling with a second assailant. She resisted at first trying to find a way to help Hegan.

Portia saw Hegan crumble and, when he was twirled around like an open parasol to face her, glimpsed the blood on his lip. She instinctively moved toward Hegan, but the taller man pushed her face down onto the roof of the Valiant and jabbed his automatic into the nape of her neck.

"Not now, brown belt." She heard Hegan's voice, as both instruction and warning. She resisted the impulse to strike back, laboriously honed through her life. It felt unnatural. As she'd never encountered men with guns before, Portia rested her hands on the roof of the car.

The Moldovan Menace continued searching Hegan and found the .45 tucked into his waistband. It too was of no consequence and got tossed into another trash heap. MM looked over at his partner and shook his head.

With his automatic at her head, her assailant began a slow, deliberate investigation of Portia's body. His hands wandered down each side and along her arms, snaking around her neck and down her chest. He fondled each breast individually. Portia let him cop whatever he wanted until his guttural slobbering exceeded her patience. She tensed to resist and he tapped her firmly with the barrel of his gun as a reminder. He paused his random mauling for a moment before proceeding to caress the inside of a thigh while shifting the gun so the barrel rested at the back of her head before turning her around to face him.

"Hey!" Portia yelled as his hand roamed up to the top of her thigh. A quick jab of the gun barrel into her throat made her cough and stopped any other sound. He shifted the gun to the center of Portia's back while forcing his hand between her legs and pressing his fingers into her groin. Her lightning-fast backward sweep caught him off guard and forced him to stagger back.

"Goddamn you!" She whirled and connected with the heel of her foot to his jaw knocking him back and against the wall. His gun dropped. She readied the heel of her hand to punch his ticket when Mr. Moldova yelled "*Nyet!*" She saw his gun against Hegan's head, with the hammer cocked. Portia realized Hegan was a nanosecond away from being executed and backed off. Hegan was not a linguist but recognized *nyet* when he heard it and realized the thugs were not locals. *Good deduction, Hegan! Eh, what?* He reproached himself.

Portia was now defenseless as the taller man brushed off his clothes to compose his dignity and regain control. He grabbed her by the throat and slapped her face before dragging her to the passenger side of the Valiant.

"Get bag. Empty. Now!"

Portia, slowly recovering, took her purse from inside the car and spilled its contents onto the hood of the Valiant. Hegan was shoved to the front of the car while the objects in Portia's bag were sifted quickly.

The tall man found nothing of value in the purse and indicated that to MM with a shake of his head.

"Open!" MM ordered Hegan, pointing to the trunk which revealed an old umbrella and spare tire. Disgusted, he instructed the other man to check the backseat. The one-eyed thug applied his vise-like grip to the arms of Hegan and Portia, moving them like cardboard figures for a better vantage.

MM rushed forward when he heard his associate call from inside the car. He was disappointed when the big discovery was a distinctive white bag with golden arches on it.

He opened the bag and announced his find. A string of *nyets* did not stop him from taking a bite until he saw green slime oozing out from under the bun. He tossed the bag and burger across the alley like it was toxic waste.

The Moldovan Menace shook his cardboard figures, asking, "So? Where?"

"Hey, that's the only guacamole burger I've got." MM received a facsimile of a sincere smile but was not impressed. He grabbed Hegan's face in his hand and squeezed until blood ran from his lip and dripped from his chin. The wagging of his stubby finger told Hegan they would meet again.

The Ram truck's horn blasted three times and its engine roared to life but MM didn't move.

"You. Turn!" he commanded Hegan. As Hegan complied, Portia feared they would both be killed. She could no longer be silent.

"Wait!" she yelled, hoping to stop the inevitable. She got no response from MM.

"What? You speak? Huh?" MM grabbed her by her neck and pulled her alongside Hegan. "Talk!"

"I've got money," she blurted. "Take me to the bank. I'll give you money. A coupla thousand."

"Nobody wants you fuckin' money." He spit. "Euros." He grabbed Portia's throat and threw her into a pile of debris. Before she could get on her feet, MM drew back his fist and slammed it into Hegan's spine. The Mondolvan Menace watched Hegan drop to the ground and smiled. His information about the cop's weakness was correct.

"What you doing?" followed by another blast of the horn. This time MM backpedaled to the truck and jumped inside. A quick

Vincent Panettiere | 241

U-turn in one of the loading docks, and they roared out of the alley as they entered.

Portia raced to Hegan's body. She noted the poor job he did of hiding his pain, and she saw the anguish on his face as his body writhed. For the moment she could not respond in word or action. Hearing Hegan's labored command—"Get the burger!"—dissolved her paralysis. As if by example, Hegan struggled to get to his feet, first crawling toward the Valiant and then pulling himself up by inches from the bumper to the taillight and finally bending over the trunk to catch his breath.

Portia was a study in ambivalence. She took a step to help him stand, but decided any help from her would wound his pride and took a step back. She had to find the burger, but she wanted to take him to the hospital. One conflicting thought after another. It was an odd dance to silent music until—

"The burger!" sounded like Hegan's dying breath.

Portia sprang into the rubbish. She desperately rummaged with her hands and feet and without thinking or feeling, combed through the area where she thought it had been tossed.

Hegan staggered toward the front fender in time to hear Portia exclaim, "I found it." She brought the burger to Hegan. He opened it and took out the mini audiotape, wiped off the slime on his chinos, and put the tape in his pocket.

"My gun and badge. Should be easier to find." Hegan struggled to remain on his feet and, leaning on the Valiant's hood for support, pointed to a smaller pile of newspapers and bottles. Again, Portia kicked through the rubbish until she heard the scrape of metal against concrete.

"Here, I think. Yeah. Got it." She lifted the gun by its handle with two fingers as though it were a dead rat or unstable explosive device.

Hegan returned the gun to his holster. "The badge is by that puddle." Portia fetched it. "I think they overreacted, don't you?" He made a courageous attempt at a smile in her direction.

"Give me your hankie and don't make jokes." Hegan struggled to reach into his back pocket for the handkerchief, but the pain produced by twisting his arm and rotating his torso was too great. "I'll get it," Portia said after several failed attempts.

Hegan waited until her hand was in his back pocket before speaking again. "Hey, watch your hands. I'm not a piece of meat, you know. I won't be objectified." Hegan's attempt at humor was not at his best.

"You're a mess. You make jokes. Don't you realize this is serious?" The anger in her voice covered fear, relief, shock.

"Gee. Why didn't I think of that?" he said in a voice as weak as his body.

Portia refused to encourage Hegan, hoping he'd get serious. She wiped the sweat from his face and cleaned some of the blood from his lip. "You may need stitches."

"I'm fine." He opened the car door.

"My ass!" Portia grabbed the keys from his hand and linked her arm with his.

"And a lovely ass it is," Hegan said, taking her arm without protest. Slowly, she led Hegan to the passenger side and helped him onto the seat.

"Where's the nearest hospital."

"No. No hospital."

"Don't get stubborn on me, Hegan."

"I know a better place," he said and motioned for her to get the car started.

Portia drove the Valiant out of the alley and Hegan, slumped against the door, motioned for her to turn right and continue straight ahead. She drove in silence for the next few minutes, occasionally looking at Hegan who massaged his temples.

"You have nothing to say?" she said.

"What about?"

Portia abruptly pulled to the curb and stopped. "Back there." She could not allow herself to be more descriptive.

"Oh, that. We almost got killed. But we didn't. We know who they are. They don't know what we've got. So, we get more points."

"Hegan, we were terrorized and worse. All you give me as explanation is some la de da verbal shrug of the shoulders. And I'm supposed to accept that?"

Hegan's pain caused him to speak in slow, short bursts. "No doubt they want the tape. First they searched Ariel's place. Again at Daley Plaza. Today they got up close and personal. Three times. The same Ram truck. Windshield was fixed. You still believe in coincidence?"

"Okay. No. But who?"

"You hear one of them say *nyet*?"

"Yeah, I guess. Can we stop playing Trivial Pursuit?"

Hegan was theatrically silent. When Portia looked over she found his eyes slowly tracing her thigh from the front edge of the driver's seat back to where it met the curve of her lower cheek.

"Are you lookin' to buy or just browsin'?" she asked, in an accent that was a poor imitation of Mae West.

Hegan went along. "Let me guess. Uh... uh... Dolly Parton."

Portia gave him a playful backhand swipe on his shoulder. "Noooo. Mae West," she said with some laughter in her voice. "Guess I'll never refer to my ass again."

"You also have a beautiful smile," Hegan observed.

"Okay, okay. Let's get back to this *nyet*."

"Not yet. Trying to figure..." Hegan told Portia about seeing Faraci and his men at the paddock as Italian Scallion was led by Ariel's assistant. He explained his initial theory about Faraci and who killed Ariel. "As of this afternoon... all I can say is *nyet*."

* * *

"A florist?" Portia's disbelief reverberated through Diversey Street as she opened the door to Clay's shop. Hegan shuffled inside as Clay came running from the floral arranging room in back.

"What did I tell you? What did I tell you?" Clay's question with implied answer greeted Hegan when he least needed reminding.

"Don't be a Jewish mother, Leon. Call Wu." Hegan said as Clay wrapped his massive arms around him. Clay carried Hegan to his arrangement table in the back of the shop. Hegan's arrival had interrupted Clay's arrangement of spring flowers for a customer. Shears and discarded plant material cluttered the arrangement table.

"Do I look Jewish?" Clay hissed into Hegan's ear as they approached the table.

Hegan's eyes sparkled as he savored his response. "Don't know. Haven't seen if your schlong was circumcised or not."

"And you won't neither."

"What was I supposed to say, 'don't be a black mutha?' Give me credit for sensitivity."

"I'll give you credit. I should drop you, you crazy son of a bitch." Clay noticed Portia, who looked dazed and rudderless.

"Hey you! Miss." Clay yelled over his shoulder. "Get all that crap offa there."

Portia continued to struggle with the state of Hegan's well-being and did not immediately react. "Hey! Do it now!" Portia's response was herky-jerky. She tried to move as quickly as she was physically able. "Just throw that crap on the floor," Clay instructed as he shifted Hegan's weight.

Portia flung herself into the task and after a few seconds had cleaned the table of all but the arrangement. She carefully lifted the overfilled vase and placed it to the side.

"Get me some of that butcher paper," Clay told her and pointed to a spool of paper attached to the wall. "Cut a piece long enough for the table." She did and positioned the paper so that the table was covered.

Clay, gently placed Hegan on the table. Portia wet some paper towel and washed Hegan's face.

"I got something better than that." Clay handed Hegan a healthy shot of brandy. "Martel. Just what you like." Hegan rolled onto his side and tossed it down.

"Leon this is Portia. Ariel's sister."

Clay reached out for Portia, His hand swallowed hers. "Ma'am, I'm sorry for pushin' you around. But this guy here—" Clay interrupted himself by grabbing the cell phone from his belt and hitting speed dial.

"Wu. He's here" was all he said. Then Clay turned back to Portia. "If you knew—"

"Leon, I need some more brandy. Now!" Hegan said, eager to interrupt.

"What? When did I become your house nigga, boy?" Clay took the glass and Hegan grabbed his shirt. "Keep quiet, Leon. Don't say a word." Clay understood.

"If I knew what? You were saying, Leon?"

Clay busied himself checking roses in the refrigerated case before returning with more brandy. "Sorry, Miss. I didn't hear you."

"Before. What were you going to tell me? If I knew what?"

"Tell you? Oh..." Clay's charm machine went into high gear. "Just that him and me, we been friends for years and years. And I couldn't bear to see my longtime, good friend in pain."

"Thank you for your concern, Leon," Hegan said with faux humility.

Before Portia could figure out what had just happened, Danny Wu dashed through the shop and into the back room carrying a plastic shopping bag.

"Woo, woo. Choo, choo!" Hegan called out, showing the effects of one too many Martels.

"Hiya, Mike. Leon. You order one from column B?"

Hegan introduced him to Portia who stared at Wu's white apron.

"Is your office nearby?" she asked with affected naiveté.

"Across the street," to Portia. "Strip, Mike. Just your shirt," he said.

Portia looked through the shop window, but her vision was partially obscured by plants and arrangements. Through the foliage she could barely make out the sign that read Fortune Garden.

"Wu's the chef over there," Clay explained.

"Best bumble bee shrimp west of the Mississippi," Wu said.

"We're east of the Mississippi," Portia said.

"There, too." Wu took a wooden box out of the shopping bag. He opened it to reveal a set of acupuncture needles, a bottle of alcohol, and some cotton pads. He cleaned Hegan's back with a pad soaked in alcohol then wiped it dry with a cloth towel.

Portia could not stand by and watch amateur hour. "Look, I know you mean well, but he has to go to a hospital."

"Easy," Clay whispered to her as if his soft tone was enough. "Be patient and you'll see."

Clay's words caused Portia to defer to his knowledge of Hegan. Her body language was not as certain.

Deftly, Wu let the tips of the fingers on one hand cross Hegan's back from one side to the other. From neck to waist and back, like a Geiger counter looking for metal on the beach.

"Here?" He gently pressed a forefinger a third of the way down Hegan's spine on the left side.

"Bingo!" Hegan responded.

Wu carefully inserted a needle then proceeded to point out five more places and, with Hegan's concurrence, indicated by a series of *oofs*, *ahhs*, and *oohs*, placed more needles.

Portia stood back and away from the action. This was beyond her knowledge or awareness. Hegan seemed to be responding and that was all that mattered.

As Wu continued to manipulate the needles, Clay occupied himself at a utility table in the back of the room. He lined a Spanish olive wood basket with moss and then searched the refrigerator for some flowers.

Wu changed locations and placed a needle in Hegan's heel.

"What did you do?" Hegan asked and Portia tensed.

"Do? You tell me." Wu said.

"It's heaven," Hegan told Wu. Portia relaxed and released a quiet, nervous laugh that went unnoticed by all except Clay.

"That's progress," Wu said. "Now I see the trouble." He removed all the needles in precise order and then started massaging Hegan's neck and back with strong, chubby fingers.

"Phew! You got the spot, Danny. You have the hands of a saint."

"Save your misplaced kudos, Mike. All I want is the hands of Michael Jordan."

"Jordan's a has-been. Gone years." Clay boomed out from the far end of the room.

"So? He's still the best."

"Okay," Hegan conceded. "You've got the hands of Jordan. But the rest of you looks like a baby sumo wrestler."

"Gee, thanks." Wu squeezed Hegan's neck.

"Ouch!"

"Sorry. I'm feeling a lot of heat. You took a bruising."

"No shit."

Clay saw Portia all but shrink into a corner of the room, fear and impotence holding her in place. He brought her a mug of hot tea and motioned for her to join him away from the table.

248 | A WOMAN TO BLAME

"Thanks, Leon." She sipped the tea and could not suppress a need to confide, which was part of Clay's plan. "He was in such pain, but he wouldn't let me take him to the hospital. I hope..." She nodded in Wu's direction.

"Danny Wu? He's got the best hands in Chicago since Michael Jordan. What's more, he makes house calls."

"But a chef!"

"And he's a good chef, too. A regular Ming Dynasty Renaissance man." Clay added some pastel gerbera daisies to the moss and then noticed Portia's bewildered look.

"That guy punched him in the back," she said, trying to make sense of what was inexplicable to her. "One punch and Hegan fell like a tree."

"Wasn't the punch," Clay advised, adding African violets and some other exotic flowers to the arrangement. "You see, Mike got shot in the back two months ago. Slug's too close to his spine. At first, docs were afraid he'd never walk again."

Clay added a Bird of Paradise. "He went to help his sister."

"Teresa? I met her this morning."

"She's the sane one in the family. Even if... but I digress. Anyhow, every time her old man got drunk, he beat her up."

"This is Eddie Perino?"

"Right." He turned to her. "Say, you do get around. So they get divorced 'cause she got fed up and rightly so. This day, sometime after the divorce, the ex drops by without calling like he's supposed. But Teresa's on the phone with Mike. Even though we're playin' cards, he called her every night. Mike races over and they're battlin' on the street out in front. Mike tries to talk some sense into the guy and he pulls his gun."

"Perino shot Mike?"

Vincent Panettiere | 249

"He's the one. Mike threw Teresa out of the line of fire and caught one in his back."

"I flipped him on his back." Portia spoke softly, but with alarm. "Any injury?"

"Yeah. Mike always thought of himself like a champion thoroughbred. Every case was a race to the finish line. Now the cops are makin' him retire. Don't know what he's doing foolin' around with you." He added "No offense" to be polite, shaking his head in disbelief. "And he says he don't gamble." Clay snorted as he added ferns to the arrangement and quickly sprayed the flowers with water.

Satisfied Hegan and Wu were occupied, Clay leaned over to Portia and whispered. "I never told you nuthin', 'cause if he finds out, he'll kill me." He wagged his knockwurst-sized finger at her for emphasis.

Portia nodded to confirm that she understood – both the need for silence as well as the insight Clay had provided. Before she could respond to Clay, Wu pushed past.

"Gotta start dinner menu. See ya."

"Thanks, Danny. You're looking at a new man," he said to Portia, smiling.

"Maybe you can fool the lady. But this is Leon."

"Would you accept reconditioned?"

"Better." Clay smiled at Portia who, warmed by the affection radiating from the big black man, found herself smiling back at him.

Leon gave Portia the arrangement she'd watch him make. "No! For me? It's beautiful."

"Take care of him." Clay nodded over at Hegan, who was getting ready to leave. Portia followed him to the door then looked back at Clay for reassurance. She returned the thumbs-up he gave her.

Hegan insisted he was fit to drive, but Portia refused to surrender the car keys. She drove the Valiant toward his house since it was closest to the florist. Every few minutes she would glance over to check on his condition, half expecting him to disappear, vaporize on her like so many other good people and happy moments had. But each time she looked he was there in the passenger seat, observing street life as they passed from the bustle of neighborhood shopping districts to the serenity of residential areas.

He'd risked his life for her. Why? Was she lucky or entitled? The universe making restitution through the sacrifices of a stranger. He was a stranger; a few days interaction did not make a lifelong friend. But as a person who knew psychic pain, surely she could be touched by the physical pain of another, particularly one who knew he could die or be paralyzed, a slower form of death.

Once, he caught her glance but did not question it, and she quickly turned back to the traffic. Again she looked and he seemed content being a passenger. For a moment she had the unusual feeling he was hunkering down, healing within. These quiet moments with him were becoming familiar, even natural. Before allowing serenity to intrude, her anger started fermenting again. As often happened, she was angry at herself. Vigilance must be maintained at all times.

No one can be trusted. No one can get close. Succumbing for an instant will bring pain or worse.

Lower the periscope. Seal all compartments. Dive, dive, dive! Take her to the bottom. Rig for silent running. She was now in her defensive mode. A growl escaped.

"Hmm? What was that?" Hegan inquired. "There's a grizzly bear in this car."

"Oh, traffic," she said.

"Yeah."

Portia looked over at him to make sure she hadn't compromised her defenses. She hadn't. He understood.

She heard Hegan thank her for driving when they were only a few blocks away. Gratitude could penetrate her defenses, as could understanding, caring, and that most potent, though elusive, offensive weapon—love. Luckily no enemy possessed that threat. *Easier to buy weapons of mass destruction than acquire love*, she thought and decided to end philosophizing for the day. Still, she had to resist attack. No one shall pass. Think *For Whom the Bell Tolls*. No passaran! All this reaction for what? For a simple, ordinary thank you? And she wondered why the corners of her eyes were traitorously moist.

Portia followed behind Hegan as they entered his house. She placed the arrangement on the living room table and, guided by the polar star of her gender, went to the kitchen. Though she was not domestic she heard the words "I'll make tea" spill from her mouth more out of charity than female destiny.

Hegan put on a table lamp in the living room. "Make beer." He pointed to the refrigerator and waited for her to open the door and take out a bottle of Old Style.

"Are you sure this is good for you?"

"Thank you, doctor." Hegan took the beer, popped the cap on the edge of the butcher-block counter, and took a long pull. "Aah! Mother's milk. Have one."

"No, no. I'd rather have tea."

"Weren't breast fed, huh? Whatever." He watched as the embers of emotion ignited across her face.

"What did you say about my mother?"

"I never mentioned your mother." Then he remembered. "You mean that crack about breast fed? That wasn't... look, I never... That wasn't meant to imply your mother. An expression. I love a good bottle of beer; to me it's better than mother's milk."

Portia shook her head to clear the sudden rise in anger. "I'm sorry. You must think—"

"Nothing to apologize for. And don't try to guess what I think. Not that I'm a complete tabula rasa—blank slate, if you didn't take Latin in high school. What I think doesn't matter."

"You see, my mother... I feel so bad for her. How she must hurt. She's not well. Her youngest daughter..."

"I saw how you favored your mother. At the funeral. You were so protective."

"You know, mother-daughter stuff."

"Sure. Seemed more than that. But what do I know?"

Portia resisted the urge to hurl barbs or unload her baggage and bobbed her head a few times in nonresponsive fashion.

He broke the silence. "Hungry?"

"Not really. If you're up to it, maybe you can take me home." When he didn't spark to that idea, she countered with, "Better, I'll call a cab."

"Let me make you dinner. Then you can go home."

Grateful, understanding, caring were the words battering the walls of her castle.

"Do you have any wine?" she asked. "White?"

"Sure do." Hegan opened the refrigerator and took out a bottle. "Chardonnay. From the Anderson Valley in California. Supposed to be pretty good." He uncorked the bottle and poured her a glass.

"To us." Hegan raised his beer bottle in a toast. Bottle and wine glass clinked. And he added, "The survivors."

At first the substance of the toast surprised Portia and caused her to step back emotionally.

"We did. We are." Portia exhaled and sipped some wine. "Very pleasant."

"Yeah? Good. A friend of mine in the Bay Area recommends different kinds to me whenever we talk. Guess that wine's been in the fridge about six months."

"Never opened."

"No reason to." He lied, remembering he'd planned to serve it at dinner the night of Lucy's accident.

"And I'm a 'reason'?" she said taking another sip and raising her eyes to look at him over the top of her glass. *What am I doing? Flirting?* She thought.

"Not a reason," Hegan said. "You wanted a glass of wine. Very simple. It pleases me that you like it. Now, for dinner you have a choice of chicken curry, beef bourguignon, or Chinese takeout."

"Really? You can make the chicken and the beef dish?"

"Sure." He was serious.

"I'm impressed," she said, partly due to the wine and also because she was seeing another side of Hegan. "Can you make the beef with baby carrots and noodles?"

"Sure. Whatever you want." He watched her face turn from an open expression of surprise and elation to the color of deep gloom.

"'Whatever I want' is 'deep as a well and as wide as a barn door' to quote a line from *Romeo and Juliet*."

"A Shakespearean scholar?"

"I'm not. Some things, once absorbed by osmosis, never leave. Now you know the size of my wants."

She took a deep breath, and Hegan decided he need not respond until she'd finished.

"Know what these wants are I can't have?" She drained her glass before continuing. "To see my sister alive. To hear her voice, to embrace her. Could I have some more wine, please?"

Hegan began to refill her glass, and as he poured, she lifted it to her lips without looking, causing some wine to spill.

"But I can't have what I want most! I know that. A part of me is missing and lost forever. What I can have is finding who killed her and making sure he or they never take another breath."

"You want to kill them?"

Portia snapped her head around to observe Hegan. "Why, of course."

"We'll find who killed Ariel, but I can't and I won't let you kill anyone."

"Yessh, I will." She wagged an index finger at him, which was her last gesture before her knees bent and she slumped toward the counter, dropping the glass which broke and spilled wine on the floor.

Hegan caught her before she slid to the floor. She'd only had a glass and a swallow of wine. He tried to imagine what would make her weaken and then he heard her say. "Valium... at the florist. Just kicked in." She tee-heed and closed her eyes.

"Guess you're not hungry."

"Not hungry," she mimicked. "Sleep."

Hegan carried Portia up the stairs to a spare bedroom in the back where his niece and nephew stayed when they visited. Furnished in early juvenile, the room contained two single beds. One had sheets with characters from *Sesame Street* and the other sheets with football, baseball, and basketball players depicted. Portia was asleep when he covered her with the athletic-themed sheets.

Returning to the kitchen, Hegan ordered takeout and then located the Caribbean resort brochure found in Ariel's possession. He dialed the phone number on the back—1-800-555-2565—and waited to be connected.

A woman with a distinctive Caribbean lilt in her voice answered. "American Airlines."

"American?" Hegan thought maybe the brochure was old and the number changed.

"How may I help you?"

"This is American?" He wanted to be sure.

"Yes, sir. How may I help you?" she asked. *Pleasant*, Hegan thought, *not like some phone operators who sound like they're doing you a big service by answering.*

"That's okay. Thanks. I'll call back."

Hegan found the slip of paper he took from LoFrisco's apartment and gave that number a try: 1-800-555-2545. Again, he waited to be connected.

"This is Lufthansa," a woman with a Caribbean lilt in her voice said.

Hegan hung up without speaking. The easy explanation was that, coincidentally, two women taking reservations for major airlines immigrated to the States from Jamaica or some other island in the Caribbean. He also recalled that many companies outsourced their call centers to former British-controlled islands to employ cheap English-speaking labor. This was a more likely possibility, he concluded. Yet, he wasn't entirely sure and dialed Information. The numbers he was given for both American and Lufthansa did not match the ones he'd just dialed. He called anyway. The American operator sounded like she was from somewhere on the east coast, maybe Maryland or Pennsylvania. The Lufthansa operator had an indiscernible Midwestern quality in her voice, definitely not German and not Caribbean either.

Hegan wanted to be absolutely satisfied, convinced beyond any contrived intellectual contortions that might intrude on his reasoning ability. He asked each operator if the airline had more than one reservation number and specifically if it had more than one eight hundred number for reservations. Both operators said they did not. Now it was absolutely clear to Hegan that the numbers on the brochure and on the pad in LoFrisco's apartment were not used to make airline reservations.

Hegan decided to check on Portia and found her sprawled out on little Mikey's bed in a deep wine-paired-with-Valium-induced sleep. He took off her shoes and thought to dress her in one of Teresa's pajama tops which she wore when she and the kids stayed over. But he knew that in the morning Portia would demand to know how and why he'd undressed her, who gave him permission to look at her naked breasts and all the rest just because he wanted her to be comfortable. He decided: (a) he didn't need the complication; and (b) she was too zonked to feel uncomfortable. He returned to the kitchen, opened another beer, and started trying to piece together all that happened in the last twenty-four hours.

"Somebody wants Ariel's tape," he muttered. "They're desperate enough to almost kill two people, one a cop. Twice. The only faces I saw could be connected with Faraci, who is heavy into gambling. A horse and its trainer are dead. Now the Moldovan ape..."

Hegan's battery wore down, and all he wanted to do was rest his head on the dining room table for a few moments.

CHAPTER THIRTEEN

In the morning, Portia found Hegan asleep at the kitchen table, his head resting on his arm. She felt a momentary impulse bubbling up from somewhere deep within, an urge to run her fingers through his hair. But she quickly gulped it back into hiding .Instead, she searched for coffee.

Sunlight and the aroma of freshly brewed coffee woke Hegan. He grunted and stretched, but did not look up until he heard, "You slept there all night?" When he turned, his neck was too stiff to straighten. "Hold it. Don't move or you'll pull a muscle," Portia told him as she ran water in the kitchen sink.

"I never knew that." Hegan stopped talking once she put a warm towel around his neck and began a massage. He felt her steady pressure, keeping his eyes closed to better concentrate on her fingers. He also decided not to recover too quickly. And, when occasionally he felt her hip against his side, he knew that was an excellent idea.

"Your hands are better than Danny Wu's."

"Thank you." She removed the towel and lowered her head to better observe his neck.

With his eyes closed, Hegan was able to hear and feel her breath. "And you're more beautiful."

"Two compliments early in the morning. You must sleep on the table more often." She immediately regretted her awkward attempt at humor. Portia finished massaging his neck and changed tone. "There! Should be much better." The words exuberant and encouraging.

Hegan sat up straight, swiveled his neck, and heard it crack. He turned to see her for the first time. "Hey. Look at you. That's my football jersey."

Portia's hair was still damp from the shower, and she was wearing an old Chicago Bears jersey with the number thirty-five on it. "Do you mind if I borrow it?"

He shook his head and smiled at the incongruous match of jock wear with robo sculptor.

She looked down at the numeral. "So you're old number thirty-five?"

"Not me. That's the number Rick Casares wore in the fifties and sixties when he played for the Bears."

"It's significant because...?"

"Casares was one of a lost breed of running backs. He ground out the yardage four yards at a pop. Nothing flashy, like some of the guys today. Wide receivers with Sharpies in their socks dancing in the end zone. 'Four yards and a cloud of dust' was the expression. There were other guys, like Alan Ameche of the old Baltimore Colts."

"And then there's Mike Hegan," Portia interrupted, "Who gains ground inch by inch. Nothing flashy. Patient. Steadfast." She regarded him with begrudging admiration, struggling to relinquish her core of distrust.

He was lost in old-time football. "Did you know that at one time Casares had gained more yards than any Bear other than Bronco Nagurski?"

"Sorry. Who?" At a moment when she was feeling closest to him, Hegan was off in the land of iron men and leather helmets.

"Nagurski. He's an immortal."

Vincent Panettiere | 259

"Shakespeare *is* immortal. NagoWho? *Was* a football player." As he sheepishly nodded in agreement, she brought him a cup of hot coffee.

"Okay. You have a point."

Hegan stood up with some effort and stretched to reacquaint his muscles with his bones. He sipped the coffee slowly before taking the cassette out of his pocket. He struggled to open a catch-all drawer in the kitchen. First revealed were a hammer and screwdriver. In quick succession came matches, cocktail napkins, candles, string, rubber bands, picture hanging hooks, and miscellaneous items beyond identification. Hegan slowly threaded his fingers toward the back of the drawer and produced a microcassette recorder.

Portia knew this moment would come. Another step on the journey to closure. Her serenity on this morning was shattered just as she was feeling comfortable with Hegan—in his space, with his presence, inhaling his masculine scent from his football jersey.

Portia refused to look at the tape recorder and turned away. She knew it was an act of petulance, an expression of self-indulgence. Also fear. Portia had experienced much worse in her life. She braced herself and turned to Hegan.

"I've stuck my courage to the sticking post. To loosely quote the old bard."

"You know, that's exactly what the old Bronco would say." He raised his eyebrows in wonderment.

In the moment she was amused, Hegan slipped the tape into the player. Her face flooded with uncertainty and dread. He pushed the Play button.

"If you're listening to this, Portia, I hope I'm standing next to you and we're laughing. If not—"

Ariel switched off the microphone.

"Nooooo! I can't," Portia cried.

"Easy." Hegan shut off the tape and stroked her arm. "I know hearing her voice is painful for you. I'll go to another room." He stood to leave.

The initial shock dissipated, Portia stopped Hegan. "No. We're in this together," she said calmly. "Remember, you told me *our* investigation?" He nodded and she indicated that he continue.

Hegan clicked on the machine and after a moment of dead air, Ariel's voice sounded.

"I'd been working for Zenda Farms out of Ocala for five months. The day I got the job I called you and we were so happy. We screamed and laughed and talked so fast that we couldn't hear each other. I was ecstatic and you were happy for me."

Hegan stopped the tape and looked at Portia. She was smiling at the memory. He waited a few moments. "I was so happy for her. What a break. A big farm in Ocala. Horse country. She'd run the operation, chose the horses to train. Great opportunity for anyone—especially a woman in her midtwenties."

"Who's this guy Zenda?"

"That's not his real name. At least not originally. Ariel told me he wanted to be more American and changed it. He's from one of those old Russian republics. Wish I could remember.

Zendofsky. That's it. I think."

"Could be the *nyet* connection."

"Can't be. He loved her. Admired, more likely. Ariel gave up trying to describe their relationship to me." The tape started again.

"April twentieth. A month later I'm in Miami with The Scallion. I like to call him 'The Scallion' because it reminds me of 'The Donald', Mr. Trump. Anyhow, I've been waiting to take The Scallion to Pimlico for a long time. This would be his first big test. Today he looked great in workouts. Great times. Fast. Slick."

Hegan shut off the tape. "Hear that? Fast? I was there the day he finished last. Either he prematurely aged in four months or he was fixed." He punched Play again.

"I broke up with Steve last night. On the phone. At last I'm free."

Now it was Portia's turn to shut off the tape. "See? Steve. That's Steve Gorman, the older guy. There's your motive. Not that he was married, but that she broke off the relationship."

Hegan listened attentively. She was entitled to her theory. "And The Scallion? A coincidence? Like the Ram truck."

"Okay. Okay. That piece of the puzzle doesn't fit. Yet!"

"All the pieces have to fit. That's why it's a puzzle. When you join all the pieces, you see the big picture." He was being pedantic, to be sure, but also determined to move ahead without getting lost in the weeds.

Ariel's voice was beginning to bring less comfort with each bit of the recording. Portia shrugged to cover what she truly felt and started the tape.

"The reason I'm keeping this umm..." Her voice weakened as if on the verge of tears or struck by a tinge of fear. Hegan shut off the tape. He saw Portia tense.

"We have to hear this," he told Portia.

"I know."

Hegan rewound the tape. "The reason I'm keeping this umm... diary... is that I'm being followed. By the same car, every night when I leave the track. I've talked to the cops, but you know how cops are. Never one around when you need one."

Hegan saw Portia wipe tears from her eyes and stopped the tape. She gave him a weak smile and he pressed the Play button.

"After a few weeks, Zenda, the owner, tells me to work more with Frankie. Calls himself the assistant trainer. The guy is a loser. One of those smart-assed New York types who knows everything and won't listen. So I tell Zenda, 'Look I'm the trainer and don't need the fat guy.'"

They heard Ariel's voice raise in outrage.

"So, Zenda says I look tired. Wish he wouldn't be so goddamn paternal. I've had all the 'father love' I need for a lifetime. Including you, make that two lifetimes."

Hegan shut it off and looked at Portia, his face asking questions about what he didn't yet understand.

"That's okay. I'm fine." Portia spoke calmly, but inside she was sucking it up, like a gasping marathon runner or triathlete with the finish line in sight.

"Guy's name is LoFrisco. A loser. Fat slob. But, I said that. Rather than do what I tell him, he hangs around trying to pick my brain. Like he was the heir apparent trying to learn all my secrets before replacing me. Don't know why I'm so paranoid. Maybe it's the car thing. But, hey! Good news. I'm not being followed anymore."

Portia turned off the tape. "What does that mean?"

"Could mean anything or nothing."

"What do *you* mean?" Portia insisted. "I've come too far to accept anything that happened to Ariel as insignificant or coincidental. All must be defined, have meaning, be explored, absorbed, concluded."

"There's a range." Hegan placed his hands on the table, palms facing each other, and spread them two feet apart. "On one end of the spectrum there is no meaning."

"That's not an option," she interrupted.

"Let me finish. Here," he wagged his left hand, "is no meaning. Nothing malicious or suspicious. For example, a worker who left the track at the same time took the same route. Or a parent taking children to soccer practice."

"And they stopped because... ?" Portia challenged.

"Got fired, changed jobs, soccer season ended or the kids stopped playing. Any number of reasons." He looked over at Portia who still watched his left hand.

"Over there," he wagged his right hand, "we have all the harm that might happen. But nothing happened to Ariel in Florida. We know this. Did her call to the cops work, or was she never in danger to begin with? We don't know."

Hegan saw dissatisfaction spread across her face.

"But here," Hegan moved his right hand just to the right of center, "is where we could find a hint, though it's not obvious to us right now. In this position it could be that whoever was following Ariel did it for a reason and got what they wanted. So they stopped."

"Who, who, who?" She hammered at him.

Hegan was struck by her intensity. Her anger remaining so close to the surface. He thought she'd beaten all her anger out in her studio the night of the funeral.

Recovering, he continued. "She was no longer followed. Good news! You heard her?" Portia nodded before Hegan remembered.

"Hey! I saw LoFrisco lead The Scallion to the paddock area for the race. Ariel's 'not available' and he gets his big chance." Hegan was silent for a while, relishing the discovery and the momentum that was building. "Now there's a nexus? Definitely a ten dollar word."

"Confluence is a ten dollar word. Nexus is only worth five."

Hegan was pleased she could express some levity. "Okay. Five. Here's the best part about LoFrisco. I saw Johnny Faraci exchange nods with him at the paddock." He saw Portia's eyes widen. "Wait a second. A few days later... after the race, when LoFrisco has vanished from the track, I went to LoFrisco's apartment."

"And? Come on, Hegan. Stop fencing with me."

"I convinced his landlady to let me in. How doesn't matter. It was a basement apartment. Trashed. Someone got there ahead of me. Didn't know what they were looking for until now." He nodded at the tape recorder. "I found a phone number on a blank pad by the phone."

"A number on blank paper? That's a neat trick."

"Under the light there was an impression. I carefully traced over it with the side of a pencil. It was an eight hundred number. I called it last night and got Lufthansa reservations."

"Now all we have to do is call Lufthansa and find out what flight he was on," Portia said with excitement.

"Except..."

"Hegan! Are you trying to drive me mad? Except? Except what? Tell me."

"Shhh. Let me finish. I also called the eight hundred number on the brochure we found in Ariel's possession. Remember, with Randy?" Her nod told him to continue. "And..." Hegan paused playfully, but Portia didn't bite. "That number was for the American Airlines reservation desk."

"You'd think the number on the brochure would be for the hotel. Blue... something."

"Blue Lagoon. On St. Vincent in the Grenadines."

"Ariel's plane ticket was for St. Vincent."

"She wrote eight hundred S-T-V in the sand."

Portia gasped as she heard Hegan make the connection which took them further but not yet all the way home.

"What doesn't figure is that S-T-V on the dial pad comes out numerically to 7-8-8. Those are not the first three numbers for Lufthansa or American. Besides," he stopped and looked at Portia, trying to decide the best way to share the new information with her. "Besides, I checked with eight hundred information last night, and the numbers we have are bogus."

Portia's shoulders slumped and she hid her face in her hands for a minute, but Hegan could see it was for some kind of mental composure and not to conceal tears.

"Let's continue," Portia finally said, giving him a weak smile of encouragement. Hegan started the tape.

"Today, by accident, I found a syringe in LoFrisco's kit. He told me he was diabetic. First I knew of it. A genetic condition, he explained very casually. Thank God we leave tomorrow for races in the Midwest and up in Chicago. Maybe the sleaze will stay in Miami. Oh. The Scallion's forelock was sore and he scratched at Pimlico. He'll be okay in a few days, more than ready for Arlington." Ariel stopped speaking and an audible click was heard.

Portia reached over and stopped the machine. "Do you have any more of that wine?"

Hegan took an exaggerated look at his watch and gave Portia a glance with raised eyebrow. "Let's see. Eleven thirty in Chicago, an hour later in New York, and at least six thirty in London. Cocktail time."

"If that's a yes, pour it. Otherwise, I'll pour it myself."

Hegan poured the wine, extended the glass to Portia, and then abruptly pulled it back. "You take any Valium yet this morning?"

"No. Sorry about yesterday. I was so stressed."

"No such thing as stress," Hegan said and handed her the glass.

She sipped quickly and fired back. "What makes you the authority?"

"You don't feel stress. You experience life. The conditions of life can be solved by using innate human intellect. We just have to apply that intellect without emotion and social baggage—which is what we euphemistically call stress. But rather than acknowledging and accepting responsibility, we neurotically burden ourselves with the hows and whys of our response to the problem."

"Thank you, Dr. Phil. Now, try condensing that into a fortune cookie."

"*Cogito ergo sum*. I think, therefore I am. Thinking equals human existence. Using human intelligence, we handle existence. The concept of stress is used to prevent us from thinking so we shrink from solving problems. An avoidance technique." He raised his voice to falsetto. "Oh, I'm so stressed, I couldn't possibly... . Blah, blah, blah."

With practiced ennui she asked, "About the fortune cookie?"

"Deal with it," Hegan said, turning on the tape recorder.

"Got a strange call from Zenda last night. Something about his accountant wanting to know why so many calls were made from the phone in the barn to an island in the Caribbean. Saint something. Never heard of it. He thought I was making the calls. As if I have time to gab on the phone."

Hegan pushed Pause. "Somebody was calling Saint Vincent, and the idiot didn't even think he'd be discovered." Again the tape played.

"I became curious about that fat guy. One day I watched him go into and out of a barn we use for storage, not horses. Why would he spend so much time there? A few minutes later I heard strange voices and hid in a stall. They spoke a language I didn't understand but sounded like how Zenda talks when he's on the phone. Maybe it was all my imagination. I peeked over the stall after they left. One was bald and the other tall. Before I could check what they were doing, a truck pulled up and more men ran into the back of the barn. They loaded what looked like stacks of bricks wrapped in plastic onto the truck, covered them with a tarp and roared off, sending gravel shooting everywhere."

Hegan paused the tape again. "Bald and tall?" Portia understood.

"When I thought it was safe to come out," they heard Ariel say, "I went into the back room and found wooden pallets with stacked bricks—I thought. Only each brick was a stack of twenty and fifty dollar bills. What the hell? I'd never seen so much money. I split real fast. Leaving the barn, I saw the bald guy and the tall one come toward me. Whoa! Scary. I gave them a wave and a holler about looking for the fat guy. They both shrugged like they no speaka da English. The look in their eyes was enough to make me shiver in the heat."

Hegan stopped the tape. "Stacks of U.S. currency? Don't think there's a mint near Ocala."

"Meaning, what?" Portia said.

"Back there in the alley I called the bald guy the Moldovan Menace. The other guy looked like a former heavyweight boxer. Now we know they're both connected to fat Frankie, who works for Zenda and also knows Faraci. The money is either stolen, which I doubt unless it came from the billions missing in Iraq, or counterfeit. More likely. Are they all working together? Or is somebody playing both sides against the middle?"

He pressed Play again. "Back in Chicago. Good to be home. Steve wants me back. The Scallion handled the trip like a true champion. We won a few races and placed a close second in two. The Scallion was trailered all the way from Miami and he held up beautifully."

Ariel's tape clicked off and on quickly before she continued.

"I'm being followed again. Some kind of black truck this time. Have to wonder if it's the same folks or new ones who have such an interest in me. Can hardly concentrate at work. Wonder if I'm losing my mind. Some recessive gene gone amok. One of mother's relatives. Remember? And those fits of mother's when we were kids. Epilepsy we were told. Was she genetically mad or made that way by you-know-who? As if that's not enough, I found that creep LoFrisco on the office phone in the barn. All hand-over-mouth, like hush-hush conspiracy stuff. One thing: he's not whispering words of love. Imagine a woman under all that flab. Yech!"

Ariel's last words were followed by about thirty seconds of silence. Hegan checked and found the tape still running. He turned the tape recorder back on. Ariel's voice was heard began again.

"I got home to find the back door forced open and the drawers in the bathroom trashed. Figured it was some neighborhood kids looking for drugs. Cops came. Same old story. Told me to get better locks. Yeah, right."

Portia turned off the tape. "Again, she's followed. There's a break in. In Chicago! This must mean something. Don't give me random chaos theory."

Hegan was thoughtful in his response. "It's very possible LoFrisco was making those secretive calls to Saint Vincent. But we don't know for what reason. Let's listen to the rest of the tape." He pressed play.

"Steve called. Said he's separated from his wife and wants us to get back together. He promised to take me to a romantic island in the Caribbean. I don't feel very romantic toward him, but Steve can be very persuasive. Finally, I agreed to have dinner with him tomorrow, the twenty-fifth. That's all. No harm can come of that. I'm strong enough to resist and wise to all his tricks. Especially the puppy dog eyes. 'We'll see,' I told him. At the least, he'll pay for dinner. At Chez Helene. He wanted to meet at a place on the near North, but I want to be seen in a more public place. My hunch is tomorrow night will be the last time I see him." The tape ended and clicked off.

"The day before she died," Portia said, sobbing softly. She reached for a paper napkin and blew her nose with a goose honk. "This is all very trite."

"Trite? I had that once in a French restaurant."

"You would," she said, her words spoken lightly.

"Someone knew Ariel made tape recordings." Hegan was trying to find order. "Speaking into a tape recorder is not so unusual. Why the interest from Frankie, Zenda, and the others? Why the fear?"

"Don't forget Gorman. She slept with him."

"Gorman's afraid of what? Ariel's gonna blackmail him? I can't believe that."

Portia pressed her theory that Gorman was afraid of losing his marriage. Hegan reminded her of Gorman's separation. That he wanted to spend more time with Ariel. Travel. Get closer.

"Gorman was not a suspect." Hegan said.

Hegan took a coin out of his pocket. "Heads, Zenda. Tails, Gorman."

"Tails."

Hegan remembered a trick he'd learned in grade school. He held the quarter tail-side up so that after several spins in the air, convincing the unsuspecting victim the flip was legit, the coin would land with the opposite side showing.

With a flourish he flipped and Portia kept her eye on the rotating quarter. It landed.

"Heads." He showed Portia and then went off to shower, whistling a happy tune.

* * *

Approaching the Merchandise Mart from the Wells Street side, Hegan realized he'd only viewed the mammoth structure at a distance. Looking up at the twenty-five floors occupying the length of two city blocks, he was dwarfed and overshadowed by the monolith. For a brief moment, the mass of concrete seemed to morph into a monster from *Lord of the Rings*. Suddenly, it symbolized the obstacle preventing him from solving Ariel's death. While Hegan had been clueless on other cases before, this was the first time he felt imperiled by a building.

"I've only seen this driving by," Portia said, intruding. "Massive, but interesting in an over- powering sort of way if you like concrete."

"Fortress architecture from the Depression," Hegan added, getting her attention. "Kind of make-work project."

"The late, un-great dictator of Romania thought the same thing. Only his edifices were white marble, while the people starved. This is why he is now dead."

"We at least mixed some altruism with our greed." Hegan lowered his voice, stuck out his gut and snapped invisible suspenders, imitating a Chamber of Commerce type. "'We're big and we're brawny, and we'll get the country back on its feet.' And they did, too. Roosevelt's WPA, all those projects got the country moving."

"There was that little matter in Europe and the Pacific."

"War is always good for the economy. Every president since Madison has known that.

Clinton's economy was so good that he didn't have to claim the right of preemptive strike."

They entered the building and were consumed by the long corridors leading to a shopper's Disneyland.

While Portia checked the directory, Hegan read aloud from an information pamphlet.

"Says here there are thirteen-point-six kilometers of corridors in this place. Don't know what that is in feet, but I wouldn't want to walk all of it each day."

"Zenda Stylistics, 1522-1525," Portia read.

"That Mr. Zenda sure has a way with words. Stylistics? Sounds like a failed funk group from the seventies."

On the fifteenth floor, they followed signs which took them down shiny corridors—right, left, straight, and right again. "We shoulda left a bread crumb trail from the elevator."

Portia figured Hegan rigged the coin toss. She accused him without evidence, but he was a male and genetically predisposed to the instincts of the hunter—bagging his prey or getting his way. She sped ahead so they could quickly conclude with Zenda and move on to her prime suspect, Gorman.

Hegan closed in behind Portia as they entered to find themselves in the middle of a high tech sweat shop. Two men, wizened beyond their years, worked at long tables. Using electric saws with vertical blades, they cut along patterns on top of stacks of pink material.

Behind the tables, three women rapidly sewed dresses in what seemed to be a familiar synchronicity.

Vincent Panettiere | 271

Hegan approached the bald cutter who was stooped over one table as he created a piece of a cloth jigsaw puzzle. "Bob Zenda?" Hegan asked. The man didn't answer. When Hegan asked again, he pointed to the other table.

Hegan approached the other cutter. Taller, with wavy hair, he resembled the brooding- Russian-émigré-with-noble-bearing character actor Mischa Auer played in old movies. A cigarette dangled from his mouth, its long ash threatening any second to fall onto the table. "Bob Zenda?" Hegan raised his voice.

The cutter looked at Hegan with soulful eyes, took the cigarette out of his mouth, and flicked the long ash on the floor. Before he could speak he was interrupted by the shrill voice of a woman calling, "Manny! Manny! Where are the goddamned side panels?" Manny returned to his work without speaking.

Hegan turned in the direction of the voice to find a diminutive woman bearing down on him. Pencil behind her ear and tape measure around her neck, rhinestone-rimmed glasses perched on her nose, she was on a mission and would not be denied.

If she were an Egyptian galley, her pace would be considered ramming speed, he thought, and then she was in Manny's face.

"Manny! The side panels? Today, Manny. Today." The shrillness in her voice said that to deny her what she demanded would be a personal affront. "I'm dying here," she added in case Manny didn't think she was serious.

Hegan saw Portia was spaced out, on one of her trips to Alpha Centauri. There, but not there. She was zealous, focused, committed, he conceded. But she was cautious with new experiences, needing adjustment and threat assessment before engaging. Hegan decided to approach the older woman instead.

"Excuse me. Where's Mr. Zenda?"

"What?" She noticed Hegan for the first time. "Who are you? What do you want?" She spit out the words at fifty-caliber speed.

"I... we have an appointment to see Mr. Zenda," he said, tipping his head in Portia's direction.

"You came in the wrong door. This is the sample room. You want the office and showroom," she explained to her first grade pupil. Before Hegan could respond, she turned to the other cutter. "Hey, Leo. You on vacation? Get movin'."

Hegan tried to explain that the directory in the lobby said suite 1522, but the woman didn't care. "You want Zenda? Huh? That dreck on rye?" Hegan nodded to each question and she pointed. "Around the corner."

Hegan took Portia by the hand, bringing her back to reality and started toward the showroom. The woman yelled after them as an afterthought.

"Hey, what's your business?" They didn't turn back as she yelled, "Manny! Manny! Cut! Cut!"

No one was in the showroom, and it looked like visitors were not expected. A few dresses hung on pipe racks in a corner, and stylish, Romanov-era chairs were arranged in rows around three sides of a highly polished parquet floor. They could hear the murmur of voices beyond the showroom and followed the sound.

Bob Zenda's office was a study of his conflicted psyche. His face smiled back from framed photos of him standing with horses and their jockeys. Multicolored pushpins fixed sketches of dresses and swatches of fabric to a corkboard. Cartons of takeout were on his desk next to an ashtray that could not hold one microgram more.

The current object of his attention was a young, leggy model in a short skirt who angled herself atop a pedestal. Donald, the tailor, who fashionably used one name, directed the model from his knees as he pinned up the hem of the pink dress she wore.

"Turn darling, turn," he instructed.

"Peoria has seen nuthin' like this, Donald. Not to mention Kiev," Zenda said, observing her legs more than the style of her frock.

Donald stood and faced Zenda. "This will never do." He wagged a ruler at Zenda. "You can't skimp on quality."

"Quality, schmality. All they know is if Sears sells it, they buy it. Ain't that right, honey?" he said and patted the model's flank. "Besides, a friend got me a good price on pink rayon." For emphasis he fingered the material, accidentally catching her lower cheek between two fingers in the process.

Zenda liked what he felt so much, he instructed the model to turn, and when her back was toward him, he reached under her skirt and stroked the inside of her thigh. She looked over her shoulder and smiled down at him, while Donald fussed with the belt around her waist.

"Dr. Zenda, I presume?" Hegan asked, and the trio turned as a unit toward the door to find Hegan and Portia. "You're the noted gynecologist?" Hegan said, eyes on Zenda's hidden hand.

Zenda did not remove his hand. Instead, he replied with impatience, "Yes? What is it?"

"I'm Mike Hegan, Chicago Police Department. I think you know Portia from the funeral. Ariel's sister. We called... ." Hegan wondered how much stimuli was needed to get a response.

"Oh, Portia. I've been meaning to... That's all, Donald." Zenda said. He removed his hand, extending it toward them. Neither took the offer.

"That's all? Oh no, it's not. I need your undivided attention. I won't be responsible—" Hegan was surprised by Donald's reaction, but Zenda seemed angry.

"*You're* not. *I* am. Get out!"

Donald took the model by the hand and helped her off the pedestal. After they left, Zenda closed the door and indicated for Portia and

Hegan to sit. The sofa, layered with material samples, sketches, patterns, and newspaper proof sheets offered no room.

"Make yourself comfortable." They stood. "You called. Now you're here. So? What?"

Hegan followed protocol and showed his badge. "I believe Ariel, your trainer, was murdered."

"I'm sorry about your sister," Zenda told Portia with a respectful half bow as salute. "A fine young woman." Then he growled at Hegan. "What's this about murder?"

"The evidence says murder." Hegan stood his ground.

"Murder? I... I'm completely at a loss," he said, leaning on the desk for support. Zenda collected himself and placed a cigarette in a long, black holder, lit it and blew smoke toward Hegan. "I thought the DA said suicide?"

While Zenda was allowing nicotine to flood his bloodstream, Hegan noticed a stack of pink material on Zenda's desk and peeled off a piece for inspection at a later time.

"Afraid not." Then Hegan changed the subject and pointed at the material. "Silk?"

"As a dressmaker, you'd make a good cop. Not silk. Rayon. A great deal. Let me tell you, it pays to have friends who have friends at bankruptcy court."

"Rayon. Huh. You coulda fooled me. Same stuff as back there. Lots of it here."

"Here, there. All over. Like I said, a great deal. So much, I got no place to store it.

I got more in my garage at home."

"You store any in your box at Arlington?"

Zenda sputtered. "You nuts? That's no place... my box is for business."

Vincent Panettiere | 275

"That was Italian Scallion's most important race, and you didn't watch from your private box? No friends or associates gathered to drink champagne and celebrate?"

"Da." Zenda lapsed into his native tongue. "Yes," with icy inflection. "We sat in grandstand to be closer. For victory celebration. No champagne. No celebration…." His shoulders sagged.

Portia rose to join the fray. Hegan's arm outstretched in her direction told her not to participate.

"You don't come here to talk schmata talk with me."

"Pink threads were found on Ariel's clothes the day she died," Hegan said, raising the stakes.

"So?"

"Hegan, can I have a word with you? Please." She grabbed his arm then gripped it by the sharp points of her finger nails arm pulled him out of the office. "What's going on? You're hiding vital information from me!"

"I'll explain," he said calmly, but firmly and got "No!" in response. Hegan had no time for temperamental scenes. "Be calm. Keep quiet. I'll explain later."

They returned. "Everything okey dokey between you two?" Zenda expressed with mock concern. Hegan ignored the question and went direct. "Mr. Zenda, can you tell me how that pink rayon fiber got on Ariel's clothes?"

"You're asking me?" Zenda took a last puff and stubbed out the cigarette, sending up a miniature Mount St. Helens cloud of ash from the receptacle.

"Did she ever come here to visit you?"

"No. Never. She had no business here." Hegan sensed annoyance in his tone.

"Maybe she visited your box at the track. And that's how—"

"Maybe she got shtupped up there for kicks," Zenda said an impatient tone in his voice. Maybe aliens abducted her. What are you asking?" his voice rising.

"Shtupped?" Portia asked.

"He'll explain it to you later," Zenda responded as Hegan bore in with "By you? I noticed you have a fondness for young women."

"Hey! What are you, the sex police? Don't think you can strong arm me. I'm from Kiev," he said in a louder voice. "Some native American and I ain't talkin Apache woulda called a lawyer by now. My wife's pirogi are heavier than your questions."

Hegan was locked and loaded. "Or maybe she was locked in your skybox and raped."

"Murder? Rape? My life is hard enough. I don't need to help you write trashy novels. I'm busy. Show yourselves out."

"Okay. Fine." Hegan took Portia by the hand. She resisted, causing Hegan to stop. Then he turned back to Zenda. "One last question."

"What's the matter? My English so bad you don't understand? No more!"

Hegan didn't hesitate. "Is Frank LoFrisco still on your payroll?"

"May he drop dead. Wherever he is. Why do you mention that stinking slob to me?"

Hegan couldn't remember when any of his questions got such an energetic response.

Portia watched in disbelief as what she thought would turn into a dry hole suddenly teemed with life and expectation.

"He speaks highly of you." Portia heard Hegan respond and wondered when he would stop being such a wiseass.

"His tongue should fall off," Zenda said, "along with his dick. LoFrisco forged my name to two payroll checks and cashed them at the track. He beat me for four hundred and fifty thousand. But I told your boss all I know."

"Captain Rosen knows about this?" He couldn't imagine Rosen being implicated, but he also couldn't reveal his independent and unauthorized work.

"No, not... who's Rosen? Perino. He's in charge. Look, you find the stinking bastard and there's twenty-five in it for you."

"I'm a professional, Mr. Zenda. Tipping is not allowed."

"The twenty-five's in thousand dollar bills. Not a tip. A reward."

"I get my reward from helping the people," Hegan replied thinking he sounded like Dudley Do-Right. He had one last question. "How have your investors reacted to the loss of your trainer and your prized thoroughbred?"

"What investors?" Zenda said ignoring Hegan by cleaning his ashtray.

"You know, the bald guy with the eye patch and the other one who looks like that Russian heavyweight."

"How... who... ?"

"I think Ariel mentioned she'd seen those guys at your place in Ocala and wondered if they were new investors. She said Frankie knew them." Hegan said a little prayer, hoping the use of a dead person's name would not bring bad karma. Then he worried about mixing religions.

Zenda cursed Frankie in Russian and English. "Oh, those two." He waved them off as insignificant. "Friends of a friend. On holiday from Kiev. They liked horses and went down to see the place. Back home by now."

Hegan indicated he found the answer plausible, even though every instinct and brain cell knew better. He helped himself to a swatch of the pink rayon. Zenda expressed no reaction.

"Thank you for your time, Mr. Zenda," Hegan said.

"Don't mention it and good luck," he said walking them to the door. "Maybe I helped a little?"

"Yes, a little," Hegan said. "Now we have to figure out who raped her."

Hegan and Portia were out of the room before Zenda could respond.

CHAPTER FOURTEEN

As they were driving to the university, Hegan got a call from Randy Crimmins on his cell phone—usually off and ignored, now open for this call. The thread on Ariel's skirt matched the two swatches. All Hegan needed now was a DNA match to find her killer. An hour later, Hegan parked the Valiant across from the Mathematics Hall. He directed Portia's attention to the ivy-covered walls, hoping to deflect her concerns.

"Look at that ivy," he said as they got out of the car in front of the English-Tudor-style building. "If you were a wall, would you want something growing all over you?" He shuddered for emphasis. "And it's bad for the masonry. Makes holes, weakens it. Starts to disintegrate. Then you have to rip off all the ivy. Repair the holes. And I betcha they'd replant it. Insane."

This was Hegan's first visit to the campus since he'd investigated the body in the swimming pool the day Lucy died. Portia had no way of knowing his obsession with ivy was a way to lessen his anxiety as well.

"Definitely," she said with gusto, getting into the same spirit as Hegan.

"Let's see what your prime suspect has to say," Hegan said, climbing the steps two at a time. When he got to the top he turned to find Portia standing below with arms folded and head downcast. "What?" he called to her.

Portia looked up when he returned to the bottom of the stairs.

"Don't make fun of me. I won't be criticized for having an opinion."

"I wasn't. I have my prime suspect; you have yours. I'm sorry."

"How easy to say I'm sorry, but the wound doesn't heal that fast."

This is one of these times, he thought, *when Oy! is the only logical response.*

"Listen to me, Portia. I wasn't trying to wound you." He lifted her chin and looked straight into her eyes. "I would never hurt you."

Hegan saw that Portia understood him, but she was quickly off into another realm. "My father used to say 'I'm sorry' to me, and the words have never meant the same."

"Not now," she said before Hegan could ask a follow-up question. "Let's go talk to my prime suspect."

Portia, speeding ahead once again, located Gorman's office on the second floor. She tapped on the partially open door.

"If you're a student, my office hours start in thirty minutes. Please respect my schedule." The superior tone from within the office dissolved her reticence.

Portia entered the office to find Gorman with his feet up on the desk, his face wreathed in pipe smoke, reading a newspaper; oblivious to anything or anyone else.

"Professor Gorman, I'm Mike Hegan of the Chicago Police Department."

Feet and paper dropped simultaneously. Pipe in his teeth, he blew a mouthful of smoke over his shoulder. He was now face to face with Portia and Hegan.

"Portia? I'm surprised to see you. How are you holding up? I'm so saddened," he said dolefully. "She was very special. I wanted to come to the funeral, but I figured it was for family... you know, private."

"You had no right to be there." Words fired as bullets. "I chased you away. Remember?"

Gorman put down his pipe and reserved direct comment or reaction. He turned to Hegan "You're with the Chicago Police?" He extended his hand, and then quickly and playfully pulled it back. "You're not going to read me my rights, are you officer?" Hegan picked up the paper, saw it was the *Daily Racing Form*, and returned it to Gorman.

"Detective Sergeant," Hegan corrected. "Miz Sutherland thought you could help me solve—"

"As a professor of mathematics, my métier is solving problems," Gorman said.

"Did you know Ariel Sutherland?" Hegan was not going to be jerked around by some arrogant, self-important pedant, particularly one who taught math, the subject he barely passed. *This could be my day to get revenge on all my beady-eyed math teachers*, he thought.

"Of course I knew Ariel," he said slowly. We were good friends. Portia can attest to that," he said gesturing at Portia who he saw looked away.

"We met for the first time at Ariel's house, didn't we Portia? Why are you asking me about Ariel, Sergeant?"

Hegan saw anger rise in Portia as she resisted losing control. Yet her eyes glowered at the man she accused of killing her sister.

"The DA ruled her death a suicide, and I've been sent out to help some politician cover his privates. Know what I mean?" Hegan went into his gee-whiz-aw-shucks routine. "Maybe get some information from someone who... knew her well, shall we say."

"I knew her, but..." Gorman sputtered.

"Did she seem depressed to you?" Hegan wanted Gorman off balance. No professorial filibustering.

"Absolutely not. That's why it was such a shock. When I heard. On the TV. I was stunned." He took a deep breath "Still, I don't understand why you're investigating a suicide."

Portia had enough of this two-steps-up, one-step-back dance. "You kept her in the affair against her will!"

"Please restrain yourself, Miz Sutherland." Hegan had to present an objective demeanor.

"It's a very unusual case," he told Gorman.

"Ariel was a very unusual woman," Gorman responded one male to another.

"She was confused. Intimidated by older men, father figures, particularly if sex was involved."

"Please control yourself, Miz Sutherland. One more time and you'll have to leave the room."

Hegan's intensity surprised Portia, causing her to merely nod and sit back in the chair across from Gorman.

"I wanted to break off with Ariel long ago. I knew she needed someone of her own generation. Her response was always the same. She found younger men too immature. She was quite loving and wanted us to continue. Ariel was very dear to me."

"You were married!" Portia erupted.

"I was. We separated just before Ariel died."

Hegan had seen a lot of scum in his career, but Gorman seemed sincere. Or he was a better actor than Olivier.

He reached over, patted Gorman's hand, and gave him a knowing, we-guys-understand-each-other nod. "You don't have to explain to me. When was the last time you saw Ariel?"

"We had a quiet dinner the night before... ."

"Where was that?" *A logical follow up question*, Hegan thought. *We'll take it slow and easy.*

"The Beau Rivage. Downtown."

"And you just had dinner?" Hegan sounded casual as a surfer.

"Why, yes," he said while examining his pipe.

Vincent Panettiere | 283

"The autopsy report found traces of semen. Did you have sex with Ariel that night?" Hegan thought Gorman should know the male bonding portion of the afternoon's entertainment was drawing to a close.

"Uh... this is really quite personal," he said, his voice just above a whisper.

"So is murder." Hegan leaned over and whispered directly into Gorman's face.

"Murder? I thought you said suicide." Gorman looked from Portia to Hegan and back.

"Murder?" Hegan asked lightly. "Did I say murder? How Freudian. But you're a mathematician, so you may not have studied Freud." Again, he leaned closer to Gorman. "We're all adults here. If you're the one who had sex with Ariel the night before she died, I can rule out foul play." Hegan tried his best, summoned all his strength of will, but couldn't resist. "I can rule out foul play, Professor, but I can't rule out foreplay."

Quietly, but with practiced anguish in his voice, Gorman told Hegan in a low voice that they'd "made love" after dinner.

Hegan hated soft-spoken people. They were all phony, using the appearance of gentility and civility, hiding behind a manipulative facade. A trick to disarm. They speak softly so you'll pay attention to their every word. The world was loud. Get used to it.

As Gorman concluded his admission of intimacy with Ariel, Hegan started salivating. Gorman may have loved Ariel, but as for having sex that night, he was lying through his clenched teeth.

"Did she like it rough?" Hegan yelled. *Take that between the eyes.*

"Sergeant! Please! Enough of this badgering." Hegan was pleased he'd rocked the prof's world, but didn't know if it was the question or the shout that made him react.

"Her eye was cut and her lip was swollen."

Gorman was visibly shaken by that bit of information, not made public in any of the broadcast or news reports. "I-I didn't hit her. I never thought... I'm sorry."

"If you didn't attack her, maybe she punched herself in the eye and cut her lip before killing herself. That'd make her a most unusual suicide. Almost like the suicide who stabs himself in the back." While Hegan regarded Gorman's denial as genuine, for now, he wanted the professor to absorb a lasting image of Ariel's face to motivate his cooperation.

Gorman said nothing. He checked the clock on the wall of his office. "I'd love to continue our chat, but I have a student conference momentarily. If you'll excuse me. I'll be at least half an hour. Maybe we could reschedule for another time." He stood so they'd get the message.

"You've been very helpful, Professor. Thank you for your time." Hegan helped Portia up from her chair and they left.

Gorman, alone and shaken, felt he should make a call and reached for the phone. The knock on his door signaled the student from his calculus class. At least he hoped it was and there would be no more surprises.

Portia and Hegan hurried down the hall without saying a word. By the time the Valiant was in sight, Portia could barely contain her rage.

"He did it! I told you. He lied about dinner. Ariel said they went to Chez Helene and he said Beau Rivage. Did you hear?"

"I heard." Hegan knew they couldn't prove where the couple had dinner, unless someone took a photo. More importantly, it didn't matter. Gorman had lied, but not about dinner. Hegan needed to know why.

"He lied about having sex with Ariel that night. Whoever killed her, raped her. That's the DNA we'll find in the semen on the tampon."

"DNA? We don't know who raped her. Where'll we get DNA?"

Hegan slowly pulled Gorman's pipe from his jacket pocket. "First we'll eliminate Gorman as the killer, because the DNA from his saliva will not match that from the semen."

"If your theory is correct and Gorman didn't kill her, why does he want us to believe it was a suicide?"

Hegan was silent "You don't actually believe Ariel killed herself?" she asked.

Hegan shook his head. "That's what Gorman wants us to believe. He feels guilty about something."

"You think he knew she'd be killed or knew the killer?" Portia made her contribution. Hegan didn't respond.

They sat in the Valiant without speaking. Portia let the new information settle and decided her theory was no longer simple. "What are we waiting for?" she asked.

Hegan started the engine. "I'm trying to figure out if I believe in cause and effect or in coincidence." He backed the Valiant out and started on a series of left turns that brought him to a vantage point where he could observe the entrance to the Mathematics Building. "With any luck, we may have shaken the professor enough to scare him into doing something foolish, which could be in another eight minutes if his student meeting lasts half an hour. For now, we wait for the professor to solve our problem."

Automatically, Hegan turned on the radio and caught the refrain from "Margaritaville."

"Wastin' away again in Margaritaville. Searchin' for my lost shaker of salt. Some people say that there's a woman to blame, but I know it's my own damn fault."

The words once again hit home, and he abruptly shut off the radio.

Hegan took the offensive as a more acceptable means of defending himself from any questions Portia might be planning to ask. "Before... what you said about father figures and sex. And earlier, how 'I'm sorry' had no meaning for you..."

Portia knew the time had come. She would try to be objective while hiding her vulnerability as best she could. "Our father," she began and the words at first sounded prayerful, "the Shakespearean scholar, lionized at university teas, not only branded us with the names of two of Shakespeare's characters to reflect further glory upon himself, but the good doctor..." The words caught in her throat and she stumbled but continued. "The good doctor proceeded to brand us with our first sexual experiences as well." She gagged and coughed and wondered if it was merely a physiological response to the moment or reaction to some reflex memory. "Each time, after he'd finished with us, he'd say 'I'm sorry.' I escaped after three years by going away to college. Then it was Ariel's turn to be favored. She ran away at fifteen and never went back."

Hegan was quiet and respectful of Portia's revelation. "This is why you have no use for men?"

Portia took the question with restraint but remained silent. She was surprised to find the constant, gnawing dread she carried lighten. She wasn't happy and she wasn't giddy. She was relieved.

"Lookee, lookee. Here comes cookie." Hegan said, which brought an unexpected giggle from Portia.

"What language are you speaking?"

"The prof cometh." Hegan pointed to Gorman leaving the Math Building in such a hurry that he left a sea of students in his wake.

"What's the lookee, lookee all about?"

"You never saw Leo Gorcey in the Dead End Kids movies? Damn, you are culturally deprived."

Gorman's pace indicated he was on a mission. Hegan slowly followed him until Gorman walked down a one-way street. He circled the quad, trying to keep Gorman in sight without hitting pedestrians. Portia provided an additional pair of eyes, warning him not to hit preoccupied coeds as they held intense cell phone conversations.

And then, in the flick of an eyelash, Gorman disappeared. Four eyes on him, then nothing. Portia remembered Hegan's last bout with frustration at Ariel's house. She waited for his eruption. This time he was quiet. No ranting and particularly no blaming. Hegan's restraint was significant, Portia thought.

Hegan decided to wait. He parked with a view of the entire quad then let time pass. He knew all might be fruitless. He was also aware, in some hidden place, that this unorthodox approach was the only one he could take.

"Beautiful day." Hegan said. "Sun's warm. Birds chirp. Flowers grow. Warm. Too warm. Days like these, wish I had a convertible

And then the wait was over. Hegan saw the top of convertible retract. It was parked across the quad. A Sebring convertible. Behind the wheel in all his pedantic glory was Gorman. Hegan started the car and Portia reacted. He pointed to the Sebring.

"Voy-la," he said and pulled away.

"A linguist and a detective. What more could a girl want?"

"What more could a *woman* want?" Hegan corrected.

"Excuse me! A linguist, a detective, *and* a feminist." She laughed.

"Don't get carried away," he said and she laughed again.

"Older kids get all the responsibility," Hegan said out of nowhere as they entered the expressway heading downtown toward the loop. "I saved my sister and got shot. You sacrificed yourself but couldn't save..."

Portia just listened. She was aware he'd revealed the shooting for the first time but didn't ask for specifics. There'd be time later. She allowed herself a quick glance at him and felt the outer ring of her defenses slip away.

Gorman led them south past the marina and exited for Meigs Field, the airport for private planes located on the shore of Lake Michigan.

"Aw geez," Hegan moaned.

"Don't tell me. Your back?"

"I'm fine." Hegan tried to wave it off.

"If that moan I just heard wasn't pain, it came close."

"Meigs Field is my death."

"Please tell me this was a prediction from Madam Mona on the astrology channel."

Hegan shook his head while closely following Gorman as he proceeded toward a single hangar at the southern boundary of the field.

"Either I'm in some undiscovered Charlie Chan movie, or I misunderstand the connection between pain and death. How can you not be in pain but nearing the place of your death?" Portia was confused about Hegan, her feelings and their relationship. On a practical level she was more concerned about accompanying Hegan into any circumstance that was preordained to be fatal for him, lest she unwittingly become collateral damage.

"Flight simulator. A computer game. I take off from Meigs Field and always, always, always crash into the John Hancock tower. No matter how long I stay in the air, fly to Wisconsin and back, I always crash. I've never taken off and landed at Meigs Field."

"A computer game," Portia sputtered. "All that..." As Portia sorted through a series of responses, starting with one that was profanity laced and others which contained more elaborate imprecations, Hegan unbuckled his seat belt and opened the car door.

"Stay here," were the last words she heard as he left the car and zigged his way behind the cover of a Piper Cub and Gulfstream then zagged around a few parked cars toward the hangar.

Hegan reached a door on the side of the hangar. He listened, but the sound of planes taking off and circling prevented him from hearing anything. Slowly entering, he found three corporate jets in various states of repair. Or the reverse. Hegan couldn't be sure. He'd never heard of a chop shop for corporate jets but anything was possible.

Intent on their work amid the whir of drills and scrape of metal on metal, no one noticed or paid any attention to Hegan as he affected the bearing of someone who belonged. Nodding with satisfaction and interest, Hegan was in the center of the hangar when one of the workers, eager to help, pointed him toward a double door in the back.

Hegan pulled the double doors open with a flourish, expecting at the least to find a corridor leading to other rooms. Instead he was facing half a dozen older men who went about their business purposefully oblivious of the intruder. These were not Cuban artisans hand-rolling Churchills with gnarled, tobacco-stained hands. They were not retirees kibitzing and playing checkers.

Hegan stood in the middle of a gambling and policy bank. Half of the men worked at two cafeteria-style tables, counting and tabulating policy slips with the aid of an old-fashioned, hand-cranked adding machine. The others sorted, counted, and stacked currency.

"You got business or didja miss the tour bus?" A man closest to the door wrapped two rubber bands around a six-inch-high stack of greenbacks as he spoke.

"There's this guy..." Hegan started out in his better-to-be-called-stupid-than-called-dead persona. Before the man could respond, Hegan heard an undertone of sound. Then, muffled voices.

The man saw Hegan respond to the voices. "Bet I know who you want," he said.

Hegan was about to speak when the whole room stopped to listen.

"I was supposed to be protected!" The voice was Gorman's. Then there was silence. Hegan inferred that whoever was in the room with Gorman now spoke in tones too low for others to hear.

"But you promised!" Gorman's words did not have the soft, cultured, superior tone of the pedant with the power of life or death over a college career. It was the whining plea of someone with petty power, overmatched and overwhelmed by a force he could not control.

The man dealing with Hegan turned to face the others. Almost as one, they tittered to each other, sharing a private joke at the expense of some stupid slob to break the monotony.

"That's him, huh?" the man asked Hegan. "A wimpy-lookin' guy bitchin about life bein' unfair? Wanted The Man to kiss his boo-boo and make it better?"

Hegan imagined how Gorman's class would respond to that description of him. He replied, "Could be him. He talkin' back there to The Man?"

"You kiddin'? Come down here and get his threads dirty? Don't bet on it."

"I'll see him myself!" Gorman shouted as he opened the door to the back office and caused all the men in the room to ogle him as they would a fatal highway accident. Gorman saw Hegan in front of the room, but didn't stop to exchange pleasantries or slink his way out of an embarrassing situation. He ran. The rear door to the outside gave him the quickest egress, and Gorman was gone before Hegan could send a signal to his legs to move.

Hegan maneuvered the obstacle course of men and tables. He tried to get a quick glimpse of who was in the office with Gorman, but the door was closed. Would've been an extra dividend, but no matter. Then Hegan was outside and running—not full-bore, but as best he could.

Portia saw Gorman running away from the hangar. She got out of the car ready to intercept Gorman if he came in her direction. She hoped he would resist and give her the chance to kick him into submission.

Next she saw Hegan valiantly limping, trying to catch Gorman who by now had reached the Sebring. Portia got back into the car and sped off toward Hegan. She skidded to a stop and he slid into the passenger seat.

Hegan pointed for Portia to follow Gorman while he gasped for breath. "We've got to stop Gorman before he gets himself killed."

"Why?" she asked.

"The ol' professor has had dealings with Faraci. You noticed he was reading the *Daily Racing Form* when we visited." Portia hadn't a clue. "I bet the prof is in debt up to his square root. And there's nothing Faraci likes better than an addicted gambler on a losing streak."

"Sure. That's obvious. An addicted gambler keeps on losing money."

"When he owes too much, that's when Faraci can ask for various favors."

"I can't imagine what a college professor... Ariel!"

"With those deductive powers, you'd make a good Beverly Hills cop."

"Never thought I'd want the son of a bitch to live."

Hegan saw Gorman head for the expressway and motioned for Portia to turn into the nearby marina. She hesitated.

"Do it!"

"He's getting away!" Portia said, watching the Sebring disappear up the entrance ramp.

"Turn! Now!"

She did, against all her instincts, and entered the marina. Portia stopped the Valiant where Hegan indicated next to a ramp leading down to a dock. He shot out of the car, and she had to sprint to keep pace. Halfway down the slip, he turned and backpedaled, taunting her with, "Can't you keep up with a cripple?"

Portia saw Hegan near a berth where a twenty-foot cigarette boat was docked. She tore down the ramp as Hegan leaped aboard and joined him.

"What do you think you're doing?" the boat owner demanded. He looked surprised but determined to repel all boarders. Hegan flipped his badge as Portia leaped aboard.

"You can come with us or stay behind. I don't care. Just keep out of my way," Hegan said as he untied the aft line and moved forward.

The owner was a man in his midsixties, radiating the glow of good health and wealth that comes with early retirement from a large corporation. Maybe a CEO who cashed out before the bottom fell. While he may no longer be of use in the boardroom, the boat told the world he didn't lack for machismo.

Hegan couldn't wait for the owner's decision. He revved the throttle and commanded the owner to get the forward line. No sooner had the line slipped from the cleat than Hegan gunned the engine, sending Portia and the owner sprawling onto the deck.

The boat was docked just inside the entrance to the marina, and within seconds, Hegan had it out into the open water of Lake Michigan. By that time, both Portia and the owner had crawled aft and taken refuge in the cockpit behind Hegan who was in his glory. *Nothing like a wide expanse of water and a fast boat at full throttle*, he thought, *while Gorman has to fight traffic*. He chuckled to himself.

"Where we going?" the owner asked Portia, who shrugged and bounced above her seat as the boat hit the wake of a tugboat pushing a scow. "That's okay," he shouted above the cigarette's twin engines. "I like surprises."

Fifteen minutes later, Hegan eased back on the throttle and the boat putted to a gliding stop alongside the dock below Navy Pier. He tied the bow rope to a cleat, motioned for the owner to handle the aft line, and hurried up the ramp with Portia in tow. At the top of the ramp, a line of limousines had stopped, blocking their progress. A wedding party. Hegan saw the young Chinese bride wore a red wedding dress and remembered white was the Oriental color of mourning. Not the best way to start a marriage.

He pulled Portia out of the crowd of well-wishers and into the empty foyer of the Chicago Clipper. Hegan saw that the restaurant's staff was busy preparing the outside deck for the wedding reception.

"Here?" Portia asked.

"Faraci's headquarters. He's a caterer, don't you know?"

"He takes bets and caters weddings?"

"Hey, marriage is always a gamble."

Portia poked Hegan in the stomach without much gusto. Marriage was not for her, but she had hoped to see Ariel married and settled with a loving husband and children. The poke was more a weak attempt to acknowledge his wisecrack than a defense of marriage.

"If the police know Faraci is here, why don't they shut him down?"

"An old Chicago tradition," Hegan said before noticing the Sebring convertible stop and Gorman rush toward the main door. Hegan checked to find the restaurant staff bustling about and silently positioned himself and Portia on either side of the entrance.

Gorman burst through the door. Hegan grabbed him by the lapels of his jacket and bounced him against the wall. Framed commendations from the Zagat guide crashed to the floor and glass shattered.

"Let me go. I don't know anything." Gorman struggled to break free as Hegan's fists pressed against the prof's larynx. Then Hegan tossed Gorman aside.

"I'm tired. Your turn, brown belt." Hegan released Gorman and backed away. Gorman rushed into the main dining room and Portia sped after him. Taking two steps, she was airborne and drop-kicked Gorman across a table in the center of the room sending plates, flower-filled vases, salt and pepper shakers, sugar packets, and chairs in every direction.

Gorman rolled onto his back and glared at Portia. There was no other woman in the world he'd rather pummel, and he didn't care if the cop was a witness. He had to move fast. She was certain to attack again. He popped up from the floor and grasped the back of a chair, determined to surprise her with a swing he knew would connect with her skull.

The sole of her right foot crashed into Gorman's sternum. He was convinced the shock disrupted the electrical impulses of his heart and he would die. Hegan rushed in and prevented Gorman from completely losing consciousness.

"Grab one side," he instructed Portia. Hegan took the other and they dragged the stunned Gorman toward the entrance as the wedding party and guests streamed inside.

"Can't hold his liquor. We're designated drivers. Don't drink and drive," Hegan said to the startled onlookers until they'd passed the crowd and the Sebring was in sight. At the car, Hegan cuffed Gorman's hands behind his back, found the car keys, and dropped him prone on the back seat. Though the sun was still warm and inviting, Hegan raised the convertible's top.

They heard groans coming from Gorman in the back of the Sebring. Portia twisted around to find him slowly waking up. Hegan knew he was out on the ledge all by himself and had no master plan for dealing with Gorman.

CHAPTER FIFTEEN

Gorman opened one eye and got a glimpse of Hegan behind the wheel. His body ached and the handcuffs were cutting into his wrists.

"This is kidnapping. I'll—"

"Protective custody. You're in my class now, Professor. I am holding you as a material witness to murder."

Gorman had never been in handcuffs before. Humiliating, even if no one he knew saw him and he was hidden out of sight. He felt weak and powerless which, on immediate reflection, he realized was the purpose. *Deprive me of my freedom. Mitigate my manhood.*

"You can't do this to me," he wailed.

"Those are my handcuffs on your wrists. It's done." They'd driven past the zoo when Hegan got an idea. "However, if you're cooperative, I'll take them off when we get there."

"Where?" Portia and Gorman said in unison.

"We'll be there in twenty minutes," Hegan called over his shoulder to Gorman and met the question in Portia's face with a canary-eating grin.

Twenty minutes later, as the Sebring entered the familiar parking lot of Wilmette Beach, Hegan told Portia in a whisper that she could stay in the car rather than revisit the scene of Ariel's death. Portia showed her middle finger to Hegan, and he received it as a signal of her participation, with maybe a hint of hostility. He parked near the stairs that led to the beach.

"Sit up," he commanded Gorman, opening the car door.

"I'm not getting out with these cuffs on. It's humiliating." Gorman was determined to wrest control of his being through the naked potency of his superior intellect and will.

Hegan spoke over his shoulder toward the back of the car without making eye contact with Gorman. "You're smart, professor. Which means, if you don't get out of the car right now, I'll drag you out. Academic ass first."

Hegan reached into the back seat and grabbed Gorman by his shirtfront. It tore slightly.

"That's a fifty dollar shirt!" Gorman moaned.

Hegan grabbed a larger clump of material and pulled. Out he came, feet first. Once they touched the ground, the rest of his body, hunched over and arms still pinioned, came out as well. Gorman stood with his back to the car, head downcast and ashamed. His expression of disgrace and embarrassment was palpable to Hegan.

As Hegan removed the handcuffs. Gorman didn't speak and his head remained downcast.

"Don't run or I'll have to shoot you," Hegan said to Gorman.

"He won't get far." Portia spit the words, affecting her best film noir diction. "I knocked you down before, Professor. And I'll do it again. With pleasure."

When Gorman asked where they were taking him, Hegan simply pointed to the stairs leading to the beach. Holding Gorman's elbow, Hegan guided him toward the spot where Ariel had been found. When Hegan looked back at Portia from time to time he saw dread etched on her face as she trudged along behind.

The yellow police tape had long since been blown away by the offshore wind. Hegan could only approximate the spot, but he figured Gorman didn't know.

"I wanted you to see where Ariel died," Hegan said, his words softened by a stiff breeze from Lake Michigan.

Gorman's downcast head sunk closer to his navel. "My God! I didn't know. I never knew anything. You've got to believe me."

Portia jumped into Gorman's face.

"She came down those steps and staggered to this spot. Her arms reached out for help and no one came. Her knees sunk to the sand. She collapsed and died here. Right here. Because of you!"

Hegan pulled Portia away. He put his face next to Gorman's ear so there would be no mistaking his words. "Take a good look, Professor. A young woman died here. Her name was Ariel. She was not some young, impressionable fuckee of yours. She was flesh and blood. People loved her. She died too young. I am going to get the son of a bitch who killed her. Whether you help or not." Before Gorman could respond, Hegan slapped the cuffs on him again and pushed him toward the stairs.

With Gorman once again tucked away in the back of the Sebring, they drove for thirty minutes or more in silence. Though Portia watched Hegan's tirade with Gorman from a distance, she was affected by the emotional heat it generated. She saw in Hegan an intensity of anger and pain that was similar to her own. His prolonged silence, driving as if on automatic pilot, gave her concern. Was his anger building to a destructive end? They'd come too far together for him to self-destruct before reaching their goal.

Hegan interrupted her thoughts by pulling off the road and onto a residential suburban street. He kept driving until the road left the solid brick houses on well-manicured lawns and reached the open spaces of the countryside. Much of what they saw, mostly fields and barns, had not changed for a century. Hegan remained silent, and Portia looked at him gripping the steering wheel.

Next the road bisected a heavily wooded area and then forked. Hegan pulled the car over and skidded to stop on the shoulder's loose gravel. He said nothing, staring at the point where the road veered in two directions. They were surrounded by trees. The tallest and thickest tree at the point of the intersection was dying. A gash four feet from the ground exposed its core to the elements and disease. Above the gash the rest of the trunk angled downward at twenty degrees. Its limbs were bare of leaves, but it had not yet the ashen, ghostly color of a wooden corpse.

"What day is today?" Hegan broke the silence.

"Friday," Portia replied She could not fathom what was happening to Hegan as he continued to stare at the tree.

"I mean, what date?" She told him it was July twenty-fifth. He nodded with understanding.

Without thinking, Portia reached across the seat and touched Hegan's hand which continued to grip the steering wheel. She stroked it and gently prodded one finger free at a time. Hegan either wasn't aware or let Portia have her way, unable or unwilling to resist. When his hand was free, she placed it on her thigh and cradled it with both of her hands. Their fingers interlaced, but his gaze remained on the tree.

"Tomorrow was supposed to be my wedding day. Six months ago on this road, my Lucy couldn't see in the driving rain and skidded on a patch of ice into that tree. The one that's almost dead." Only Hegan's chin moved toward the dying tree at the tip of the fork. "Coma. Died." Hegan's eyes were moist when he turned to Portia.

She shared his pain, wanted to comfort, but could think of not a single word or phrase more profound than the usual trite or inconsequential. To speak those words would only trivialize his feelings and his tragedy. She said nothing. But she lifted his hand and placed a soft kiss on its palm.

Hegan sniffled and smiled. "The tree lived longer than she did. Look at it. Not quite dead. Still hanging in. Like us." He pulled his hand away and took hold of Portia's shoulder. "You and me. Hanging in. We'll live longer than that tree," he assured her with a throaty chuckle. Hegan started the car, made a U-turn at the fork, and sped off in the opposite direction.

As summer dusk gradually turned to dark, the Sebring pulled in front of the Calvary Baptist Church. A spirited, up-tempo rendition of "Closer Walk with Thee" rolled out of the open windows and into the street. Hegan listened for a bit, tapping his foot, and then got out.

"Be right back," he said before jogging up the church steps and entering the front door. The harmonic blend of voices from behind the lectern at the front of the church bathed Hegan in a rhythm and spirit that put life in his steps.

Clay led the choir as they sang, swayed, and clapped to what Hegan barely identified as a spiritual song. The tune was lively and he felt its joy. Hegan's spirituality was superficially deep. Fine for other folks, but nothing on which he cared to spend much time. Clay moved his girth with ease and grace, his rich baritone at times rising above the choir as he brought the song to a resounding close. Clay mopped his sweat-streaked face with a towel draped over the lectern.

"That's it, ladies and gents. See you Sunday. Until then, be righteous." Clay stepped off the riser in front of the choir and returned to the center aisle. Charlotte, the nurse who'd tended Hegan, joined Clay. She took him by the arm in a way, Hegan noted, that was more proprietary than casual. "Hey!" Clay waved as he spotted Hegan at the rear of the church. "You remember Charlotte," he said.

"Leon tells me you've made a complete recovery. Great!" She was warm and strong, a combination Hegan knew would captivate Clay.

"Getting much better, thanks to your tough love approach. 'Lie still, Mr. Hegan!'" he mimicked in falsetto. "Could you excuse us for a minute, Charlotte?" Hegan didn't wait for permission, but directed Clay halfway to the front of the church and out of hearing range.

Charlotte couldn't hear the words, but she didn't miss Hegan's animated exchange or the look of thoughtful disagreement on Clay's face. Ultimately, she saw Clay reach into his pocket and unhook a key from his key ring. Hegan took the key and dashed. He had no time for good-byes.

* * *

The moment he thought to link his pager to the transponder, he knew it was a stroke of genius. When it sounded for the first time, he and Louise were covered in sweat. She'd reached satiation an hour before. He could delay, like stopping a videotape to take a piss. Checking the transponder was more important. He abruptly pulled out, and ignored her cry of displeasure while fumbling for his pants on the floor by the bed. When he took the pager from his pants pocket and checked, the numbers corresponded to the transponder. Hastily, he jumped into his trousers, buttoned the middle button of his shirt, and, in bare feet, padded out of Louise's split-level to his sedan.

The transponder was in the trunk. He saw the red numbers glow in the partial darkness just before the lid was fully raised. When he checked the coordinates, he knew his subject was heading southeast. Since the Sebring was on the move, he decided to bring the equipment inside where he hoped he could resume with Louise without much need for preparation. Without trying, he envisioned her curvaceous Italian cheeks—pasta ass, he called them. Yet he was reminded of his standards. He wasn't in need of some monstrous boot-tee, as the *melanzane* called them. Substantial and shapely cheeks. That's what Louise had. Those cheeks, arched and leaning over a stack of pillows... there was nothing better. As he placed the transponder on the kitchen counter and headed toward the bedroom, he knew he wouldn't need much encouragement to continue.

* * *

The Sebring entered the alley behind Clay's florist shop later that night. One street light barely illuminated ten feet of the alley, and Hegan groped for the lock before inserting the key.

The door opened and Hegan found the alarm system where Clay told him it would be. He deactivated the alarm and turned on the lights in the arranging room as Portia entered, then returned to the Sebring for Gorman.

Hands cuffed behind his back, Gorman was seated in a folding chair in the center of the room, but behind the arranging table so that he was hidden from any inquiring eyes who might peer through the front window. Gorman was tired, disheveled, and cranky.

"You are heading for a lawsuit that will spin your head into orbit. It will end your career, destroy your reputation, and make you unemployable anywhere in the state. As we sit here, my family has filed a missing person report, and every law enforcement agency in two counties is hunting for me."

"No one looks for you until after forty-eight hours." Hegan drew up another folding chair and sat on it backward, facing Gorman. "Okay, professor. Final exam time." Gorman pressed his lips together presenting a thin line of opposition to Hegan. His lips were sealed, but his body language spoke of his disdainful superiority.

"Did you kill Ariel?"

Gorman did not expect a direct assault and flinched at the words.

"No! I've told you," he said in a tone indicating not only his contempt for Hegan but the belief his interrogator was illegitimately conceived.

"Talk, or I'll set the karate kid over there," meaning Portia, "on you again. She whipped your ass twice. Remember?"

"I've got rights." Gorman sounded tougher than before.

"You're not under arrest. I'm protecting you. We're just friends, interested parties, talking. Who killed her?"

"I don't know." Gorman knew being stubborn was his best chance. His will was stronger than theirs and he'd outlast them. Hegan's palm cracked across the side of his head, making his ear ring and Portia gasp.

"Wrong answer. Let's try again. Who killed Ariel?"

The sting of the slap had receded. *If that's the best he can do*, Gorman thought, *I'm not worried*. "I don't know," he said looking straight at Hegan and smiling. Hegan smiled back and backhanded Gorman on the other side of his head. Two ears rang in stereo. Gorman shook off the slap and rose off the chair, trying to stand, only to be met with a violent shove from Hegan that sent him over the chair and onto the floor.

"My shoulder. It's dislocated," he called up to Hegan, lying with all his weight on his arms. Hegan lifted one foot and placed it squarely on Gorman's chest, keeping sustained, firm pressure on it for several seconds. Gorman screamed as loud as he could and Hegan stepped away.

"Yell as loud as you want. No one will hear you. The question remains. Who killed Ariel?" Hegan lifted his foot toward Gorman's chest.

"No more." Gorman tried to turn on his side until Hegan stepped on his ankle. "I gambled," Gorman began.

"Faraci?" asked to Gorman's surprise.

"Not originally."

"When we visited your office, I didn't think you were preparing a lecture on Copernicus from the tout sheets." Hegan helped Gorman onto the chair. "Now is the time to be precise and explicit, professor."

Realizing false bravado was useless, Gorman related how Faraci gave him ten thousand dollars as payment for information on Trujillo, a university janitor who made "loans."

"He charged outrageous interest, and I got in over my head." At the mention of Trujillo's name, Portia shot Hegan a questioning look. He put a finger to his lips before continuing.

"He *gave* you? Faraci's not a charitable foundation. He's a mobster. What were you thinking?"

Gorman felt Faraci would convince the janitor, being an illegal alien, to seek an alternative source of income. He firmly believed the transaction was quid pro quo. One hand washed the other. Done. No debts. Except, six months later, after Gorman relaxed and felt all was well, he received a call from Jeff and was summoned to meet with Faraci.

"I refused to meet with him. It was inconceivable that we had further business. Then Jeff told me I was an accessory to the murder of Jose Trujillo."

"I can't believe Faraci would kill one of his own." Hegan said.

Gorman reverted to haughty professorial demeanor and shot Hegan a look reserved for dumb students. "Jeff, Faraci's thug, told me the Russians ran Trujillo. The Ivanoffs or a name like that."

Hegan absorbed the information and told Gorman to continue. With his defenses permanently breached, he gave them the rest.

Gorman said he was scared but convinced he could reason with Faraci. A derisive snort from Hegan made him pause. Several weeks later, Gorman arrived on time at the designated Michigan Avenue street corner near the latest Donald Trump edifice. Faraci's black Escalade pulled up and Gorman entered, trying not to exhibit any signs of fear. Faraci was not alone.

"I was introduced to somebody named Frankie. Faraci wanted me to work with this big slob and provide him with information. What kind, he didn't tell me. I agreed to meet Frankie at Arlington Park where we would go over specifics. On that first day he introduced me to Ariel."

"Why?" Portia demanded as a way of releasing her frustration.

"At the time, I had no idea." Gorman fell silent and grimaced as if reliving his pain.

"That's it?" Hegan prodded, shaking Gorman loose from his thoughts.

"We walked around the barn area. Frankie made inane comments, and I wondered if this was all I had to do, listen to his ramblings."

The turning point came, Gorman said, when Frankie started making suggestive comments about Ariel—she was young, hot, alone and needed sex. Frankie leered at him like a hungry wolf when he ordered Gorman to "date" Ariel. Then he pumped his fist in a downward angle, up and back, to indicate the specifics.

"I was appalled by the implication. Immediately it became a command. Frankie told me Faraci wanted me to become intimate with Ariel. I absolutely refused. Not because I'm so holy, 'cause I'm not, and not because I couldn't be attracted to her. I hate being told what to do."

"Lot of good that stance did you," Hegan said, unable to resist.

Gorman's pride had ebbed hours ago. He continued without responding. "I was in my office two days later and looked up to find Jeff looming over me. Like he came out of a puff of smoke. Didn't say a word, just laid five photos on my desk. All of them with me and Trujillo in the bodega. In one, Trujillo waved the envelope of cash. Cash I got from Faraci."

Within days of Jeff's visit, Gorman was in Dover, Delaware. Frankie got him a pass to Delaware Park, and it was Gorman's job to pursue Ariel. When they "accidently" met again, he told her he was an accountant interested in learning about the economics of horse racing for a client.

He nodded when Hegan asked if Ariel had believed his story.

"Then what?" Portia jumped in, on the edge of control. "Did my sister fall to her knees in worship? Then suck you off?"

"Easy," Hegan said softly.

"Don't... don't distort..." Gorman explained he was very nervous at first. Ariel was cordial and gradually he relaxed. By the end of the day, he asked her to dinner and was surprised she accepted.

"Okay. Okay," Portia blurted. "You had dinner. When did you fuck her?"

Gorman's voice was strained and thin. "Wasn't like that."

"So, what was it like fucking my sister?"

Gorman found a vein of strength and exploded. "None of your fucking business! Your sister was not some holy virgin—"

"I know. Our father fucked her first."

"Hold on," Hegan said.

"I can still be quite charming, you know. Of course, she was younger..."

"And gullible and easily manipulated," Portia spat across the room, fighting her own war.

"Which worked in my favor," his tone back to its haughty peak. "This enabled me to ask questions about her horses and later provide Faraci with the information he needed."

"What kind of information?" Hegan asked.

"On some of the horses she trained at smaller parks. Like Delaware and—"

"Arlington? Italian Scallion?"

Gorman simply nodded. A warm, gentle smile crossed his face as he remembered. "She was lovely and eager and interested. Something my wife lost years ago."

"Enough with the soap opera," Portia snapped.

Hegan intruded. "So, the first favor was to seduce Ariel. You did that willingly, but there were other favors? Fixing races?"

"At our last in-person meeting, I told Faraci the idea was absurd. Why would Ariel listen to me? I drew the line. Faraci reminded me of the body found in the university pool. Christ! That hit me between the eyes. I-I felt like that guy in *The Godfather*. Remember the horse's head? That's when I realized the body was a message—not only for the

Russians but for me. I had to do what he wanted." Gorman exhaled, ruined and drained.

"We'll take a break now for a few minutes, Professor." Hegan went over to a shelf above the prep sink, took down a ceramic mug with yellow daisies on it, filled it with water and held it to Gorman's mouth. He gulped and was grateful.

"I hope we're finished."

"You should know, Professor, I was assigned to investigate that body the morning it was discovered in the pool. Same day as my fiancée's car wreck. We identified the head and hands that matched Trujillo's torso. That means I'm very much involved. So, we're not finished until I say we are. Continue."

Gorman said he tried to ask Ariel questions about her horses, how they were performing and their chances of winning, but she refused. She wanted Gorman to tell her about the university and talked about her plans to attend someday. She missed not having a formal education. She knew he was married and had a family, but didn't care, happy for the time they spent together.

Portia squirmed in her chair. This was too much information about her sister, whose image had reached a venerated state since her death.

Gorman related how Jeff paid another unexpected visit and showed photos of Trujillo's dismembered body, torso and appendages. Gorman had no idea how the photos were taken or how Jeff possessed them. Clearly this was another example that Jeff and his former Special Ops buddies could do anything at any time.

Jeff also hinted there was other evidence that would implicate Gorman, so for the sake of his family, his career, and his ability to breathe freely—if at all—he should indulge Faraci just this once and do the favor. The favor involved Ariel. Of course they knew about his affair. Jeff laughed as he told Gorman they knew from the very first day. He gave Gorman dates, places. Even date and location of their first night together.

"He played a tape of Ariel moaning and me encouraging her to orgasm." Sweat stained Gorman's shirt and mingled with the grime already present there.

"They what?" Portia asked.

"They arranged the whole thing," Hegan surmised. "A match made in loan shark heaven. Take one horny, snotty professor who gambles on the horses. Someone whose ass they saved, but whose ass they still own. Add one naive, young woman who never had a boyfriend, not even one her own age, but who knows how to respond to the attention of dominating, older men. And the fix is in."

Gorman glared at Hegan. "Once again you don't have all the facts. Faraci knew your father and I worked at the same university," he told Portia. "Ariel Sutherland, this rising star of a trainer in Florida, was his daughter. He made sure I chatted your father up about Ariel."

"My father helped you!"

"No, no. Not help. I got some information about her from him that enabled me to break the ice, so to speak, when I met her in Delaware."

Hegan found it more difficult to accept Gorman's naiveté. "You had to know there'd be a fix. Come on. Faraci wasn't concerned about your sex life. There'd be some result at the track he had to control."

"All I know is Italian Scallion had the buzz. A strong reputation. Winning races on the way up from Florida. Faraci wanted him fixed so he'd lose at Arlington."

"Why?" The word escaped Hegan's mouth without thought. It made him feel foolish asking such a dumb, obvious question.

Hauteur returned to Gorman's face for the first time since he'd been trussed and hustled from the Chicago Clipper. "I wasn't exactly his confidante. But let me help you with simple arithmetic. He was a rival of the Russians..."

Hegan summed up his conclusion for Portia. "The Ivanovs are connected to Zenda whose horse is trained by Ariel. Scallion loses and Faraci hits his rivals where they live. If that happened, Faraci would do… what? Reduce the vig or cancel your debt entirely? Silly boy!"

Portia looked confused by what she'd heard and recapped, trying to understand. "Okay. You get my sister to fix the race, Faraci would win and then you don't owe them any more money."

Gorman shook his head. He was back in the classroom, instructing once again. "Faraci didn't want to win. Faraci wanted someone to lose."

"Who?" Portia spat out question.

"Hegan just told you. Zenda's friends bet on Italian Scallion. He loses and they lose."

"Let's say we buy this theory," Hegan said. "Why would Faraci—"

"The fat guy said something about a vendetta. You know those wops. They always got a hard-on for something. The evil eye. Vengeance. Yeah, that's what it seems to me. Though the fat guy never said exactly. Revenge for some slight. Payback. That's why he wanted Italian Scallion to lose."

"Whatever." Hegan couldn't care less about Faraci's vendetta. "You know something is behind the fix. What did you do next?"

"I raised the issue with Ariel."

"Was it, like, pillow talk while you were fucking my sister? Huh?" This time Portia would not be restrained. "Something like, 'What can you do to fix a race? Now spread your legs?'"

Gorman ignored her, his mind wandering back. "All I did was raise the issue. I asked her to help me out. She got furious. That's when I knew the affair was over. We hung out for a few more weeks and had a farewell dinner to be civil."

"The night you had dinner. Tell me about that." Hegan shifted speed into slow and easy.

Gorman squirmed like a school boy who had wet his pants. "I never... I didn't... . You have to believe me. We ate. We talked. She meant a lot to me. Our relationship was over. She was so dear, so warm. I couldn't blame her."

Gorman recalled they walked down a hill from the restaurant and crossed the street. Near the corner, Ariel got into her car and drove off. He never saw her again.

"Did you tell LoFrisco?" Hegan asked.

"I told them over and over. Finally, one day they backed off."

"Just like that. One day they stopped?" Portia's question mocked Gorman's answer.

"You should know better," Gorman said. He turned to Portia. "Finally, maybe a week before the race. LoFrisco tells me they don't want any more help to fix the race. They'll do it themselves." He stopped talking and they all waited for the next clue down the path to the unknown.

"But?" Hegan asked. "There's always a but. You should know that, Professor." Gorman was silent. "But, what else did they want?" Hegan pressed.

"All I had to do was one more thing for them and they'd cancel my debt. I told them I'd pay them in full. If I had to mortgage my house. Sell it, even. Whatever. I wanted out and was determined to pay my way out once and for all. I'd never gamble again, get help. I couldn't stand them or being near them or hearing their stupid voices."

Hegan saw Gorman was on the edge of a crack-up and softly asked, "Did they agree? Once the money was paid in full they'd leave you alone?"

Gorman needed no prodding to continue his revelations. He'd fully regurgitate, no matter the consequences. "Naturally they'd take payment in full. But now they needed something other than money. 'What else?' I asked. As a way of keeping me in line they reminded me of the Trujillo photos and Ariel's tape, which would go to the cops and my wife unless I did one more thing for them."

"Which was?" Hegan knew they were close and didn't want Gorman to lose his nerve. Gorman had to know he was as much a threat as anything Faraci could serve up.

"All I had to do was take her to dinner. That would pay off the money I owed."

Portia could be contained no longer. "Basically you were a delivery boy? Did you understand? Did you know? Was there a germ of an idea in your stupid head that you were leading Ariel, my sister, to her death?"

"They weren't supposed to—"

"Who raped her?" Portia elbowed Hegan away to get closer to Gorman. Frustrated, she slapped Gorman with her open palm when he professed not to know. Portia was not discouraged. "Why were there rope burns on her wrists?"

Gorman looked at Portia, pleading with her to take his answer as truth, but she would not and slapped him repeatedly until Hegan pulled her away.

"You lied to us in your office." Hegan's cadence was that of a kindergarten teacher. "Didn't you, Professor?" Gorman opened his mouth to speak, but Hegan wouldn't let him. "I'm convinced you didn't have sex with Ariel or rape her that night. What I don't understand is who killed the horse."

* * *

During the two hours he spent with Louise, his pager sounded indicating the transponder picked up signals from half a dozen directions, from northwest to north and then southeast before remaining stationary for more than three hours. He followed the coordinates and narrowed the

Sebring's location to a three-block area on Diversey Street. For several hours he cruised the surrounding streets but could not get a steady, pulsating fix. As a last resort, he drove slowly through back alleys until, in the midst of a section poorly illuminated by one street lamp, the transponder gave forth the signal he'd been waiting for. Up ahead the dark shape of the Sebring gave him visual contact as well. All he had to do was wait.

He drove out of the alley and parked across the street, but not directly in front of the florist shop. All the shops were closed and he was unlikely to be disturbed by foot traffic. The odd car that passed by would get a glimpse of someone taking a nap, if they even bothered to look twice.

Knocking off Gorman would not be easy. Hegan's friend owned the shop and Gorman would not be alone. Getting both of them would bring a double pleasure but create too much heat. He'd end up the victim if both were missed. He needed a sure shot. Percentages told him they'd exit from the rear, closest to the car. No need for Hegan to bring the car in front and attract attention. He expected they would leave at daylight, which in July would be just after five. With his back to Lake Michigan and the rising sun, he could get a shot off without Hegan guessing its source. Now he needed to find the best vantage point for his sniper nest. The rest would be a piece of cannoli.

* * *

Hegan woke to find Portia's head on his left shoulder and her left arm across the right side of his chest. He listened to her breathing, slow, steady and mesmerizing. For a few seconds he found his breathing in sync with hers. He encircled her with both arms and felt an exquisite peace that slowly started to take him under. He woke, abruptly moved and startled Portia. The grey of dawn was sliding through the alley, into the back window.

Portia felt the tremor in her human pillow and opened one eye to locate its source. She smiled sleepily. "You moved. I was so comfortable." As he rose, Portia put her head back down using her hands as a pillow.

"We've gotta move." Hegan checked Gorman, one hand cuffed to the radiator, his head on a bag of potting soil. He looked back at Portia who was trying to get settled again. Then he realized Portia was not surprised to find her head on his chest. She sought it, wanted the physical proximity to him and was not frightened or repelled. That insight disturbed Hegan. Why, he didn't know. He was unsettled by her innocuous overture. Something was not where it ought to be. Now *he* was the one resistant to change.

He kicked Gorman in the fleshy part of his butt. "Let's go, Professor." Gorman woke up more violently than the kick necessitated.

"Huh? Wha? Don't!" he yelled until Hegan shook him into consciousness.

"You had a bad dream, Professor," Hegan assured him.

"Not the most comfy place to bed down," Gorman said as Hegan released him from the radiator and cuffed his hands behind his back again.

Portia finished throwing cold water on her face from the prep sink and dried her face with paper towels. Hegan opened the back door as the sun was shooting down the alley from the east. He shielded his eyes with one hand as he looked in both directions. No one was in sight, but he un-holstered his weapon nevertheless. A shrill beep announced the Sebring's doors had unlocked.

Hegan stepped back inside and turned to Portia who, oblivious to the possibly dangerous situation, was pulling her hair back and securing it with some kind of elastic device.

"This is why women shouldn't be in combat. The platoon would have to wait half an hour for all the women to fix their hair." If she heard, she didn't acknowledge the speech as anything more than the occasional and peripheral Hegan rant.

She looked up when he said "pay attention" in a sharper tone. "I'll take Gorman out first. Once he's in the car, you turn out the lights and lock the door. Then we'll figure our next move."

Portia nodded her readiness, both in spirit and coiffure.

Hegan cautiously stepped out the back door, checked both ways, and then reached inside and pulled Gorman out by his shirt. Hegan opened the driver's door and pushed the seat up toward the windshield. Next, he positioned himself behind Gorman and guided him toward the open door. Two shots cracked through the morning air.

"Get down!" Hegan yelled, but Gorman had already fallen. "Stay inside!" he yelled at Portia, who resisted the urge to investigate.

Hegan crouched behind the front of the Sebring and pointed his automatic in the direction of the shots. He saw nothing but the blinding rays of the rising sun.

Gorman did not make a sound or movement. Hegan turned him over to find a bullet hole in the side of the professor's head. Another had smashed through his left eye socket. He wouldn't gamble any more.

CHAPTER SIXTEEN

The robed and bearded figure was crumpled in a heap at the base of the staircase. Through his barely conscious haze he saw black athletic shoes pad down the exterior steps of the minaret where moments before they had ascended. The man carried what looked like a rifle case. He could not know that it contained the AR-15 with silencer that ended Gorman's life.

Convinced the figure on the floor remained comatose, the man enjoyed the results of his mission. His shots were dead-on. Gorman's unconsciousness was permanent. Retrieving the spent shells, he amused himself by wondering if the killing would be blamed on Al Qaeda. Now, even if the cops could pinpoint the trajectory of the shots, it would be difficult for them to determine the exact caliber of the weapon.

He remembered how the community fought the construction of the mosque and adjoining minaret because it would spoil the historical scale of the neighborhood.

Lucky for him the NIMBY-ites failed.

* * *

A wave of humidity welcomed Frankie back to South Florida as he left the plane and started up the ramp to the Miami Airport terminal. Once again he chuckled to himself and didn't care if anyone else heard, including the old broad who'd been sitting next to him during the flight from Chicago. He felt her throw suspicious glances his way the few times during the trip when he remembered what a smart guy he was and laughed quietly, the girth of his body vibrating, which disturbed her even more.

"Slick!" he said out loud to himself as he reached the air-conditioned concourse. No one took any heed, since it was just another word in mingled sentences from a mass of passengers waiting to board the return flight. He probably couldn't articulate what "slick" meant to anyone, but for Frankie the word indicated a growing self-appreciation. He knew he was safest in a crowd. Anyone who somehow discovered his destination and planned to whack him would kill or wound other travelers. Frankie saw the headline: INNOCENT BYSTANDERS KILLED BY HIT MEN. That awareness made him secure, enveloped in the streams of travelers coursing through the terminal.

Frankie had scammed Zenda and Faraci. It felt good. He figured both were screaming like stuck pigs all the while he traversed the city leaving false trails. "Goin' to Atlanta 'cause my sister had a baby," he'd told the cab driver on the way to O'Hare. Then Frankie allowed a mellow smile to seep across his face so the flow of strangers passing him could look at Frankie and know they were observing a happy man.

One more obstacle and Frankie was ready to grab his dream. First, he hit the men's room, for tactical more than physical reasons. Inside a stall, Frankie opened his travel bag and pulled out a bundle of cash. He waved it and watched it flow one way and the other. For good luck, he kissed Andrew Jackson on the mouth. Frankie wanted to avoid having to dip into his bag every time he needed money. Calculating his expenses, he'd need five grand for Bobby Jayce and, at the most, thirty for a cab to Bobby's, plus the motel, food, and a cab back to the airport the next day. Using his finger as a pen and writing in the air, Frankie divided twenty into six thousand. The first time he lost concentration. He tried again and this time calculated he'd need three-hundred twenties. When

Frankie left the stall, his left pocket had Jayce's money and the right his spending cash. Hopefully, he'd remember which was which.

Jaunty Frankie left the terminal, plowed through the humidity, and got into the first available cab. He settled his bulk and began humming a nonsensical tune like a five-year-old would do, stringing dum-de-dum-de-dums together that come from nowhere and end up in the same location.

"You happy man," the Pakistani cab driver chirped back at Frankie.

"I am," Frankie replied with a wide, self-satisfied grin.

The Pakistani saw in Frankie's grin a cross between John Candy and Reginald van Gleason but would never make the connection. "You have such big smile on face."

"My sister just had a baby. I'm an uncle. I'd give you a cigar, but I'm fresh out."

"That's okay," the driver replied. "I've taken vow. No smoking." He pointed first to himself and then to a "No Smoking" sign in red letters affixed to the dash.

"Religious?" Frankie asked.

"SmokEnders," the driver answered.

* * *

When the cab stopped in front of Jayce's, Frankie forgot which pocket contained which pile of cash. He felt the outside of his pants and, as the right pocket was not as thick, reached in. He found a couple twenties for the driver. The tip was ten dollars and the driver smiled in gratitude.

The front of Jayce's fifties-style tropical bungalow contained at least six pink, plastic flamingos, stationed at varying intervals around the perimeter of the house. Had Frankie been a connoisseur of kitsch, he might have appreciated the presence of one pink flamingo. These were all the same. He didn't see the point, though he noticed the comb on the head of each flamingo was painted a different color.

* * *

Bobby Jayce watched the cab arrive via closed-circuit TV, the camera hidden in the head of the blue-combed flamingo. An electronic eye in the flamingo with the red comb gave him advance warning that a vehicle had stopped for an extended period of time in front of his house. The signal activated a brief, shrill sound and flashing light in Jayce's workroom, provided a view of the visitor, and gave him a chance to escape if he felt threatened.

Within the confines of his modest bungalow, Jayce performed services enabling him to acquire the sobriquet "forger to the stars" after he'd helped Nixon's pal Vesco and some FBI agent from New Mexico escape U.S. authorities.

That label was not advertised freely and known only to a limited few—those who recommended him and those who needed his help. As he watched Frankie's bulk ooze out of the cab, Jayce had second thoughts about taking this assignment. He first gained notice of Frankie at Hialeah and was not impressed. There was nothing specific, but over the years his gut instinct had been reliable. Better to walk away and keep his freedom than give in to avarice and get ten-to-twenty in some fed pen.

Jayce hated fat people. He didn't believe in glandular disease, or genes, or large bones.

Fat people had no discipline. That simple. In his theory, the body was like a computer that produced what it was fed. Garbage in, garbage out. With the body, calories that went in had to come out through exercise or some other expenditure of energy. Which is why Bobby Jayce was a fanatic at working out every day for two hours.

He opened the door and let Frankie enter.

"Hey!" They greeted each other almost simultaneously, but with superficial warmth. Bobby shook Frankie's soft, pudgy, sweaty hand. Repulsed, he patted Frankie's back to wipe the slime off and led Frankie into the living room.

"Take a load off. You want a drink or somethin'?"

"Coke?"

"Only diet."

"Never touch it."

"You should," Jayce advised. "Particularly with your sugar problem."

"Sugar? What sugar?" Frankie rolled his eyeballs to the top of their sockets, indicating the story he spread about having diabetes was false. "Gimme water, then. It'll help my sugar," he said, grinning.

Jayce returned with a glass of water. "I'll be right back." When Frankie started to follow, Jacey waved him back. "Nobody's allowed in the workroom."

"Okay." Frankie, somewhat chagrined, sat back in an overstuffed sofa, the kind where the pillows enfold the occupant. He struggled to get comfortable, but each time he moved, his weight forced him deeper into the pillows. As Jayce returned with a brown envelope, Frankie heaved himself onto his feet. "Like being in a bear trap," he said.

"I hate that damned thing myself," Jayce empathized. "My ex-wife bought it, and I never sit on it. Shoulda told ya." He directed Frankie to one of the wrought iron chairs with padded cushions around a table near the kitchen that opened out onto the lanai. Then he emptied the contents of the envelope on the table.

Frankie looked on with curiosity but knew by the way Jayce fondled the documents that a certain procedure would take place. It did. "Frankie, today is your baptismal day. From this moment on, you are Frank Peters."

"Frank Peters? Frank Peters. Yeah, I can live with that. I can be a Frank Peters. That's me all right."

"Okay. Let's bring it down a notch. Enthusiasm is great, but name changing is serious.

There's your new Social Security card, passport, driver's license and birth certificate, which you'll note I've aged through a special solution." Jayce displayed with pride all the documents in front of Frankie. "Just don't get fingerprinted."

Frankie reached out to scoop up the documents but Jayce was faster and stronger. He grabbed Frankie's wrist.

"First, I need assurances. Gotta tell ya, Frankie, I don't trust a fat guy."

Frankie tried to extricate his hand. "Lemme go. You need assurances, okay. What?"

Jayce pulled back the documents with the arc of his arm like scooping a pot of coins in a poker game. "Fat guys got no discipline."

Frankie rumbled his girth in the wrought iron chair, causing the air to stir. "What's it to you? What are you, the fat police? I got no time to waste with your politically correct bullshit."

Frankie stood, towering over the more diminutive Jayce who never looked up, only pointed to the empty chair.

"Sit."

Frankie returned to his seat like a chastised grade-schooler and folded his arms across his chest in high dudgeon. Jayce took a few moments to decide whether or not Frankie was worth the risk. True, he'd done a masterful job, as usual, and was worth the money. But he didn't need the money. Besides, he knew someone who'd pay a pretty penny for information about Frankie. Make that a shitpot full of pennies. He'd make out two, even three ways. With his arms folded like a kid, Frankie made Jayce's decision easy. One less fat person in the world.

Jayce waggled his fingers, palm-up on the table, until Frankie caught on and reached for the larger wad of cash in his pants. He placed the folded bills in Jayce's hand, saw it close and disappear.

"This is the conclusion of our business. Forever," Jayce responded after pocketing the money. "Remember this." He pointed his thin, but strong, finger at Frankie's nose. "You don't know me. Never met me. I don't want any referrals from you. We will never see or speak or communicate with each other in any way. Failure to comply with these demands..." Jayce paused for emphasis and stared at Frankie but couldn't believe what he was seeing.

Frankie never liked lectures. He didn't like the tone of Jayce's voice either. "It ain't like this is a freebie," he said to Jayce and started picking his nose. No longer listening, he concentrated on a long grey booger.

Jayce slapped the booger out of Frankie's fingers and got his attention.

"And they are demands, not rules or requirements but demands. Failure to comply with these demands, get it Frankie?" Jayce stopped and looked at Frankie again but with less patience. "What are they, Frankie? You listening?"

"Yeah, I hear ya," he said unconvincingly.

"What are they? What did I just say?" Jayce's voice moved up the shrill ladder.

"Demands! That's what you said. You got your money. I'm going." Frankie stood, but Jayce's hand snatched his wrist and forced him down.

"Good boy. You heard me say demands. Remember that. If you fail to comply, you will never drink another Coke or add another calorie to your fat, disgusting body again." Jayce knew the threat went too far, but what the hell. Frankie was finished and the world would be leaner.

Frankie could not voice a word of protest. His tongue was paralyzed by the look in Jayce's eyes and he deflated. Jayce released his hold on the documents and passed them across the table. He watched with satisfaction as Frankie scooped them up—greedily, he thought, befitting one with no self-control over appetite—and stuffed them into his jacket.

"I need a cab," Frankie said, chastened.

Jayce called a cab company but gave an address two blocks away so there would be no record of pickup at his house. He watched as Frankie trudged down the street and kept him in focus for the ten minutes it took the cab to arrive and drive off. Jayce hoped Frankie had disappeared from his life forever. He returned to his workshop and made a long-distance call.

* * *

Clay arrived to open the florist shop at eight and found six patrol cars, two nondescript sedans with red dome lights twirling on their dash, and an ambulance from the coroner's office occupying parking spaces on both sides of the street. He zipped into the first available parking place three blocks away and hustled back. All the way he worried what mayhem could bring these surprise visitors to his shop. Whatever it was, Clay knew viscerally that they weren't buying flowers and somehow Hegan was involved. He prayed his friend was not on the receiving end of any violence.

A uniformed officer blocked his entrance at the front door. "Crime scene. No entrance," said the cop who drew himself up to his full height and made a display of moving one hand to grip the end of his nightstick and the other his gun butt. His legs were splayed, feet firmly planted. Clay could have lifted the cop with one hand and moved him out of the way, but didn't. He regarded himself as a man of rationality and peace. No longer would he react as he did on the football field all those years— bulling offensive lineman out of the way; instinctively springing for a fumble or leaping to deflect a pass.

In control of his feelings, Clay took a step back and looked down on the cop. Clay figured the man was on the job about two years, which wasn't enough time to adjust to situations not covered by the academy rule book.

"This is my shop. I'm the owner," Clay began as the cop settled into his stance.

"Crime scene," the cop said into Clay's paunch.

Clay pointed to the painted letters on the door. "See that? Clay's Florist. I'm Clay." He quickly reached into his back pocket for his wallet, whereupon the cop drew his Magnum.

"I got a situation here!" the cop yelled over his shoulder into the shop and then snapped his attention toward Clay.

"Easy, easy. I'm getting my ID." Clay pulled out the wallet, flipped it open, and showed the cop his driver's license.

Hegan saw Clay at the door but was in the middle of answering the questions of two detectives from the local precinct. When one paused to take a sip of coffee, Hegan covered the short distance to the door and interceded. "Hey! Put that away now! And let him in."

The cop didn't move. "Crime scene. No entrance," he said, eyes straight ahead.

Hegan sensed the cop was frozen on edge and didn't want to jar him into accidentally exploding. He spoke softly. "I called Mr. Clay. He is needed for the investigation. Please let him enter, Officer," he peeked at the cop's name tag, "Powers. I'll take full responsibility, Officer Powers."

Powers, legs still splayed, stepped aside in a way that a garden gate would swing back. Clay entered as Hegan thanked the young cop.

"Whew! Thank you, Jesus!" Clay lifted his eyes skyward.

"Hey, pal. That was me back there. Not Jesus."

"You were his instrument." Clay's faith would not be shaken.

"Only instrument I saw could blow a hole in your gut big enough to... Aw skip it. See if you can help calm Portia. She's in the back." Hegan

Vincent Panettiere | 323

had enough to worry about and didn't want to banter with Clay, which was preferable but under present conditions impossible.

This was the worst day of Hegan's career. Part of him feared he would not even make it to retirement. That he'd be canned, lose his pension, and become the latest poster boy for all that is wrong with lawless cops. There'd be politically correct knee jerking from coast to coast, like with that guy Fuhrman from the OJ case.

When the smoke cleared, Hegan knew the subsequent investigation would reveal he had dragooned a *possible* material witness, obviously against his will, handcuffed him and intimidated him into giving testimony that could not hold up in court. The short list of charges against Hegan could include kidnapping, assault, false imprisonment, deprivation of Gorman's civil rights, as well as complicity in Gorman's death. The papers would call him a one-man street gang.

Worse was Portia's reaction to the gunshots and dead figure of Gorman, as if every hysterical nerve in her body had been activated by methamphetamine. He'd resorted to the only way he knew to bring her back to reality. He'd slapped her. Hard. Twice. She'd been jolted back as quickly as her cheeks reddened. At the same speed, she'd launched her attack against Hegan, fists and legs flailing to defeat him through her formidable martial arts training. Hegan had fended her off as best he could in the confined space of the floral workroom, stalling for time until he could unlatch the spare set of handcuffs he kept in his jacket pocket.

Dodging and weaving, Hegan had firmly grasped Portia's wrist with his left hand and, allowing her to rain blows and kicks to his outer shoulder and thigh, finally snapped on one of the cuffs. He'd dragged her halfway across the confined space and attached the other cuff to the radiator where Gorman had formerly resided, then called nine-one-one.

Moisture rose to the surface of his skin while a wave of sorrow pulsed through Hegan as he remembered Gorman's death and his slapping of Portia. No matter how he sweated or blushed, neither act could be reversed, undone, made right. Each existed as mental bas-relief, three-dimensional reminders that he'd failed—twice. He was aware of past failures, though minor in comparison. This was much worse. With Portia and Gorman, he'd failed their trust in him as protector.

No one had appointed him Grand Lord Protector, though the responsibility to protect was inherent in his role as a law enforcement officer. The whole world knew this wasn't his case. He made his choice to sit on the edge of the limb, blithely sawing away, head in the clouds, focused on some inner sense of justice and obligation. The branch broke.

Regret and disappointment dissolved into the next scene of his psychic life to reveal Hegan's morose side. How quickly life—lives—can change. In his experience, the change usually was not for the better. Immediately Hegan recalled Lucy's death, less than twenty-four hours after an exquisite night of lovemaking.

Now, eight, maybe twelve, hours after finding refuge in Clay's shop, Gorman was dead, trust was broken, and a trail of felonies brought ruin in the wake of an unblemished professional career. He snapped his finger, indicating to himself the rapid finality of it all.

"Hey, Hegan. Rosen wants you," he heard a voice say as a cell phone was thrust into his face. The brief conversation with Rosen was neither a conversation nor an exchange.

Hegan only spoke two words: "Yes sir." He thrust the phone into the air, where it was taken by the same disembodied hand. Rosen was just what Hegan needed had he been inclined to jump off a building or discharge a bullet into his brain. Since Hegan intended to take neither path, he accepted the sharp command from Rosen in stride, aware of the fated, conclusion that awaited him downtown.

Hegan caught Clay's eye as he knelt next to Portia, her back against the wall, legs drawn up in a semifetal position. She seemed calmer. Whether she had been comforted by Clay or was catatonic,

Hegan couldn't tell from that distance. Clay found Hegan at the front door and learned of Rosen's summons.

Clay's unexpected absence from her side at first caused Portia to feel vulnerable. Slowly she drew upon an inner resolve that had emerged over the last few days. Strange, she recalled, tossing fists and feet at Hegan did not give her the same or any feelings of superiority and invincibility she'd felt during practice at the dojo—only a release from fear and anger, but not strength.

Clay returned to find Portia no longer needing to huddle in the corner. He used the key Hegan had given him to unlock Portia's handcuffs. The rich tones of Clay's voice soothed a raw place inside. She was grateful to him. His words of faith and redemption were comforting, even if the subjects were not what she cared much about until now. Because of those words she would forgive Hegan and try to understand her reactions to Gorman's death.

Clay accepted Portia's gratitude and offered to help if ever he could. He told her Hegan was ordered to a meeting with Rosen and not available just yet to accept her forgiveness.

* * *

The peristaltic rumblings in Hegan's stomach were loud enough to be heard the moment Captain Rosen paused in his monologue. "That you?" he asked Hegan, who once again had one cheek poised on the arm of the chair opposite Rosen's desk. Hegan nodded at Rosen, who this time officially sat behind his desk, hurling questions. "You eat?"

"Yesterday."

Rosen pushed back from the desk. "We'll go across to The Arsenal. Come on." Both were silent in the elevator, knowing it was the last place where anything of a sensitive nature should ever be discussed.

The invitation to lunch made Hegan feel he'd crawled out of the abyss, maybe not very far from the edge, but at least out of the pit. "Hey, the Cubs got a real shot," Hegan offered in Rosen's direction. Four heads in front turned back to look at Hegan. Their faces questioned his sanity, paternity, and planet of origin.

Rosen had no choice but to comment, else the others would brand him the same way they did Hegan. "You nuts?" Rosen opened. "They're twenty-six games out."

"It's only July," Hegan added. "Still early. Three months to go." The stares from the other occupants of the elevator, including Rosen, did not diminish.

"Two months," Rosen corrected.

"Maybe a wildcard," Hegan continued without much conviction. Not good enough for the crowd. "Keep hope alive?" He spoke before the elevator stopped and the doors opened.

"A real shot?" Rosen spat the words into the air like a hairball just as they reached the sidewalk where a cab stopped, blocking their chance to cross in the middle of the block.

Portia flung open the door, its edge hitting Rosen in the highest bony prominence of his kneecap, which meant it hurt like hell. "Lady!... Watch where the fu—"

Portia didn't hear or see Rosen. "Hegan, I came as soon... I'm so glad..." She threw her arms around his neck and hugged him. Hegan, paralyzed by surprise, stood with arms at his side and let himself be hugged.

"You know this broad?" Rosen asked.

Hegan stepped out of Portia's embrace and introduced them.

The Arsenal was across the street from Police Headquarters. A venerable cop hangout, it was more a clubhouse than a restaurant, a little less, even, than a bar with food. No one actually cared what they ate, but they were confident that anything heard within its walls stayed there.

Hegan watched Portia disarm Rosen before they reached the front door. He was acutely conscious of how she maneuvered herself closer to Rosen, pushing Hegan to the rear. More outrageous than that, she accidentally tripped reaching the opposite curb so that Rosen had to stem her fall by wrapping his arms around her. She lavishly gushed and cooed her gratitude to Rosen. Hegan did not believe clumsy from a woman who could stand on one leg and lash out with foot and fists like Jackie Chan.

Hegan's paralysis got worse during lunch as Portia launched her offensive. She played every card, from bereaved sister to angry feminist, throwing in determined seeker of truth and justice and hinting at her distrust of the system, which included the police departments in every city in every country.

Rosen ordered another vodka gimlet and gulped the onion when the waiter brought their burgers. Portia swallowed her Stoli on the rocks with olive and ordered another. Hegan stuck with Old Style.

Mercifully, Hegan concluded, Rosen agreed that Gorman was in protective custody and their efforts needed to focus more on his killer than any breaches—no matter how flagrant, though well intentioned—Hegan had committed.

There was one area in which Rosen remained adamant. The St. Vincent angle was too wild a leap. No connection was made. It was not on anyone's radar screen; consequently, no one would be sent by the city of Chicago on taxpayer funds to visit the island.

Portia would not quit, fueled by a third Stoli. Rosen, who up to now had shown great restraint and kind understanding, became more rigid. Hegan knew Rosen was determined to help him retire with dignity and his benefits. He also saw all that goodwill fly away the more Portia pressed her case with "that's ridiculous and foolhardy of you, Captain. And, I must say, symptomatic of the constipated thinking of a very gender-specific, piggly-wiggly kind."

A smack in the chops could stop Portia and save his future, but he'd already done that in the last fifteen hours. He did the next best thing.

Portia looked surprised when the recently filled glass of ice water came spilling off the edge of the table and into her lap. She jolted up from her seat, knocking over her coffee cup, which added its contents to the water. Hegan went to the rescue with a ketchup-smeared napkin. Mixed with the liquid, a brownish-pink hue formed on Portia's light-colored slacks, which Hegan didn't find unpleasant, though he wasn't about to ask her opinion.

"I'll take care of this, Captain. You've got more important things... Thanks for lunch."

Rosen was eager to get away from Portia. There was a disturbing intensity about her that he considered, bordering on what he felt, though not a mental health professional but with enough street smarts and experience - he had to conclude - nutso. Sure, she functioned like anybody else—work, pay bills, buy groceries, hold a conversation—but he knew once the thin filament around her psyche was breached, she'd explode.

Seeing her at work and on the verge of eruption during lunch, Rosen began to feel sorry for Hegan. Somehow she glommed onto him and hasn't let go. Poor son of a bitch, he concluded, reaching his office; it's none too soon that he retires and gets rid of all the wackos in his life.

Hegan waited while Portia went to the ladies' room to clean up the mess he'd made being "helpful." Relieved that Rosen understood the Gorman tragedy, he took sips of cool coffee and allowed himself to enjoy his escape from imminent doom.

Now more at ease, Hegan's inner voice began calling him toward the island of St. Vincent, less for the tropical breezes than for what he believed was Ariel's heroic effort to provide a clue.

Hegan decided Portia could find her way and left The Arsenal. He pushed open the front door of the restaurant and almost knocked down

Eddie Perino, who quickly removed surprise from his face and replaced it with a sneer, the kind junior high school rivals might exchange passing in the hall.

Hegan had been to college and simply flicked his disdain-filled eyes over Perino before stopping. "Hey, Eddie," he called over his half-turned shoulder. "I got a tip for you on the Sutherland case."

"Go tip yourself."

Hegan turned to fully face Perino. "The Caribbean. Place called St. Vincent." Perino revealed no more than a flicker of recognition in his eyes. It was enough for Hegan. Confirmation there was a connection between losing gamblers and the death of a young woman. For emphasis, Hegan quick-drew, Wild West style, an imaginary gun from an imaginary holster, pointed his forefinger at Perino, cocked his thumb and mockingly shot him. "Bang!" he said in case Perino didn't get the message.

Hegan took a cab back to Clay's shop. As the cab pulled up, Hegan saw only a single squad car and the truck of a glazier indicating something unusual had happened during the past six hours.

Hegan wanted Clay to know his plans in case they went awry.

"The house goes to my sister. She's also the beneficiary of my life insurance policy,"

Hegan advised Clay in the car as they drove back to his house.

"Easy. Don't get all dark and spooky on me," Clay half listened and half denied what he heard and half tried to make breezy retorts. The whole was less than the sum of those parts. Nothing added up and left him a mass of conflict.

"I'm relying on you to take care of things."

"You sure you know what you're doing?"

"As Ariel was dying, she tried to give us a clue. I can't let her down." Hegan felt this was his last chance to do right by someone who trusted him, even though Ariel didn't know who would take up her cause.

"At least tell Rosen."

"No. He made it clear. No one was to go to St. Vincent."

"What? And you, you like some warped knight, some romantic putz, you'd risk—"

"What? Tell me. What do I risk? If I'm wrong, I look like a retard or I'm dead. But if I'm right... and, Leon, I just might be right. I could get all the numbers to fall in place and *whamo!* The safe opens with all the answers."

Clay could only shake his head in response. "At least," he started, not knowing where he would end, vamping riffs along the way, "at least take the sister along. What's her name?"

"Portia? Without question, no."

"Play the odds, man."

"You know I don't gamble anymore."

"Just listen. If you go, there's a good chance you'll get killed. If you take Petulia..."

"Portia. With her, there's a two hundred percent chance I'll get killed. Tell her nothing. Tell her I'll be back in a few days."

"Where'd you go?" Clay gave in to the inevitable. There had always been an obsessive streak in Hegan. He'd known that from the early days of their friendship. Once Hegan made up his mind, it closed like a bear trap.

"Tell her I got called up to the mother ship for in-depth sexual probing by extraterrestrials, and if she plays her cards right I'll put in a good word so she can get probed too." He stuck his hand out and shook Clay's paw as the car stopped in front of his house. "See ya" were Hegan's last words as he got out.

"She'll know I'm lyin'," Clay yelled through the opened passenger window, but Hegan did not respond.

* * *

Faraci summoned Jeff to his office. "We located our friend," Faraci said, taking a short puff on his Cohiba. Jeff listened attentively while Faraci unfolded the information.

"His name is now Frank Peters." Faraci handed the man a plane ticket. "And he has moved out of the country. We don't want him to find his way back."

* * *

The stewardess announced they were making their final approach to Arnos Vale Airport on St. Vincent, a volcanic oval at the north end of the Windward Islands. Hegan knew they were closer to South America than the southernmost region of the continental United States. He'd located the island on a map. Soon he would know how it felt to stand on one of the tiniest specks on the planet.

Automatically, Hegan checked to make sure his seat belt was secure, though he'd stayed strapped in and seated during the entire thirty minute flight from Barbados. He also made sure Portia's belt was fastened as she rested her head on his shoulder where she'd been sleeping for the entire trip.

The drone from the engines in the Bombardier de Havilland made sleeping easy. He felt himself getting drowsy several times. Rest was now a luxury.

A slight crosswind buffeted the fifty-seat aircraft as it neared the runway, causing its wings to waggle from side to side. Hegan took the motion in stride, but Portia woke up startled.

"We're landing," was all he said, still miffed she was with him.

July was midpoint of the rainy season in St. Vincent which meant it could rain or not. Grey clouds loomed on the horizon as Hegan and Portia stepped off the plane and onto the tarmac. They headed for a door in the terminal marked Bwee Express and quickly found themselves in line for customs.

The official, a young man in a stiffly starched light-blue uniform shirt, inspected their Illinois driver's licenses and return tickets and passed them through. Hegan and Portia exchanged disbelieving glances, not able to fathom their informal entrance onto the island.

"They should try that at O'Hare," Hegan commented. "Maybe the planes would take off on time."

But he knew that could never happen. He'd succumbed to the lure of the tropics, where visitors look upon the easy lifestyle as a template to measure the rest of the world. No doubt the islanders look upon life in North American metropolises as an unattainable goal, longing to participate in their pulsating rhythms. They had no idea of the personal cost until they were trapped in its pull. Then it was too late.

His meanderings trailed off as they reached the baggage carrousel where another surprise awaited. The baggage area, such as it was, consisted of a corrugated tin roof with open sides allowing the pleasant breezes to flow through. On the north, Hegan could see the runway and mountains in the distance. Presently, a tractor pulled luggage carts to a stop, and handlers placed the luggage in a row before twenty or so waiting passengers.

Their luggage was in the third cart. As Hegan took a step toward the first piece, a brown hand reached for it. "This yours, sir?" a young man asked.

"Hey!" Hegan barked defensively, the way he would under similar circumstances in any big city airport. He was on guard and not ready for the pleasant, smiling face of the cabbie trying to be of assistance.

"My name is Charles. At your service, sir."

"What's the idea?" Hegan was not ready to toss aside the self-protective instincts he'd built up over decades.

"Time and tide wait for no mon," Charles responded, a cheery lilt in his voice. "Where to?"

Hegan looked over at Portia for support, but she was zoned out on the mild climate, her face turned, eyes closed, in the direction of the balmy breeze which ruffled the scarf around her neck. Hegan watched it flutter behind her and thought of Isadora Duncan, strangled to death by such a scarf. For a brief moment he entertained a similar fate for Portia. This was his trip, his mission, and she'd shanghaied him!

"Sir?" Charles asked, saving Portia's life. "Where to?"

"The Blue Lagoon." Hegan said.

They followed Charles to his cab, a bright yellow 1968 Plymouth Valiant parked at the curb no more than ten feet from the baggage area. "Look, Hegan. He's got your car!" Portia said, too loudly for Hegan's preference.

"Very good. Let's get in the car." As Charles put their bags in the trunk, Portia once again reminded Hegan of her displeasure.

"I still can't imagine how you could leave without me. If Leon hadn't called... ."

"Damn Leon" was all Hegan could say when Charles returned.

"The Blue Lagoon. A perfect choice. You want Charles take you on special tour?"

"Not today, thank you, Charles," Hegan said

The route to the Blue Lagoon took them through the middle of Kingstown, the capital and main city of St. Vincent.

"This be Kingstown." Charles seemed determined to give them a tour, whether they wanted it or not. Hegan doubted he was being stubborn, only proud of his home and eager to share it with strangers. "Capital of our fair island and its main city."

Capital and *city* were not words Hegan would use to describe Kingstown. He thought *quaint* was more descriptive. Most of the commercial buildings were one story and none seemed to have been built after the late nineteenth century.

"There be de church of St. George." Charles pointed to a neo-Romanesque church that dominated the main square. It too was made of brick and stood as a solid reminder of the glory days of British rule. "He de patron saint of St. Vincent."

"Why didn't they name the island St. George?" Hegan asked openly, without irony or sarcasm.

"Don' know, mon. Since I been born, always been dat way. Saint George de church and Saint Vincent de island."

Most of the people on the street were locals. Those Hegan bothered to identify as tourists either had assumed the easy gait of locals or appeared to be of elderly vintage.

"Where are all the tourists?" Hegan said, trying to make up for his brusque rejection of the special tour by making conversation with Charles.

"This be de rainy season. Not many tourists come so far to get wet," Charles explained. Then he shot his arm through the open window and waved a welcome to the broad back of a man who had eased out of the barber shop.

"Mr. Frank! Oh, Mr. Frank!" Charles warbled as he slowed down the cab. Mr. Frank half-turned into profile and returned a two-fingered papal blessing of a wave in response to Charles.

Hegan's mind had yet to adapt to the languid pace of St. Vincent. It whirled with conflicting approaches, trying to juggle too many new complications. He felt unprepared and out of his natural environment. And there was Portia. She was a burden, an intrusion. Now he had to act and think for two, when he was unable to determine what to do with himself.

All his rumination deflected Hegan from noticing the recipient of Charles's greeting. But, when Charles turned to give a departing wave as the taxi eased past Hegan caught a peripheral glimpse of Frankie.

"Who was that?"

"We just pass our American benefactor. Maybe you know him?"

"Just because we're Americans doesn't mean we know all our countrymen." Portia jumped in.

"Who was that?" Hegan asked again, keeping on target.

"Mr. Frank Peters."

"Yes, of course. Mr. Frank Peters." Hegan nodded at Portia. Hegan knew who was walking the streets of Kingstown. If it wasn't Frankie LoFrisco, it was a masterful recreation, almost like a Saddam Hussein double. This was information he would not share with Portia.

"You know him?" Charles asked.

"No. Sorry. There's just too many Americans, I'm afraid."

Hegan smiled at Portia, concealing his discovery.

"Dat's okay," Charles said. "But St. Vincent now have six Americans on de island."

"Uh-huh," Hegan answered without much thought. He reconsidered. "Six? Who are the six?"

Charles was willing to play along. "You and de missus," Charles said as if explaining the obvious to a child. "Mr. Frank and his lady..." Charles stopped to remember.

"Oh. He has a lady?" Something got Hegan's pulse quickening. It was another Zen moment. He knew the other two Americans were not tourists who liked to get wet. Had to be others who wanted a piece of LoFrisco or his action, whatever that is, he concluded.

Charles thought for a few moments. "Not sure, sir. My friend pick dem up. And dey disappear, like a phantom. Maybe dey go fishin'."

A phantom? Just what Hegan needed. And without his magic, phantom-catching decoder ring.

The cab started its ascent up a steep, winding road bordered on each side by deep green foliage. Here and there a stray banana tree grew wild as nature intended. Hibiscus bloomed in a variety of shades from yellow to fuscia. Occasionally there was a break in the greenery, and a glimpse of their progress up the hill became apparent.

"Look!" Portia was the first to notice the town of Kingstown laid out in miniature and the aqua-colored water lapping at the edges of the black sand beaches. Hegan gave a perfunctory look and nod of recognition to Portia, but he couldn't wait to get to the hotel, dump her in the room, and pick up the trail of LoFrisco.

Foliage bordering the long driveway up to the Blue Lagoon was kept low to give arriving guests an unobstructed panoramic view of the island and the surrounding Caribbean Sea which bordered the western side of the Island, the Atlantic Ocean on the east. The cab stopped alongside a hundred-year-old banyan tree. Its stately branches covered the cab and all else in shade for a circumference of twenty feet.

"I'm Mike Hegan," he said to a pleasant, white-haired Englishwoman at the front desk. Portia stood over his shoulder and watched as the woman checked the registration and then eyed Hegan.

Hegan pre-empted any embarrassing questions. "There are two of us now."

The woman looked relieved. "Right. Well, then. Welcome, Mr. and Mrs. Hegan, to the Blue Lagoon. And may I add my congratulations."

She plucked a large brass key off a wooden board behind the front desk and handed it to Hegan. "I've put you in Browning cottage," she said. When that reference didn't get any recognition, she added, "You know. Elizabeth Barrett Browning. 'How do I love thee? Let me count the ways.' Hmm?"

Portia could not resist. "Journey's end in lovers meeting; every wise man's son doth know. *Twelfth Night*."

"Thank you," Hegan said, smiling sheepishly. He was playing the reluctant bridegroom. Whatever that was, reluctance was a constant. Just another sword he—instead of Portia—had to beat into a work of art.

The hotel consisted of a series of cottages and low buildings surrounded by lush tropical vegetation. A porter waited for them outside the office and led them through a maze of paths to their cottage, which seemed to be at the far and very secluded end of the hotel's property. Built in the style of a Victorian-era gingerbread house, their cottage easily could have been found in the countryside of the English Lake District. This one had a bower of frangipani on one side of its entrance and tall hibiscus bushes on the other. The porter took the key from Hegan, opened the door, and set the bags down inside. He smiled at the couple before Hegan tipped him the few loose dollars he had in his pocket.

Hegan thought Portia was too quiet. He watched her as she examined the cottage, more like a large suite with a bedroom and sitting room. The cottage was bordered on three sides by a veranda wide enough to accommodate a few chairs and open a chaise lounge.

Portia stood motionless at the veranda railing for what Hegan guessed was eight to ten minutes. He knew she didn't want to be disturbed and concentrated on putting his clothes in the armoire opposite the queen-size bed. It was the only bed, a delicate matter Hegan didn't want to tackle just yet.

He returned to the sitting room as Portia left the veranda. Moist streaks on her cheeks caught the fraction of sunlight from the front window.

"You've been crying." It was a statement and a question. "Why?" He resisted the urge to comfort her, convinced Portia's force field, not always apparent, was not far off and could be activated to repel him on command. He stood still as she advanced, not certain of her intent.

Portia threw her arms around his neck. Tears trickled from the corner of her eye and down his cheek. Unlike the last time, when she'd embraced him in the presence of Rosen, he was not paralyzed and managed to wrap his arms around her at rib cage level. He could feel her taper up from the waist and also knew her hips delicately flared out below his arms.

"'You've been crying.'" She mimicked Hegan through sniffles that also dribbled on his cheek as she buried the side of her face into his neck. "Oh Hegan!" She drew her head back but stayed within his arms. "You have such a remarkable grasp of the obvious."

"Thank you, I think," he replied, looking into her eyes and not relaxing his arms. "You made fun of me, but you didn't tell my why you were crying. You'll let me know sometime between now and the end of the world?"

Portia squeezed her eyes tight to contain the welling tears and blinked them away. "This is all so beautiful. It makes me happy to be here. I haven't felt happy in a long, long time. I've forgotten. When it came back to me I was overwhelmed."

She stopped sniffling and her face brightened. "I need to take a shower."

Hegan sniffed dramatically. "You sure do."

Portia slapped him lightly on the shoulder then took his head in her hands and kissed him fully on the mouth. It was more than a platonic kiss but did not cross the border into the realm of foreplay. "Thank you," she added for emphasis.

Hegan held her for a moment longer than required. Lucy had been dead for six months and most of his libido died with her. Now, he stood with a woman in his arms, one who could restore a piece of his soul. He could feel Portia begin to pull away, unwrapping his arms from her waist. She was also drifting out of a moment in his life. Unlike the loss of Lucy, he had the ability to stop her. As she freed all of herself except for one hand that Hegan held by the wrist, he reeled her back into his arms and kissed her until they both were nearly deprived of oxygen.

"You're welcome," Hegan added for emphasis.

"Hold that thought." Portia slipped off to the shower.

Hegan did not question the kiss. It felt right, but now he had to find Frankie. He waited to hear the roar of the shower and then unzipped an inner pocket of his suitcase and took out his forty-five.

Hegan hurried from the cottage, unsure of the direction back to the main office. The first path took him in a circle until he spotted an arrow that pointed toward the main building.

Hegan emerged from the lush, verdant foliage in time to spot Charles pulling out of the circular drive. "Charles! Wait!" Charles stopped the yellow Valiant and waited for Hegan to climb inside.

"You want de special tour?"

"Maybe," Hegan began. "Your American benefactor..." Hegan sidled up to the subject.

"Ah, Mr. Peters." Charles replied. "He de one who buy de big house on de hill."

"He must live here full time then?" Hegan asked as Charles put the taxi in gear and started its descent.

"Now he do. He smart man, Mr. Peters. First he come down and set up big business. He such a happy man; he move his whole life to St. Vincent."

"I guess he opened a hotel or a restaurant. I mean, this is a tourist island. What else is there?" Hegan set up the quiz so that Charles could fill in the blanks.

"Oh no, sir. He make lots of jobs for island girls."

"Forgive me, Charles. All I see for people to do here is work with tourists. Maybe some agriculture. Do they make handicrafts like lace tablecloths or paint pottery?"

Charles shook his head then answered with pleasant derision in his voice. "Dey are all high-tech marvels."

"High tech. Really? Must be some computer assembly plant then, huh?"

"Charles show you."

The cab returned through the quaint streets of Kingstown and down the road leading out of the city. Untethered cows grazed lazily by the road as Charles took Hegan past small farms and fields of sugarcane.

At the edge of one field, Hegan noticed a cone-shaped building made of field stone. He tried to make sense of its shape and utility, finally asking Charles. "Dat very old mill, sir. For sugar. Top part gone long ago. Big sails. But de rock is sturdy, just like folks of St. Vincent."

"A windmill. For sugarcane?"

"Exactly, sir. Plenty like dat all over de island." Charles shifted into second gear and turned down a side road that ended in an ornately designed iron gate. An armed guard stood by the gate which was anchored by two stone pillars.

Hegan was not impressed by the old shotgun the guard slung barrel-down over his back.

He did wonder why such precautions were needed at the St. Vincent School for Girls, as the bronze plaque attached to one of the pillars indicated.

"Why the armed guard, Charles?"

"Not to worry, mon. He my cousin Avery." Charles waved out the window of the cab, and Avery opened the gate for the taxi to pass.

Through the windshield, Hegan saw the winding road open up to a massive colonial mansion. He thought it was most likely the largest building on the island, built of the same red brick as St. George's Church and other buildings in town. The difference Hegan spotted immediately.

Two thirty-foot satellite dishes sat at either end of the roof, incongruous with two brick chimneys in the center. Hegan recalled they were the same size dishes as he'd seen on top of the Chicago Clipper. Such a coincidence might be just that, but then he recalled his lecture to Portia about the nonexistence of coincidence unless it was on *CSI*.

"For many years dis be St. Vincent School for Girls. But today most young people leave for jobs in Barbados or Trinidad. Mr. Peters help keep our children home. He build modern wonder."

Charles parked the cab in front of the main steps and led Hegan into the building, again assuming his role as tour guide.

"Originally de building house de McBain family dat come from Edinburgh in Scotland. Dey come here one hundred, one fifty years ago. At one time, old folks say, all dis be sugar. Den come de crash and so dey pack bags and go. De Anglican father take dis over for de girls' school."

Hegan paid half an ear to Charles and the other he focused on the sights around him. The hallway that ran the width of the school was cool and quiet when they entered, but as Hegan followed Charles to the right wing of the school, he detected first a slight murmur and then a constant buzz of sound.

With a broad smile on his face Charles threw open the door to what had once been the school cafeteria. Before him, Hegan saw young island women from teens to twenties sitting in cubicles, computer screens in front of them. Charles led Hegan from row to row, and he observed that all the women wore headsets attached to a phone console. Hegan quickly assessed each console had multiple phone extensions.

"We get calls from all over de States through the miracle of de eight hundred number," Charles told Hegan. At first, Hegan thought it was a phone sex operation. When he listened and failed to hear any artificial moans of pleasure, he discarded that reasoning.

Hegan passed one of the cubicles and heard a woman answer, "American Airlines," while at another a woman said, "This is Lufthansa. How may I help you?" A third answered, "Royal Thai."

"Ah..." Hegan said to Charles. "Now I see. They take airlines reservations."

The smile on Charles' face faded, replaced by what Hegan assumed was disappointment. He wondered if perhaps he'd offended some arcane island custom. As Hegan struggled to discover what he'd done to displease Charles, movement on one of the computer screens caught this eye.

He leaned into the nearest cubicle to observe a split computer screen. On the top half was live action from the Rockingham Park race track. Below it was a list of horses, their jockeys, and their odds. The woman in the cubicle turned her head and smiled at Hegan until her phone console started to ring. "Royal Thai," she answered with the island lilt in her voice.

"Holy shit!" Hegan said so that several female heads turned at once in his direction. He gestured his apologies then turned to see Charles smiling at him.

"Royal Thai is Rockingham! American is Arlington! Lufthansa is Los Alamitos! This is a bookie joint!"

"I knew you were a very smart man. Sir." Charles seemed pleased his faith in Hegan's intelligence was not wasted. "I can show you more."

"Not today, Charles. But I would like to meet Mr. Peters. If he's here. We could do some business, maybe."

"Maybe you invest in St. Vincent too. I'll check with my cousin Esme."

Hegan watched Charles go to the end of the row and confer with a woman who stuck her head out of her cubicle and waved at Hegan. He waved back.

Charles returned. "Cousin Esme say Mr. Peters will be on de premises tomorrow."

Hegan noticed Cousin Esme watching as her information was conveyed. Hegan waved again and she returned to her work.

"We could try to visit his house on the hill?" Hegan suggested.

"Indeed we could. My taxi awaits you, sir."

"Do me a favor, Charles. My name is Mike. Do not call me 'sir' any more. Call me, Mike. Okay?"

"Certainly, Mr. Mike, sir."

Hegan accepted the compromise as they came down the front steps to the taxi.

CHAPTER SEVENTEEN

Hegan calculated the drive from the bookie operation to the mansion where fat Frankie LoFrisco, aka Frank Peters, the island's sainted benefactor, lived took about ten minutes. It wasn't precise because Hegan forgot to look at his watch. He seemed to remember how tropical islands had a hypnotic effect on visitors and was surprised to find he'd gone on "island time" so quickly, thinking he, of all people, was immune to such foolishness. But watch or no watch and even with the winding roads, he was convinced the distance was short. On an island only eleven miles wide, what trip could be long?

The house rose up from behind a broad green lawn that sloped to the sea. Gardens bordering the long drive from the main road were in full bloom and well-tended, Hegan noticed. No gardeners or other workers were in sight as the taxi came to a stop under the porte cochere.

Hegan admired the house. It was solidly constructed of stone which he concluded must have been plucked from the surrounding fields before they were "civilized" and turned into lawns and flower beds. The mansard roof had been weathered to a grey-green over the years and complemented the structure and environs. Hegan wondered where all this interest in architecture came from, almost like he'd been watching the international version of the House and Garden cable channel.

As the soft, warm breeze stirred the palm fronds above, Hegan felt at ease for the first time in months. He recalled, but did not miss, the staccato rhythms of the big city. While he felt such an admission, even to himself, was heresy, he didn't care. He was away from the noise and the dirt, which only now became apparent by their absence. Gone was the frenzy. He felt the empty pain would disappear as well.

"Move to a speck on the globe and find peace." Hegan created the perfect advertising slogan for the islands, but knew he could never use it. The hordes would descend and nothing appealing would be left to enjoy.

Hegan's reverie dissolved when he knocked on the solid mahogany front door. There was no answer. A few knocks later, he tried the latch and found the door unlocked, providing him with an unsettling mix of curiosity and legality. In Chicago, walking through the open door of a strange house uninvited was not looked upon with great favor. Yet, his instincts told him the islands' way was more friendly and relaxed than the big city. He was curious to meet this great benefactor Frank Peters.

Hegan glanced over to Charles who watched as Hegan hesitated. Charles wagged his hand at Hegan through the taxi's open window and urged him forward. Motivated by what he felt was island custom, Hegan entered the wide foyer, silent as a museum gallery. An embellished wooden staircase bisected the entry. A formal dining room shaded by closed shutters was to his left; an expansive living room, bathed in light coming through open French doors, was to his right. Hegan chose the light.

Outside, Hegan found another carefully tended garden. This one of roses bordered by weathered stones. The blooms of pastel pinks and yellows provided a wall of color beyond which Hegan could not see. He followed a slate path until the glint of sparkling blue light caused him to shield his eyes. As he carefully stepped forward out of the blinding sheen he glimpsed an Olympic-size swimming pool. At the far side, a man in swimming trunks slept on a chaise lounge. Hegan recognized the man by his girth as the same Frank Peters, née LoFrisco, he'd spotted from the taxi.

Hegan affected a Caribbean insouciance and gave the man a friendly wave while approaching.

"Hello there. Mr. Peters? Hi."

"Hey! Whadda you want?" a female voice rasped from behind a trellis covered with fuchsia frangipane. The sound of flip-flops scuffling on slate came closer and caused Hegan to turn his focus away from Frankie.

First Hegan noticed a hip-wide, four-inch fold of white abdominal skin that hung over the top of a fire-engine-red bikini panty. Working his way north, Hegan found the matching bikini bra, followed by impenetrable, dark sunglasses, topped off by short, copper-colored hair.

The cigarette dissolved her anonymity.

"You! Monica?" said in tandem.

"You got a search warrant?" she said without taking a breath.

"Don't need one. Not my jurisdiction. I was in the neighborhood. This is a social call."

"Who's that, Monica?" Frankie called in the voice of one being roused from the embrace of a nap.

"Mike Hegan," he said and quickly covered three-quarters of the distance to where Frankie was prone. *Like a beached hippo*, Hegan thought, then figured hippos didn't exactly beach, but they could get stuck in mud somewhere, sometime.

"He's a cop," Monica yelled. "The one who came by the house."

Frankie waved Hegan over with the gentility of one to the manner born.

"Kinda outta the Loop." Frankie joked. Hegan pulled up a chair and sat directly opposite Frankie's head, within sight of his mountainous belly.

"Not really," Hegan said

"Why's that?" Frankie adjusted the back of his lounge from one eighty degrees to an angle of about one thirty-five.

Before Hegan could speak, Monica joined them.

"Monica, sweetie. I need a drink."

"I just sat down."

"I'm roastin' here."

"You shoulda thought of that before I sat down. Like when I was closer to the house."

"Look, we got a guest. How 'bout it, Hegan. You want a drink?"

Hegan didn't care one way or the other. But he got a look from Frankie in generic male code and went from ambivalent "Er... uh..." to definitive. "Got any iced tea?"

"Sure. Please get us two iced teas, Monica my sweet." Monica left and Frankie showed his magnanimity. "And pour one for yourself." His laugh followed her to the end of the pool where she turned and projected two middle fingers into the air.

Frankie didn't like to fence. "Why're you here?"

"Got some questions about Italian Scallion."

"Whoa, whoa." Frankie sat up and swung his legs over the edge of the lounge chair.

"I *know* you were at the track that day."

"You got me confused, pal. I'm Frank Peters. I got a business here."

"I saw you in the paddock at Arlington, leading Italian Scallion out. I know you're Frankie LoFrisco, the assistant trainer. I'm down here because I need your help. Not official. Yet."

"Good for you. You saw somebody who *looked* like me," Frankie jerked his thumb back toward his stomach. "But couldna been me. Since I reside here. And I got a passport to prove it."

Frankie took his passport from the pocket of his shirt he'd tossed on a table nearby. He waved it at Hegan. "Take a look."

Hegan took the passport, flipped some pages and handed it back to Frankie.

Monica interrupted, carrying a tray of tall glasses filled with iced tea. After setting down the tray, she turned her back to Hegan to give Frankie his drink.

"Cut the crap, Frankie." Hegan started to cough as soon as Monica lit a cigarette and blew smoke in his direction. "I don't care if you have a passport from the moon. I can place you at the track the day Italian Scallion died."

"You gonna extradite me for doping a horse? First, down here, you gotta show cause to a magistrate. And they ain't got no treaty with no other country for doping horses." Frankie paused to let reality sink into Hegan's gut. "You think I'm as dumb as I look?"

"Let's talk about Ariel's murder. I'm sure murder is an extraditable offense everywhere in the world." Hegan wasn't one-hundred-percent-take-it-to-the-bank sure, but he hoped the sun had burned a few of Frankie's brain cells and he'd never know.

"Murder?" Monica said. Taking off her sunglasses, she glared at Frankie.

"Don't give me that. I'm Frank Peters. You saw my passport."

"Your passport is Dutch and it's expired. Somebody ripped you off, Frankie."

"Jacey, that bastard." Hegan made a mental note of another name to check out.

"Come on, Frankie." Hegan tried being reasonable. "Help me out."

"He doesn't have to," Monica said with a stand-by-your-man attitude.

"Enough," Frankie snapped at Monica. "Go away!" He was many things but not a murderer and didn't need her help. He had no time for Monica's interference. For a large man, Frankie moved like a cliché once again. He was up from the chair and swept his arm, finger extended, toward the house.

"But, you said—" Monica resisted a little.

"Now!"

The conversation resumed when she was out of earshot. "So. How'd you find me?"

"Graphite." Hegan saw Frankie's face was a blank slate. "Edge of a pencil on a pad of paper revealed impression of a phone number." Frankie's shoulders slumped. "Almost didn't see the pad by the phone. Your place was a pigsty. Totally trashed."

"No way!"

"Someone else wants you more than I do." Hegan said. "Let's talk about Ariel."

"Look. On that I'm one thousand percent clean. I only did the horse." His tone sounded like I-went-to-the-store-to-buy-milk instead of I-went-into-the-barn-and-hypoed-Scallion's-neck.

"Why the horse?" Hegan didn't want Frankie to take the lead. "Kill a horse. In public? What's that about?"

Hegan watched Frankie's Frank Peters mask fall away.

"I always loved horses," his face contorting in anguish at the remembrance. He was now the almost naked, grossly overweight Frankie LoFrisco. "I didn't want to kill him. Just slow him down," was his strained explanation.

"You did this because... ?"

"You know... he—"

"Who, he? I saw you nod over at Faraci in the paddock. That he?"

"Yeah. Faraci. Treated me like shit. His errand boy. Coulda got me the job with Zenda, but noooo. He let the chick get it. The only job I ever wanted."

"You took your revenge out on a poor defenseless animal? Frankie, Frankie. What'd they teach you in Catholic school?"

"Stuff it. All I wanted was to slow him down so Faraci'd lose a bundle."

Hegan looked over at Frankie, not ready to reveal his suspicion about the presence of other Americans on the island. Hegan decided to pump as much as he could out of Frankie should the corpulent one meet an untimely end, though Hegan knew the others could be tourists or businessmen. Yeah, right.

"So, this was your plan to screw Faraci?" Hegan asked again to settle his mind.

"Yeah," Frankie said in a low voice.

Hegan now had an opening to continue. "As a result, both Faraci and Zenda lost a bundle, and you have two enemies. Geez, Frankie. How dumb can you be?"

"I just told ya. But I ain't dumb," he snapped "This here..."—he gestured in a wide circle that included the house and maybe even the universe—"this here proves I'm smarter than both Faraci and Zenda figured I'd be. We take bets and soon there'll be online poker. And the beautiful part is I done it by scamming their money. Hah!" Frankie rested his case, smiling with boyish glee.

"Could be very profitable for you, if you keep on breathing." Hegan dipped a few fingers into the tepid water of the swimming pool. "Mmm. Like a bathtub."

Frankie brightened. His face told the world he was a lucky fellow. And smart. "What's that you said? Whadda you mean, breathing?"

Hegan explained he wasn't the only American on the island looking for Frankie. He took the news with a fatalistic awareness, as though he knew his scheming was too good to last. Once again Hegan confirmed with Frankie that he acted alone. "No quid pro quo?" With no response after ten seconds, Hegan repeated the Latin phrase. "It's Latin."

"Only dead people speak Latin."

"Latin is a *dead* language, but living, *breathing* people speak it."

"Okay, so what does it mean?"

"That for this," Hegan explained. "Or this for that. You know what I mean. You do this or that for Faraci, and he does this or that for you in return. Get it?"

"Yeah, yeah. I get it. You wanna know what was he gonna do for me."

"Exactly."

"So, why didn't you say so? You don't have to worry; Frankie was not waitin' for no one to do nuthin' for him. Frankie was empowered. Just like Monica says. I took... ." With those words, Frankie stretched out his arms so his meaty paws could grasp the air and pulled his closed fists back to his chest.

"So. Tell me. What happened to Ariel?"

"Dunno," he said and shrugged. "Looks like she fucked up."

Hegan took gentle, baby steps. "I guess Zenda musta been on the hook to Faraci."

Frankie the reclining hippo sat bolt upright. "Nah! You kiddin'? Zenda was loaded and connected. Them Ruskies stick together. Zenda was a partner with the Ivanov brothers."

Hegan shook his head to make room for the new names.

"I'm in Ocala," Frankie continued. "One day the office was empty and I nosed around.

Those "I" boys are big in laundry. Know what I mean? I'm not talkin' the restaurant or the commodities business, like they say, either."

"If not... then what?" Hegan didn't know if playing Donny Dummy would fly with Frankie, so he shrugged for emphasis.

Frankie's tone indicated a lecture was beginning. "They also got a bunch of vig boys around town. And other stuff."

Hegan erupted. "Now I know you're bullshittin'! Faraci runs all the vig boys? Come on."

Frankie regained the upper hand. "That kid they found in the pool belonged to the Ivanovs. You figure it out. The old horse's-head trick. This time it was a spick," Frankie said.

Before Frankie got too much control, Hegan pressed forward. "Tell me about Ariel."

"What's to tell?"

"Her death an accident too? Like Scallion?"

Frankie's snigger, which sounded eerily like a horse's neigh to Hegan, expressed his contempt for the dumb cop. "Could be," Frankie said.

"Okay. Look, I gotta get something for this."

Hegan feigned boredom and showed more interest in watching a sloop sail lazily across the sparkling blue Caribbean. Or was it the Atlantic? He couldn't tell.

* * *

After the ten hour journey from Chicago, which required a change of planes in Barbados, Portia was not eager to leave the warmth of the shower. The water soothed aching muscles and revived her spirits. When she stepped out onto the soft bath mat, the entire room was clouded in steam. She breathed the vapor into her lungs and found it settled her anxiety as the water had comforted her skin.

Portia wrapped herself in a bath sheet and cracked open the door so that she could clear the mirror.

"Hegan, it's all yours in ten minutes," she called around the edge of the open door, but there was no response. "Hegan? Hey, Hegan... ."

She bunched her hair on top of her head, squeezed out the excess water and went in search of Hegan. He wasn't inside the cottage, nor was he out on the veranda.

Portia leaned into the veranda railing, caught in the bright glow of sun on calm blue sea. The air felt cooler than the warm shower, but Portia decided it was warm enough to dry her hair naturally. She opened her towel so that a balmy freshet could evaporate the moisture on the rest of her body. Soon she felt her nipples respond, which brought her back to the kisses she'd shared with Hegan. This erogenous response was the most she'd experienced in more time than she cared to remember. She corrected her memory, recalling the uterine pull she'd felt that first day at the beach when they'd argued and she'd flipped Hegan on his back in the sand.

The recognition of the damage she might have caused Hegan made her shudder. Chilled, she went inside.

* * *

He'd waited in the midst of a thick banana palm for more than an hour, trying to determine if they were in the cottage. A moment before he was prepared to abandon his stakeout, Portia appeared on the veranda. Filtered through the leafy trees, the glow of the sun illuminated her face, graced some of her body, and kept the rest in mysterious shade. *Nice tits* was his first reaction; *neat bush*, his second.

He was close enough to see her nipples harden, and he wondered if she was going to do more than just dry off. If that happened, he felt himself ready to do more than watch her. But when she returned to the cottage, his moment passed.

* * *

Portia finished dressing, expecting Hegan would momentarily return from roaming the hotel grounds. She thought he was being considerate, giving her privacy before they shared a living space more intimately than before. She was not about to search for him among the circuitous paths and thick tropical vegetation. It was easier to call the front desk.

"Have you seen Mister... uh, Mike Hegan?" she asked the woman in the office.

"Not for some time, Missus Hegan. I did see him drive off with Charles, your taxi man, about thirty minutes ago. I'm sure he'll be back presently."

Portia thanked the woman and hung up. She knew Hegan had been trying to abandon her since before they left Chicago. First chance he got, he split.

"Damn you, Hegan! Damn you!" she swore at the walls of the cottage.

* * *

Frankie finished telling all he knew about Ariel. It wasn't much. Hegan needed more. He primed Frankie like an old well. "This is what I've got, Frankie. See what you think."

Hegan told Frankie the pink threads found on Ariel's body matched the material he took from Zenda's office at the Merchandise Mart and his box at the track. "The way I look at it, Frankie, the person or persons who killed Ariel stashed her the night before in Zenda's private box. She was raped there. And you helped them."

"Oh, no. Not me." Frankie knew murder was the major leagues compared to blatant theft. His protest was vigorous but did not dissuade Hegan. A fish was on the line, and he didn't care what kind it was as long as he could reel it into the boat.

"Get dressed," Hegan commanded. "We're going downtown. Wherever downtown is in this place." When Frankie didn't move, Hegan reminded him of the choices.

"Cooperate with me, and you live. Don't, and I let the other Americans find you. I don't care about you or how you killed Italian Scallion. All I want, all I've ever wanted since that day, is anyone and everyone involved in Ariel's murder."

Hegan had one more question, but it had to be set up properly.

"Maybe this will help you get off your fat ass. Who would benefit materially from Ariel's death?" He aimed his finger directly at Frankie. "Since you could benefit the most, that makes you an accessory, if not an accomplice, to whoever actually did the deed." This got Frankie's attention to a degree, but he still didn't stir.

Hegan paused to try to figure what Frankie had cooking in the back of his mind. "Just look at it," Hegan continued. "You kill his horse and he promotes you to trainer? Get real."

"That's your wet dream," Frankie said with impatience.

"Still... Zenda and the Ivanov brothers are working together. Word gets out Zenda's assistant trainer has a relationship with Faraci, and you drown mysteriously in a vat of vodka and pickled herring."

"I keep on tellin' ya. Who could know?"

Hegan shot him a who-are-you-kidding look.

"Besides, why do you think I got this set up here? You really think I believe Faraci?"

"I saw it. Neat. You won't live long enough to enjoy it unless—"

"Unless, what? You want me to make stuff up?"

"Stick with me," Hegan said.

Frankie continued to resist, suddenly becoming fascinated with some lint from his navel.

"Let me understand," Hegan said. "Faraci has Trujillo, who is a dealer for the Ivanov's, knocked off for poaching on his territory. Did the Ivanov's retaliate? Did they even know it was Faraci?"

"No. That's why Faraci's revenge is so slick," Frankie said.

"Hey, Faraci's been around long enough to know that revenge leads to a short life."

"Tell ya the truth, I think he's lost it." Frankie twirled his index finger along the side of his head, bugged out his eyes, and hung his tongue out of the corner of his mouth. "Get it?" he asked.

"I'd have to be blind not to. What about Faraci's mental capacity?"

"First off, he hates illegals. Some kinda pride thing. If his grandma could come through the front door, blah, blah. Now he finds out the Ivanovs are using illegals to cut into his business. And he knows for a fact the Ivanovs came over here with not even an empty vodka bottle to piss in. Now they got businesses, legal and illegal, making out like bandits. Which they are."

"You're telling me this whole thing—murder, horse doping, me being down here talking to you—all of this is—"

"Wait. There's more. The older brother, Vadim, lives right next door to Faraci on Lake Shore Drive. The very next condo. Drove Faraci up a tree. Like, in his face is this guy who in what, eighteen months, can afford almost seven figures for a condo?"

"So? This is because... what? Competition? Jealousy? Nationalistic pride? I can't believe what I just said."

"He's a very weird guy. His drapes are always closed, and they're lined with lead."

"Lead?"

"To protect him from radioactive rays. Thinks the CIA is trying to mess with his brain waves."

"A sweet girl with her whole life to live is dead because of some delusional—"

"That's not the reason."

"Then tell me!" Hegan took a sip of tea.

"Burnt fish is the real reason."

Hegan coughed out some tea and recovered. "No! This better be the slightest bit plausible."

Frankie laughed as he watched Hegan wipe his mouth. "Faraci hates odor. His place is shut up like a tomb so that no smell can disturb him while he smokes his stinky cigars. One morning he smells burning fish. He checks the hall and discovers it's coming from Ivanov's condo. That's how it started."

"Ariel was killed over burnt fish?" Hegan couldn't believe Frankie capable of making up such a ludicrous story. When Frankie said "there's more," Hegan hoped he would confirm the information on Ariel's tape.

"That's when Faraci got a hard-on for the Ivanovs. Killing Trujillo was payback. Meant nothing to Faraci. They made a move on Faraci, so how could they know? But, really, Ariel saw too much... knew too much."

"Now you lost me. Too much about what?"

"The new twenties."

"Must be I'm having an allergic reaction to all this sun," Hegan said. He watched as Frankie seemed to shrink within himself.

"If I help you, you gotta leave me be." Hegan's silence was an unexpected motivator. "Pink thread is used in the new twenties to prevent counterfeiting. The Ivanovs have been printing twenties at Zenda's place. Without the brothers he wouldn't be such a big horseman. Get it?"

"Holy horse apples!" he said on purpose.

"They ship stacks, like bricks, to Romania. Some goes here, some goes there. I dunno more than what little bit I overheard and saw."

"If you knew, why not—"

"Kill me? Ha! They think I'm too dumb! But ya gotta believe me. I didn't kill Ariel."

* * *

"Monica? Hey, Monica!" Frankie called entering from the pool. He threw on a pineapple print tropical shirt over his swim trunks and shoved his feet into flip flops.

With Hegan in tow, Frankie found Monica in the library. There were no books in the room formerly used as a library in such ancient times when being well-read had a value. Now the room was a repository for an assortment of exercise machines from Bowflex to ThighMaster.

Monica was on an exercise bike. Judging by the effort she expended, her pedal rate was about half a mile an hour. She listened to music through a headset and watched a tape on a TV monitor set on a table at eye level.

"Hey, Monica," Frankie yelled from the doorway. "I'm goin'. Be back soon."

Monica didn't acknowledge Frankie's voice or presence.

Once the cab pulled away, Monica placed a call from her cell phone.

* * *

"You like my cousin Avery. He de magistrate." Charles burbled from the front of the taxi.

"Avery? The one with the shotgun?" Hegan asked.

"Oh, no, mon. Dis my udda cousin Avery."

"How many cousins named Avery do you have?" Hegan kept up the questioning so that Frankie wouldn't have to think in silence and maybe change his mind.

"Five."

"You have five cousins. They're all named Avery. How can that be?"

"Me granfadda got five sons."

"Don't tell me...."

Charles read Hegan's mind. "You be right mon. Me granfadda de first Avery."

"Why am I not surprised?" Hegan played along. He glanced at Frankie who had gotten more tense since leaving his mansion. "You getting all of this?" Hegan asked Frankie who shrugged.

"Each of me grandfadda's son had at least one son. An' always de first born called Avery to honor grandfadda."

"Makes perfect sense to me," Hegan said as the taxi stopped in front of the red brick courthouse. "Wait for us, Charles."

"No matter, mon. Charles be here. My cousin Avery he be speedy fellow."

In the presence of Avery the magistrate, a court stenographer, and Hegan, Frankie recounted all he knew about Italian Scallion, Ariel, Faraci, the Ivanov brothers and Jacey. In short, he emptied the contents of his gut, which was considerable.

Hegan made arrangements to have the transcribed document shipped to Captain Rosen by prepaid air courier and returned to the taxi.

Frankie, more heavyhearted than sullen, told Hegan he would make his own way back to the mansion. He needed to figure out what the future, if he had one, held now that his most imaginative scheme had been pierced and the bubble of his ego popped.

* * *

Abandoned, inferior, worthless were the labels Portia applied to herself as her frustration with being purposely left behind by Hegan grew more intense. She had been discounting the value of her life from birth to present for at least fifteen minutes after calling the front desk. Only a slight tapping on the front door of their cottage interrupted her.

She hoped it was Hegan and was prepared to tear him a new one. But when she opened the door, it wasn't him. "What?" was the only word she got out of her mouth.

"There's been an accident," he said. "No time for conversation. Come quickly."

She did. He led her down a path away from the front of the resort and onto a side road where his car was waiting. She didn't expect him to be such a gentleman when he opened the front passenger-side door for her. The biggest surprise of all came when he dusted the back of her head with his gun butt. She would not recall the experience of being trussed, gagged, and tossed into the back seat of his rented Renault.

CHAPTER EIGHTEEN

Jeff took a cab from the airport and ambled down Bay Street, the main drag of Kingstown. He passed the Grenadines Wharf and other nineteenth century buildings. All were made of bricks brought to the island as ballast on European ships that made the return journey loaded with sugar and molasses. He looked like any other tourist. Beneath his dark shades his eyes scanned for more than a place to buy some seashells and a gaudy tropical shirt.

If this was some perverted test by that wacko guinea, Jeff was determined not to fail. Asking around at the first trinket shop for the "rich American," he learned about Mr. Peters who lived in a big house on the hill. How easy was that? With luck he could be finished in thirty minutes and on his way back to Chicago.

Maybe a cab could get him there. He searched for a taxi stand and then realized he was a long way from the big city. Spotting the first vehicle with a native driver, he stuck out his thumb. Surely that international sign would be recognized. It was. An old gent driving a battered truck loaded with palm fronds gave him a lift, stopping within easy walking distance of the mansion. All the training he learned at Fort Benning came rushing back.

Dodging a stand of bamboo bordering one side of Frankie's palatial residence, he neared an open window. Hearing no sound from within, he took bolder steps until he had a clear view of the pool. The sight of a topless woman sunning her ponderous breasts made him halt in place. He reversed direction and found the front door, partially open. Jeff again stopped to listen for any indication that others were present. The motor of an approaching car made Jeff pay attention. He hoped it would recede in the distance. The car stopped. It drove away after a door was slammed shut.

* * *

The bright yellow pineapples on Frankie's shirt were the polar opposite of how he felt. This great scheme of his was turning to dust. He had such plans and now his future was anything but bright. Somber and depressed, he paid the cab driver and lumbered to the front door of the mansion. What he didn't know was that being somber and depressed would be the high point of his day. The low came before he could call out, "Honey, I'm home."

* * *

Now that the broad was tied up like a goat staked out to welcome a hungry tiger, he could focus on his original target. Monica's call brought him back to the quaint streets of this one stoplight burg. Soon, all this would be his. And Monica would get hers too. When he saw Frankie leave the courthouse and enter a cab, he knew this was his lucky day. He indulged himself with a sardonic laugh as his rented Renault passed the cab on the winding two-lane road and sped ahead, disappearing around a hidden curve. He'd get there first and hide in wait.

He watched as Frankie got out of the cab, paid the driver, and pushed open the front door. He didn't expect that a hiss of air and loud thump would welcome Frankie home. He knew the sounds meant that Frankie would not draw another breath. *One problem solved* while another stood behind the half-open door. Luckily, he'd chambered a round in his S&W .45 while in hiding. All he had to do was create an element of surprise and enter blasting.

He rang the front doorbell. Soft chimes in the background announced a visitor. Before the door was answered, he shouldered open the door, his arms in extended combat grip. They leveled at Jeff, frozen by the sound of the chimes as he checked Frankie's neck for a pulse. Three loud, rapidly fired blasts echoed through the hall, finding Jeff in his upper torso and neck.

Monica, not surprised by the gun shots, charged through the living room door. Holding the butt of a sawed-off shot gun anchored at her hip she found him feeling Jeff's neck for a pulse.

"Thank God it's you," she said lowering the gun. "Who is he?" His reply came in the form of two bursts from Jeff's Browning .22. One shot hit her ample abdomen and caused her to fire harmlessly into the hardwood floor. The other, more deliberate, went through the side of her skull. He left three bodies.

* * *

"Let's go," Hegan said as he threw himself into the back seat. "Back to the Blue Lagoon." He didn't have to look at his watch to know that he'd been gone far longer than Portia anticipated when she entered the shower. *She'll be livid*, Hegan imagined. *Oh well.*

Before the cab could stop by the banyan tree, Hegan stumbled out the door. He struggled for a moment to gain his balance and ran toward their cottage.

"Portia!" Hegan called within steps of the cottage. He threw open the screen door and called her name again but there was no response. There was not much area to cover in the small cottage, and Hegan seemed to navigate the space in less than ten ticks of the second hand of his watch.

His first pass-through indicated all was as he'd left it, with one exception: Portia was nowhere to be found. Not until his second pass through the bedroom did he see a piece of paper stuck to the door by a Band-Aid.

Hegan ripped off the note and hastily read the message written in large capital letters, the strength of which indicated the hand of a man. Come to the old windmill on the point at the other end of the island. Come alone. Unarmed.

Gun in one hand and note in the other, Hegan raced back to the cab. Charles noticed Hegan's frantic state but could not interpret its meaning. He'd seen anxious mainlanders before. Petty arguments imported from home sometimes could not be mollified by the calm of the tropics. Old grudges festered and mutated in a foreign culture. That he understood. It was the gun Hegan gripped in his hand that defied explanation.

"Take me to the windmill on the point." Hegan puffed his words in spurts, trying to gain his breath while hurling himself again into the cab.

"Dat no tourist spot, mon." Charles thought some resistance to Hegan's uncontrollable mania could have a diffusing effect.

"I'll get another driver," Hegan said, popping out of the cab.

"Never fear. Charles at your service."

"Don't waste time," Hegan instructed, returning to the cab. "Get there as fast as you can."

"I do my best."

"Do better than best, Charles." Hegan dropped the civility and tropical bonhomie. "This is urgent. You know what urgent means?"

Charles felt there was no need for Hegan to get rude, but he wasn't about to argue with an armed man. "It mean de same in de English language no matter where."

"Make believe I've had a heart attack and you must get me to the hospital before I die. That's the kind of urgent I mean. It's the same in any language. You have to save a life, Charles."

The cab sped down from the Blue Lagoon and passed swiftly through Kingstown without running over any pedestrians or ramming any other vehicles. Within a few minutes they were in the countryside.

"How far to the point?"

"Maybe another five, ten minutes."

"What's the best way to the windmill?" Hegan didn't know what to expect, but he was not going to rush into an ambush.

"An old dirt road go across de meadow."

"Can we get there any other way?"

"It be de only road."

"How about from the point? Maybe by boat and up the beach?" A cab speeding alone across an open meadow was an easy target.

"No, no sir. No beach. Only rocks."

"Then there is another way." Hegan seized the alternative. He had no time for tourist comforts. "Look, Charles, I need your help. Take me to the rocks."

"You don't want to go dat way. Only goats go dat way."

"I'm a goat," Hegan told Charles as he leaned forward to check the magazine in his forty-five. Through the windshield Hegan saw the road bordered on both sides by tall stands of sugarcane. Soon they would come to the edge of the cane and reach the meadow, about half a mile further. "Stop here," Hegan said.

Charles stopped and turned to face Hegan who looked worried about what lay ahead. "I must get to the windmill without being seen," Hegan said in a confiding tone that did little to allay Charles's fears.

Charles was motionless for longer than Hegan desired. He counted out five twenties and gave them to the driver. Charles refused the money. "Take it. I need help." Charles said nothing and shook off the money again.

Hegan reached into his pocket and all of Charles's nerve endings instinctively seized up in fear. Hegan showed his badge. "I'm a detective. From Chicago. My... friend has been kidnapped."

"You mean de missus?"

"Uh... yes. The missus. I need your help."

"Why you not say so, mon? Charles is friend to de authorities."

Hegan exhaled audibly. "Thank you, Charles. Now, we can't waste any more time. You've got to help me get up behind the windmill without being seen."

Charles started the engine and headed straight for the cane.

"What? Where... ? We can't—"

"Charles know de way." He directed the cab between the stumps of two palm trees and, in almost biblical fashion, parted the dense stalks, revealing a decades-old rutted road which bisected two fields. Once inside, the entire cab was concealed by the green rushes.

"Before de harvest, we be hidden. By an' by, all de young folks come dis way at night for some funnin'."

"Ah! Yes. Playing hide the salami," Hegan said.

The cab stopped and Charles led the way, bending in a half crouch, trying to be stealthy.

"Now be de goat part," Charles announced as they arrived at the edge of a bluff with a panoramic view of the sea. In front, Hegan could see the calm water, but below them were massive black rocks, the result of some ancient lava flow meeting the cool sea. Any doubts Hegan had that goats could navigate their way disappeared as Charles picked his way toward the bottom of the bluff.

"Here de way," he called back with what Hegan could only describe as joy. At what? Hegan didn't know but figured it must be the tropical zest for life, no matter what the circumstances. Maybe he'd read too many travel brochures.

Hegan found a bit of dirt that hadn't been covered by congealed lava. He was not about to call it a path, but soon was a few paces behind Charles. When they reached the bottom, the path broadened by the width of two feet—not twenty-four inches, but the width of two average-size adult feet. Now Hegan could place his feet side by side instead of scuffing one in front of the other. He was grateful for any progress, however minute.

Charles stopped to get his bearings, and Hegan took the opportunity to glance back from where they'd started. It looked like they'd traversed one solid wall of rock, but the sugarcane above became a fused green expanse, with not a hint of access.

"Here de land rise up and be true path to de windmill." Charles pointed as he spoke, and Hegan saw what could be clearly defined as a path by humans and an interstate by goats.

"Where is the windmill?" Hegan whispered, though the surf crashing against the black rocks would mask any voices. Still, Hegan didn't know what sort of natural echo chamber the rocks and bluff might have created.

Charles pointed the way to the windmill. Hegan took the lead, quickening his pace as the path began its slight rise which also heightened Hegan's exposure. He dropped to the ground.

Hegan crab-crawled in the dirt until he was able to peek over without being seen. About fifty yards before him were the remains of a nineteenth century windmill. Its wooden vanes long lost to the elements, the conical structure was made of solid fieldstone. Halfway to the top was an opening which Hegan believed to be a window on a second floor.

Exposed to the elements, Hegan figured the wood of the second floor would have rotted away years ago, which meant no one could accidentally spot him, and he'd preserved the element of surprise.

Hegan slid back down the bluff and stood. He pulled out his gun and Charles cringed again.

"What you want, mon? I do like you say."

"Shh! Easy, Charles," Hegan whispered and proffered the gun butt-first. "Take this." Charles stepped back. "Take it. If I'm not out of the windmill in fifteen minutes, fire three shots and yell 'Police!' But yell it loud. Very loud."

"No way," Charles whispered.

"Time and tide don't wait," Hegan reminded him.

"I cannot impersonate de authorities." Even in the tropics there were ethical and legal considerations.

"Raise your right hand." Hegan would not be deterred or delayed.

"What?" Charles continued to whisper.

"Do it." Charles was reluctant. "Now!"

Slowly Charles raised his right hand.

"Under the power vested in me, I now pronounce you a deputy Chicago police officer. Do you swear to uphold the law... blah, blah, blah?"

Charles solemnly nodded and took the gun which was heavier than he imagined. To his surprise, Hegan grabbed it back to unlock the safety.

"Remember. Fifteen minutes." Hegan spoke directly into Charles's ear. "Bang! Bang! Then yell, 'Police!'" Hegan thrust the gun back into Charles's hands.

Charles watched in disbelief as Hegan slid up the rise and disappeared over the edge of the bluff. He peeked over to observe Hegan crawling over the coarse grass toward the old stone ruins.

Once Hegan felt he was out of sight from the second floor opening, as remote as that possibility was, he stood and slowly moved around the solid back wall of the windmill until he found the opening to a former window on the ground level.

Hegan struggled to find a footing on the edge of a weathered stone in the wall and slowly boosted himself up to peer inside. All of his weight was on one foot, and he gripped the window ledge with his fingertips. His precarious perch lasted only a few seconds before his leg cramped and he had to readjust his position. Once again his foot found a resting spot and he raised himself slowly. More comfortable, he got a better view inside and finally spotted Portia, gagged, hands tied behind her back to an iron ring implanted in a stone column which once had supported the second floor.

Hegan held his breath as he watched Portia undetected for several seconds. When there was no sound or movement in the room, he slowly slipped from his vantage point and moved around to the mill's entrance. Totally exposed to whatever or whoever hid inside, Hegan stood facing the opening where once there'd been a door. He knew he made an inviting target backlit by the bright sunlight. Inside he could only see dark recesses and shadows. He took two tentative steps to the entrance.

As he moved half the distance to Portia, his motion caught her attention. Hegan was glad she was alive and then surprised by the apologetic look in her eyes.

"Mikey!" someone said in a tone reserved for the unexpected meeting of an old friend.

Hegan turned toward the sound to find Perino moving out of the deep shadows behind the column that held Portia. "Eddie?" Hegan squinted to place the body with the voice and was entirely surprised when both matched.

Perino acted like the emcee at a family reunion, and confided in Portia with an easy confident air. "I knew he'd come. He had no choice."

His gun visible, Perino moved within ten feet of Hegan, entering the circle of light that filtered through the open roof. "Surprised you, didn't I?" Perino said unable to conceal a his contempt. "Hands behind your head. Lace your fingers. You know the drill." He laughed as he instructed Hegan. Perino frisked Hegan with one hand, while he kept the barrel of his gun pressed into the center of Hegan's spine.

"What the hell is this, Eddie?"

"You shoulda retired a week ago. But, nooooo. You hadda be a hero. Don'tcha know we got cemeteries full of heroes?" Perino shoved Hegan toward Portia. "Go over to your girlfriend." Hegan stumbled toward Portia then regained his balance as he reached her side.

"I've known you fifteen, twenty years. I can't figure it. Why, Eddie?"

"Your figurin' days are over. There's those who do and those who figure with their thumbs up their asses," Perino said, feeling in control for the first time in his memory. Their lives, Hegan and the girl, were in his hands. Finally, his life was his own. With Frankie gone, and soon these two disposed of, he could disappear forever. The operation would be his alone. No more alimony. He'd give the Ivanovs of piece of Frankie's action. Maybe even make them partners. The thought of dictating terms to the Ruskies released an enigmatic smile from Perino and then a manic laugh. Quickly he realized the Ruskies could never be trusted and his smile vanished.

When Hegan saw Eddie's smile, he thought it was a sign of some kind of emotional grandiosity. The laugh convinced him Eddie was nuts.

"Don't do this, Eddie." Hegan took a tentative step toward Perino, not knowing where he was headed or why. "Whatever hook you're on, let me help. No harm, no foul." Hegan was exhibiting some weird fraternal, twelve-step empathy and it made him sick, but he continued. "Together, we'll beat the bastards. Whoever... ."

Hegan halved the distance to Perino but didn't arouse his defenses. "You had chances," Perino said as if he truly had to defend his position to Hegan. It was grandiosity. The Mussolini gene, Hegan figured.

"For what? I'm blind here. Help me help you, Eddie." Hegan knew Perino would see through the act any minute, but he continued and became more animated. His arms flailed about theatrically, like the wings of a pelican preparing for flight.

"Easy, Mikey." Perino gestured with the gun and Hegan froze in place about three feet away. "You wanna help? Where's the tape?"

Hegan smacked both palms against his temples. "And I call myself a detective. All this is about some tape? Plain as the spit on my face and I didn't figure." Hegan was twirling and whirling and flapping his arms, hoping to distract Perino with his manic behavior and get close enough to knock the gun away.

"We had the suicide story knocked until you stuck your dick in the case. That's when the odds turned against you. Nobody who knows the real story is still breathin' except you two."

Portia suddenly realized Perino's admission and tried to force sound through her gag.

Perino heard her and waved Hegan back over to Portia. "You two lovebirds belong together. For now. Let's hear what your fuck buddy has to say for herself." Perino ripped the gag from Portia's mouth.

"You killed her. You killed my sister. You motherfucking bastard!"

"And I did her too. Tasty piece of ass. Nicely broken in," Perino said. *What the hell does it matter?* he thought. *I got them both by the little curly ones.* He laughed again, with too much mirth, like a man nearing the edge.

Perino backhanded Portia's face. When Hegan took a step forward, Perino pointed his gun straight at his chest. "That's for motherfucking me now, and this is for motherfucking me in my office." A second backhand left its mark and Portia's face reddened.

Hegan had to stall and decided to play into Perino's weakness—his naked self-importance, his need for recognition and appreciation.

"And you killed Gorman too. Nice work," Hegan said appreciatively. "We thought we were home free,"—he nodded over at Portia—"didn't we?" Hegan saw Portia's face clouded with rage and unable to respond.

"I owe you one, Mikey. I come down here after Frankie, but some guy beat me to him. Now I got you two lovebirds. So, that's three birds with one stone."

"You offed Frankie?" Hegan was again his fraternal, twelve-step self.

"I told ya. Some punk did it. Looks like some mercenary you see guarding the stooges we got running I-rack. He got his. Shoulda stayed in I-rack." Perino snarled and shoved Hegan hard against the stone pillar. Hegan grimaced and crumbled to the floor as one of the protruding stones hit the vulnerable part of his back.

Perino watched rage build in Portia's eyes as she watched Hegan, powerless to help him. He was thankful she wasn't free.

"Why'd you kill them?" Hegan was determined to play to Perino's vanity.

"What do you care? Knowing won't help you. You'll never use the information."

"I know, I know." Hegan slowly stood, his body supplicating more out of pain than design. "I could never figure this case out, Eddie. You amaze me. All the time. I never knew."

Perino relented. Nothing before mattered now. "The broad—"

"Ariel!" Portia spit out.

"Oh, that was her name?" Perino laughed, happy to twist the dagger.

"You fuck!" Portia jutted her jaw at him, challenging Perino to smack her again.

He did.

"Anyhow, Ariel," he said with effeminate emphasis, "knew too much. We asked her about the tape. She refused. Nobody could reason with her. The boyfriend, that college guy, was useless. Gotta say, I'm kinda glad."

Perino shot Hegan a glance, saw he'd be no trouble with the bad back then got up close to Portia. "She was a nice piece of ass. Nice tits like yours." He noticed Portia's mouth open trying to respond but words failed her. "Yeah, I saw you out there on the porch. Now, your sister... she was tight. But no virgin."

Portia tried to spit at Perino, but nothing came out of her mouth.

Hegan wanted to distract Perino from Portia "Why Gorman?'

"Who?"

"The college guy."

"Too risky. Maybe she told him stuff. Like pillow talk?" He laughed in contempt of their intimacy. "You've been a big help to me, ex-brother-in-law." Perino was feeling secure enough to go up to Hegan and pinch his cheek in a gesture of false affection. Perino left Hegan at the sound of a car approaching.

Suddenly Perino stepped back toward the door, glanced out and waved to whoever arrived in the car.

"Why Frankie?" Hegan asked.

"Frankie saw the whole operation. Same as the broad."

"He's got a slick deal going here," Hegan reminded Perino.

"Had! Now it'll be my slick deal. I'll run Frankie's operation." Perino checked the open area in front of the mill. No one was in sight.

"You'll run it with Monica?"

"A good girl, that Monica. Was." Perino leered at Hegan and took a quick look out the window. "Okay, we gotta go."

Hegan knew he had to call on all his strength if they were to survive. He watched Perino approach Portia and began extravagant, even lunatic, movements as he limped closer to Perino. "Oh boy! I'm ready for retirement. Shoulda left years ago. My brain's in cement."

Perino regarded the gimpy, unarmed Hegan as no threat. He focused on untying Portia then reconsidered, stopping to squeeze her breasts with one hand, the other holding his piece to her temple.

"Your sister's were smaller," he sneered before rubbing his open palm between her legs. "This feels about the same." Untying Portia, he laughed at her anger which all but paralyzed her speech.

"You…" was all that escaped before he pushed her toward Hegan.

"Sometimes we get too smart when it's too late," Perino said, tossing a casual look at the gyrating Hegan, then strode out to meet the car.

"Let's go, folks. Your ride's here," he said for his own amusement.

Portia rubbed her hands to increase circulation. She saw Perino quickly look away and flew at him. The sole of her foot hit him squarely in mid-spine. An electric charge, that paralyzed and weakened, shot through Perino's gun arm. His hand opened and the gun fell out.

Perino tried reaching for the gun, but Hegan got to it first while Portia twirled and kicked and leaped at Perino. She looked like the vanes of a windmill gone haywire.

"Bastard! You raped her and beat her and poisoned…." With each word Portia made contact with another part of Perino's body, and he fell to the ground.

Hegan approached, holding the gun on Perino. His legs were unsteady, and he hoped Perino wouldn't notice.

"Trying to impress your fuck buddy, Mikey? You can't win. You heard the car. I got the place surrounded with my men."

"I saw you wave. Could be another bluff by a chump. I like my odds."

"You're still gambling on lost causes, Mikey. Long shots are for dreamers. And losers.

You shoulda learned to play the favorite."

Hegan leaned over and pulled Perino up by his shirt. Perino stood, feeling recharged, and allowed himself to be escorted toward the entrance.

"Stuff the lecture, Eddie. You're a stupid, crooked cop. You didn't find us here. I led you here, you dumb bastard." Hegan was bluffing, but thought deflating Perino's outsized pride might give him an edge.

Perino lunged for the opening, but Portia took two leaps and knocked him down before he could reach safety. Perino lifted his body half up from the ground.

"Get fucked," he spat out as Hegan got closer.

"I've watched you, Eddie," Hegan said with contempt. "When you get self-confident, you lose your head. You thought you could beat Teresa and you'd never get caught. Now you think you can kill Ariel, Gorman, and whoever."

"And you!" Perino laughed.

"You'll never do it." Portia wanted in on the party.

"There's two reasons why," Perino said and gestured to the two native men who silently entered from either side of the structure, rifles in their hands. "I think we got ya covered, Mikey. And I don't mean your bets." Perino pulled the gun out of Hegan's hand and smacked the barrel across his face. Hegan staggered. Portia quickly grabbed his arm and kept him from hitting the ground.

As the two gunmen led the way, Perino pushed Hegan and Portia forward. He looked up at the clear blue sky and took in a deep breath. "Ah. Beautiful day for a swim," he said.

Portia realized she was holding onto Hegan for more reasons than just breaking his fall. He represented the security and stability she needed. The absurdity of that realization under present circumstances was ironic and funny, a morbid kind of humor that made her burst out laughing.

Hegan thought she'd snapped and stopped their forced march to hold her. But she was consumed by laughter and her body rippled uncontrollably. Even Perino pushing them did not stop Portia, who Hegan thought looked more like the deranged Vivian Leigh in *Street Car Named Desire* than the woman he'd been close to for the last few days.

"Move it," Perino demanded. At his command they shuffled forward a few steps, but still Portia was not composed. "She's flipped. Knew it the first day we met. It's in the eyes. You musta seen that, Hegan. She's got the eyes of a maniac—like they're looking off, over your shoulder at something no one else can see."

Hegan noticed they were being positioned close to the edge of the cliff. A quick glance down and he estimated they were two hundred feet above the surf that crashed on the jagged black rocks below.

Hegan embraced Portia and spoke into her ear. "Snap out of it! I need you. Now! Listen to me!" Portia stopped laughing and started crying.

"Look at the dumb broad," Perino said to the gunmen. "Now she's crying."

The two native men stood with their weapons in a more relaxed way than Perino anticipated when he'd hired them off a fishing boat from the Grenadines. They were part of a gang of smugglers who had a violent reputation, plying the islands to service the underground economy of the region.

Hegan wiped Portia's tears with his shirttail. "I need you, brown belt. You hear me?" Portia raised her eyes to his and nodded.

Perino waved the two riflemen toward Hegan and Portia when three shots were fired in rapid succession from behind the windmill.

"Halt! Police!" drifted across the meadow.

The native gunmen wheeled and fired blindly in the direction of the shots as Perino crouched, trying in vain to find a place of concealment in the open meadow. Distracted, he forgot about Portia and Hegan, anticipating where the next volley of shots might originate.

Once they'd fired back, the gunmen were frozen in place, unable to predict if they'd be attacked and trying to calculate how quickly they could reach their vehicle about a hundred yards across the open space. In that brief moment of indecision, Portia leaped at them from behind and took both down with a scissor kick.

The jolt knocked one into an uncontrollable roll to the edge of the cliff. At the last possible instant he grabbed onto a tuft of grass with one hand while the other clawed at the dark rich earth without securing a grip.

The other gunman fared better. He took the sole of Portia's foot squarely in his nose causing him to gasp for air while he attempting to stem the flow of blood streaming into his mouth. Coughing and gasping, he dropped his rifle and ran toward the road, looking for help.

As soon as Portia moved toward the gunmen, Hegan flung himself on the crouched Perino. The surprise and sudden weight of Hegan's body on the smaller man caused his gun to be dislodged. Hegan and Perino grappled with each other until Charles raced toward them.

Perino, thinking Charles was another member of his squad, pushed Hegan away. "Shoot him," he urged Charles and pointed at Hegan.

Charles was nervous as he gripped the gun with both hands eager to return it to Hegan.

"Here, Mr. Mike," he said relieved when his responsibilities had ended.

While Hegan and Charles were occupied, Perino located his weapon and crawled toward it. Charles, saw the object of Perino's intent and, with newfound bravado, kicked it away with soccer-style panache. Perino sought a diplomatic solution.

"You gotta understand, Mike," he pleaded.

"You want understanding? See a shrink." Hegan commanded Perino to get up as he kept the barrel of his weapon pointed at Perino's head. "There's rope in the mill, Charles. Get it."

Portia joined them and launched into Perino, who had drawn himself up and was about to stand. Portia's foot caught him in the side of his head and knocked him prone.

"Enough!" Hegan yelled at Portia.

Charles returned with the rope, and Hegan gave Portia the honor of tying Perino's hands behind his back. Portia yanked Perino upright by his pinioned arms, causing him to yelp.

"Shut up, scum. Or should I say motherfucker?"

Perino spit at Portia and she whaled him with a series of backhand slaps across his face, stopping only when a shot was fired. She turned in the direction of the shot and saw the other gunman had managed to scramble onto the cliff. She looked at Perino, who was unscathed, and then to Hegan. She saw blood seeping through her shirt as she dropped to her knees.

CHAPTER NINETEEN

The sound dissipated in the open space, sounding more like the pop of a champagne cork and maybe a little louder than the back fire of an old Keystone Kops jalopy. Hegan reacted only when he saw Portia slump on her knees.

When Portia fell, Charles felt honor bound as a deputy police officer to bring her assailant to justice. He snatched Perino's .45 where it lay on the ground and released the safety as Hegan had demonstrated. Charles fired at the smuggler, who dropped his rifle and ran.

"Halt! Police! Halt!" Charles yelled with each wildly fired discharge as if he didn't want to hit his target. The hail of bullets sent tufts of dirt flying into the air, causing the gunman to choose between dodging bullets or shielding his eyes from the flying debris with his arms. He ran in erratic, uncontrolled bursts, stumbling and finally losing his balance and sense of direction before slipping over the edge and down to the sea.

Charles returned to find Hegan on his knees Portia cradled in his arms. The bullet from the old rifle had found Portia's left side.

"Get their car," Hegan yelled and directed Charles to the edge of the meadow.

Charles opened the door of the box-like vehicle, one of those old East German heaps. The Trabi. With keys still in the ignition, Charles started the car and gunned it across the meadow.

Portia's breath was shallow as Hegan held her in his arms. Waiting for Charles to arrive, he saw movement in his peripheral vision. Perino, hands tied behind his back, struggled to stand. "Don't!" he yelled at Perino, who froze.

"Untie me. I can help. Together we can save her."

Hegan felt something wet against his skin. Portia's blood had saturated the front of his shirt. He looked at Perino and back to Portia. "Two choices and neither of them good," he muttered.

"Just like voting for president," Portia replied, her voice barely above a whisper.

"Portia, you idiot," Hegan said, clutching her head to his chest as Charles pulled up beside them and opened the rear door.

"Come, Mr. Mike. Hold her arms. I take de feet and we lay her in back. Hospital not far."

"What about him?" Charles asked, nodding over toward Perino as they lifted Portia and placed her in the back seat.

"We can't. Turn the car around and wait for me." As the car pulled away, Hegan charged at Perino who backed up awkwardly until he was against the stone wall.

"Eddie, you're a scumbag!" Hegan yelled and lofted his foot into Perino's crotch. "Gee, Eddie. That felt good." Perino screamed in pain and sank to his knees. "Stick, around. I'll be back."

Hegan jumped into the back seat and knelt on the floor, pressing his shirttail onto Portia's wound. Charles stepped hard on the gas, and they jounced across the meadow to the road.

"Hey, Charles!" Hegan yelled over the sound of the 6.8 liter engine. "You need new springs back here."

"Ain't my car, mon. S'okay. I never sit in de back." Charles laughed, downshifted, and followed the winding road into Kingstown.

The rear seat of the car seemed like a trampoline to Hegan as he tried to keep Portia horizontal while at the same time applying pressure to staunch the bleeding. The two functions required more stability than he could achieve careening down the winding road. He straddled the hump above the transmission casing—awkward at best, but this mission called for dexterous skills he could not master. All the while his knees were pressing on some grainy substance, small pebbles, perhaps, that were fast becoming permanently affixed to his kneecaps.

The blood flow seemed to lessen, and Hegan hoped it was more from his attempt to keep constant pressure on the wound than from total depletion. Portia perspired heavily, and he tried to keep her forehead dry. To what end, he didn't know; just that he had to. Using two fingers pressed together, he swiped the droplets from her brow like windshield wipers.

Portia eyes fluttered open as the car lurched more severely. "Be careful!" Hegan yelled at Charles.

"Sorry. But I drive for her life, mista."

Hegan regretted yelling. It was a visceral response.

Hegan apologized as Portia's hand darted up, grabbed hold of Hegan's shirtfront, and pulled him down. He thought it a clumsy way to ask for a kiss. And it was. Through her hazy vision, Portia found Hegan's lips and kissed him as if it was the last kiss of her life.

Hegan didn't want to kiss her. Not this way. He allowed her to use his mouth as she wished. When she stopped pressing her lips to his, he said, "We'll have lots more time for this later." He hoped it would not turn out to be a lie. "Just rest."

Unwilling to take orders or suggestions, even for her own benefit, Portia kissed Hegan one last time and dropped back onto the seat.

More sweat formed on Portia's forehead, and once again he wiped it off with his fingers. Instead of transferring the moisture to his shirt, he tentatively placed his finger on the tip of his tongue. This communion with Portia's salty essence joined him with her in a way that no official ceremony could. If she lived, he'd tell her. If not... .

Charles started blasting his horn the moment he entered the driveway to the hospital's emergency entrance. He stopped with a lurch and both passenger doors flung open. Alerted by the blaring horn, hospital attendants streamed toward the car. With careful urgency, one helped Hegan out of the back. His knees were stiff and bleeding through his torn pants. Two orderlies lifted Portia out, placed her on a gurney, and whisked her into the hospital.

The moments he spent sitting on a hard bench in the hospital corridor ticked by an hour at a time. *Like an eternity*, he thought, and realized that overused expression was shorthand for the interminable vigil of loved ones in pain and crisis.

Charles's voice popped the bubble of his thoughts. "Here be de doctor, Mr. Mike."

A tall man wearing blue scrubs approached Hegan. "I am doctor Stoddard, Mr. Hegan," he said reaching out to shake Hegan's hand.

Tall as an NBA shooting guard, Stoddard had to lean down to speak with Hegan even while seated.

"We stemmed the flow of blood," he began softly, in the maddening superior tones of the Oxford educated. "And found—"

The rest was a blur, a block of words with no meaning, and on the way back to Chicago he didn't want to attempt a recreation. He sat alone, contemplating obsession and risk. He took the risk and others paid the price. But the words were relentless. At first appearance, only a flesh wound. Decrepit ammo. Destabilized. Disintegrated. Circling her organs like the space shuttle, nicking each along the way. Wholesale devastation. All the way back they echoed in his head to the degree that no amount of mini Stoli bottles could obscure.

* * *

Clay visited Hegan the same day he saw the headline: CHI DICK BUSTS RUSKIES. And then the subhead "Girlfriend Slain Saving His Life." Hegan didn't answer the doorbell. After three or four rings, Clay started to pound on the door, but found it swung open with no effort. Not a good sign. He called out to Hegan, hoping to scare any intruder into making an escape attempt. Doomed to be ill-fated. No intruder and no Hegan as Clay pushed on into the living room. He found Hegan stretched out on his sofa, eyes closed and arms crossed over his chest in repose.

"Holy God!" Clay cried out. No empty liquor bottles or beer cans nearby. That was one good sign. "What in holy hell did you do?"

Hegan shot bolt upright and pulled out the earbuds connected to his iPod. "Trying to get some fucking sleep!"

Clay jumped as the assumed corpse rose and spoke. "Lemme tell ya, Hegan. This ain't the first or the last time you'll be hearing this: you're an asshole!"

"And I'm happy to see you too, you stinking pile of buffalo chips."

Greetings and salutations concluded, Clay showed his concern. "Start at the beginning," he said. But where? And then came the torrent. By the time Hegan finished, the light of this late-July evening had begun to fade. Over dinner at Kaz's—turkey leg for Clay, a beer and pickles for Hegan—the three decided to pay for Portia's funeral. She'd be buried with Ariel. The Sutherlands had not responded to Hegan's numerous calls, either to their home or the professor's office. He did not expect them to attend.

Kaz surprised Hegan with a question. "You know who came around a few days ago asking about you?" Hegan crunched into a pickle and shrugged.

"Can't be Madonna, 'cause I'm not a baseball player. Angelina was taken and Mother Teresa is dead. So?"

"Diana. You remember. She plays poker with us."

"Diana? Oh, yeah."

"'Oh, yeah,' he says. You forgot she spilled ice water on your merry men?"

Hegan took a pull on his beer so he wouldn't have to speak and nodded toward a table in the rear corner, site of the now-infamous event.

"How come you always sat next to her when we played poker at Henry's?" Clay saw an opportunity to give Hegan a well-deserved zotz.

"You guys writing a dossier for Captain Rosen? How do I know where I sat?"

Kaz didn't ease up. "Then, whenever she got up your eyes followed her like two lasers. I wouldn't be surprised if you wrote your name on both halves of her tush." Kaz concluded with a flourish and lusty chuckle.

"Enough," Hegan countered. "This is like being Suzanne Pleshette in *The Birds*. All pecking at me. Okay. Okay. I remember. Diana from poker. So?"

"What's with the so? She's a nice kid. That's all." Hegan shrugged again, and Kaz put all his chips into the pot. "She wanted your number."

"I'm a cop. I'm unlisted. Did you tell her?"

"Yeah. I told her your number. Couldn't hurt."

"What? How many more dead women do you want on my conscience? Aren't three in six months enough?"

"You're blaming the *women* for dying, Hegan?" Clay blurted, almost apoplectic and choking on a gulp of water.

They absolved Hegan of any responsibility and tried to convince him he was acting irrationally. "Maybe you should see a shrink," someone said in the blur of words Hegan ignored. He heard nothing, while insisting that any woman who came into his life ran the risk of premature death. He'd rather sleep with a camel.

"That can be arranged," Clay offered seriously. "Problem is, you snore." Hegan managed a weak smile.

"Worse that can happen is she'll call," Kaz said. Hegan started to protest, but was cut short. "And you'll slam the phone down in her ear. Proving you're a major asshole. And she'll never call you again. Ya see, Mikey? Life is in your hands." Kaz left them to tend to other customers.

* * *

After Portia's funeral, Hegan formally announced his retirement, filling out the forms under Captain Rosen's watchful eye. Distrust of Hegan and his tricks ran deep. As Hegan's pen left the paper, with the last letter of his surname formed, he heard Rosen sigh.

Hegan returned home, opened a bottle of Old Style, and turned on the Sox game from Detroit. Slowly, he tried to wrap his mind around the events of the last few weeks as Harrelson's folksy voice droned in the background.

First, the Feds took down the Ivanovs, based on Ariel's tape and after hauling several thousands in bogus twenties from Zenda's barn. Zenda quickly lost his stable of horses and his dress business. Then, Rosen sent two trusted detectives to St. Vincent with extradition papers for Perino, who had been arrested after Charles contacted his cousin Constable Avery. Hegan volunteered to accompany them, but Rosen declined. Even though the local authorities wanted to try Perino for two murders, they eventually acceded. Another of Charles's cousins, Judge Avery, suggested that turning Perino over to the Chicago cops would improve St. Vincent-U.S. relations. As if.

He added Portia to the list. She was a pain in the ass, but he'd grown closer to her. Now she'd be a constant source of regret.

And finally, only Faraci, the catalyst, remained unscathed. If not for the burnt fish maybe he and the Ivanovs would be in business together. For now, Faraci could take comfort in the FOR SALE sign on Condo 32C.

Hegan was alone. There would be no more missions to accomplish in the near future. Clearly, he was without a job and a lover. He did have loyal friends and for that he was grateful.

He spent the next few weeks scanning the Internet looking for law enforcement positions in one-stoplight towns out West. At one point he thought of returning to St. Vincent as a constable, whatever that was.

One day, about noon, Hegan got a call from the public safety supervisor of a town called Weedley, located in Northern California close to the Oregon border. They needed a police chief. Would he be interested? Hegan tried to place the town among the blizzard of emails he'd sent. The doorbell rang and he put the caller on hold.

There was Diana on his doorstep. "Hi, Mike," she said with her 1,000-watt Ingrid Bergman smile. She crossed the threshold before Hegan could think of treating her like a Jehovah's Witness.

"Come in" was all he could blurt out after she was deep into his living room.

"You never returned any of my calls. Thought I'd drop by to see if you were still alive," she said as she inspected his bookshelves. "*Bartlett's Quotations?*" Hegan told her it was one of those books left over from college that he kept for some unknown reason.

"You remember one quote?"

"Er... not really."

He wondered why she picked that rather than any book from his collection of Hemingway, Gore Vidal, or even William Goldman.

"Objets d'art, I see," she teased, picking up a model of a classic Maserati.

"It's a Maserati 200. I made that in eighth grade. The same car driven by Juan Fangio in the Italian Grand Prix."

He had thought of Diana occasionally during the months since she'd become part of the poker group at Henry's. Once his obsession with finding Ariel's killer became paramount, he'd dismissed any social activity. Never did he envision her sailing into his house as if it was her residence.

He watched her circle the living room.

"Do you mind?" She seemed embarrassed, apologetic. Hegan shrugged.

"Just as long as you don't ask for my tax returns."

"I'm an amateur voyeur," she explained.

"Maybe you should see a shrink," Hegan countered without shame but with a smile.

"If I start talking to myself, I'll really be in trouble." She watched Hegan who was torn between continuing the conversation and the blinking red light of his hold button on the phone. Hegan held up one give-me-a-second finger and leaned toward the phone. The light disappeared. He might not become the police chief of Weedley, California, after all.

"We miss you at poker," she said, wandering from the living room and into the kitchen. She whistled a long trill. "Look at this. A kitchen fit for Emeril. You any good or is all this to impress your conquests?"

Hegan's first instinct was to give some kind of modest "aw shucks" response. Then he gave the invader a closer look. He noticed the two-piece, light-grey pantsuit, plum blouse, and short-heeled black pumps. With her leather brief case, Diana could be any member of the executive class rat pack or an insurance salesman. Firm thighs, trim waist. Formidable and huggable.

She was a smart woman, and he loved smart women. Beautiful women, like the models in the *Sports Illustrated* swimsuit issue, were intimidating and out of his reach. But a smart woman was a challenge. Intelligence always gave him the urge to compete. Bring his A-game. Lucy was like that. Was he lucky enough to find another Lucy?

She waited patiently and felt his eyes scan her body. "You find the bar code yet?" Diana asked. She did a slow pirouette, to Hegan's surprise, so he could get a better look. He admired the lazy curve of her cheeks as they met the top of her thighs.

"Not yet." Those words began a challenge Hegan had longed for ever since the early days with Lucy. He upped the ante. "You have time for lunch?"

Diana's last client canceled and she had the afternoon free.

"I'll make us lunch," Hegan said opening the refrigerator and pulling out a carton of eggs, some mushrooms, and a block of Jarlsberg; placing the ingredients on the counter top.

"I've missed all those times when we played poker and I'd go to powder my nose. If you know what I mean."

He shook a look of confusion from his face. "You? A therapist? Doing a line of coke?"

"Think again, Mike," she countered, hands on her hips. "We're playing poker at Henry's. Clay's dealing a new hand. I get up to 'powder my nose' and you do what? I know what you did. I felt your eyes on my butt. I miss them."

Hegan saw the image in his mind and blushed.

"Rosy cheeks are becoming on you, Mike."

Hegan turned from her to attend to lunch, hoping his blush would subside. The cheese and mushroom omelet accompanied by al dente asparagus, crusty bread, and a bottle of Pinot Grigio leveled the playing field.

"I didn't come here expecting lunch. Kaz and Clay kept me informed of all that happened."

Hegan admitted it was a tough six months. Now, he was no longer driven. His job was done. He'd turned the page.

Diana listened, hearing words and at the same time trying to intuit their true meaning. She knew his job was done, but doubted he had turned the page. "If you ever want to talk about it, I'll listen. As a friend. As a poker-playing buddy. That's all I wanted you to know by coming here. Why I barged into your space. However, it is truly amazing what you can find out about a person by paying a surprise visit." She wandered back into the living room.

"Like a welfare worker," Hegan said, throwing the reply over his shoulder while preparing coffee.

"Hey! A sax. Do you play?"

Hegan's relationship with the sax was as strained as his ability. The only tune he remotely remembered was "My Funny Valentine." Diana insisted. Hegan lifted the tenor sax from its stand, pulled off the mouthpiece, and wet the reed in his mouth. He started tentatively and slowly gained the confidence of a high school band member. His version was light-years from that of Gerry Mulligan or Stan Getz. The words appeared in his head, and he heard her sing them softly:

"my funny valentine...you make me smile with my heart....Is your figure less than Greek? Is your mouth a little weak, when you open it to speak are you smart?...stay little Valentine stay. Each day is Valentine's day."

She glowed and applauded. With a diffident bow, something in his heart glowed too.

"Next time, you'll come to my place," Diana said, presuming there would be another time together. "I'm even better in the kitchen than you are." She gave him a peck on the cheek.

"We'll see," he challenged.

"Yes, we'll see." she said and gave him another kiss.

* * *

Dies Irae *all over again*, Hegan thought two weeks later as he tried to decide what to wear. Summer casual? Chinos and a Hawaiian shirt from L. L. Bean. Or formal summer casual? Chinos, Hawaiian shirt and navy blue blazer.

Hegan arrived at Diana's condo across from the Lincoln Park Zoo with a bunch of multihued Shasta daisies he got from Clay, who also gave him the third degree. Was he serious? How many times had he seen Diana?, etc. He also carried a bottle of Merlot from the Anderson Valley—another recommendation from his friend in the Bay Area.

"You're one of those," Diana said, opening the door. "On time to the second. Dinner is not quite there yet, so you'll have to wait." She took the gifts and gave Hegan a peck on the cheek.

Now it was Hegan's turn to wander her living room, what there was of it. No extensive wall of books or the equivalent of an old-fashioned Maserati. Maybe a Madame Alexander doll with one eye and torn dress? No luck.

A modern, cream-colored sectional dominated one wall. A scrawny potted plant rested on the windowsill. There was a barrel chair with reading lamp and ottoman in the corner by the window. A book on African wildlife rested as if soldered in place on a glass-topped coffee table.

"Ever been to Africa?" he asked rifling some pages. Diana glanced over from the kitchen.

"No. A friend gave it to me. Never read it. Just left it there."

There was a dining alcove off the kitchen. Diana returned and placed a wooden salad bowl on the dining table between two unlit white candles in crystal holders. She returned to the kitchen, and Hegan found her smiling in his direction for no apparent reason. He tried to force an embarrassed smile back at her, feeling like an awkward, pimply-faced teen suddenly being asked to the prom by the homecoming queen. He heard the oven door close, and at almost the same time Diana appeared at the end of the sectional. She sat, legs tucked under her, and stretched one arm out until it was within inches of his shoulder.

"Give me your hand."

Hegan hesitated for a moment. Why did she want his hand? He stalled. "What's for dinner? I heard the oven door—"

"Come on, give," she said, her voice both soothing and flirtatious. "I'm baking some halibut. I hope you like fish."

Having to decide on his preference for fish as well as surrendering his hand, Hegan felt confused, like he'd suddenly been awakened after a long night of drinking. "I dunno... I guess. Don't have it much. Actually, not at all."

"That's okay. Most guys don't like fish. They want"—her voice dropped lower—"manly food. Meat. Like cavemen." Her cave-man-style grunt, seeming so out of character, made them both laugh. Hegan then realized he knew almost nothing about her.

Diana would not be sidetracked. "Your hand. Give it." She reached closer to make it easier for Hegan. It was and he did. Her fingers fit between his, and she pulled so that he had to scoot closer.

"Tell me about your day. Your life. I want to know everything."

Her rapid-fire directives disarmed Hegan. "You mean like therapy?"

Her face erupted into the Ingrid Bergman smile he'd first noticed at Kaz's. Her eyes danced with amusement. "Not at all. As two people who barely know each other.

Hegan easily recalled their first meeting. That opened the closet door and out tumbled memories and experiences he couldn't remember storing so long ago. He wondered why he shared them with her with such ease.

Diana was amused and regaled. A quick smile. A burst of laughter. Flashing eyes revealing the warmth of heart. When had Hegan been so touched? In answer, the cold breath of that January day slowly crept up his spine. He resisted with all the strength he could find, turning his focus onto saying whatever would make her smile and laugh. He wanted to feel the warmth of her heart through her eyes over and over and over.

"Noooo" He stopped as Diana jumped up. "Noooo!" again as he heard the oven door bang open. The kitchen fan whirred. He knew.

He found Diana in the kitchen, near tears, trying to act in the same rational way she would advise her clients as she stared at the burnt-to-charcoal halibut on a baking sheet in the sink, now getting drenched by water.

"I'm sorry. I talked too... ." He stopped talking and wrapped his arms around Diana, holding her closer than he'd ever imagined. She didn't try to break free. She didn't try to flip him on his back karate-style. Just as he realized how much he delighted in holding her, chivalry and a cramped arm got the best of him and he let her go.

Diana continued to mourn the loss of the halibut as her tears watered the frangipanis on Hegan's shirt. "Hey, come on. We'll go to Kaz's. Don't be sad." Diana's forlorn expression did not brighten. She looked up at him and nodded.

"What about the salad?"

Hegan picked up the salad bowl and cradled it in his left arm. "Let's go." Before she opened the door, he stopped. "Did I ever tell you what Goethe said?"

"Goethe?" Her voice rose an octave, her inflection filled with astonishment and enough unexpected joy to lighten her mood. So like Hegan. So out of the blue. Over the rainbow, even. She couldn't wait.

Hegan would not be denied. "Something like this: 'man thinks he controls his actions, but his existence is controlled by destiny.'"

"I can see that," she said, trying to keep from laughing.

"Pretty neat, huh?"

"Yeah. Neato." She exhaled and tried to stifle a laugh but without much success. The result was a combination donkey bray, guffaw, belly laugh, and wheeze.

"Maybe next time, I should make dinner?" Hegan said

THE END